Second Chance
(Chances Are #2)

By P.T. Dilloway

Copyright 2013 by P.T. Dilloway
ISBN-13: 978-1492200642
ISBN-10: 1492200646

Part 1
Identity Crisis

Chapter 1

I take one last look in the mirror. For a moment I don't recognize myself. Earlier that day I spent a hundred fifty bucks (with tip) at the beauty parlor for the stylist to give me a perm and dye it red. Neither was my idea; I let Maddy choose my new look for me. She had run a hand through my straight brown hair and said, "It's so boring like this. You need some flair."

I could have pointed out how straight and brown her hair had become in the last year, but she would have countered she was already taken. So I kept my mouth shut and let my daughter talk the stylist into the perm and red hair. Not a carrot-orange red or rusty chestnut red, but a deep burgundy, like a glass of red wine. When I asked Maddy why that color, she said, "Red is so passionate and it goes really well with your natural skin tone." That was a nice way to say I'm as white as a ghost.

I touch the wavy red hair now and wonder if it really does give me some flair. It certainly is different. So are the clothes. I wear a short black jacket, short black skirt, white blouse, and tall black boots, all designer labels. Those weren't Maddy's idea. I bought them about a year ago with the credit card of a dead man. The outfit is gorgeous, fit for a movie star, a far cry from the faded T-shirts and torn jeans I usually wear.

I've done what I can with the makeup to cover up some of my natural skin tone. Although it's been a year since an experimental drug known as FY-1978 changed me from crusty old Detective Steve Fischer into young Stacey Chance, I still can't put on makeup. Tess has tried to teach me, but most days I don't wear more than lipstick if I can help it. Tonight's effort doesn't look too bad. I've got a little pinkness to my cheeks and some definition to my eyes and lips. Maybe I'm not ready to pose in *Playboy*, but at least I don't look like a kindergartner finger-painted all over my face.

"Stacey, are you all right?" Tess asks through the door. "Do you need any help?"

Tess doesn't know anything about my real past. To her I'm an abused runaway who wants to get on her feet. I've become like a surrogate daughter to her, a replacement for her daughter Jenny who died of cancer four years ago. I don't mind her mothering most of the time, especially on nights like this, where I need all the help I can get.

I open the door for her. Her face goes pale and she puts her hands to her mouth. "Is it that bad?" I ask.

"No, dear. You look gorgeous," she says. Tears actually come to her eyes. "You look so grown up now."

"Thanks," I say. I am by all estimates nineteen years old, a grown-up in the eyes of the law. In the eyes of Tess is usually another matter. "You think he'll recognize me?"

"Of course he will. If he doesn't he's no kind of gentleman for you."

I smile a little at this. Sometimes Tess sounds like a character from a Tennessee Williams play, a faded

Southern belle who entertains "gentlemen callers." At those times it's hard to believe Tess is two years younger than I would be if not for FY-1978.

Seth Barnes waits downstairs in the living room. He's as shocked as Tess when he sees me. "Stacey?" he asks.

"It's still me," I say. I give my hair a little toss. "You like it?"

"It's great," he stammers.

Seth has cleaned up a little himself. He wears a white button-down shirt and dark blue pants, very different from the polo shirts and jeans he usually wears to Chemistry 102. That's where we met, in the lab when the professor assigned us as partners. We kept our minds on our experiments throughout the class, so it came as a little bit of a surprise when he asked me out after our final exam. I had considered it myself, but it's a new experience for me to ask out a man.

Tess makes us wait so she can take a picture, as if I'm going to the prom. She hasn't graduated into the digital age yet, so I'll have to wait a few days to know how the pictures turn out. I probably have my eyes closed or I'll just have that terrified look I usually have in photos of me as a woman.

Of course tonight I'm terrified for a good reason. I've never gone on a date with a man before. I think of it as "a date with *another* man" before I correct myself. I'm not a man, not anymore. Dr. Palmer did a whole bunch of tests to prove I'm completely female, except for my memories. I have gone on a couple of dates before with other women, most notably Maddy's partner Grace. We even made love in Grace's bedroom before I came to my senses and realized how wrong it was to steal my daughter's lover. Since then Maddy has set me up a couple of times with girls she knows, but it hasn't worked out. They were perfectly nice, but there was no chemistry between us.

None of them gave me the same nervous flutter in my stomach as when Seth and I worked together in the lab. I still remember when our hands touched for the first time as we reached for a beaker at the same time. We stammered apologies and laughed like idiots, which only proved he wanted me as much as I wanted him. Now's our chance.

He takes me by the arm and leads me out to a Pontiac Grand Am. It's old, but still in good shape. He tells me about how he's tweaked the engine and suspension systems. I'm so nervous I don't pay attention to the details. From the tremor in his voice, I figure he babbles out of nervousness. What a pair we are, scared as a couple of junior high kids on their first date.

We agreed through text messages to go to the latest superhero action movie at nine o'clock. That gives us a couple of hours for dinner. He pulls into the parking lot of an Applebees-type place I haven't gone to before. As the hostess leads us to our table in the back, I can feel people stare at me. I force myself to walk with my back straight and proud, like a princess. A princess with her prince.

Seth grabs his menu and uses it to shield his face. "You want an appetizer or anything?"

"If you want one," I say. I'm not really hungry at the moment. I don't know if an appetizer or anything else will stay down.

I order an iced tea to drink and wish I could make it a Long Island iced tea. There are plenty of places in the city that will serve a nineteen-year-old without question, but those are harder to find out here in the suburbs. A chain restaurant like this certainly won't serve a minor and God knows I don't look a day over eighteen even with the makeup, hair, and clothes.

While we wait for the waitress to come back with our drinks, we say nothing; we just stare at our menus. Another time I might order a steak, but tonight my lack of appetite and girlish modesty prompt me to look at the salads instead. "We could split something if you want," I suggest.

"We don't have to. I have plenty of money."

"I didn't mean that. I just thought if you're not hungry—"

"Oh, I'm sorry. I didn't mean—"

"It's my fault," I say. I lower my menu so he can see my eyes and cheeks that are probably redder than my dyed hair. "I don't mean you're poor or anything. It's just that I'm not very hungry right now. I'm a little nervous, you know?"

His face goes red too. He smiles at me. "I know. I'm really glad you said yes."

"I kept hoping you would ask me."

"You did?"

"Yes." Seth looks surprised at this, probably because he's not exactly *GQ* material. He's gawky, about six inches taller than me, with some leftover teenage acne on his cheeks. His black hair sticks up no matter how much goo he puts in it. Then are the ever-present glasses with black plastic frames that make him look like a control room extra in a movie on the moon landing. In short, Seth is a nerd. *My* nerd.

The waitress shows up and I decide to order a Cobb salad while Seth gets the chicken fingers. The waitress leaves again and we're left with silence. Seth looks down at the table, unable to look me in the eye.

"Are you taking any classes this summer?" he asks.

"No. I thought I'd take a couple of months off."

"That's a good idea."

"What about you?"

"I'm taking a music appreciation class."

"Sounds like fun."

"Have to do something to complete my art elective."

"Yeah, I guess."

"I got accepted to USC. My counselor says all of my credits should transfer."

"USC? That's so far away."

"I know."

"So this is a one-shot deal?"

"Well, no. We have the whole summer—"

"Then you'll be gone."

"Maybe you could transfer too in a year."

"Yeah, right."

"If you want."

"Maybe."

"I'm sorry. I shouldn't have asked you out."

"No, it's all right. I'm glad you did."

"But you're not happy now."

"Well, no," I say. "I thought we'd have more time to get acquainted."

"Yeah." He wipes his glasses with a napkin to buy some time. "I don't have to go to USC. I could go somewhere closer—"

"USC is a good school. I wouldn't want to hold you back," I say with such iciness that he reels back like I've slapped him. I can't believe after all this time he finally asks me out and then says we have no future. Not that I was about to get our wedding invitations printed, but I thought we might have a little more time to see if we really do have some chemistry. There's not much point to it now.

    We don't say much until the waitress brings our entrees. Then we spend most of our time eating; we look down at our plates so we don't have to look at each other. What a wonderful evening.

***

    We still see the movie, mostly because I don't want to explain to Tess why my date lasted only ninety minutes. Seth buys the popcorn and sodas, though I make him buy separate tubs of popcorn so I don't have to share with him. Then my hand won't touch his like in the lab.

    In the second half of the movie, when the hero gets his suit and starts to bust criminals, Seth puts his hand on my thigh. I move a seat over. I cross my arms and try to focus on the movie, but I never liked comic books much as a kid. I preferred detective stories, the old hardboiled kind with guys in trench coats and fedoras. I used to own a trench coat, though by then only hipsters wore fedoras.

    What am I doing here? I ask myself. Steve Fischer wouldn't be here; he wouldn't sulk because some broad will move away in a couple of months. At nineteen years old Steve would have welcomed that because it meant he could get laid without all the bullshit of a *relationship*. He wouldn't have prepared for the date all day either; he would have just combed his hair, slapped on some aftershave, and then got dressed in a rumpled shirt and trousers.

    Why do I care if Seth will leave in a couple of months? We're just lab partners, not married. And I'm only nineteen years old, way too young to settle down. This isn't *Little House on the Prairie* for Christ's sake; most girls nowadays don't get married until their late twenties or early thirties, if at all.

I slide back to the seat I vacated. I lean over to put my head on Seth's shoulder. "I'm sorry," I whisper.

"For what?"

"For acting like such a bitch. I mean, we should just try to have fun, right?" I put my hand in his hair as I say this.

"Yeah," he says. He puts his arm around me to keep me close.

As the movie goes on, I let my hand wander down from his hair, along his chest, and then to his crotch. Right as the hero works up the courage to finally kiss his girl, I give Seth's junk a little pat. "Stacey?" he whispers.

"Don't you like it?"

"Um—"

"Let's forget the rest of the movie and go out to the car."

"What? Why?"

I start to knead the crotch of his pants as I say, "Take a guess."

He bats my hand away like it's a poisonous snake. "What the hell is wrong with you?" he says loud enough that some in the audience shout for him to shut up—some more vehemently than others.

I storm out of the theater; I knock over his popcorn and Coke in the process. He catches up to me in the lobby, where he tries to take my arm. "Stace—"

"Shut up and take me home," I say.

In the car I again sit with my arms crossed. "What's your problem?" I finally ask. "You're supposed to fool around during the movie."

"Usually you stick to making out," he says. "You're not supposed to give me a hand job in public."

"It was dark. Not like anyone was going to notice."

"What happened to you?" he asks. "Why are you acting like this?"

"Like what?"

"So...aggressive."

"Maybe I thought one of us should be."

"If this is about dinner, I'm sorry I didn't tell you sooner."

"I don't care about that anymore. I just want to enjoy the time we have. Even if that means they throw us out of a movie."

"And right into jail for public indecency."

"They'd give you a slap on the wrist," I say, the voice of experience. "Especially when they see how hot your girlfriend is. You'd get a warning officially and unofficially a pat on the back."

"That's not funny."

"I'm not joking. I know how things work. My uncle is a cop."

"Even so, it's not right."

"Fine, be a pansy."

"Stacey—"

"If you want to show me you're a man, then take me to wherever the kids go to make out. Then you can make a woman out of me."

"Jesus, Stacey."

"So you're not a man? You're a sissy?"

"God, I wish I'd listened to everyone about you."

"What the hell does that mean?"

"Everyone I asked about you said you were a dyke. I mean that girl you hang out with—"

"Maddy? What's wrong with her?"

Seth must sense he's crossed a line, because his face starts to look scared instead of angry. "Nothing. I'm just saying she's a lesbian."

"That means I'm one too?"

"Well you have been going out with girls."

"Maybe I'm just experimenting. That's what college girls do, isn't it?"

"I don't want to be an experiment."

"Then what do you want? To be my boyfriend? You think I'll be your little woman, sitting at home pining for you while you go to USC?"

"No—"

"Then what do you want from me?"

"I don't know."

"Then take me home."

I let him walk me up to the front door and then give me a kiss goodnight. It's not because either of us want to so much as I know Tess is watching. Seth's kiss is a dry one that lasts a few seconds. "Goodnight," he says.

He doesn't ask if I want to go out again. The answer to that is obvious.

Chapter 2

I tell Dr. Palmer about my date while I'm on the exam table. Unlike our first exam, I don't lie with my feet in stirrups. I sit fully-clothed on the table in jeans and a tank top to make it easier for her to take my blood. "Why did he tell me that?" I ask. "Why did he even bother asking me out if he was planning to leave in a couple of months?"

"I don't know," Dr. Palmer says. She stabs the needle into my arm. I hardly notice, not after we've done this every three months for the last year. "You know more about men than I do."

"Yeah, I guess." I thought about it most of the night, after I gave Tess a much different report on what happened so she won't worry about me. As far as Tess knows, Seth and I are an item, on our way to marriage.

"When I was nineteen, all I thought about was getting laid," I say.

"Men are supposed to be more sensitive than back in the '70s," Dr. Palmer says. "But you did really like him, didn't you? Before he told you about going to USC?"

"Yes. I mean, I wasn't thinking about marrying him yet."

"Then what were you thinking about?"

I can only shrug. I think about it for a couple of minutes while Dr. Palmer puts the tube of blood into a container to be sent to the lab for analysis. "I guess I thought we could be friends."

"Friends with benefits?"

"What?"

"It means you're friends, but you also fuck when you want."

"Oh. No, not really. I thought it'd be more like when Debbie and I started going out."

"So you did want to marry him?"

"No!" I feel my face turn hot as I get flustered. "I didn't think about marrying Debbie right away. We went out for like six months before we started to get serious about it. Then it was a whole year before I got up the nerve to propose."

"And his leaving ruined all that?"

"Well what's the point? We could go out a few times and then he'd have to leave."

"You could always talk on the phone. Chat on the Internet or whatever kids do today."

"Maybe, but it wouldn't work. I mean these long-distance things usually don't."

"Wasn't he worth seeing if it would?"

"I don't know." I sigh and shake my head. "I've really made a mess of it, haven't I?"

Dr. Palmer puts a hand on my shoulder; she must sense I'm about to cry. Ten months ago I'd already have begun to sob like a little girl with a skinned knee. I've gotten a better handle on the female hormones since then. "It's all right, Stacey. You're just confused. It happens a lot, especially when you're young."

"But I'm not young, not really."

"You've only been a woman for a year. I've been at it over forty years and I still get confused."

"Thanks for trying to cheer me up."

"Well, let me ask you something: why did you try to touch him in the movie theater?"

"I don't know. I was sitting there, pouting about him moving and then I got thinking."

"What were you thinking?"

"I thought that's what a girl would do, sit there and sulk. Steve Fischer wouldn't have done that."

"But you're not Steve. Not anymore."

Dr. Palmer opens a drawer to take out her purse. She rummages through it for a minute. Tess would cluck her tongue at that; she makes sure I keep my purse nice and organized so I can find anything the moment I need it. The doctor finally takes out a business card. She passes it across the desk to me.

"Dr. Robert Macintosh," I read from the card. "You want me to see a shrink?"

"I think it would help. He's a friend of mine. He mostly works with children, but he takes a few older cases too."

"Great, a *child* psychologist. That's just what I need."

"He's very good. I think he could help you."

"With what?"

Dr. Palmer leans forward and clasps her hands together. "Look, Stacey, I like talking to you. I care about you, a lot. You're like my favorite niece."

"You'd send your niece to a shrink?"

"If she were in your situation? Absolutely."

"What am I supposed to tell him about my situation? I tell him what Artie Luther did to me and he'll have me committed."

"You don't have to tell him that part. He gets kids like you all the time who are gender confused."

"'Gender confused?' Is that what you think I am?"

"Yes."

I get up to leave, but Dr. Palmer is faster than me. She takes my arm and then looks into my eyes. "Remember what you told me about your date? You couldn't decide whether you were Stacey or Steve. You started out as Stacey and then you let Steve take over once your feelings were hurt."

"I'm not schizophrenic."

"I'm not saying you are. I'm just saying you haven't decided who you are yet, whether you're Stacey Chance or Steve Fischer. Dr. Macintosh can help you sort that out."

"How? He can't change me back."

"You don't necessarily need me to make a serum to change you back. Girls become boys all the time. It just takes a little surgery."

"But I wouldn't really be Steve. I'd just be Stacey with a fake dick."

"Still, the option is there if you want it."

"Well I don't. And I don't want to be Stacey either. I want to be *me* again." Now I start to cry like I used to. "I want Maddy to see me as her dad again, not some freak who got surgery. Don't you get that?"

"I do." Dr. Palmer wraps me in a hug. "Look, just go to one session. That's all I'm asking. If it doesn't help then you don't have to go back. OK?"

I sniffle and as always feel like an idiot to sob like this. "I guess."

She musses my expensively-coiffed hair. "Good girl. You want me to call Tess?"

"No, I should get to work. Grace is expecting me."

"OK." Before I leave, Dr. Palmer says, "I like your new look, by the way."

I blush a little at the compliment. I run my fingers through my wavy hair. "You think it gives me some flair?"

"I think you'll have boys eating out of your hand. If that's what you want."

Is it what I want? I think about that as I leave Dr. Palmer's office.

Chapter 3

I'm the oldest patient in the waiting room. There are other adults, but they're the mothers and fathers of the children here to see Dr. Macintosh. I sit on a plastic chair and read an article on Justin Bieber in *Teen People* while I will myself to stay in my seat.

In the opposite corner is a little girl, ten or so, who plays with her cell phone like most kids do these days. She wears a plaid skirt and white blouse, probably a school uniform. As if she senses my eyes on her, she looks up at me and smiles. I turn back to my magazine. When I glance over a few minutes later, she's back to playing with her phone.

What the hell am I doing here? I'm not a little girl like the one in the corner. For that matter, why is she here? When I was ten, the most stress I had was to worry whether my dad would spank me if I didn't do my chores, said a dirty word, or got into his stash of porno magazines I wasn't supposed to know about. Of course nowadays everyone has to go see a shrink to have their heads examined. The little girl in the corner is probably hopped up on Prozac or Ritalin or something.

The receptionist calls my name and shows me into the doctor's office. The moment I see the toys scattered on the floor and the wallpaper of puffy clouds against a blue background, I want to run again.

The doctor himself doesn't fill me with confidence either. He doesn't look much different than Seth, except he doesn't have the acne and his dark hair lies neatly on his head, without the help of mousse or other goop. Like a stereotypical college professor he wears a tweed jacket with a white shirt—no tie. When he stands up to shake my hand, I notice he wears blue jeans. Typical yuppie, I think. I wonder how old he is. From the lack of wrinkles on his face, I bet not much over thirty. There's no picture of a wife or girlfriend on his desk, just a picture of a boy about ten years old who looks like a miniature version of him, probably his son. So maybe not everything's peachy keen in his world.

"Welcome, Ms. Chance," he says. "You come highly recommended from Clarita."

"What's she said about me?"

"Let's talk about that. Have a seat."

"Isn't there a couch?"

"I can have one brought up if you want. Or we could try out those nice chairs facing the window." He motions to a pair of white fabric armchairs that face a window overlooking downtown. I walk over to the edge of the window and just about press my nose to the glass. If I squint I can see Lennox Pharmaceuticals's lab where Dr. Palmer is probably laughing her ass off.

When I turn around, I see Dr. Macintosh in one of the white chairs, legs crossed so he can balance a pad of paper on his lap. "You can stand if you want. Some patients prefer it."

I throw myself onto the empty chair and sprawl like a petulant child. Dr. Macintosh doesn't seemed fazed by that; he probably has that happen a lot. "So, Stacey, you wanted to know what Dr. Palmer said about you?"

"Are you going to ask why I want to know that?"

"My idea of psychology isn't just to sit here asking you why all the time. It's not asking about your parents either, unless you want to."

"So what is your idea of therapy?"

"I want you to talk about what you want to talk about." He motions around the room, at the pile of toys, the stupid cloud wallpaper, and the window. "I want you to feel like this is your sanctuary. You can be yourself here. No one's going to judge you."

"Except for you."

"I'm not here to judge you. I'm here to help you." He looks down at his notes. "Dr. Palmer says you're bright, a little shy, and like a lot of girls your age, you're confused. Would you say that's accurate?"

"My teachers might argue about the bright part." I've managed a consistent 'C' average so far in college, except in Chemistry 102, where I had Seth to help me.

"Well, maybe she doesn't mean bright in terms of schoolwork. Maybe she means you're street smart. Is that more accurate?"

"I guess."

"You've spent a lot of time on the streets, haven't you?"

"Did she tell you that?"

"A little bit. She says you come from an abusive home, that you ran away when you were still a child. How long ago was that?"

I shrug. "About three years."

"And what did you do during those years?"

"I survived."

He nods and writes something down. "I can understand if you're not willing to talk about it yet. We'll get back to it later."

"If I decide to come back."

"You think you won't?"

"I don't know."

"Are you afraid of what you might find out about yourself in therapy?"

"What? I'm not afraid."

"I'm just trying to understand you, Stacey. Just like I want you to understand yourself."

"I do understand myself."

"If that's so, then why are you here?"

"Because Dr. Palmer made me."

"I've known Clarita since I was an intern. She's a very smart lady. If she thinks you need my help, then I think you need my help. The only question is whether *you* think you need my help. Do you?"

I think about it for a minute and turn to look out the window. I think about what happened on my date. It's obvious I'm a mess, but what good will it do to talk to this schmuck? "I don't know."

"Let's talk about it. Why did Dr. Palmer think you should see me?"

"Because I'm confused."

"About what?"

"About who I am."

"That's not so unusual, not in a girl your age. When my sister was nineteen she went and joined the Peace Corps."

I turn back to the doctor. "She wanted to save the rainforest or something?"

"That's part of it, but she also wanted to learn what she was capable of."

"And did she?"

"Somewhat. She met a very nice man in the Sudan. When she came back, she was big as a house."

"She got fat?"

"Pregnant. She gave birth to my nephew a week after getting back. That's his picture on my desk."

"Oh. I thought—"

Dr. Macintosh cuts me off with a laugh. "I know. Family resemblance."

"So you think I should join the Peace Corps and get pregnant?"

"Not unless you want to."

"Then what should I do?"

"That's up to you. Whatever will help give you some direction."

"That's not really helpful."

"Maybe our sessions could help you find out what you need."

"Maybe."

The doctor checks his watch. "Our session is almost up for today. I want you to strongly consider coming back in a couple of days so we can continue."

"I'll think about it."

As I get up to leave, Dr. Macintosh says, "Dr. Palmer was almost right about you."

"Almost?"

"I think you are bright and you are confused."

"You don't think I'm shy?"

"No. I think you're secretive. I think whatever you endured from your parents has made you turn inward, to keep people from learning too much about you. It's something I see more often in my male patients. You know, most men think talking about themselves with a doctor makes them a sissy. What would you say to that?"

"I thought most of your patients were kids?"

"See what I mean? You answer my question with a sarcastic comment."

"It wasn't so sarcastic."

Dr. Macintosh gets up from his chair and then takes a few steps towards me. "Stacey, if we're going to help you, you need to stop being so defensive. Remember what I said at the start? This place can be your sanctuary. It's where you can be yourself without fear of anyone laughing at you or hitting you. You're safe here. I'm not here to hurt you or judge you. I'm here to help you get in touch with yourself, with the person you've been holding back, hiding deep inside all these years."

As he talks I back up until I'm against the door. It's a good thing I've learned to contain my emotions or else I'd be a wreck right now. Not only the doctor's words, but also his passion in them, make me want to believe him. Maybe Dr. Palmer was right about this whole therapy thing. Maybe he can help me.

"If you want to stay a little longer, it's all right," he says. "I can step out for a few minutes if you'd like to be alone."

"No, I'm fine," I say in almost a whisper. "I've got to go."

"I hope I'll see you again, Stacey. If that's what you want."

I nod to him and then turn to open the door. I force myself to go over to the receptionist's desk. "I'd like to make an appointment for another session," I say.

Chapter 4

Grace senses right away there's something wrong when I show up for work. "What's wrong?" she asks. "Things not go well at court?"

I've never told Grace the truth about myself, so she thinks I'm still a runaway from an abusive home. I take advantage of this when I need to take some time off for things like my appointment with Dr. Macintosh. I usually tell her I have to see a lawyer to maintain the restraining order against my fictitious parents. I don't feel good about it, but it's better than to try to explain the real reason for my absence.

"Oh, sure," I say. I force myself to smile. "It's just hard, you know?"

"I'm sure it is." She puts an arm around me. Even after a year there's a part of me that would like to pull Grace even closer to kiss her. I always remind myself that time is over. It will be over so long as Maddy loves Grace. I won't betray my daughter again. "I can't imagine what you're going through. It must be awful."

"It is."

"I wish you'd let me and Maddy go to support you."

"That's nice of you to offer, but I really want to keep this in the family."

"I understand," Grace says, though I can see from the way her mouth twitches that she doesn't. One of these days I'll have to bring her to Dr. Palmer's office with me so she can learn the truth about me.

"Thanks. How are things here?"

"The same as usual."

Which means dead. Grace only gets a handful of customers in a day. If not for the inheritance from her mother, she probably would have had to close this place down long ago. Then we never would have met and I might never have run into Maddy at the Kozee Koffee down the street.

Grace smiles at me and then changes the subject. "I have some good news. You're looking at the new assistant treatment counselor at Windover Rehabilitation Clinic."

"You got the job? That's fantastic!" I give her a hug this time. Grace had gone to a second interview a few days ago but hadn't heard back from them. "When are you going to start?"

"Next week. I thought that would give me time enough to wrap things up here."

"You mean to sell everything off?"

"No!" She gives me a playful slap on the arm. "You remember our deal, don't you? When I get a job, all of this becomes yours. If you still want it."

"Oh. Well, I'm not sure—" my voice trails off as I think of my appointment with Dr. Macintosh. Do I want to run the store? I wouldn't be able to go to school, not full-time anyway. I might still be able to take a few classes at nights, after the shop closes.

Proprietor of a bohemian clothes shop in the garment district is a lot different than my last career. Steve Fischer had been born to be a cop; he would never want to run

Grace's store. Yet my job here is what brought me closer to Maddy and Grace—my friends. "I don't know," I stammer. "It's a big step."

"I know. You wouldn't have to take official control. I could still be the owner for all the taxes and whatnot. You could just be the manager. I swear I wouldn't get in your way. You can do whatever you want with the place."

When I look Grace in the eye I can see she wants me to accept. As much as she wants to be a psychiatrist, this shop belonged to her mother. It was her mother's dream to have something of her own after she divorced Grace's father. Grace desperately wants someone to help keep that dream alive. Since there's no one else around, it falls to me.

"That sounds OK," I say.

"Thank you so much." I'm not prepared for her to kiss me. The way she staggers back a moment later, I don't think she was either. "I'm sorry. I got a little excited."

"It's all right. It is really exciting."

"Well, um, I think the best idea would be to keep the receipts for the week and then we can go over them on the weekend."

"Sure," I say.

"Hey, what's with the long faces?" Maddy calls out from the doorway. "Someone die?"

"No," Grace says. "We were just talking about Stacey taking over the store."

"Really? So that means—?"

"Yep."

"That's great!" Maddy's kiss is a lot longer and less awkward than mine with Grace. There's still a part of me that shivers when I see my daughter kiss another woman, that old-fashioned father in me who always thought I'd give Maddy away at the altar. If she does get married it will probably be in a courthouse with me in a dress as a witness.

After she lets Grace go, Maddy says, "OK, kids, we have to go celebrate."

"I'm not sure that's a good idea," Grace says.

"Well I think it's an awesome idea," Maddy says. "What do you think, Stace?"

"I don't know—"

"You two are such sticks in the mud. Come on! Grace has a new job, Stacey's taking over the store, and I just finished finals. We all have a reason to get plastered, right?"

"I can't," I say. "I'm not old enough to drink."

"Oh, the hell with that. I know plenty of places that won't card you."

Grace takes Maddy's arm. "Madison, stop it. We've talked about this. Stop trying to pressure Stacey into things she doesn't want to do."

"I'm only trying to get her to loosen up a little."

I remember what Dr. Macintosh said about me being defensive. "I guess a drink or two wouldn't hurt."

"That's the spirit!" Maddy claps me on the back hard enough to stagger me. Sometimes my daughter doesn't know how to control her enthusiasm. That relentless enthusiasm is what makes her so special to me and Grace, but sometimes it can be annoying. She takes my hand, and pulls me towards the stairs leading up to the apartment she shares with Grace. "We'll have to find you something to wear. I have this green dress I think would be perfect for you."

I look back at Grace to plead with her to save me, but she just smiles and gives me a little wave.

**

The green dress is a little big on me, which is a good thing because it means the skirt covers my knees. I still don't like to show skin around Maddy, no matter how many times she says I have great legs and boobs. While Maddy means well, to hear that from my daughter only makes me more reluctant to wear anything sexy when we're together.

Maddy shows plenty of skin in a little red dress. In the cab on the way over, I made sure to keep my eyes on the window so I wouldn't get too good of a look at her legs—or anything else. That old-fashioned father in me always wants to throw a blanket around her and then drag her home to lock her in her room until she's sixty. The rest of me reluctantly accepts the idea Maddy is twenty-three years old and free to make her own decisions.

Grace shows less skin than either of us. She looks almost dowdy in a long tan skirt and a yellow T-shirt. She's gotten a lot more self-conscious about her body since she turned thirty. She should probably go to a therapist herself for that, although I'm sure most women struggle with that, unless they're oblivious like Maddy.

The cab drops us off at the Open Mic, a karaoke bar in the garment district. "A karaoke bar?" I ask.

"It'll be fun," Maddy says. "We can have a few drinks and then get on stage and mangle a few songs." Maddy squeezes Grace's knee. "Remember when you did like six tequila shots and then got up there to do 'Girls Just Wanna Have Fun?'"

"Not really," Grace says. Her face turns red.

"Oh my God, Stace, you should have seen it! First it sounded like someone was skinning a cat on stage. Then about halfway through she threw up on the first row! To finish it off, she dove off the stage, right into the lap of this really fat chick. Grace started making out with her, thinking that elephant was me. Can you believe it?"

I can't contain my laughter at this story, in large part because it's so uncharacteristic of Grace, who's usually so calm and in control of herself. Maddy is the one I imagine would get drunk, throw up, and then jump off a stage. "That's so awful," I say.

"I wish I'd brought my phone to get some video of it. It would have got like a million views on YouTube."

"Well this time you can be the one to make a complete ass of yourself," Grace says.

"Oh I don't think I could ever top that," Maddy says.

No one cards us as we go inside. The karaoke bar isn't nearly as bad as some of the clubs in the city. It looks mostly like my old watering hole, except there's a stage at one end with a karaoke machine, a microphone, and a couple of stools. A drunk blond girl looks ready to fall off her stool at any moment as she butchers one of those Lady Gaga songs Maddy downloaded onto the iPod she gave me for Christmas.

A waitress shows up to take our orders. Maddy orders a mojito. Grace gets an appletini. "Just a club soda," I say.

"Come on, Stace—"

"She doesn't have to drink if she doesn't want to," Grace says.

"OK, I'll have a beer," I say.

"We don't serve beer here."

"You don't? What kind of bar is this?" I ask.

"I'm sorry, but—"

"Just bring her a sake," Maddy says. She pats my hand after the waitress is gone. "That's rice wine. It's pretty good."

We talk about Grace's new job while Maddy drinks another three mojitos and I drink two bottles of sake. Grace trails behind us; she sips at a second appletini. I'm into a third sake when Maddy climbs onto the stage. She talks with the emcee about what song she'll perform. "No, I'm not going to do that one. Here, this one."

Maddy sits on the stool and gives us all a drunken smile. "This song is for the love of my life, Grace, and my best friend, Stacey. OK, girls, I'm going to show you how it's done."

Despite Maddy's best attempts, I don't know much about popular music since the early '70s. I still recognize the song she sings as the Cyndi Lauper one Grace mangled years ago. Maddy's version isn't much better, except she doesn't throw up or jump off the stage. She sings most of it in an off-key baritone that contrasts greatly with what should come out of a young woman's throat. Grace and I break into peals of laughter and put our hands to our ears.

Maddy breaks off the song to glare down at us. "Oh, I suppose you could do better?"

"Not me," Grace says. She gives me a little push. "I bet Stacey can."

"Me? I can't—"

"Oh, come on, don't be such a chicken," Maddy says. She looks around at the rest of the audience. "Hey, who wants to hear little Stacey sing?"

The bar patrons begin to applaud. Some even whistle. Maddy leads them in a chant of my name while my face turns so warm I expect to combust at any moment. Grace gives me another push. "Go on, Stace. It'll be fun."

I remember again what Dr. Macintosh said. I suppose to make a fool of myself in public is a great way to break out of my defensive shell. I take Maddy's hand so she can pull me up onto the stage. "What am I supposed to do now?"

"Just tell this guy here what you want to sing. He'll bring the words up on this screen and you sing them," she explains. She pushes me towards the emcee. "What do you want to sing?"

"Do you have any Creedence?" I ask.

"Creedence Clearwater Revival? God, that's the kind of shit my dad listened to," Maddy says.

I'm tipsy enough to stand up to my daughter. "Well maybe he was on to something," I say. I turn to the emcee. "You got 'Bad Moon Rising' in there?"

He nods to me and then brings it up. I remember when I sang this song to Maddy in the car a few times, or at least I tried to; she always whined about my music being yucky. I sit down on the stool and find myself in front of a roomful of people, most of whom stare at me in anticipation. "Hi," I whisper into the microphone. "Um, my name's Stacey and I'm going to try singing this."

Maddy leans into the mic to add, "She's a karaoke virgin so don't be too rough on her."

"Thanks," I say.

"That's what I'm here for," Maddy says. She pats me on the back and then goes down to sit with Grace. I'm alone with the emcee on the stage as the song begins.

The words start to appear on the screen, but I don't need them. I just close my eyes and remember all the times I sang it to myself on stakeouts. Except back then my voice sounded like a car backing over a gravel driveway. Now it's so high and thin, like I've sucked down a couple of balloons filled with helium.

At least that's what it sounds like to me. The audience has a much different opinion. The place erupts with applause as I finish. I open my eyes to see Maddy and Grace gape at me in shock. What did I do wrong?

My first thought is to bolt from the stage. Then I hear people call for an encore. I look helplessly around the stage, not sure what I should do. Maddy climbs onto the stage and puts an arm around me. She pulls me in for a hug. "That was beautiful," she whispers.

"It was?"

"Yes. Why have you been keeping that a secret?"

"I don't know," I stammer. "What do I do now?"

"An encore, dummy." She gives me another squeeze and then goes over to the emcee; she whispers something in his ear. When Maddy returns, she says, "Here's something a little newer for you. This is me and Grace's song, so don't mess it up."

The song the emcee brings up is called "Angel" by Sarah McLachlan. I've never heard of it, but obviously Maddy has. This time I can't close my eyes. I keep them focused on the screen so I can follow along with the prompts.

When I finish, there's more applause than before. I turn to Maddy and Grace and see them both in tears. Was it that bad? So bad the emcee comes over to take me by the arm. He leads me off the stage, accompanied by the crowd cheering.

I expect him to tell me not to ever come back, but instead he says, "Listen, kid, that was the best I've ever heard in this place. How'd you like to do it again?"

"Um, I don't know. I should ask my friends."

"Forget about them. Look, I'll give you a hundred bucks to come back and do a set."

"You want to pay me to sing karaoke?"

"OK, make it three hundred. If you wow them like you did tonight, we could make it a regular thing."

Three hundred bucks to sing a few songs off a screen? I've never imagined myself as a singer before, but I could sure use the money. I owe Jake and Tess a few grand already for my tuition and textbooks at school. "Sure," I say. "I'll give it a try."

Chapter 5

When the receptionist shows me into Dr. Macintosh's office this time I find him already in one of the armchairs. "Hello, Stacey. Have a seat."

I sit in the chair opposite him and keep my body tightly compacted this time instead of sprawled out. I look down at my sneakers and say, "I guess you aren't surprised I came back."

"I'm very glad you decided to give therapy a chance to help you," he says. "So have you thought about what we discussed before?"

"A little. I got a couple of job offers since last time."

"Really? That's wonderful. What sort of jobs?"

"Well, my friend Grace owns this little second-hand clothes shop in the garment district. She's been studying to be a shrink like you. She got a new job over at the Windover rehab clinic. You know where that is?"

"As it happens I've had a couple of clients about your age admitted there."

"OK. So she's going to be working there and she wants me to take over the store for her."

"Is that what you want to do?"

"I don't know. I really like being there, around Grace and Maddy."

"Maddy?"

"Madison. She's my...friend." I always have to resist the urge to call her my daughter. "She and Grace live together. As a couple, you know?"

"They're lesbians. There's no shame in it. Is there?"

"No, of course not."

"You're just not comfortable talking about that."

"Well no offense, but this is only our second session."

"I see. You're trying to spare my feelings."

"It's not like that. The way I was brought up, we didn't talk about stuff like that."

"Your parents didn't tell you about sex?"

"Not really. My dad tried to give me the whole 'bird and the bees' thing once. He was so embarrassed he didn't make a lot of sense. And my mom, she would ground me if she heard me so much as mention a woman's breasts."

"Are you attracted to women?"

"What?" I don't realize until then that I've slipped up. I've remembered Steve Fischer's adolescence in the '60s instead of Stacey's adolescence thirty years later. "Oh, well, some women."

"So you'd say you're bisexual?"

"I don't know." Like at the karaoke bar I feel so embarrassed I'm ready to pass out.

"You don't have to be embarrassed, Stacey. A lot of girls your age aren't sure about their sexuality yet."

I remember what I said to Seth in the car about experimenting. "Yeah, maybe."

"Are you a virgin, Stacey?"

My head snaps up. The doctor stares at me so calmly I'd like to punch him in the face. "Why are you asking me that?"

"It's just a question. There's no right or wrong answer."

"No, I'm not a virgin."

"How many partners have you had?"

I remember to answer as Stacey and not Steve this time. "One."

"Was that partner male or female?"

I can't stop myself from crying. "It was Grace. We'd already kissed once and then after Maddy's dad's funeral, we went back to Grace's apartment and…did it."

"You made love?"

"Yes."

"And you enjoyed it?"

"Yes."

"But you and Grace aren't still together, are you?"

"No. I decided—we decided—it was better for her to stay with Maddy."

"Why is that?"

"Because Maddy is my friend. I can't hurt her like that."

"You value her happiness over your own?"

"Maddy and Grace were already together. What happened between Grace and me was just a fling. It was a mistake."

"But you still care about her, don't you?"

"Yes."

"You love her?"

"Part of me does."

The doctor smiles at this. He reaches over to pat my knee. "Stacey, in my experience love is never part way. You're all-in or not. So you do still love Grace?"

"Yes."

"But you don't think of yourself as a lesbian?"

"No." It sounds crazy even to my own ears. "Look, I might love Grace, but she's just one woman. There have been others I didn't care about nearly as much."

"You didn't make love to any of those other women?"

"No. What kind of girl do you think I am?"

"There's no need to get upset. I'm not judging you. I just want to get the full story. That's why you're here, remember?"

"Sorry."

"You don't have to be sorry either." He puts down his pen and folds his hands. "I think a lot of your confusion stems from your feelings for your friend. You love Grace but you don't think your love is as important as Maddy's. Does that sound right?"

There's no way I can explain to the doctor exactly how complicated things are. Maddy's love is more important because she's my daughter and as her father I want the best for her. "Grace and Maddy helped me when I didn't have anything. It wouldn't be right for me to break them up. Is that wrong?"

"I'm not here to discuss right or wrong."

"That's a nice copout."

"If you really want to know, I think you're a good person, but you're making yourself miserable."

"So you think I should turn Grace down?"

"Is that what you want?"

"I don't know what I want."

"You mentioned another job offer."

"Oh, that. It's kind of silly."

"How so?"

"Well, we—Maddy, Grace, and me—went out to this karaoke bar the other night. Maddy pulled me on stage and made me sing. And I guess I was really good. That's what the owner of the place said. He wants to pay me three hundred bucks to sing again."

"And you turned him down?"

"Hell no. I could use three hundred bucks."

Dr. Macintosh smiles at that. "But you don't think you're a singer?"

"I never really thought about it before that night. I'm probably not that good."

"Well, let's find out. Go ahead, sing something."

"Now?"

"Why not?"

"I don't have any lyrics or any music—"

"Just sing anything. 'Twinkle Twinkle Little Star' if you want. That one's popular with most of my patients."

I take a moment to gather myself and then I sing "Twinkle Twinkle Little Star." I keep my eyes closed so I can't see Dr. Macintosh's reaction until I finish. I don't open them until I hear him applaud softly.

"You have a lovely voice," he says.

"You really think so?"

"It's gorgeous. Almost angelic." He raises an eyebrow, no doubt when he sees how red my face turns. "That embarrasses you?"

"I guess no one's called me angelic before, except maybe Tess."

He nods. I figure our session must be almost over because the doctor gets up. He goes over to the desk. Maybe he'll fetch a prescription pad to give me some medication. Instead he comes back with a hand mirror. He holds it out to me. "Go on, look in the mirror."

"I know what I look like."

"Just indulge me, please."

I take the mirror from him. I stare into the glass at my face. My eyes are still a little red and puffy from my earlier tears. I didn't shower this morning, so my hair looks wild, the wavy strands like Medusa's snakes. "What do you see?" Dr. Macintosh asks.

"A girl," I say.

"A pretty girl?"

"No."

"Why not?"

"I look tired. And dirty."

"You can always get more sleep and take a shower. Look deeper. What do you see?"

I stare into the mirror some more. I'm drawn to my eyes. They're still blue like before. I don't know anymore if they're Steve's eyes or Stacey's eyes. With my longer lashes and eyeliner, they look more like a girl's eyes.

I put the mirror down. I start to cry again. "I don't know."

He wraps an arm around my shoulders. "That's all right, Stacey. That's what you're going to find out here. OK?"

"OK."

He rubs my back the way Tess does when I get upset. "I have a little homework for you if you're up to it."

"What?"

"I want you to look in the mirror for ten minutes a day, every day until our next session. When you do it, I want you to think about what you see. Then we'll talk about it next time."

"All right," I say and punctuate it with a sniffle.
"I'll get you some tissues."
"Thanks."

He gives me a few minutes to cry myself out and then clean up a little. Throughout it all he sits with his arm around my shoulders; he must sense I need the company. I should ask Grace if it's unprofessional for your shrink to hug you. At the moment, I don't care.

Chapter 6

I stare into my compact for the entire train ride to the garment district. I try to do as Dr. Macintosh suggested. I hold out the little circle mirror to show as much of my face as possible. I've seen myself hundreds of times before and yet it's like the first time I saw myself in the mirror after I woke up as a woman. Has my nose always been this tiny? Did I always have that mole on my left cheek? God, I should really pluck my eyebrows; they've just about grown together.

My features start to change in the mirror. They blur for a moment before they reform into the ones I saw in the mirror for fifty years. Of course they changed a little with time, the wrinkles around my eyes, the creases on my forehead, the gray hairs along my jaw, and the bloated redness of my nose. I could tell Dr. Macintosh all about this face; it's the face of an old, broken man, a man worn down by too many years and too many miles. It's the face of a man divorced from his wife and estranged from his daughter.

I snap the compact shut as the train nears my stop. I still don't know what to tell Dr. Macintosh about my new face. I'll have to try again later, see if anything comes to me. I doubt it. Stacey's face is still too new to me. It's a face without much history.

When I enter Grace's shop—soon to be my shop if I want it—I find her and Maddy in the back room, to go through some clothes people have traded in. "Ready for the show tonight?" Maddy asks.

I haven't given any thought to my actual performance so far. I probably should; it's nine hours away. My knees turn rubbery at this thought. Grace grabs one arm and Maddy the other before I can collapse. "I think I need to sit down," I mumble.

They walk me over to a stool, which I gratefully sink onto. I look down at my feet, at the worn sneakers not nearly sexy enough to wear on stage. I'll probably have to wear heels; I imagine myself on stage in the heels; I trip over a microphone cord or something and then topple into the front row. "This is a really bad idea," I say. "I'm not a performer."

"Come on, it'll be fun," Maddy says. "It'll be just like the other day. You go up there and do your best."

"But it's different this time. I'm not some drunk girl doing karaoke. People will expect me to be professional, you know?"

"Most people will be too buzzed to notice. They probably won't even hear you."

"Maybe."

Grace takes her turn to try to comfort me. "Think what a great opportunity this is. You have a chance to do something not a lot of other people get to do."

"Really?"

"Maddy and I couldn't do it. You've heard us sing."

I think of what Dr. Macintosh said when I sang for him. "You really think I'm good?"

"You're amazing. If you tried out for *American Idol* you'd get to Hollywood for sure," Maddy says. "After that it's just a popularity contest."

"But if you don't want to do it, that's all right," Grace says. "We'll still support you."

I think of my first session with Dr. Macintosh. He said I needed to get out of my shell more. I did when I got up on that stage and look what happened: I found a hidden talent and got a chance to make three hundred bucks. I can't back down now, can I?

"Thanks, guys. I'll do it."

"That's great!" I'm always torn when Maddy hugs me. Part of me is glad for the warmth and comfort of a friend. The rest of me remembers all those times when little Maddy would wrap her arms around my neck as I carried her to her room. The latter can't happen anymore. "Have you thought about what to sing?"

"What? Oh, I don't know. I thought I'd wait until I got there like before."

"No no no," Maddy says. "You can't just wing it. You got to practice."

"I do?"

"It's a good idea," Grace says. "It'll help you feel more comfortable when you get up there."

Grace has a good point. If I have a solid game plan beforehand, I won't panic as much once I get there. "What do you think I should sing?"

"Not more oldies," Maddy says. She puts a finger down her throat for emphasis.

"I don't know much else," I say. "We weren't big into music in my house."

"Let's go find something," Maddy says. She takes my arm and yanks me off the stool.

***

The first time I was nineteen, my music collection consisted of records piled up in my apartment. Creedence Clearwater Revival was always my favorite, but I also had Led Zeppelin, Springsteen, the Stones, and of course the Beatles. Those are all "oldies" now, the kind of music that makes Maddy gag.

Her music collection is contained on her laptop and cell phone. I haven't heard of any of it and most of it I don't want to. I certainly can't imagine myself on a stage to sing about some boy who broke my heart or how hot I am or shit like that. The grumpy old man in me grumbles that music was a lot better in my day.

We listen to clips for an hour before Maddy shakes her head. "Jesus, Stace, you may have a great voice but you got a tin ear."

Grace is there to pat me on the knee. "Don't worry about it. You sing whatever you want. It's your show."

"Even oldies?"

"Sure. Hey, I got an idea." Grace brings up more music. Hers is the complete opposite of Maddy's, the kind of music popular before I was born.

"That's not even oldies. That's *prehistoric*," Maddy says.

"Ignore her," Grace says. "I think you'd be great at this. Real old school music."

"I don't know," I say. "It's a lot to learn in a couple hours."

"Well, what do you know?" Maddy asks.

Oldies, I think. I remember when I used to sing Creedence in the car, how little Maddy would whine about it to make me turn it off. She would have me put in one of her Disney tapes, usually *Beauty and the Beast*—

"Disney," I say.

"What?"

"Disney songs. Like *Beauty and the Beast. Aladdin. Lion King*," I say. I list the movies Maddy watched endlessly as a child.

"I don't know," Grace says. "These are grown-ups, not kids."

Maddy elbows her partner in the ribs. "Don't listen to her. I think it's a brilliant idea. I used to have all of those on tape. Mom probably threw them out though." Her face brightens with a smile. "But hey, that's what iTunes is for, right?"

***

I get home at six o'clock, which is about ninety minutes earlier than usual. Tess is already in the kitchen, hard at work on a pot roast. "That smells good," I say.

She jumps a little at this. "Oh my. You gave me quite a start."

"Sorry."

"You're home early."

"We closed early." I look down at my feet and shift my weight; I always feel awkward in Tess's presence. There's something regal about her that makes me feel like a child. "Actually, I'm going out tonight. There's this karaoke bar—"

"A bar?"

"It's not like that. I'm just hanging around with Madison and Grace—"

"Oh, I see," Tess says. She's known Madison ever since Maddy was born, but that doesn't mean Tess approves of her lifestyle. "A place like that isn't fit for a girl your age."

"But I'm not going to drink. I'm going to *sing*."

"You can sing right here in your room."

"They're paying me to sing. Three hundred dollars."

Tess stares at me in disbelief. She's never heard me sing before, not even in church. "How long are you going to be there?"

"I'm supposed to go on at nine. It'll probably be an hour or two."

"You know I don't like you going out on your own at night."

"Maddy and Grace will be there." That's not a point in my favor. I hasten to add, "Maybe you and Uncle Jake could come too? I'd really like you there for support. Please, Aunt Tess?"

Tess thinks for a moment and then nods. "If it's that important to you, sweetheart, we'll be in the front row."

"Thanks." I shift nervously again. "I thought maybe you could help me get ready. I don't want to make a mess of it."

"Certainly. You just go upstairs and I'll be up in a few minutes."

"OK." I kiss Tess on the cheek and then bound up the stairs to get ready for my big night. In a couple of hours I'll be a professional singer.

Chapter 7

Maddy and Grace are in the club. Maddy grabs my hand and squeals. "Look at you! That's such a great dress."

"That dress is really nice," Grace says. She wraps me in a hug and pats my back.

"You really think it looks all right?" I ask. The dress is one of the expensive ones I bought last year, a strapless red number I'm surprised Tess let me wear out of the house.

"Gaga has nothing on you," Maddy says and I decide to take that as a compliment. Maddy and Grace share pleasantries with Jake and Tess. Maddy motions to the front of the room, by the stage. "We already got a table. You can sit with us."

"That's very thoughtful," Tess says.

There's someone else with a front-row seat. It takes me a moment to recognize Dr. Macintosh. He sits on the opposite side of the room from my little fan club. When the doctor waves to me, I excuse myself from the others.

"Shouldn't you be backstage?" he asks.

"I guess," I say. I look down at my shoes, heels that cost almost as much as the dress. "I'm not really into the whole showbiz thing."

"That must be your aunt and uncle," he says.

"Yes."

"And your friends? Madison and Grace?"

"Yes." I can feel my cheeks turn warm as I remember what I said about Grace during our sessions. "Grace is the taller one."

"I see. She is attractive, isn't she?"

My head snaps up. I glare at Dr. Macintosh. "Did you come here to spy on me?"

"Of course not. I came to support you."

"Well you have a funny way of doing it."

"I'm sorry," he says. He smiles at me. "It's hard to leave it in the office. That's why I try not to get involved with patients."

"'Involved?' Is that what we are?"

"Not in that sense. I only mean I don't usually visit with patients outside of the office."

"Then why are you?"

"Your little audition this morning piqued my curiosity."

"I see. Plus you get to see my friends and family, right? Get a little background on me?"

"Stacey—"

"I hope you enjoy the show. We'll talk about it in our next session."

I turn on my heels, something that would have killed me a year ago. I summon what dignity I have to march back over to my friends and family. Jake, being a cop, is already watching Dr. Macintosh. "Who's that?" he asks.

"A teacher from school. He came for moral support."

"Maybe we should ask him to sit with us," Tess says.

"No!" I say. I don't want Maddy and Grace to realize I'm seeing a shrink. "I'm going to get ready."

"You want any help?" Maddy asks.

"I'd rather be alone," I say. "So I can get my head together."

Before I can leave, Grace takes my hand. I hope Dr. Macintosh doesn't see this. "Just remember to breathe. If you get nervous, close your eyes and imagine you're somewhere safe, all by yourself."

"OK. Thanks."

Maddy crushes me in a hug. "Break a leg, kid."

I just hope I don't take that literally.

The emcee raises an eyebrow when I give him my song selections. "This isn't a nursery school, you know," he grumbles.

"I don't know many other songs."

I stalk over to a stool. I remember Grace's advice and take a few deep breaths to force air into my lungs. The last time I was on stage to perform was in second grade. I played one of the wise men in the Christmas pageant at church. I only had one line: "We seek the chosen one." When it came my turn to speak, my mind went to mush. All I could get out was, "Hi." After that I was relegated to the chorus or backstage.

This is a lot bigger than a church pageant. It's a long way from the Hollywood Bowl too, but it's still a professional gig. If I do this right, I could land other gigs, ones that pay even better. In time I might even be able to cut an album, go out on tour with some big act. My stomach churns as I think of myself on stage at a sports arena, so tiny against a sea of humanity.

I shouldn't be here. I should be at home, on the couch to watch *Grey's Anatomy* with Tess while Jake works in his study. Or else I could be out at a movie with Maddy and

Grace. I would sit off to one side and try to focus on the movie while Maddy and Grace focus on each other.

I'm still on the stool when I hear the emcee announce me. He calls me a "talented songbird." Jesus. I'm not a songbird. I'm not some little nightingale or mockingbird who jumps around on a little trapeze in a cage for someone's amusement. Am I?

I hear the audience applaud. It's now or never. I turn to look towards the emergency exit. Then I think of Maddy, Grace, Jake, and Tess. I won't let them down.

***

The karaoke bar is standing-room only. There must be two hundred people in here. Word must have gotten around about my last performance. I take a deep breath and wish I'd rehearsed some patter for when I came up to the microphone.

Like my last public performance, I squeak, "Hi." The microphone at least works. I clear my throat into it. "I'm, um, I'm going to sing a couple of songs. I hope you enjoy them."

I'm grateful for the screen with the words on it, because my mind has turned to mush again. I've heard "Beauty and the Beast" a thousand times at least, but I can't remember any of it as the music begins to play. While the intro plays, I take another deep breath to clear my mind.

I have to force the first words out of my mouth. I practically read them off the screen. Shit, I think. Everyone will laugh at me. Someone will probably put it on the Internet so the whole world can make me a punch line.

I'm about to bolt when I hear a shrill whistle. "We love you, Stacey!" Maddy shouts.

The tension melts away. I smile as I think of all those times with Maddy in the car, when she sang this very song. Now it's my turn to sing it for her. I turn away from the screen, to focus on her. I don't need the screen anymore.

I almost do what Grace suggested. Instead of some imaginary happy place, the rest of the karaoke bar falls away. It's just me and Maddy, back in the car. I see Maddy as she was back then, the way her chubby face lit up as the music played. Those were some of the best times between us, before I slipped out of her life.

The rest of the bar comes back in a rush as I finish. I flinch as I hear the applause, which reminds me there are other people in the room. Maddy of course leads the cheers and gives another shrill whistle. I feel my face turn warm from so much attention.

The next song goes a little more smoothly. By the third one I get the hang of it and let myself go with the flow of the music. I even risk a look around the bar at some of the other people who've paid their hard-earned money to hear me sing.

My gaze settles on Dr. Macintosh. He sits in the corner, legs crossed as if he's in one of our sessions. All he needs is the pad of paper and a pen. I'm sure he's taking mental notes to discuss with me later. He meets my gaze and gives me a nod. There's a smirk on his face; he's probably congratulating himself about my progress.

The two kids about my age behind the doctor also smirk. It's a different kind of smirk, though. I stumble over a line of the song as I realize they're ogling me. One shouts, "Take it off!"

I turn back to Dr. Macintosh. He's still got that smirk on his face. He's not as overt as the others, but it's still the same. He's not here to take notes; he's here to make a move on me. I imagine he'll go back after the show to butter me up with some compliments. Then he'll lean down to kiss my lips—

I stop singing. For a moment I just stare at the audience. "I'm sorry," I mumble into the microphone.

Then I run.

***

Some internal guidance system directs me back to the place where my new life began—more or less. The change actually happened underwater, at the bottom of the harbor. I still remember how I watched from the outside, like one of those out-of-body experiences, as I went from Detective Steve Fischer to a young woman who would eventually be named Stacey Chance.

I'm not at the bottom of the harbor this time. I'm on a park bench by the waterfront, outside a private marina. There are a variety of boats in the marina, some with sails and some with plain old motors. Some are the size of an RV while others are more the size of a destroyer. This is the place where Stacey was born.

I woke up on a metal pier at the edge of the harbor. I can't get to it right now, not unless I want to jump into the harbor and swim to it. I'm not that desperate, yet. For now I'm content to sit on the bench and hug myself in a vain attempt to warm myself. This dress isn't suited for a chilly night.

I don't know how I got to this place. All I remember is I ran out of the karaoke bar. How long ago was that? From the look of the sky it's still night, probably no later than midnight. I've run for a couple of hours at most. I don't feel that winded from the effort. This body always has run well.

When I woke up in this place the first time I ran all the way from here to my old apartment. I didn't have anything but an oversized jacket and galoshes I stole from one of the yachts in the harbor. At least this time I have the dress and my shoes. The latter comes as a surprise. The last time I ran around the city in a panic I kicked my shoes off and cut the hell out of my feet. Maybe my subconscious remembered that. It probably helps that I've gotten used to women's shoes since then.

Something touches my shoulder. I spin around and gasp. "Hey," Maddy says. "We've been looking all over for you."

"Well you found me."

"What are you doing here?"

"Have to be somewhere."

"You mind having some company?"

"It's a free country." I slide over so Maddy can sit down next to me.

"You really had us all worried. Jake put an APB out on you."

"Really?"

"Tess is totally freaked. I think she thought you'd do something, you know?"

I stare at the water and think of how easy it would be to jump in and swim until I tire and drown. Or I could jump off a building. Find something sharp to slit my wrists. There are plenty of ways to kill yourself in this city if you want to do it bad enough. Tess has probably thought of all of them right now.

"I'm sorry," I say. "I didn't mean to worry her."

"It'll be fine. I can call her. If you want me to."

"Like I said, it's a free country."

"How long are you planning to stay out here?"

"I don't know."

"Well you should probably find something a little warmer to wear before you turn blue."

"I'm fine."

"I wish Grace were here. She'd know what to say. Talking with crazy people is what she does."

"You think I'm crazy?"

"Would a sane person leave in the middle of her set?"

"That doesn't make me crazy. Just a coward."

"Was it stage fright? From where I was sitting you were doing really good. It was unbelievable, really."

"Thanks."

"So why'd you stop?"

"I don't know. I felt sick."

"You felt so sick you ran halfway across the city?"

"Fresh air does me good."

"Come on, Stace. I thought we were friends."

"We are."

"Then why can't you tell me what's going on?"

"Maybe because I don't know myself."

Maddy puts her arm around my shoulder. She pulls me against her body. The warmth of her body helps to take some of the chill off. "It's all right. I'm sure you can find somewhere else to perform."

"I don't want to *perform*. I'm not one of those organ grinder monkeys." I tear myself away from Maddy and get to my feet. "I don't want to be a singer, I don't want to run Grace's store, and I don't want to go back to college!"

"Then what do you want? Huh? Just tell me and I'll help you do it."

I stare at her helplessly, unable to say what I really want. I want to be her dad again. I thought being Maddy's friend would be enough, but it's not. I want her to run to me for advice, not to dispense it to me like my big sister. "I—"

Before I can say anything else, I feel something prick my shoulder. At first I think I've been shot again, but when I look down I see it's a tranquilizer dart, the kind used to put down escaped zoo animals. "What the—?"

My legs turn to goo; I drop to the ground. Maddy starts to scream, but then a gloved hand clamps over her mouth. Before I pass out, I see black shapes surround us. I figure before long I'll end up back at the bottom of the harbor, only this time I won't wake up.

Part 2
Lab Rats

Chapter 8

I've been in hospital rooms a few times. You can't be a cop for thirty years in this city and not wind up in a hospital once or twice. In my case it was three times, if you don't count the time Big Al pulled a bullet out of my shoulder.

So I have enough experience to recognize the beeping and humming of hospital machines to monitor my vital signs with my eyes still closed. I lie suspended in that place between sleep and wakefulness; my last moments of consciousness come back slowly to me. Maddy and I were on the waterfront, by that private marina where I first woke up as a woman. We argued—until a tranquilizer dart hit me in the arm.

I know I ought to wake up and raise some hell about the situation, but I'm still groggy from the tranquilizer dart. I wonder what they gave me? I wonder too if it will have any interaction with the FY-1978 still in my blood? Dr. Palmer has cautioned me about that a few times. I try not to even take an aspirin if I can help it in case some allergic reaction causes me to grow a third arm or something.

I open my eyes. It's dark in the room, but the light from the machines is enough for me to see I'm not in a hospital room. Overhead I see steel beams instead of ceiling tiles. There's not enough light for me to see where the roof is, but it's probably a few stories up. Where the hell am I?

I try to sit up; I don't get very far. Something holds me down. I turn my head to the side, enough to see straps that hold me down to a bed that's a glorified gurney. I try to move my legs, but they're strapped down too. At least they let me move my head around.

I turn my head to the other side and see the machines that monitor my vitals. I have no idea if the numbers are good or not. Beside the machines are two metal stands with plastic bags that hang from them. The one that's full is probably an IV for nutrients. The empty one could be one I already used up.

I thrash around on the gurney, but the straps are too strong for me to break. Then again at the moment they could be made of paper and I might not be able to break them. My limbs feel like someone filled them with wet sand. I try to move around anyway, until I see part of the reason for my weariness.

My left arm looks like that of a drug addict. The skin is paler than Kristen Stewart's in those *Twilight* movies Maddy likes to watch. Someone's taken my blood with a needle. Why someone would do that is obvious: FY-1978. Did Lennox Pharmaceuticals decide to take a few unauthorized samples from me? Or maybe I had a reaction to the tranquilizer and Dr. Palmer took some blood to analyze. This might be some secret company lab where they can keep it quiet.

I won't get any answers on my back. I want to scream, but I can't. My throat is too dry. I spend another minute to work up some spit into my mouth. What finally comes out is more of a wheeze than a scream.

But it's enough. I hear footsteps.

***

I close my eyes a second before a light comes on. I open my eyes slowly to give myself time to adjust to the light. With the light, I can see I'm not in an actual room, just an area sectioned off by some dark green curtains. The ceiling is as high as I imagined before, which means I'm probably in a converted factory or warehouse. But why?

The curtain parts and I get my first visitor. It's an Asian woman, dressed in a white smock that looks more appropriate for a butcher than a nurse. The woman is probably four inches shorter than I am, but ten pounds or so heavier. When she smiles, wrinkles spread out from the corners of her eyes and mouth; she's probably in her early forties then. Her teeth are yellowed and crooked, which means she doesn't make a lot of money at whatever she does.

"Hello Stacey," she says.

"I know you?" I croak.

"Not yet. I am Qiang, your caretaker." She bows slightly to me. There's a thick accent to indicate she didn't come here very long ago from the Far East.

"Where—?"

She shushes me and then presses a warm hand to my forehead. "Relax," she says. "I will not hurt you."

"What—?"

She cuts me off again; this time she dribbles water into my mouth. I swish it around for a few moments, to taste for anything funny in it. It seems like regular lukewarm water. I swallow it and wait to pass out again, but I don't.

The water loosens up my throat enough that I can ask, "Where am I?"

"You are safe."

"Where?"

"That I cannot say."

"Can't or won't?"

"I cannot say."

"What about Maddy? Can you tell me where she is?"

"Your friend? She is being cared for."

I think of all those little pinpricks in my arm. Are they "caring" for Maddy in the same way? "What do you want with her?"

"I cannot say."

"Goddamnit, if you hurt her—" I try to break through the straps, but I'm still too weak. Qiang pushes me back down and pins me by the shoulders.

"Do not move. You will hurt yourself."

"You mean you'll hurt me."

"I have no wish to hurt you. I am here to care for you."

"If you want to care for me, how about letting me go home?"

"I cannot do that."

"Then give me a phone so I can call my uncle."

"That is not possible."

"Why not? You got him in here too?"

"I cannot say."

"Lot of help you are."

Qiang squints behind her glasses at my monitors. "You must relax, please."

"How can I relax when I don't know where I am or what you're doing to me?"

Her hand moves to stroke my hair. She smiles at me again. "Do not worry, you are in no danger. Neither is your friend."

"Prove it. Let me see Maddy."

"You will, in time. When you are strong enough. For now, rest. Relax."

"I don't want to, you—" I don't see the needle, but I feel it prick my neck. A few moments later, I'm asleep again.

***

The next time I wake up, the room is dark again. My throat is moist enough that I can call out for Maddy. If there aren't real rooms in this building then maybe she'll be able to hear me. My voice still isn't very strong; I can't even hear an echo of my attempted shout. My singing career might be over before it ever began.

I start to laugh at this thought. The hoarse laughter hurts my tender throat, but I can't stop myself. I laugh until tears come to my eyes. I can't do anything to wipe them away, not with my hands tied down. This only prompts me to laugh harder at my ridiculous situation.

The first thing to do in a situation like this is to evaluate my surroundings. It's too bad my "caretaker" couldn't have left a scalpel or some other sharp implement where I could grab it. From what I can tell I have on a standard hospital gown, so there aren't any pockets where I might find something useful. My head can't move enough and the straps are much too strong for me to bite my way through.

With that established, I wiggle my hands to see if there's any slack to my bonds. They stay as tight as before around my wrists. I try my legs with similar results. I try to think of something else. My hands can move enough to feel the sides of the gurney. I poke around to search for a piece of metal that might break off for use as a shiv. I can't find anything weak enough for me to break off, not in my current condition. For the moment I'm trapped about as well as anyone can be.

I've got to do something. I can't just lie here while they do God only knows what to my daughter. I start to thrash against the straps again; I hope I can get one of those surges of adrenaline they talk about in the news that lets a mother lift a car off of her baby. All that happens for me is I tire myself out after a couple of minutes. Tired and defeated, there's nothing left to do but scream, "You monsters! Let her go!"

My little tirade finally gets some attention. It's not Qiang who answers. A man's voice hisses, "Don't worry, Mr. Fischer. We have no intention of harming your daughter, so long as you're a good girl and cooperate."

It's too dark for me to see who's said this. I turn my head as much as possible, but I still don't see anyone. "I don't know who you're talking about," I say. "My name is Stacey—"

The light comes on and my whimper swallows the rest of my sentence. When I've blinked most of the green and purple blobs away, I see the man who's spoken beside the gurney. Like Qiang he's Asian, only he wears a black suit and horned-rim glasses. He's got one of those Bluetooth things on his left ear; is that so he can keep in touch with Qiang and any hired muscle he's got here?

He bends over the gurney to look into my eyes. I try not to flinch at this. I have to be strong, try to intimidate him. That won't be easy since he holds all of the cards right now. "Your daughter looks so much like you. It's uncanny."

"She's not my daughter. She's my friend. I don't know who this Mr. Fischer is, but he's got nothing to do with us."

The man steps back. He smiles beneath his mustache. "There's no need to lie, Mr. Fischer. I know all about FY-1978. I know more about it than you do. Perhaps even more than your friend Dr. Palmer."

"Did you take her too?"

"No need. We already have her work."

"How?"

"We have our sources."

"Who are you?"

"Oh, how impolite of me to forget that. My name is Dr. Huang Ling."

"Ling? Are you—?"

"Yes, he was my father." Ling's eyes narrow behind his glasses. "He was the one you murdered the first time we tried to obtain the FY-1978 formula."

"I didn't kill him. That was Artie Luther and his goons."

"Don't lie to me. I know everything. You were the one who convinced my father to balk at Mr. Luther's offer. If not for your interference, he would have bought the formula and left without incident."

I laugh at this. "You really think that? Lex was never going to let your father walk out of there alive. Soon as he had the money, he would have had those guys in the Mercedes mow your father down. You can count on that."

I wait for Ling to slap me or maybe wring my neck, but he doesn't. He only nods slightly. "There's no way to know for certain, is there? I will still hold you responsible for his death, as I am bound to do by family honor."

"So that's what this is about? Revenge?"

"That is only a pleasant secondary benefit." He grabs my left arm at the elbow and runs his thumb along my track marks. "I am mostly concerned with is your blood."

"Why? You already have the FY-1978. You probably got the original formula and Dr. Nath's notes too."

"Very true, but that is still not a working model of the serum. For that, we need your blood."

"Fine, you have my blood. Now let us go."

"I'm afraid not. You would most certainly tell your friend the police officer. We can't afford any interference at this juncture."

"What am I going to tell him? I don't know anything except your name. You'll probably be back in China before we could find you."

"Perhaps, but I see no reason to take the chance."

"That's no reason to keep Maddy. She doesn't know anything."

"That is also very true. You haven't told her who you really are, have you? She thinks of you only as her dear friend." When he touches my hair, I flinch. "You wanted to protect her, like any father would. That is why my father wouldn't let me go to the meeting with Mr. Luther."

"He was a smart man then, wasn't he?"

"Not smart enough to avoid his fate."

"Look, I'll do whatever you want. Just let Madison go. She's not part of this."

"I'm afraid not. Her presence will guarantee your cooperation with our experiments."

"What experiments?"

"You'll find out, in time. For now, you need to rest. Miss Qiang will give you something to help you sleep."

Before I can say anything, I feel the needle in my neck again. Once more everything goes dark.

Chapter 9

There's no clock or window so I can't keep track of time. Every so often I wake up for a few minutes, long enough to see I'm still strapped to the gurney. I make a feeble attempt to break the straps that hold me down. When that fails I call out for Maddy. I never hear her answer me.

Qiang comes in a minute later. She touches my forehead and then says her usual, "You must relax. You are safe here."

"I want to see my daughter. I want to see Maddy!"

I never see the needle until it's too late. There's the slight prick in my neck and then everything begins to fade again. I'm not sure how many times this cycle repeats itself. Everything runs together into one long nightmare.

One time I wake up and things are different. I hear a rumble like a car's engine. I can't see anything but a hazy brown light. It's warm around me. I feel my breath against my face. They must have a bag over my head. I try again to free myself. It doesn't take Qiang so long to come to me this time.

"Do not worry, Stacey. Everything is all right."

"Where are you taking me? Where's Maddy?"

Qiang doesn't answer me; she lets the needle do it for her. I feel it prick my neck and then the hazy brown light turns to blackness.

The next time I wake up, something is different. There's more light in the room; sunlight comes through a crack in the wall. When I turn my head, I see a wall with a chalkboard on it. There are wrinkled signs with the letters of the alphabet written in cursive.

I'm in a classroom. From the dank smell of the place, not one that's been used for a while. They must have taken me from that warehouse to an old elementary school, one that's been closed down. That narrows my location down to about two-dozen possible places. That is if I'm still in the city. By now they might have carted me across the country, or even across the ocean to China.

There's another difference I note when I start to thrash around on the gurney. There aren't any straps to hold me down, so my thrashing lands me on the floor, hard. I lay dazed for a moment before I sit up. I don't have on a hospital gown anymore; I'm clad in dark blue pajamas. I roll up the left sleeve of the pajama top. I have to squint in the darkness to see the skin of my elbow. It's still pale as a ghost, but there aren't so many puncture marks.

My muscles have atrophied from all that time spent on a gurney. I have to grab onto the bed in order to lever myself into a standing position. My knees are still wobbly after a few moments on my feet. I plant one hand against the wall to help support me as I survey my new prison.

Dr. Ling and Qiang have been careful not to leave me anything too useful. There aren't any tools around. No loose boards I can pry apart. The closest to a weapon I can find is a mildewed history textbook. I flip through the table of contents; the textbook stops after the Watergate scandal. Either this school closed thirty years ago or they didn't bother to update their books for a while.

The door is solid wood, on which is still a cutout of a centipede with a mortarboard atop its head. I try the knob, but of course it won't open. If I look around I might find something I can use to pick the lock. I doubt they're so stupid as to not have another lock on the outside, probably a padlock. If I'm really valuable to them they might have a fancy computerized lock on the door.

The boards over the windows are on the outside. I give them a few good pushes anyway, or as good as I can do in my weakened condition. There's nothing in the room I can use as a battering ram, just the gurney and a bedpan. Out of desperation I look up at the ceiling. Maybe if I can climb up on the gurney I can free the tiles.

I manage to stand on top of the gurney for all of two seconds before my knees buckle. I drop onto the gurney; it collapses onto its side. I hit my head on the floor hard enough that I see stars. As I lie on the floor in a daze again, tears come to my eyes.

Then I hear a tap on the wall. "Stace? Is that you?" Maddy's voice hisses.

I crawl over to the wall. I give it a tap. "Maddy?"

"Stace?"

"Are you all right? Are you hurt?"

"I'm fine. Just a little tired. What's going on? Where are we?"

"We're in an old school. I'm not sure where."

"Who are these people? What do they want?"

I've never told Maddy anything about Lennox Pharmaceuticals or FY-1978. She and Grace think I'm a nineteen-year-old girl who ran away from her abusive parents three years ago. Through the wall of an elementary school-turned-prison isn't how I want to explain the truth.

"I don't know," I say. "They're doing some kind of medical tests on me. Have they done anything to you?"

"No. This Chinese lady keeps giving me a shot to knock me out."

"Me too." I press against the wall. I wish I could break through it so I could hug Maddy, tell her everything's going to be all right. Or maybe she could do the same for me. "We're going to get out of here. It'll be fine."

"Sure it will," Maddy says. I can hear her bitterness through the wall.

"No, listen, can you stand on your bed? Try to pop one of the ceiling tiles."

"I'll try."

I'm not sure how long it is before she taps on the wall to get my attention. "It's no good," she says. "It's too small."

"That's all right," I say. I try to keep my voice calm. "We'll find another way. Is there anything you can use for a weapon?"

"All that's in here is the bed, a bedpan, and a globe. I don't think those would do much."

"Probably not."

"How long have we been here?"

"I don't know. I'm sure Uncle Jake has everyone out looking for us."

"They'll never find us here," Maddy says. I can hear her muffled sob through the wall. "What are they going to do to us?"

Maddy's tears make me want to cry again. I tell myself I have to be strong right now. "Madison, listen to me," I say. I muster as much authority as I can with my songbird voice. "We're not going to die here. We're going to find a way out. I promise."

"Sure," she says.

"We just have to stay calm and think."

"All right."

I run through everything I already tried. Maddy's done it with her cell too. Dr. Ling's done a nice job with the place. But there has to be a weakness somewhere. We just need to find it and exploit it.

I hear a metallic rattle at the door, probably that padlock I imagined. "Someone's coming," I whisper to Maddy. Then I hurry to put the gurney back. It's hard work given how weak I am. I jump on top of the bed as Qiang appears through the doorway.

She carries a metal tray. I worry at first that it might be another shot or surgical tools or something like that, but then I smell food. "It is time to eat," she says. "You need to get your strength back."

"So you can take more blood?"

"I hope not."

If I weren't so weak I'd try to knock her down and then make a break for it. Dr. Ling probably has guards somewhere, but it would be better than to sit around and wait for him to dispose of me like so many used needles. At the moment, though, I doubt I could run ten yards before I collapse from exhaustion.

She sets the tray on the end of the bed. It looks like some kind of stew, a roll, and a glass of milk. "Shouldn't you be serving fried rice and egg rolls?" I ask.

"I thought this would be more to your liking," she says. "I can send it back."

The pained expression on her face indicates I've actually hurt her feelings. Maybe there's a way out of here after all. "No, this will be fine," I say. The utensils she gives me are plastic, not strong enough to even give her a nasty scratch.

I dig into the stew. That's not part of the act; I'm really hungry after nothing but IV fluids for however long it's been. "This is good. Did you make it?"

"Yes. It is a family recipe."

"So you've made it for your family?"

"I did."

"But not anymore? They didn't come to America with you?"

The pained expression comes across Qiang's face again. "This is not an appropriate conversation. I will pick up your tray in a few hours. Does your bedpan need changing?"

"No, not yet. Wouldn't it be easier to let me use the bathroom? I assume there's one in this place somewhere."

"That would not be acceptable. The bedpan will have to suffice." The way she marches out of the room with her back ramrod straight and legs stiff tells me she's trying not to break down after what I said. Something in her past haunts her, something about her family. If I can work on her a little bit, maybe she'll help me and Maddy escape.

Qiang stops by the next time while I thumb through the history book. I didn't do so well in my American history class at community college, despite that I'd lived through the last fifty years of history. "I don't suppose you could get me something else to read? A newspaper maybe?"

"I will ask about that."

"Dr. Ling, right? He's the one running the show?"

"It is not my place to say."

She takes the tray from where I left it on the floor. I left her a little present in the bedpan too. She picks up the bedpan delicately, but doesn't show any sign of revulsion. She's probably done this before. "So are you a nurse back in your country?"

"Dr. Ling says I should not answer such personal questions."

"I see. He's probably watching us right now, isn't he? This is a real nice prison he's built for us. How long is he planning to keep us here?"

"I do not know."

"Is he going to hurt Madison?"

"I do not know."

I jump off the bed. I take a few steps towards her. I lower my voice to make sure Maddy can't hear me through the wall. "I have to know: is he going to hurt my daughter?"

"I do not know."

She starts to walk away, but I lunge at her. I grab her shoulder. "Tell me!" I can't get any farther before someone comes through the door. Something heavy hits me in the back of the head.

I'm out before I hit the floor.

***

I wake up to something cold against the back of my head. With a groan I reach back and feel an ice pack with a hand on it that's not mine. I open my eyes and see Qiang beside me. I'm back on my bed, the top part of the gurney up so I'm in a reclining position.

"You should not have done that," Qiang says.

"No kidding," I grumble.

"You must not try to escape. You will only end up hurting your daughter."

Qiang's probably right about that. I might be too valuable for Ling to kill, but Maddy isn't. "Is she all right? Did they hurt her?"

"No, she is fine. For the moment."

"Can I see her?"

"I am afraid not."

"I won't try to run again. I just want to know she's all right."

"That is not possible." She takes the ice pack from my head and then smoothes down my wet hair. "You must try to relax. We have no wish to harm either of you."

"Yet. But when they're done with us, what do you think is going to happen? Those friends of yours will put a couple of bullets into us and then drop us into the river."

"Dr. Ling would not do that. He is an honorable man."

"Just like his father, right? Did he ever tell you how his father died?"

"That is not relevant."

"He was trying to buy the formula—the one in my blood—from a gangster named Artie Luther. The deal went sour and he got shot."

"That is not relevant," she says again, but I can see her face tighten.

"These aren't nice people, Qiang. Do yourself a favor and get out of here as soon as you can because chances are you'll end up in the harbor with us."

"Dr. Ling would not hurt me."

"Oh no? You, me, and Maddy can compromise his little operation. If any of us goes to the cops, he's screwed. You really think he'll keep us around?"

"He promised—"

"Promises aren't worth a damn from people like that."

I'm not prepared for her to slap me. I've been hit a lot harder, but the sting is still enough to bring tears to my eyes. Qiang seems as surprised about it as I am. She presses the ice pack to my cheek to take away the pain. "I am sorry, Stacey. I did not mean to strike you."

"It's fine," I say. I push the ice pack away from my face. "What did he promise you? Money? A job? Love?"

"My daughter," she says. Then she turns on her heel and storms out.

***

I wait a little while before I go over to the wall I share with Maddy. I tap on the wall and hope she's not asleep—or something worse. "Maddy? Are you all right?"

I sigh with relief when I hear Maddy say, "I'm fine. How about you?"

"Just a little headache thanks to Dr. Ling's friends."

"Who?"

"Dr. Ling. That's his name. The guy who took us. He hasn't been in to see you?"

"No, just that woman. I know this sounds weird, but she seems nice."

"I know. But we have to remember she's the enemy."

"Right." Through the wall I hear Maddy sigh. "What do you think Grace is doing right now?"

"Probably thinking about you." Thinking about *us*, I want to say.

"I miss her so much. I didn't even get the chance to say goodbye to her." I hear Maddy start to cry.

I desperately wish I could break through the wall so I could hold her. All I can do is sit there and say, "It'll be all right, Maddy. You'll see Grace again. We'll find a way out of this."

"I know," she says with a sniffle. "I'm going to sleep now, OK?"

"Sure. I'll be right here, though if you need anything." I fetch the pillows off the gurney, and make myself a nest by the wall. For hours I listen to Maddy cry before her sobs finally turn to the soft breathing of sleep.

Chapter 10

Now that there's a little bit of light in my cell and no one constantly drugs me, I can keep better track of the days. The plastic utensils Qiang gives me for my meals can't do anything to a person, but the prongs of the fork can scratch the wall. That lets me keep track of how long Maddy and I have been here.

As the notches start to pile up, I continue to work on Qiang. But since she mentioned Ling's promise about her daughter, Qiang has all but clammed up. She still encourages me to eat and relax, though now with an iciness in her voice. Maddy's noticed the difference too. We spend a lot of our time talking through the wall. I read from the history textbook sometimes to help us stay occupied.

Other times Maddy talks about life outside of this awful place. I start to feel like a priest in a confessional as she opens up to me. "Last Christmas Mom finally asked me the Question."

"What question is that?" I ask.

"When am I going to settle down and make her some grandchildren?"

"Really?"

"Yeah. She just blurted it out over dessert, after Number Four went to watch football or something like that."

Number Four would be my ex-wife's fourth husband, the third after me. I've never met any of them; Maddy hasn't reintroduced me to my wife yet. I haven't been adamant to make that happen either. "She does know about you and Grace, doesn't she?"

"Sort of."

"Sort of?"

"She knows I'm a lesbian. She was really cool about the whole thing when she found out. We had one of those Lifetime talks on my bed when I was fifteen. She said all that stuff about how it's OK if that's what makes me happy and everything."

"Well, that's good," I say. That's been my opinion of Maddy's lifestyle as well, not that I ever got the chance to have a heart-to-heart with her about it. "So she knows you can't really make a baby, doesn't she?"

"She knows." Maddy stops to laugh bitterly through the wall. "Mom doesn't know shit about computers, so I guess she went to the library to ask the librarian about it. Can you see that? This old lady asking some dried-up librarian about how lesbians make babies?"

I force myself to laugh. It's hard for me to think of Debbie as an "old lady." She's only forty-nine. To a girl Maddy's age that's ancient. "That's pretty hard to believe," I say.

"It gets better. After she asked me, she brought out all these brochures."

"Brochures?"

"For sperm banks. She even offered to make me an appointment."

"Wow. And you didn't take her up on it?"

"God, no! I'm only twenty-three. You think I want to have a baby?"

"Well—" Despite how awkward it would be, part of me relishes the idea of being a grandfather. Of course I wouldn't really be the grandfather; I'd be Aunt Stacey.

"Don't tell me you're part of that old school who thinks every woman should have a kid before she's thirty? I mean, you don't want to have a baby, do you?"

"No!" I say maybe a little too quickly. My reasons are a little different than Maddy's. Besides my body's age, I'm not sure what would happen if I tried to carry a baby with FY-1978 in my blood. "I'm sure you'll be a great mom someday."

"Yeah, maybe. If we get out of here." Neither of us says anything for a while after that. Then Maddy says, "I guess I'll hit the hay. Goodnight."

"Goodnight," I say and then the door to my cell bursts open. A couple of Dr. Ling's goons march in. Before I can get up, they yank me away from the wall by one arm. "Stacey?" Maddy shouts through the wall.

"It's all right, Maddy. Everything will be fine," I shout. I hope she can hear me as they drag me away.

***

The goons drag me through the door of an office. It probably used to be the principal's office back in the day. Now it's Dr. Ling's office. He hasn't done much with the space, just cleaned up the wooden desk and brought in a new leather chair. There's also a lamp on the desk that provides the only light right now. The shadows from the lamp give his face a sinister look. That's probably the idea.

"Have a seat, Mr. Fischer," he says.

The only other chair is a plastic one meant to accommodate kindergartners. I feel like a fatty as I sit down on the chair and hear it creak dangerously. Not to mention the way my ass spills over either side of it. This is more intimidation, so that I have to look up at him as if he's a lot bigger than me.

"It's a pity my guards interrupted you when they did. Such a touching moment."

"Why don't you just tell me what you want?"

Dr. Ling nods and then opens a folder on his desk. "It seems we're ready to begin trials of the new serum."

"Hooray for you. I suppose that means my usefulness is at an end, right?"

"Not quite. As I said, we're ready to begin trials. That does not mean the drug is complete yet."

"If you're not going to kill me, then what do you want?"

"I thought you should be here to witness this momentous occasion."

"I'd rather you let me see my daughter."

"Don't worry, you'll see her soon enough."

"What the hell do you mean by that?"

One of the goons who brought me in returns. This time he carries a little TV set. He sets it down gently on Ling's desk. Ling fusses with the cords before the screen comes to life. "Very good," Ling says. He turns to the guard. "You may leave Mr. Fischer and I."

After the guard stomps out of the room, Ling turns the TV so I can see it. The screen is about as grainy as the surveillance cameras in your local 7-11. I squint a little to make out a room similar to mine, with a chalkboard that dominates one wall.

In the corner is Maddy.

She looks about like I remember, though a little paler and thinner. Her hair is longer too, down to almost her waist. At the moment she has the hair on her right side pushed back as she presses one ear to the wall. "Stace? Are you all right? Are you there?"

"Her concern for you is very touching," Dr. Ling says.

"Whatever you're going to do to her, don't," I say. "She hasn't done anything. She's innocent."

"We're not going to harm her. At least not if my calculations are correct."

"Calculations? What—?" I stop as I remember what Ling said. His version of FY-1978 is ready for trials. *Human* trials. He of course doesn't want to use it on me and pollute the gold mine in my veins. And why try it on Qiang or one of his henchmen when he has a perfectly good guinea pig in Maddy? "No! You can't!"

"Of course I can."

I launch myself across the desk. Before my hands can grab Ling's throat to wring the life from him, one of Ling's guards yanks me back by the hair, hard enough that my scalp burns with pain. The guard tosses me back onto the chair. He doesn't pull a weapon; he just crosses arms with biceps bigger around than my head. Any time he wants, he could snap me like a twig.

"Relax, Mr. Fischer. Your daughter should be fine."

Or she could end up as a man, the inverse of what happened to me. Or she might gain another head. Or she might turn into a puddle of goo on the floor. No matter what, I know no good can come from her being injected with FY-1978. "Please don't do this. Test it on me."

"You're much too valuable to waste on a first trial."

"Then find someone else. Grab some bum off the streets. Just not my daughter. *Please.*"

"There's no time for that, Mr. Fischer." He opens another folder. "Your daughter is a fine specimen. She's in remarkable health. You should be proud."

"I am. That's why you have to find someone else. There must be—"

"It would take weeks to find another specimen so suitable for our tests."

"She's not a specimen! She's my daughter!"

"Be that as it may, she's going to be a part of history now."

The door to her cell opens and two goons as big as the one who looms over me storm inside. I feel a surge of pride to watch Maddy throw herself at them. She kicks one in the crotch and he doubles over. The other one she tries to hit in the throat, but he blocks the punch with one massive forearm. He shoves her against the wall as if she's made out of straw. "You son of a bitch!" she shouts. "Try that again."

He doesn't need to. He reaches to his hip for his pistol. That's enough to cool Maddy's bravado. "What do you want?" she asks, her voice calmer.

"We only want to give you a shot," Qiang says from off-screen. She appears on the screen with a syringe. "It won't hurt."

"I don't want any more shots. I want to go home with my friend."

"You will be able to go home soon," Qiang says. "After you take your medicine."

"Yeah, right," Maddy says. "Where's Stacey? What did you do to her?"

"Your friend is fine. We took her for some tests."

"Probably to test if she can float with a rock tied around her ankle."

"She is unharmed—for the moment. If you choose not to cooperate, we may be forced to take drastic measures."

"Leave her alone! She's just a kid."

"We do not wish to hurt her, or you. Please, relax. Let me administer your medicine."

I silently urge Maddy to hold out, to keep them from injecting her with the serum for as long as possible. But she doesn't. She wants to help me, keep me safe the way I want to for her.

"All right," she says. "Just make it quick."

Qiang is quick. She brushes hair away from Maddy's face with one hand. With the other she stabs the needle into the side of Maddy's neck. As Qiang presses down on the plunger, I start to cry.

Maddy's body goes stiff, her mouth locked in a wordless scream of pain. Qiang helpfully eases Maddy onto the floor, where she remains motionless for over a minute. Maybe we'll be lucky and this batch will be a dud. Maybe nothing will happen to Maddy.

We're not that lucky. The first changes are subtle. Her hair starts to darken. It goes from its natural light brown to darker shades until it's black. Too bad that's not all that happens. Next I see her face reshape itself. Her cheeks turn pudgier. As for her eyes, they seem to narrow as if she's squinting—

"She's turning Chinese," I whisper. I turn to Ling, my fists clenched. "You son of a bitch, what are you doing to her?"

"The serum uses gene therapy. I simply added some strands borrowed from Miss Qiang."

"Why would you want to do that?"

"Imagine if my government had such a serum in its possession, one that could make its agents look like ordinary white Americans. Or black Americans. Or any other ethnicity imaginable. Are you starting to understand?"

I understand perfectly. Dr. Nath invented FY-1978 ostensibly as a cosmetic drug—a Fountain of Youth in a syringe. She had greater hopes to use it to treat cancer, AIDS, Parkinson's, Alzheimer's, and other diseases. Dr. Ling's come up with an entirely different use for it, one that might be even more profitable. A drug that could make it easier than ever for insurgents to infiltrate American society. The Chinese could use it to sneak over thousands of agents who could seamlessly blend in. So could anyone else willing to pay the right price.

"You watched a few too many James Bond movies," I say.

"Perhaps, but you can't deny the potential of this formula."

"It's fucking crazy," I grumble.

I turn back to the screen to see the drug isn't done with my now-Chinese daughter yet. Her pajamas look looser on her than before. As I watch, her hands and feet disappear inside the material. She's probably in her early teens right now. I pray for that to be as far as it goes, but it's not. Her body continues to compact within the pajamas.

Her head shrinks at the same rate. As it does, despite the differences from her changed ethnicity, I see the face of my little girl. My little girl from before I left her, when we were still a somewhat happy family. "Oh God."

She gets even smaller, so small that the top of the pajamas go down to her ankles. She's a toddler now, five or maybe even four. How much younger will she get? Will she revert back to an infant? Maybe she'll disappear entirely.

But she doesn't. Ling and I stare at the screen for a good two minutes to make sure she's stopped shrinking. I let out a sigh of relief. My daughter might be a toddler again, but at least she's alive.

Ling shakes his head. He takes a cell phone from off his belt. I can't understand what he barks into the phone, but it doesn't sound congratulatory. When he finishes, Ling turns to the guard. "Tell Miss Qiang to get some blood samples for me to study. And take Mr. Fischer with you. We'll need his help to calm the child down when she wakes up."

The guard seizes me by the collar. As he drags me away, I scream, "You son of a bitch! I'll get you for this!"

Chapter 11

I pass Qiang in the doorway. She has a couple vials of little Maddy's blood. "You monster! How could you? How could you do that to my daughter?"

Qiang stops. She looks back at Maddy on the floor, engulfed by her pajamas. "I am sorry, Stacey. I did not mean for this to happen."

"You're as bad as he is," I hiss at her. Then the guard shoves me into the room.

They leave me alone with Maddy, though I'm sure Ling still watches us with his cameras. I rush over to her and kneel at her side. I touch one of her pudgy cheeks to make sure it's still warm. I put one hand against the potbelly that bulges against the pajamas to make sure she's still breathing.

I grunt as I lift her up. Despite a couple of weeks of recovery, I'm still weak from all that blood they drained out of me. I barely manage to get Maddy over to the gurney. She whimpers a little as I set her down.

I stay by her bed for a long time and remember how I used to watch her sleep the last time she was this age. Like then she looks so peaceful, so angelic that it nearly brings tears to my eyes. I've never seen anything so beautiful before or since as my little girl as she sleeps.

The tears start to flow again when she sticks her thumb in her mouth. I watch her happily suck on her thumb, a habit her mother and I spent a lot of time and effort to break her of. I finally started to dip her thumb in vinegar while she slept, so when she put her thumb in her mouth it would taste awful. A couple weeks of that and she broke the habit. I guess I'll have to try it again.

As I used to do, I pull the blankets over her, up to her chin. Then I stroke Maddy's black hair while she sleeps. "It's all right, honey. Daddy's here. I'll find a way out of this for us."

In her sleep, Maddy whimpers again.

***

I try to stay awake for when Maddy finally wakes up. As the hours go by, my eyelids start to get heavy. The sounds of her gentle breathing eventually lull me to sleep.

I wake up to a shriek. As I jump to my feet, I know the shriek came from Maddy. She screams as she stares at her tiny, chubby hands, the thumb of the left one coated in slobber. "Oh my God!" she screams. Her little football-shaped eyes focus on me. They've turned brown now instead of their natural blue. "Stace? What's happened to me?"

"It's all right," I say.

"The hell it is! I'm a baby!"

"I know. Just calm down. Let me explain."

"You know? Did you help them?" Her pudgy cheeks turn red and tears bubble up in her eyes. "Did you do this to me?"

"No, of course not. Dr. Ling had me in his office. I saw the whole thing."

"What did they do to me?" She looks around frantically, for a mirror I'm sure. There aren't any mirrors in here. No glass either. Then I see the metal tray from Maddy's last meal.

"Stay right there."

"Don't go, Stace. Please."

"I'm not going far, all right?"

"OK."

I grab the tray from the corner of the room. It's not a perfect mirror, especially in the dim light of the room, but it's better than nothing. I bring it over to Maddy and press it into her hands. She holds the tray up in front of her face. The tears start to flow even faster. "I'm a fat *Chinese* baby!" she wails.

All I can think to do is pat her gently on the back. "I know, honey." I pull her into a hug, to force her not to look at herself. "It'll be all right. We'll find a way to change you back."

"What did they do, Stace? Tell me!"

I let go of her and then crouch down so my eyes are level with hers. "They gave you an experimental drug. It's called FY-1978. It's an anti-aging drug."

"Anti-aging? It turned me into a baby!"

"I know." I wish Dr. Palmer were here; she could explain it a lot better than I can. Even Dr. Ling would be an improvement right now. "That's what it does, make you younger."

"Why am I Chinese?"

"He put some Chinese DNA in the serum."

"What?"

"I don't really understand it either. All I know is they gave you this drug and it made you like this."

"Why?"

"They used you as a guinea pig, to see if it worked."

"It worked all right."

"It sure did."

Maddy picks up the tray again. After a minute, she hurls the tray away. "I don't wanna be a baby!" she sobs.

"I know, sweetheart." I hug her again. There's not much else I can do at the moment. I rub her back, the way I used to when she would cry. "We'll find a way to fix this. I promise."

Like when she was a child before, she cries herself out after a few minutes. Once her sobs have turned to sniffles, she goes limp in my arms. I ease her back onto the gurney. I stroke her hair while she drifts into sleep again. Before she falls asleep, she whispers, "Don't go, Stace."

"I won't. I promise."

***

I keep my promise. There's still nothing to sit on, so I sit on the floor. I lower the gurney as much as I can so she won't have to look too far to find me. Then I wait.

As I wait, I stare at her. I try to memorize her new face so I can tell if anything's changed. It seems like she's stopped regressing, but what if she hasn't? What if she gets younger? What if soon she's down to two years old? What if she becomes a baby again? I didn't change many diapers the first time around; I can't imagine I'd be any better at it this time.

The door opens after what I figure is at least three hours. I expect Dr. Ling's goons to march in and haul me away. It's just Qiang. Oddly enough she carries a pair of oversized department store shopping bags.

"How is she feeling?" Qiang asks.

"She's sleeping," I whisper.

"Good."

Qiang sets the bags down by the gurney. Then she bends over the bed. She brushes hair away from Maddy's face to feel her forehead. Qiang nods to herself. "No fever," she says.

"She's just tired. Regressing eighteen years will do that to you."

"Yes, I am sure it is very difficult for her."

"Like you'd know."

"No, I would not. But you do. That is why I hope you will help her."

"Of course I will." I take Maddy's hand, the one not in her mouth at the moment. "I'd do anything for her."

"Good. After she has rested, we will need to perform some tests on her. Dr. Ling wants to verify that the regression has stopped."

"Yeah, great. So what's he going to do then?"

"That I do not know."

Maddy mumbles something I can't understand with her thumb in her mouth. Her eyes are still closed. She must be dreaming. From the way her body begins to twitch, I doubt it's a good dream. I squeeze her hand. "It's all right, Maddy. I'm here. You're safe."

She calms down a little at that. I keep hold of her hand and hope that will allow her to sleep peacefully. The poor kid deserves some rest after what she's been through. Qiang is right that I know a little about what Maddy's going through, but to go from a fifty-year-old man to an eighteen-year-old girl isn't as difficult as Maddy's transition will be.

While I hold Maddy's hand and she dreams, Qiang unpacks the bags. The first bag contains clothes: shirts, pants, sweatshirts, pajamas, and even underwear all the right size for a little girl. Qiang unfolds a pink T-shirt with a unicorn on it. "I hope these will fit her. I could not be sure of her measurements."

I don't say anything, though I imagine the real problem will be to get Maddy to wear little girl clothes like these. But then the alternative is for her to run around in a pajama top six sizes too big for her. In the end she'll have to make the practical choice.

From the other bag, Qiang takes out toys. She sets a teddy bear on the gurney, at Maddy's feet. There are also a couple of Barbie dolls and a baby doll. Lastly, Qiang produces a pile of coloring books and a box of crayons. "I thought these would help keep her entertained once she is more active."

"Good idea," I say. I take the teddy bear and press it against Maddy. The bear is almost as big as she is. She mumbles in her sleep and then lets go of my hand to wrap her arm around the bear. As she pulls it close, I hear her mutter Grace's name.

I choke up a little as I imagine her disappointment when she wakes up.

***

The bear is the first thing to go. There's a moment of disorientation when Maddy wakes up with the stuffed toy clutched to her. I see her eyes go wide at the sight of the teddy bear she imagined was Grace. With a sob, she hurls the bear away, against the wall.

I rush over to her side and help her to sit up. She looks down at her bulging stomach and then holds up her tiny hands. She starts to cry again. "It's real," she says. "It's all real."

"I know," I say.

"I'm still a baby."

"You're not a baby. You're a big girl."

"You're just saying that."

"Madison, listen to me: you're not a baby. And you won't be so long as you remember who you are. Right?"

"I guess."

I see the clothes Qiang's left in a pile on the floor. "I know, how about we get you dressed? That'll make you feel better."

"Maybe."

I bring the clothes over for her to inspect. As I expected, she isn't thrilled with the choices. "These are baby clothes," she says. She throws the unicorn T-shirt on top of the teddy bear. "I want my real clothes!"

"I know, honey, but those won't fit right now." I go through the pile and take out a purple sweatshirt and sweatpants. Besides that they're a little less girly than the other clothes, they should also stretch enough to fit. "Why don't you try these for a little while?"

"I don't wanna."

"Madison, please. It's just for a little while. Unless you want to go around naked."

"Maybe I do."

"Now Maddy, is that what a big girl would say?"

She thinks about this for a moment before she shakes her head. "No." She snatches the clothes away from me. Even with the gurney at its lowest setting, I have to take her hand to help her get down. Besides the sweatshirt and sweatpants, she takes a pair of underwear and socks as well into a corner. "Don't peek."

"I won't." I want to ask if she needs any help, but that would make things much more awkward. So I sit on the gurney and face away from her. I hear her grunt a few times. I hope Qiang guessed right about the sizes.

I get my answer when Maddy waddles up to me. The sweatshirt is tight on her, enough that when she raises her arms, I can see her bare belly. It's hard to resist blowing a raspberry on that cute little tummy sticking out. It's almost as hard not to pinch her adorable cheeks.

I do pick her up and help her back onto the gurney. She sits next to me; her feet dangle in the air. Qiang didn't provide a pair of shoes for Maddy, probably to keep her from running away. Not that she could get very far in her present condition.

"What do we do now?" Maddy asks.

"There's some dolls. Or coloring books."

"Those are for babies."

"They don't have to be." I pick up the Barbie dolls. I pass one with black hair to Maddy. "We could pretend the gurney is Grace's shop. That doll is you and Barbie is Grace—"

"She wishes."

I smile legitimately for the first time in what seems like forever. "Yeah, she does. And the redheaded one will be me. I'm helping a customer find something to wear. And Grace—" I pause as I try to think up a story. It's been about forty years since I played with toys and I never played with dolls—those were for girls.

"Grace is telling me about her new job," Maddy says. "It's not much fun sitting around listening to all these addicts whine all the time. And I tell her that at least she's helping people."

Maddy snatches the Barbie away from me. She presses its face against the doll that represents her. "Then we kiss and your face turns all red like it always does—"

"It does not!"

"Does so. You're so embarrassed to see two girls kissing."

"I've kissed plenty of girls."

"But you didn't really like any of them. You like boys."

My face turns red for real. I think of that awful date with Seth for the first time in weeks, or maybe even months. Things had been so much simpler back then. "Maybe I do."

"Boys are gross."

"Some are."

Maddy starts to make her dolls walk away from me. "Grace and I go upstairs and—" Maddy can't finish. She throws the dolls to the floor and then starts to sob.

"Don't cry, Maddy. It's all right."

"I was just thinking. I'll never get to…you know with Grace again."

"Of course you will. We'll find some way to make you a grown-up again."

Right on cue, the door opens. Qiang comes in; her face brightens with a smile. "Hello, Madison. Are you ready to go on a trip?"

"Where?"

"To see some nice men. They want to make sure you are feeling all right."

"You mean doctors want to probe me," Maddy says with a sniffle.

"Yes. We want to make sure you are not getting any younger."

"Younger?"

"Don't worry," I say. "You're not getting any younger. You're fine."

Maddy isn't convinced. She presses against my side. "Can Stace go with me?"

"I am afraid not."

"I don't want to go alone. I want Stace!"

"I am sorry, little one. That is not possible."

As Maddy starts to cry again, I pat her back. "It'll be all right. They aren't going to hurt you. And I'll be right here when you get back."

"You promise?"

"I promise." I give her a short hug. "Go on with Qiang so she can take care of you."

"All right," Maddy says. She takes Qiang's hand to hop off the gurney. Before she leaves, Maddy turns to wave to me. I wave back. I just hope that's not our last goodbye.

Chapter 12

Over the next few days, Maddy adjusts to life as a toddler. She sleeps most of the time. I can't really blame her; sleep is about the only way to escape the madness of this situation. When she is awake, she lies on the floor and colors in the books Qiang bought. To amuse herself, she picks outlandish colors for people's skin and hair. She shows me a princess she's colored with dark blue skin and bright red hair. "You like it?" she asks.

"It's great. You're like a miniature Picasso."

Her lips tremble at that. She doesn't like when I reference her small stature. "I'm sorry," I say. "I didn't mean—"

"No, you're right. I am pretty miniature right now." She forces a smile as she pats her belly. "Except here."

She turns back to her coloring. Later I see her working diligently on another princess. For this one she uses the peach crayon for the skin and dark brown for the hair. I kneel down beside her as she finishes. "Is that you?" I ask.

"No, it's Grace," she says. She colors the skirt of the princess's dress tan, so that it looks somewhat like what Grace wore the night we disappeared.

The real problem comes when Maddy tries to write Grace's name in the margin. Her first attempt is so shaky that it's illegible. Maddy tries again; she squints as she concentrates on the page. This next attempt is legible, though the letters are uneven and wobbly, like a kindergartner's. Maddy throws the crayon down and then begins to cry at last.

As I always do, I pat her back and mumble what encouragement I can. "It's not fair," she mutters. "I didn't do anything."

"I know you didn't."

"Then why are they doing this?"

"I don't know, honey," I say. I wonder if I should finally come clean to Maddy about why Dr. Ling wanted me. With how broken up Maddy is already, I decide against it. She's been through enough already.

"I didn't do anything!" she wails again.

"I know." I hug her close until she's cried herself out. After that she's ready for a nap. Before I help her onto the gurney, she tears the picture she colored of Grace out of the book. She hugs it to her chest like the teddy bear as she falls asleep.

She's asleep for about an hour when the door opens. It's Qiang again. "Haven't they tested her enough?" I ask. In the past few days they've poked and prodded little Maddy in just about every way possible, which included X-rays and an MRI.

"I have not come for Madison. Dr. Ling wishes to see you."

I look down at Maddy, the picture of Grace still tight against her chest. "Tell him I'm busy."

One of Ling's thugs steps into the room. "I am sorry," Qiang says. "It is not a request."

I bend down to kiss Maddy's forehead. "I'll be back soon," I whisper.

***

Qiang and the guard don't take me to the principal's office. Instead the guard shoves me into the school's kitchen. There's still a rusty stove and sink, but the rest of the equipment is gone. On the steel counters now are computers, folders, and beakers. This must be Dr. Ling's lab, where he and his minions work on their version of FY-1978.

Another guard appears and wheels in a gurney like the ones Maddy and I sleep on. For all I know it could be the one from my cell. He stops it beside me. "Get on, please," Qiang says.

"Why?"

"I cannot say. Please do it or else we will do it by force."

"Yeah, sure," I say. "I could use a nap anyway."

As soon as I'm on the gurney, one of the goons starts to strap me onto it. That is until Dr. Ling says from the doorway, "The straps won't be necessary. Will they, Mr. Fischer?"

"No."

"Good." Ling comes to stand beside the gurney. He still wears a black suit, but now he also wears rubber gloves. I figure he wants to take some more blood from me. It's been a few days since they last did that.

It's not a syringe Dr. Ling takes out of his pocket. Instead it's something that looks like a meat thermometer, the kind you put in a Thanksgiving turkey. "You going to cook me?" I ask.

"Not at all. I designed this little device to measure your cellular decay."

"So?"

"It tells us how old you are based on the amount of decay in your cells, sort of like counting the rings of a tree."

"You've used it on Maddy already?"

"Yes. Your daughter's reading came back at four-point-nine."

"That's about what I figured," I say. "Did you tell her that?"

"There's no need. All that matters is the result has been constant."

"So she's not regressing anymore?"

"Not from what we can determine."

Without warning, Ling jams the meat thermometer into my elbow. I wince with pain, but try not to cry in front of him. Like a thermometer, he leaves it in my arm for a couple of minutes. Then it begins to beep. He yanks the gauge out of my arm. He holds it up so I can see the red digital numbers: 18.7.

"How much of a margin for error is there on that?" I ask.

"I estimate about a point-two differential."

"Great." Which means I could be eighteen-and-a-half or just about nineteen. Too bad Dr. Palmer doesn't have one of these things. If I get out of here alive, maybe I'll tell her about it. "Now that you found that out, can I go back to my daughter?"

"Not yet. Take off your clothes."

"What?"

"Remove your clothes. Unless you want one of my associates to do it for you."

"Why do you want me naked?"

"There's no need to be shy, Mr. Fischer. I've seen you naked several times while you were unconscious."

"You son of a bitch!" Before I can move, one of the goons has a meaty hand on my shoulder to press me down on the gurney.

When the other thug starts to grab my pajamas, I kick at him. "Let me do it," I hiss at him. Ling says something in Chinese that backs the goons off.

A minute later, I'm naked on the gurney. I want to brush my hair forward to cover myself, but Dr. Ling stops me. "I'm afraid I can't let you do that," he says. He snaps his fingers. Three guys in lab coats appear; I'm not sure where they've been hiding all this time.

They start to fasten diodes all over my body. I see why Ling didn't want me to cover up my breasts when one of the technicians fastens diodes to my nipples. "Is that really necessary?" I say.

"Yes. We must have complete coverage of your body to observe an accurate result."

"What are you doing to me?"

He reaches into his jacket for a syringe. It's filled with a dark red liquid. Though it looks different from Dr. Nath's version, I know it has to be FY-1978. "No! You can't!"

"We must. Thanks to your daughter's sacrifice, we have altered the formula. It should be perfect now."

"But I already have the serum in my blood."

"Very true." Dr. Ling touches one of the diodes on my arm. "That is what these are for, so we can observe the interaction of my serum with that in your blood."

"But isn't that going to fuck up the test of your serum?"

"Perhaps. At any rate, we have taken enough of your blood. You have no more use to us than your daughter."

I turn to Qiang, the only one even remotely friendly in this room. "Don't let him do this. Please!"

"I am sorry, Stacey. I cannot interfere."

I try to rip the diodes off to at least buy some time. I get the ones on my nipples loose before the goons stop me. They press my arms down. One of the technicians tightens the straps around my hands so I can't move them again. There's nothing I can do then except thrash around and scream.

"Keep her steady, please," Ling says. The goons hold me down; one presses a hand over my mouth to silence my screams.

I close my eyes so I can't watch. There's the prick of the needle in my neck. Just as before, my entire body goes numb almost immediately. The goons let me go. I want to scream, but I can't. I can't do anything but lie there and wait.

***

The last time this happened, I had an out-of-body experience. While at the bottom of the harbor, I watched myself change from a middle-aged man into a teenaged girl. Because of that, I didn't feel any pain as my body compacted and reshaped itself.

This time there's no out-of-body experience. I'm still in my body as the changes begin. Though I'm numb, I can still feel my body change. The very first thing I feel is like someone pressing down on my nose, as if to jam it into my brain. After that comes pressure below my eyes as if someone is trying to push my cheekbones into my eyes. I'm becoming Chinese like Maddy.

"Good, very good," Dr. Ling says. "No signs of drug interaction so far."

He helpfully turns my head to the side, where I can see a monitor, like the one we watched Maddy on before. As I figured, my face has already rearranged itself, my nose smaller and my cheekbones higher. My hair has straightened and turned black too. As I watch the monitor it starts to feel like someone's jammed hot needles in my eyes. I want to scream, but my vocal chords are still paralyzed. I wish I could just pass out, but that doesn't happen either.

My vision turns red for a few seconds. When it clears, I can see on the monitor that I've got the same slanted eyes as everyone else in the room—and Maddy. I'm Chinese, like all of them. I wish I could cry from these new eyes, but I can't do that either.

Nothing happens for a minute. I still can't move. Dr. Ling sticks the meat thermometer in my arm again. When it beeps this time he says, "Sixteen-point-four. Very good, gentlemen." A few moments later, he says, "Sixteen-point-two. Sixteen-point-zero. Fifteen-point-nine." He turns to his technicians and barks at them in Chinese. They answer in the same language, though with far less authority.

Something's gone wrong. I'm getting younger. Though I can't move my limbs, I can feel pressure on all of them, like someone's put my bones in a vise and is cranking it like mad. On the monitor, I can see my body shrink as I continue to regress. I watch as my breasts go from C-cups to nubs that would hardly fit into a training bra.

Prepubescent. That's what I am now. A little girl, though not so little yet as Maddy. My mosquito bite boobs flatten out completely while the rest of my body continues to shrink. As I compact, my midsection turns flabby. Not as much as Maddy, just a little potbelly.

"Ten-point-eight," Ling says. His voice is on the edge of panic now. Maybe his formula isn't right yet, or maybe it has interacted with the FY-1978 already in my blood. Whatever's going on, I doubt he can stop it. Before long I'll be a toddler like Maddy. Maybe I'll go all the way back to an infant. Or maybe I'll turn into so many stem cells.

I feel the hot needles in my eyes again. My vision blurs. I can't see the monitor to watch the rest of the change. "Ten-point-two," Ling says with disbelief.

As sudden as it began, it stops just as quickly. I still can't see the monitor, but I can't feel the pressure on my bones anymore. Maybe it's stopped. Maybe this is as young as I get. "Ten-point-zero," Ling says. "Holding steady."

I wish I could smile at that. Ten-point-zero. That means it's my birthday. I'm ten years old now. With that thought, I finally pass out.

Chapter 13

When I wake up, I can't see much. I can only see blurs of light on one side of the room. The rest of it is a dark blob. My entire body feels leaden and weak, like they've drained out all of my blood this time. I'm tempted to go back to sleep, but not yet. Not until I make sure.

I have to concentrate as hard as I can just to move my arm. I raise my hand up to my face. It looks like a light brown blur against the dark blur of the background. I take a deep breath and then move my hand closer. It's about a foot away from my face before I can see it clearly.

What I see is a hand darker than my own, the skin almond-colored instead of pasty white. The fingers on this hand are much smaller than I remember. They're chubbier too. It's a child's hand. The last moments of consciousness come back to me. I'm ten years old, just a little girl.

Like a little girl, I start to cry. Maybe I'm not as young as Maddy, but I'm still a child. I can't drive or smoke or drink or even see a PG-13 movie, not unless someone older is with me. I doubt I'll get a chance to do any of those things, not after Dr. Ling has finished with me.

I must be back in my cell, because I hear Maddy's voice through the wall. She shouts, "Where's Stacey? I want Stacey!"

"I am sorry, Madison. Stacey is not feeling well."

"I want Stacey!" Maddy howls.

Her voice wakes something inside me. I have to get off this bed and go to my daughter. She needs me. I'm still her father, even if I'm ten years old. With a groan I roll towards the edge of the gurney. Some helpful person has put up the rails on the sides. I'll have to roll over those too.

That would be a lot easier if I were still a man. Even at nineteen I could manage it. At ten, it's impossible. Especially since I'm not only ten, but still groggy and sore from the change. I give the rail a few feeble pushes, but it doesn't budge. I decide to change tactics and try to lift myself over it. That works just as well. I'm too weak to do it. With a choked sob I collapse onto my back to stare up at the whitish blob of the ceiling.

That is until I hear Maddy again. "Leave me alone! I want Stacey!"

I roll onto my side. Then I roll as fast as I can towards the rail. I slam against it hard enough to make me wince, but I stay on the gurney. I'm not about to give up just yet. Instead, I roll all the way to the other end. I bang against that railing. I go back and forth, to build up enough speed to send me over the railing.

It takes about five tries before I get the speed I need. Physics has never been my strong suit, so it's no surprise I miscalculate. Instead of flying over the railing, I end up on top of it. I whimper as I try to swing my legs around. Again this would be a lot easier at full size. At pint-size, I have to stand on my toes to touch the floor. Before I can steady myself, my hands slip off the railing.

I fall onto my back and land in a heap on the floor. I take a few deep breaths to clear away the cobwebs. Ten years old or not, I've got to get on my feet, over to the door. I roll onto my stomach and then do a sort of push-up to raise my chest. From there I struggle to get traction with my legs. I scramble for a few seconds before I collapse back to the floor.

I start to crawl. It's slow going at first since I don't have much strength in my limbs. With my blurred vision, it's hard to tell how far I've gone. I try not to worry about that.

I crawl for a few minutes before I hear the door open. I squint, but I can't make out more than a dark shape in the doorway. "Who's there?" I ask. My voice sounds so tiny now, as if I've taken a hit of helium.

The blob grows larger before me. I try to back away, but I'm even slower in reverse. At last the blob takes on a shape. It's Qiang. She kneels down beside me and puts a hand on my shoulder. "Stacey? What are you doing?"

"I heard Maddy. She needs me."

"Madison will be fine. You must rest."

"No! I want to see her."

"You are not well. You need to rest."

"I want to see Maddy!" My voice sounds so childish that it gives me pause. "Please? Just for a few minutes? So she knows I'm OK?"

Qiang considers it for a moment. "All right. For a minute."

She hooks one arm under my armpit to help lift me to my feet. I'm at least a foot shorter than her now, so that my head leans against the side of her breast. We take one step and then rest for a moment. It would be easier for Qiang to carry me.

I'm exhausted by the time we reach Maddy's cell. The thought of lying down for a while sounds really, really good. "I don't think I can make it," I tell Qiang.

She finally does carry me. I hear her grunt softly as she scoops me up in her arms. I lean my head against her chest; my eyes flutter. One of her hands strokes my hair. "Stay awake, Stacey. Just a little longer."

"OK," I whisper.

My eyes are closed as she carries me into Maddy's cell. I'm almost asleep when I hear Maddy say, "Stacey? Is that you?"

I open my eyes, not that it does much good. All I can see is a pink-and-brown blob in the distance. I try to squint, but I can't squint enough for it to make much difference. "It's me. It's Stacey."

"But you're so little."

"I know."

Qiang carries me over to the gurney. Maddy slides aside enough that Qiang can set me down next to my daughter. Maddy crawls on top of me to look into my eyes. "Are you really Stacey?"

"Yes."

I'm not prepared for Maddy to throw herself at Qiang. Her tiny hands claw at Qiang's eyes. Qiang easily deflects the attack. She lets Maddy tire herself out. My daughter sinks down next to me on the gurney. She puts her head on my flat chest. "Oh, Stace," she says.

"It'll be all right," I say. "We'll find a way out of this."

"Sure we will," Maddy says.

I will my arm to drape across Maddy's back to stroke her hair. "I'll be fine, Maddy. I just need some rest."

"But—"

"You have to be good until then. All right? Do what Qiang says."

Maddy is close enough that I can see the tears in her eyes. "OK."

"Good girl." Then I fall asleep.

***

When I wake up, Maddy isn't around. I still can't see much more than light and dark blobs. I try to squint, which again doesn't help. From nowhere a hand touches the back of my head. I turn and see Qiang a little behind my bed. "It's all right," she says. "No one is going to hurt you."

"Maddy?"

"Madison is sleeping. As you should be."

"How long have I been out?"

"Twelve hours."

"That long?"

"You have been through quite a lot."

"No kidding."

"How are your eyes?"

"I still can't see much. What's wrong with me?"

Qiang bends down. She looks into my eyes. "You have her eyes."

"Whose?"

"Ming's. My daughter. She was nearsighted like you are."

"Was? I thought your daughter—?"

"She may still be alive. I have not talked with her in ten years. Not since she was arrested."

"What did she do?"

"She was a student. She wrote something critical of the government. They took her from me. They put her in prison."

"And Dr. Ling is going to get her out?"

"Perhaps. He has much influence in my country."

"That's why you're helping him?"

"Yes. It is the only way to save her."

"And all you have to do is sacrifice me and Maddy."

Qiang says nothing for a while. Then she reaches into her pocket. I'm not sure what she's doing until I feel something heavy on my face. The background becomes a little clearer, though there's still some blurriness at the far edges. I touch the side of my face and feel the pair of glasses.

"Thank you."

"Those were Ming's."

"You kept them with you? All the way to America?"

"They are one of the few things of hers I have left."

I start to take the glasses off. "I shouldn't take these."

Qiang puts out a hand to stop me. "She does not need them. You do."

I let her resettle the glasses on my nose. "Thanks."

"I brought you some clothes, if you feel like getting dressed. There is also food if you are hungry."

"I'd really like a glass of water."

Qiang takes a glass off the silver food tray. She puts the cup to my lips; she tips it so all I have to do is open my mouth. Cool water rushes down to soothe my dry throat. When I signal I've had enough, she pulls the cup away.

She brushes hair away from my face. "You look just like her at that age. It is remarkable."

Not so remarkable since Ling said he used Qiang's DNA in his serum. "I'm sorry about your daughter. I'm sure she's still alive."

"I hope so." Qiang forces a smile to her face. She holds up the clothes she's brought for me. There's a pastel yellow T-shirt and a pair of white sweatpants. She's even brought a pair of white Crocs for me to wear.

I struggle to get off the pajama top that's become like a nightshirt since the change. Qiang finally helps me out of it. It's strange to see my chest so flat and brown. I put a hand on my belly and pinch the roll of fat there. "This is really happening," I say.

"I am afraid so."

I lift my arms up so Qiang can put the T-shirt on me. She gathers up my hair to pull it out of the shirt. It's so long now that it goes all the way to my thighs. "I really need a haircut."

"You look very pretty."

"I'm sure."

Qiang's come prepared with a compact. It's no surprise that in the mirror I see a little Chinese girl. The glasses Qiang gave me are bright red and so big they take up most of my face. That makes me look even younger than I already am. My nose is little more than a bump and my cheeks pudgy, though not as much as Maddy's.

Qiang tears a strip off of the old pajamas. With this she ties my hair back into a ponytail. It still dangles down past my rear, but at least I won't have hair in my face so much. "Such a beautiful child," she says.

"I guess." I turn away from the compact; I don't want to see my cute little face anymore. Like Maddy I don't want to be a kid. I want to be a grown-up again. Whether I'm Stacey or Steve doesn't really matter. I just want to be able to take care of myself. As it is, I can't even pull on my own underpants. Qiang pulls on the sweatpants for me too. Then the socks that match my pants and the Crocs.

"Can I see Maddy again?" I ask.

"If you feel up to it."

"I do."

It's still a long, slow walk for me. I make it under my own power this time. Maddy stirs as we enter the room. She rubs her eyes before she focuses on me. "Hi Stace."

"Hi."

"The glasses look cute."

"Thanks."

She manages to crawl off the gurney all by herself. "You want to color?" she asks.

"Not right now," I say. Qiang helps me over to the gurney. I need her help to get on top of it. Maddy tugs at Qiang's blouse until the woman picks her up. Qiang sets Maddy down next to me. Maddy has the teddy bear, which she presses against me—a present. "Thanks."

"Are you going to be all right?" Maddy asks.

"I'll be fine. I'm just tired."

"OK." Maddy lies down next to me, the teddy bear between us. I drape my arm over the bear, my hand on Maddy's shoulder. That's how we fall asleep.

Chapter 14

Maddy and I are both on the gurney in her room when the door opens. I scramble to find my glasses to see who it is. "Qiang?" I ask.

She appears at my bedside. She finds the glasses before I do and pushes them onto my face. "I am sorry, but you two must go. Right now."

"Go? How?"

Qiang puts a finger to her mouth. "Be very quiet. I must get you out of here. Tonight."

"What's going on?" Maddy asks.

"Dr. Ling is preparing to take you back to Beijing with him."

"Beijing? China?"

"Yes. Once there you will be subjected to further studies—including dissection."

"So he is going to kill us," I say.

"Yes. In time. After he has finished his studies. I must get you out of here tonight, before he can take you from here."

"How are we going to get out of here?"

Qiang points up to the ceiling. I remember when Maddy tried to climb up there. She was too big back then.

We're not big anymore, though. "Hurry, children. Dress warmly. It is chilly outside."

She helps us put on a couple extra layers, which for me consists of a sweatshirt and a jacket. Maddy looks like the Michelin Man in three layers of clothes. "Very good. Now, we must go."

"Wait," I say. "If you do this, Ling isn't going to free your daughter."

Qiang nods sadly. "I know. But she would not want me to let two innocent girls die, even to save her own life."

"Thank you," I say.

"I am sorry for everything."

"It's not your fault," Maddy says. She hugs both of us.

The moment lasts only a few seconds before Qiang pulls away. She gets up on the gurney so she can reach the ceiling tiles. She pushes one away. Then she bends down to pick me up. "Go straight to the first junction and then turn right. At the next junction, turn left. That will take you outside."

"What about you?"

"I will meet you outside. I cannot fit in there."

"Oh. Right." I let Qiang pick me up. She hefts me into the ceiling and gives me a push into an air duct. It's a tight squeeze even now. Too bad they don't make air ducts like in the movies where a grown man can walk upright through them.

I crawl forward a few feet, enough so Qiang can lift Maddy up. I wish I could turn around to help her, but there's not enough room. I wait until I hear her grunt behind me. "Stace?" she whispers.

"I'm fine. Try to keep a hand on my shoe."

"OK." I feel Maddy's hand on the bottom of my Croc. Then we start out. It's slow going; I don't want to make a lot of noise or lose Maddy. Since she's smaller than me, she's bound to tire before I do.

"How are you doing?" I ask as we reach the first junction.

"I'm fine," she says. I can hear the indignation in her voice as she says, "I'm not a baby."

"I know." I think for a moment to remember what Qiang said. Then I go to the right. We crawl down the air duct until we reach the next junction. By then I can hear Maddy breathing hard. There's enough room with the junction so I can turn around to look back at her. It's too dark to see much. I reach out to touch her cheek. Her face is warm and slick with sweat. "We can rest for a minute, OK?"

"I can do it," Maddy says.

"It's all right. I'm feeling a little tired still," I say. "Come here."

I let Maddy crawl up against me, that way we can talk easier. It's not just that she's little; she's also dressed in all those clothes in a warm air duct. I stroke her sweaty hair and whisper that everything will be fine. I hope she believes me.

After a few minutes, Maddy's breathing is regular enough for us to head out again. The hard part now is to remember which duct we came to the junction from. They all look the same in the dark. In the end I take a guess and hope we don't get lost in the ventilation system.

I crawl for a little while, until I see a grate up ahead. I hope it's the right one. Even before we can reach it, I smell what passes for fresh air in the city. "Come on, Maddy," I hiss. "We're almost there."

I don't hear anything. "Maddy?"

There's no answer. Shit, I lost her. I have to lie down and then awkwardly roll over so I can turn around. I crawl the way I came and whisper her name. Where did she go?

After a few frantic minutes, I literally run into her. She squeals from either pain or surprise as I topple her. "Stace?"

"Maddy, where did you go?"

"I was tired."

"Why didn't you tell me to stop?"

"I did! You didn't hear me," she whines.

I wish I could see Maddy's face right now to look her in the eye. Instead I fumble around until I find her shoulder. "Madison, please, we have to get out of here. Don't you want to see Grace again?"

"Yes."

"Then we have to go. Come on." We settle back into crawling position. "Try to keep up this time."

"OK."

We waste another twenty minutes at least to backtrack to the grate. This time we make it together. I can hear Maddy pant hard from the effort. Even for a little girl she's badly out of shape. "You can rest now," I say. "I'll try to get this open."

I push at the grate. Nothing happens. Didn't Qiang loosen it? Maybe we're at the wrong grate. Maybe it's a trap, a test set up by Dr. Ling.

I decide to change tactics. I roll onto my back and then kick at the grate. It takes three times before my little Crocs finally knock the grate loose. It makes way too much noise as it hits the ground. At least now we can get out of here.

Except when I look down, I see it's at least a ten-foot drop onto to solid concrete. I'd probably break both of my legs if I jumped. "What's wrong?" Maddy asks.

"We need a ladder or something."

"Where are we going to get one of those?"

"I don't know."

"This is stupid," Maddy whines. "We should have stayed in the room."

"Be quiet," I snap. "I need to think."

"Who put you in charge? You're younger than me. I should be the one in charge."

"Well if you can think of something, go right ahead."

"I will think of something. That'll show you."

"Oh, girls, there you are!" Qiang whispers. "I thought I had missed you."

"I think we went to the wrong place," I say. "Can you help us down?"

"Just a moment."

We have to wait at the edge of the grate for a couple of minutes. I worry Qiang has abandoned us, until she returns with a couple of old crates. She sets these on top of each other and then stands on them. That gives her enough height so she can almost reach the grate. She can't reach all the way, which means she'll have to catch me.

I whimper at the thought I'll fall ten feet and break my legs. "It will be all right," Qiang says. "I will catch you."

I whimper again in response. It's so high up and I'm so little. Then I hear Maddy ask, "What's taking so long?"

"Nothing. We're going now."

I get down on my back again. I let my legs dangle out of the grate. I feel Qiang grab them. She pulls on my legs until my waist dangles in the air. Then she wraps her arms around my waist. With a tug she pulls me out the rest of the way. I let out a scream, until I remember we have to be quiet.

"I have you," Qiang says.

"Thanks," I say. I wipe tears from my face. Qiang puts me down on the crate so I can climb down. Once I'm on the ground, Qiang starts to encourage Maddy to come to the edge.

"It's so high," Maddy says with a whimper.

"You can do it," I call up to her. "See, I made it. I didn't get hurt at all."

"But I could fall."

"You're not going to fall. And even if you do, Qiang will catch you. And if she doesn't, I'll break your fall. All right?"

"OK," Maddy says, though she still sounds skeptical. I hear metal creak as Maddy settles herself into position. "Here I come."

Maddy slides too fast out of the duct. She's already falling before Qiang can grab her. Qiang reaches out to grab Maddy on the way down, but all she catches is Maddy's left sleeve for an instant. Everything goes in slow motion as I watch my daughter's tender little head tumble towards the concrete.

I do exactly as I promised. I lie down in the spot where I think Maddy will come down. It turns out I'm right. She slams onto my chest, all fifty pounds of her. It feels like someone's fired a cannonball into my stomach. The wind is knocked out of me; I gasp for air. Maddy rolls off of me. She slaps at my cheek with one hand. "Stace? Are you all right? Did I hurt you?"

I shake my head, still too winded to speak. I wheeze for a minute or so. Finally I manage to say, "I'm fine."

Qiang comes down and helps me sit up. She pats the back of my head. "Such a brave little girl."

"Thanks."

"Now you must go."

"What about you?"

"I cannot. I must make sure Dr. Ling does not find you."

"How are you going to do that?"

She pats my head again. "Do not worry, little one. I will take care of everything. You must get Madison to safety. She is depending on you."

"All right," I say. I give Qiang another hug. "Thank you."

"Now go, my children. You must hurry."

I take Maddy's hand. Then we run. We get about a block away before there's a flash of light. I turn in time to see a column of flame rise from the school that was our prison. Qiang's work, no doubt.

We're on our own now. I turn to Maddy. She cries as she too probably thinks of Qiang, our caretaker. I squeeze Maddy's hand. "Come on, let's go."

Part 3
Second Childhood

Chapter 15

The world looks a lot different at four feet tall. Everything's so distorted by the change in perspective that it's impossible for me to get my bearings. Maddy, about a foot shorter than me, has trouble too. She finally throws herself onto a park bench. With a huff she says, "Where are we?"

"I'm not sure. But we have to keep going."

I try to keep us away from people when I can. In the middle of the night, anyone you encounter isn't likely to be friendly. Sometimes this means we have to skirt an alley or duck behind some bushes as a drunk or bum or junkie stumbles past. When we come upon a hooker on the corner, I grab Maddy's hand to hustle her along before anyone can stop us.

We finally come to a place with two intact street signs. Now I can get our bearings. We're on the south side of the city. The garment district is halfway across the island. We could always take a train, except we don't have any money. I doubt we could jump the turnstile either.

I don't want to see Grace right now anyway. She probably wouldn't believe our crazy story and even if she does, it would be a hell of a shock to find out her partner has been changed into a five-year-old girl. Jake is the one we need to talk to. He knows all about my experiences with FY-1978.

The problem right now is Maddy. She gets tired quickly, which prompts her to whine like a normal toddler. Three times an hour we have to stop for a five-minute break so Maddy can rest her stubby legs. Despite the rests, she still lags; her feet shuffle along the sidewalk as we go. "How much farther?" she asks.

"I don't know."

"Where are we?"

"The south side. There's probably a liquor store or something around the corner."

"You said that three blocks ago."

"Well, we just have to keep looking."

"Can't we find somewhere to sleep?"

"No. We have to get to a phone first."

Maddy kicks at the sidewalk. "This is stupid."

"Madison, stop it. Let's go a little farther. All right?"

"All right."

I peek around a corner and check to see if it's safe. Ahead I see a sign for a market. It's still lit up. Light spills onto the sidewalk. "I found something," I tell Maddy.

She trots over to join me. Before I can stop her, she breaks into a run. I catch up to her easily enough and grab her shoulder. "Maddy, slow down. We can't go running in there."

"Why not?"

"We don't know who's in there. If he calls the cops, we'll never see Grace again."

"Oh. OK then."

I take Maddy's hand and lead her to the front door of the market. I peer inside. There doesn't seem to be anyone inside except for the shopkeeper, a middle-aged

Asian man. I see a payphone in the back, next to a cooler of beer.

The door is a lot heavier than I expect. It takes all the strength in my tiny muscles to prop it open enough for Maddy to squeeze through. I slip out of the way so the door can shut behind me. The shopkeeper looks down at us. His eyes narrow; he doesn't get many little girls in his store in the middle of the night.

"What you want?" he says.

"We need to use your phone," I say. "My sister and I got lost and we need to call our daddy so he can pick us up."

"Phone over there," the shopkeeper says. He motions to the phone.

"Thanks." The problem is for me to reach the phone. I have to drag a plastic soda crate over so I can reach. I punch in Jake's home phone.

Tess answers the phone. "Hello?"

"Aunt Tess, it's Stacey."

"Stacey? Oh, thank God! I've been so worried. We all have. Where have you been?"

"I'll explain later. Is Uncle Jake there?"

"Yes, he's right here. I'll wake him up." I hear Tess try to rouse Jake. "Jacob, wake up! It's Stacey. She's alive!"

"What?" Jake asks, his voice still thick from sleep. He grabs the receiver and then says, "Who is this?"

"Stacey."

"What's wrong with your voice? You been sucking helium?"

"No. I'll explain when you get here to pick us up."

"Us? You have Madison too?"

"Yes, she's with me. Hurry, Jake, please. I'm scared."

"All right, sweetheart. Just stay calm. Where are you?"

"I don't know. It's a market on the south side."

"That narrows it down to about two hundred places."

"Just a second." I let the phone dangle and then gallop over to the counter again. The shopkeeper eyes us, especially Maddy. I get the address from him and then run back to the phone. "Jake? You still there?"

"I'm here. Where are you?" I give him the address. Then he says, "I'll be there in twenty minutes. Are you going to be all right until then?"

"Yes. We'll be fine." I clear my throat into the receiver. "But we'll look a little different than before."

"What?"

"Just hurry. Please." I hang up the phone. Now all we have to do is wait and hope no one else gets here first.

***

The shopkeeper turns out to be a nice guy. After I tell him our daddy will be here in twenty minutes, he invites us to sit behind the counter with him. I'm reluctant, but Maddy goes for it right away. He helps her onto a stool.

"How old you girls?" he asks.

"I'm ten and she's five," I say.

"I have daughter her age," he says and motions to Maddy. "She sleeping right now."

"I wish I were sleeping too," Maddy grumbles.

"How you girls get here?"

"We missed getting off the train. Then we went around and around for a while, until we wound up here," I say. It seems like a slightly plausible scenario.

The shopkeeper buys it. "You safe now."

The bell over the door rings. I see Jake come up to the counter. He looks at the shopkeeper and then at Maddy and I. He turns his head to look around the rest of the store. He probably thinks Maddy and I are the shopkeeper's daughters.

I jump off my stool and hurry around the counter. "Daddy!" I squeal to sell the moment to our host. Before Jake can react, I've got a death grip on his leg. "I knew you'd come."

"Stacey?"

"It's me, Daddy," I say. I give Jake a wink.

He stares at me; his face pales. But he's experienced enough to shake it off. "I've been very worried about you, young lady. Where have you been?"

"We've been trying to find you. Then we found this nice man's store and he let us use his phone."

"That was very nice of him." He turns to the counter. "Madison? Come on, honey. It's time to go."

"OK, Daddy." She hops off her stool. A few seconds later she's attached herself to Jake's other leg.

"Thank you so much for taking care of my girls," Jake says. "What do I owe you?"

"No charge. I glad to help."

"God bless you, sir."

Then Jake bends down to scoop Maddy up. I let go of his leg to follow him out to his car. He's taken his Fairlane, probably because it's faster. He helps Maddy crawl into the backseat and then buckle up.

"All right, kids, time to go home."

Chapter 16

Maddy falls asleep about two minutes after we leave the market. Once we're sure she's out, Jake asks, "What the hell happened?"

"It's a long story. You remember the guy Lex tried to sell the FY-1978 formula to?"

"Some Chinese guy. But you said he was dead."

"He is. His son did this to us."

"How?"

"He made his own version of the drug. He put a Chinese woman's genetic material in it. Voila, Maddy and I are a couple of little Chinese girls now."

"Jesus Christ. Is it permanent?"

"I don't know. We need to ask Palmer about it."

"Right. In the morning. For now we have to think of what to tell Tess."

"Just tell her we're a couple of little runaways."

"You already told her you're alive. She's expecting you."

"Oh. Shit."

"Don't swear. It sounds weird."

"Sorry."

"How old are you?"

"Ten. Maddy is five."

"Five? Jesus Christ," Jake says again. He reaches into his pocket for a cigarette. Before he lights it, he looks in the backseat at us two innocent children. Then he tosses the cigarette out the window unlit. "What a fucking mess. You really have a knack, you know that?"

"Tell me about it."

***

Maddy is still asleep when we get to Jake's house. She stirs for a moment as Jake lifts her out of the seat. "Are we home?" she asks.

"We sure are, sweetheart," Jake says.

"OK." Then she's out again.

Tess is already at the door. She must have heard the old muscle car's engine a mile away. Her face turns pale just as Jake's did. "What's going on? Who are these children?"

"It's me," I say. "Stacey."

"Stacey? But you can't be. You're—"

"Too little?"

"Yes."

"We'll talk about it inside," Jake says. He brushes past Tess as he steps inside. Maddy still hasn't woke up.

"Is that...*Madison*?"

"Yes," I answer.

"Oh my." The way Tess wobbles, I worry she'll faint. She grabs the edge of the doorway to steady herself. Then she follows us inside.

While Jake takes little Maddy upstairs, I settle onto the couch. I'd like to sleep too, but we have to explain things to Tess. We can't hide this one from her.

Tess sits on a chair across from me. She studies my face, to look for signs of the old Stacey. "Would you like something to drink? Or some cookies? I have some chocolate walnut ones. They're Stacey's favorite."

"I'm fine," I say.

"Are you cold? I could get a blanket."

"I'm all right." I pat my stomach. "I've got a couple layers on."

"Oh, I see." She clears her throat. "Those are very pretty glasses."

"Thanks."

"Are they real?"

"Yes. My eyes aren't very good." I take the glasses off. "I can't really see you right now. You're just a big blur." I settle the glasses back onto my face.

Tess stares back at me. I look down at my feet and swing them back and forth while we wait for Jake to return. I sigh with relief as he tromps down the stairs. "I put her in Stacey's bed. She should be all right."

Jake settles onto the couch next to me. He puts an arm around my shoulder. "Now, why don't you tell us the whole story?"

***

When I've finished the story, Tess gapes at me. As I did with Maddy, I didn't tell Tess about why Ling abducted me. I let her think it was a random abduction. "I don't believe it," she finally says. "How could a drug turn Stacey into *this*?"

"I can't really explain how it works," I say. "I just know it does work. Go ahead, test me. Ask me something Stacey would know. Like maybe what happened to the sheets on Jenny's bed the first night I was here?"

Tess's eyes widen at that. She must remember how I woke up my first night as a woman in her house with blood on my sheets from my first period. I'm sure Tess didn't tell anyone else about that; she's much too discreet.

"Oh my. I think I'll go get some water," Tess says. "I'm feeling a bit piqued."

Jake watches her go and then pats my shoulder. "It'll be all right. I'll go talk to her."

"I'm sorry about this, Jake."

"It's not your fault. How could you have known someone was going to do this?"

"I shouldn't have gone off alone. I made myself an easy target. And they got Maddy—" I can't say anything more. I start to sob. Jake pulls me close and rubs my back the way I did with Maddy when I was still a grown-up.

He waits until I've cried myself out before he pushes me back. "I'd better go talk to her. You'll be all right?"

"I'll be fine."

I grab the TV remote from the coffee table and then curl up on the couch. There's not much on at five in the morning, mostly infomercials. I stop on the Disney Channel. It's some show about teenagers and their phony problems. God, I'm not even a teen anymore. What's the word they use nowadays? A *tween*. That's what I am. Between being a toddler and a teen. It sounds better than *prepubescent*.

I feel a hand on my back. I assume it's Jake, but then I hear Tess say, "Stacey? Do you want Jacob to take you up to your room?"

"I can make it," I say. I sit up to prove to Tess how spry I am.

She touches my hair and grimaces a little. "This is going to take some getting used to," she says.

"I know."

"But I want you to know, I'll still love you no matter what you look like on the outside. You're like a daughter to me and I'm going to take care of you, no matter what. Understand?"

"I understand." I lean forward to hug her. "I love you, Aunt Tess."

"I love you too, dear."

I don't ask, but Tess scoops me off the couch. She carries me upstairs. I'm too tired to put up a fight about it. Tess's body feels so warm right now that I just about nod off on the way up.

She turns on the hallway light so she can see into my bedroom. From what I can see, everything is the same as before I left. The only difference is little Maddy on my bed. She's still curled up on her side, thumb in her mouth.

"Oh my," Tess says again. "The poor dear."

Tess pulls back the covers enough so I can scramble beneath them. I squeeze in beside Maddy. Before I can drift off to dreamland, Tess takes my glasses. I hear them click down on the nightstand. Then she bends down to kiss my forehead. "Goodnight, dear."

"G'night, Aunt Tess."

Chapter 17

When I wake up, my hand touches something wet and cold. I blink my eyes open. Most of the room is a blur, but I can see a dark stain on the sheets, where Maddy had slept. Then the smell of the stain hits me: urine. But I haven't wet the bed in over forty-five years.

I hear a sniffle from the corner of the room. I fumble around until I find my glasses. It's dark in the corner, but I can make out a small, round lump surrounded by a pink blanket. I roll off the bed and then pad over to the lump. "Maddy?"

"Go away," she says.

"Maddy, what's wrong? Did you have a bad dream?"

"This is a bad dream. I wanna wake up!"

I sit down next to Maddy, close enough that I hope she can feel me through the blanket. "Maddy, what happened?"

"I went pee-pee. On the bed."

"Oh." So it was Maddy responsible for that stain on the sheets. "That's not so bad."

"Is too. Only babies wet the bed."

"It was just an accident. No one will be mad."

"I'm mad." Maddy finally turns so I can see her face. Her eyes are red and puffy from crying. How long has she been here in the corner? "I'm just a stupid baby."

"No you're not. You're still a grown-up inside."

"Grown-ups don't pee-pee in bed."

"Sometimes they do."

"Not normal ones. I never did."

"Come on, it's no big deal. The first night I was in this room I got blood all over the sheets."

"Blood?"

"From my period. It was really nasty. I didn't even know about tampons or anything. You know, because of my parents."

Maddy stares at me. "You're lying."

"I am not! Ask Tess when she wakes up. She was there. She cleaned it up."

"But you were a grown-up when you came here."

"I know. I had a little accident. That's all." Of course I was even more freaked out about it than Maddy was about wetting the bed. Since then it's become a funny story: the eighteen-year-old girl with her first period.

I reach beneath the blanket to touch Maddy's hair. "When Tess wakes up, we'll explain and clean it up. She won't be mad. I promise."

"OK."

"Now, how about I go get a towel and you can go back to sleep?"

"I guess."

I pad down the hallway so I don't make any noise. Tess is a light sleeper, even lighter since I'm sure she'll listen for any sign of distress. I creep into the bathroom and find a beach towel. Debbie used to do this the last time Maddy was a toddler. Like the thumb sucking she eventually grew out of wetting her bed. I hope it's just because of all the stress from the previous night, not something that will continue.

I make it back to the bedroom; Tess doesn't wake up. I spread the towel down over the wet stain on the bed. Maddy climbs up onto the bed and plops down onto the towel. Before long she's asleep again, thumb planted in her mouth. I watch her for a few minutes before I take off my glasses. There are tears in my eyes before I fall back to sleep.

***

The next time I wake up it's almost noon. When someone touches my shoulder, I think it must be Qiang to take more blood from me. "No more tests," I mumble.

"I'm not going to test you, dear," Tess says.

I wake up and see a peach-and-gray blob. Tess presses my glasses into my hands. I put them on and most everything comes into focus. I blink a few times, still not entirely used to the glasses. "Hi. Sorry about that. Thought you were someone else."

"No one's going to hurt you now. You're safe."

"I know."

I turn and see Maddy is already gone. The towel is still there. "Maddy—"

"She told me. Poor little dear was all broken up about it."

"It is a big adjustment."

"Yes, it is. It's good she has a big sister like you to help her through it."

"Yeah, I guess," I say. But who will help me get through it?

Tess gives me a hand to help me out of bed. I see a pile of clothes on the vanity. "I fetched some of Jennifer's old things from the attic. I hope they'll fit you until we can buy you some new clothes."

"I hope so."

She leaves me alone so I can change. In some strange coincidence, Tess has picked out a pastel yellow T-shirt. There's a picture of the Grand Canyon at sunset on it, probably from a trip the Madigan family took years ago. The shirt is a little snug over my tummy, but it'll do. The blue jeans are a couple sizes too big; the legs droop down past my feet. I have to wear the same underwear and socks; Tess's pack rat mentality didn't extend that far.

I pick up the brush that still has some of my red hairs in it. I start to run it through my black tresses and note how much thicker they are. Longer too. I look for something to tie my hair back with. I see a white plastic headband. I brush my hair back from my face and then put on the headband. It looks appropriate for a little girl like me.

Tess waits for me outside. "You look very pretty, dear. I like what you did with your hair."

"Thanks. Can we get it cut soon? It's so long."

"Certainly. After you go see the doctor. And after lunch."

Jake shows up as we finish our lunch. "Hurry up, kids. We've got to meet Dr. Palmer in an hour."

"Where?"

"At St. Vincent's."

"Not Lennox?"

"We thought that would be more *discreet*." Jake puts some emphasis on the last word. I know what he's thinking: Dr. Ling had a mole at Lennox. Until we know who that was, it would be best to stay away from there.

We take the station wagon this time. There's a booster seat in the center of the backseat. "I found that in the garage," Tess says. "I think it would be best, Madison—"

"But car seats are for babies."

"I know, but it's the law. All little girls have to use a booster seat."

"Why doesn't Stacey?"

"Because she's not as little, dear. When you get to be as big as Stacey, you won't need one either."

"It's not fair," Maddy says. Her face turns red as if she's ready to throw a tantrum.

"It's only for a little while," I say. "Until you're grown up again."

She looks at the seat and then back at me. "OK."

Tess helps her buckle in. I manage my own safety belt and note how much less belt I need now. Maddy looks miserable on the plastic seat; her rear spills over its sides. I pat her on the back. "You're such a brave girl," I tell her.

"Thanks."

Tess gets into the passenger seat and then we're on our way.

***

Dr. Palmer meets us in the main lobby. Just like Jake and Tess, she goes pale when she sees us. She puts a hand to her mouth, probably to silence whatever curse words she was about to say. Then she squats down so she's eye-level with us. "Hello, Madison. Hello, Stacey." She touches each of us on the head as she says our names. "You're looking very pretty."

"So I've heard," I grumble.

"It really is you," Dr. Palmer says. "And you still remember who you are?"

"Yes."

"How old are you?"

"Ten."

"No, I mean how old are you really?"

"Eighteen-point-seven."

"That's pretty exact."

"I'll explain later."

Dr. Palmer turns to Maddy. "And how old are you, Madison?"

"Twenty-three. Or I was. Now I'm five."

"Yes you are."

"And you can make me grown up again?"

"That's what we're going to find out."

She takes us to an elevator, which deposits us on the third floor. From the pastel wallpaper with borders of cartoon animals, I know this is the pediatrics wing. Much as I hate it, I know it makes sense. We'll be a lot less obvious here than in the oncology or burn wards.

There's an empty room already set up for us. I use a stool to climb onto the exam table. Jake lifts Maddy up to sit next to me; he ignores her protests that she can do it herself. I pat Maddy's back to reassure her everything will be all right.

But the moment she sees Dr. Palmer with a syringe, she begins to shriek. "Stay away from me! Don't touch me with that!"

I put my arm around Maddy and pull her close. "It's all right, Maddy. The doctor needs to take some blood so she can study it. So she can make us better."

"He needed our blood too," Maddy says. She presses her face into my T-shirt. "She's going to make us littler."

"Dr. Palmer wouldn't do that. She's a nice lady," I say.

"How do you know?"

"Because she's my doctor."

"She is?"

"I've been seeing her since I was this age—the first time."

"You have?"

Dr. Palmer jumps in to say, "That's right, sweetheart. Stacey is a good friend of mine. She's my most favorite patient in the whole world."

"And you're not going to make us littler?"

"No, of course not. I promise. I just need some blood samples so I can find out what that evil man did to you. That will help me find a way to make you better."

"Well...OK." Maddy still holds my hand and looks away as Dr. Palmer takes her blood. Despite how many times I've had my blood drawn in the last couple of months, I feel a nervous flutter in my belly at the sight of the needle. When Dr. Palmer pulls out the needle, she puts a Snoopy Band-Aid over the hole. I try to tell myself that's all they have in the pediatric wing.

Once she has the samples, Dr. Palmer sits down in a chair. She pats Maddy's knee. "I don't want you to expect any miracles. It could take a while to find a way to change you back. But I promise I'll do everything I can for you two."

"What do we do until then? I don't wanna be a baby anymore."

"You'll just have to make do the best you can, sweetheart. I'm sorry. I wish I could wave a magic wand to make you better, but I can't. It's going to take a lot of hard work."

"OK."

"I should have some preliminary results in a couple of days. In the meantime, don't do anything foolish. Try to live as normal as you can."

"We'll try," I say. I know all too well how hard it is to find a way to reverse FY-1978. I only hope this time Dr. Palmer has more luck with it.

***

Dr. Palmer tries to make an excuse to get Maddy out of the room. "I want to catch up a little with my favorite patient," she says. I could kill her when she tousles my hair as she says it. In part because it's demeaning, but also because Maddy sniffs out there's something going on.

"What are you going to talk about?" Maddy asks.

"Some boring stuff."

"Then why can't I stay?"

Tess comes to our rescue. She puts an arm around Maddy's shoulder. "How about we go down to the cafeteria and buy you some ice cream?"

Maddy looks at me and then at Tess. "OK. As long as you aren't talking about anything important."

"I promise it's dull as dirt," Dr. Palmer says.

We wait a couple of minutes to make sure Tess and Maddy are gone. Then Dr. Palmer says, "OK, young lady, tell me the rest of it."

So I tell her most everything that happened since I woke up in Dr. Ling's makeshift prison. It's good Jake is there, so I won't have to tell him all of this again later. Dr. Palmer stops me a couple of times, to ask me about the equipment I saw. "This 'meat thermometer' you mentioned, that's what told him your age?"

"Yes. He says it measures cellular decay. Like counting tree rings."

"That's a simplistic way of putting it, but it's more or less true. Keep going."

I tell her all about what the first batch of serum did to Maddy. Then about what the second batch did to me. "He put all these diodes on me to check for interaction between his formula and Dr. Nath's."

"Was there anything?"

"No. But he was disappointed with the results. He didn't want me to get so young."

"So maybe there was a reaction. His formula could have reacted with the stuff already in your blood and sent it into overdrive."

"He was going to take us back to China. Qiang says he was going to dissect us after he learned everything he could."

"That doesn't surprise me." Dr. Palmer sighs. "We've dealt with Ling Pharmaceuticals before. They're real sons of bitches, as you can see. And the regulations over there are a joke. That lets them get away with all this mad scientist bullshit."

"At least he got what was coming to him," I say.

"I will have to give you and Maddy both a proper physical. We have to see what all that shit he gave you did. I mean, you look like a normal ten-year-old on the outside, but we don't have any idea what's going on inside."

"He already did some tests on both of us."

"Well, since your friend blew up his lab, there's no way I can get a copy of those results." She looks up at Jake. "I'll set it up and then give you a call. We'll run everything out of here for the time being. Did Ling say how he knew about our formula?"

"No. He probably has someone working on the inside. You know how money can make people do things," I say. I glance at Jake.

"In the meantime, I'd suggest getting a proper eye exam. You'll probably need some real glasses made for you specifically, not some dead woman's daughter."

Jake claps me on the shoulder. "Looks like we got a full day ahead."

"The fun never stops."

I'm about to hop off the table, but Dr. Palmer puts a hand on my knee to stop me. "We need to talk about Madison."

"What about her?"

"I think you know what I'm talking about."

"No. I don't."

Dr. Palmer sighs. I make a lot of people do that. "I'm talking about mental regression. You've seen the signs. The way she whines. Throwing tantrums when she doesn't get her way. How she clings to Stacey, who is for all practical purposes her big sister. Coloring with crayons. Playing with dolls."

"Wetting the bed," Jake adds.

"She's sucking her thumb too when she sleeps," I say. "So what? She's been through a lot in the last couple of months."

"Exactly. Her mind has been traumatized by all of this. She doesn't know how to handle it, so she's reverting back to her five-year-old self."

"What are we supposed to do about it?"

"We should bring Dr. Macintosh in on this. He has experience working with traumatized children. He could help her deal with it." Dr. Palmer pats my knee. "It wouldn't be such a bad idea for you to see him again either. He's been calling me every day to ask about you."

"He has?"

"Well I can't blame him the way you ran out of that bar."

"You were there?"

"No, but I've heard about it. What happened?"

"I had some stage fright."

"Right. Anyway, I'm not as concerned about your mind. You've already been through a few traumas."

"And you're too damned stubborn to become a sweet little kid," Jake adds.

"That too. The point is, Madison doesn't have that experience. She needs some help to sort everything out. Otherwise she's going to keep regressing until there's nothing of the adult Madison left."

I can't argue with that; I've already seen the symptoms myself. "What are you going to tell him?"

"I suppose I'll have to tell him everything."

"Everything? Even about me being…you know?"

"Oh." Dr. Palmer tilts my chin up to look me in the eye. "I'm sorry, Stacey, but I think he needs to know the whole truth if he's going to help you and Maddy."

"But why? Who I was before doesn't have anything to do with Dr. Ling."

"If he's going to help us then he needs to know the truth."

I remember the way he eyed me, the same way as those drunk boys at the bar. What will he think when he finds out I was born a man? "I don't wanna tell him."

"Why not? Stacey, what's wrong?"

"He'll think I'm a freak."

"He won't. Dr. Macintosh is a scientist, like me."

"He'll hate me for lying."

"He's a good person. He's not going to judge you." She gives my hand a squeeze. "Trust me, Stacey. Please?"

I look her in the eye and see how serious she is about this. "All right, you can tell him."

"Thank you. That's very grown up of you."

"Can we go? Maddy's probably finished her ice cream by now."

"Sure, you can go." She pats the roll of fat that bulges over my pants. "You both could use to lay off the sweets, especially Madison. I don't want either of you developing diabetes. You've dealt with enough needles already."

"I'll try to keep my girlish figure," I grumble.

Chapter 18

We separate at the eye doctor. Tess takes Maddy home for a nap while Jake and I stay there. We'll have to get a cab to take us back, unless Jake wants to try to take me on the train.

"Can't I go with them?" Maddy asks with a five-year-old's whine.

"No, dear. You need to get some rest. You've had a busy day."

"Have not."

"It's for the best, dear."

"Trust me, it's not going to be any fun," I say. "It'll be as bad as all those tests Dr. Ling ran on us."

That prompts Maddy to shiver. "I don't want to go then."

With that, Tess drives off; Jake and I are alone again. "I don't know what's wrong with these," I say. "They aren't so bad."

"Palmer's right: you need glasses made for *your* eyes. I don't want you going blind because you insist on wearing these ugly old things."

"They're not ugly. I like them."

"You look like the Chinese Sally Jesse Raphael."

"It's a good thing I'm not ten years old or I'd have no idea what you're talking about."

"Stop being such a baby and go in the damned store."

Jake holds the door open so I can slip inside. It looks more like a car dealer than an eye doctor. There are rows of glasses all along the walls. Sales reps in gray polo shirts chat with other customers, to help them try on glasses.

Jake puts a hand on my back to steer me past the rows of glasses. A saleswoman spots us and then heads our way. Her forced smile gives me the urge to cling to Jake's leg the way Maddy used to do to mine when she got scared. She bends down to focus on me. I whimper out of fear at the way she looms over me. "I bet you're here to get some new glasses, aren't you?"

"Yes," I mumble.

"We need to get her an eye exam too. Can we do that today?"

"Of course! But first I'll need to get some information about both of you."

She takes us over to a table so we can start to fill out the paperwork. "All right, sweetie, what's your name?"

"Stacey."

"And what's your last name?"

I look up at Jake, not sure what I should say here. We didn't really think this far ahead. Just like before, it's Jake who renames me. "Cha...Chang," he says. He pats my back. "She's a little shy."

"Am not," I mutter.

"And how old are you, Stacey?"

"Ten."

"Oh, so you're a big girl, aren't you?"

"Yes," I say with teeth clenched.

"And is this your daddy?"

"I'm her grandfather," Jake says. "Jake Madigan."

"I see. Does Stacey have insurance, Mr. Madigan?"

"No. We'll pay cash today."

"Not a problem. I'll just need to get the rest of your information." Jake has to give the woman his address, phone number, and all that stuff. My part in this interview is over. The saleswoman hardly looks at me until she finishes the paperwork. "And that should do it for now. There will be a short wait before the doctor can see you. In the meantime you can browse our selection."

I wait until the woman has gone to glare up at Jake. "Chang? That's the best you could come up with?"

"At least it isn't Ling," he says.

"Gee thanks, *Grandpa*."

"Well you have to admit I don't look like I could be the father to a ten-year-old Chinese girl."

"I guess." I sigh. "We really have to work these things out ahead of time."

"Let's hope it's the last time. Come on, let's go find you something. Try not to make it too expensive. I'm not made of money."

"Right." We wander around the store for a few minutes. Most of the glasses look the same to me. The only glasses I've ever worn are sunglasses, so I have no idea if the shape or styles matter.

Then I see the perfect pair. I stand on my toes, but they're too high for me to reach. I point up at them; my hand trembles with excitement. "Let me see those."

"Are you serious?"

"Yes! They're perfect." The glasses in question have rectangular frames like most of the others that are a lot smaller than the ones I wear. The difference is they're the same red as the ones Qiang gave me.

I take the old ones off to try the frames on. The lenses are glass, so I have to lean close to a mirror to see my face. I look slightly more grown up in these and except for the color they're less conspicuous than Ming's old glasses.

I turn to Jake. "What do you think?"

"I think you look ridiculous."

"Well *I* like them. They're cute."

"Why would you want to wear those?"

I look down at my old glasses, the ones Qiang's daughter wore. "She saved our lives. Her daughter's going to die in prison because she helped us. I just want to honor her memory, you know?"

Jake considers this for a moment and then nods. "If that's what you want, we'll get them."

"Thanks, Grandpa."

***

The eye tests are almost as bad as those Dr. Ling subjected us to. Instead of jamming needles into my arm, the doctor blows puffs of air into my eyes. Next he tries to put eye drops in to dilate my eyes. I blink at the wrong time the first two times, so we have to do it a third time. That's all before we get to the more traditional test where I stare at the wall to read letters off the chart.

I fail that test miserably; I only get to the third row of the chart. The doctor smiles and says, "Very good, Stacey." As he writes down the results, I know he can't believe how bad my eyes are. If I have to stay in this body, I'll probably be blind by the time I'm twenty.

To finish, I stare into what looks like a bulkier Viewmaster so he can try different lenses. "Number one or number two?" he asks. There doesn't seem to be much difference between them.

"Number two, I guess." We repeat this a few times before he scribbles a prescription for me. I don't know what the numbers mean, but I'm sure they're bad.

By the end of the tests, I'm ready to go home and take a nap. I can't just yet. I have to get my new glasses. The doctor talks to Jake, to tell him about the tests they ran to make sure I don't have glaucoma or anything like that.

The doctor gives me a pair of roll-on sunglasses to wear outside until the eye drops he gave me wear off. Then he reaches into a pocket of his lab coat. From the pocket he takes out a red sucker. "And here's a little something for being such a good patient."

"Thank you," I mumble.

"I'll see you next year. OK, Stacey?"

"OK." God, I hope not.

Since we already have the frames picked out, it's not hard to get my new glasses started. The same saleswoman as before waits on us. She makes me try the frames on again, just to make sure I want them. "They look very pretty," she says. To Jake she says, "It should only be an hour to get these made. Two at most. You can wait here if you want or—"

"I think we'll come back in a couple hours," Jake says. "I bet someone is really hankering for a milkshake about now."

"Right," I say without enthusiasm.

The sunglasses the doctor gave me don't work very well in Ming's old glasses. They unroll and slip down my face. The moment they get out of position, it's like someone's shined their high beams right into my eyes. I look down at the sidewalk all the way to a diner a block or two away.

"You all right, kid?" Jake asks.

"It's these stupid drops he gave me."

"Oh, those. They'll wear off in a few hours."

"Sucks until then."

"Yeah, it does."

We make it to the diner, where we take a booth in the darkest corner. I press myself as far into that corner as I can, though it's still too bright. If the doctor thinks I'll do this every year he can go fuck himself.

"Uh-oh, looks like someone isn't very happy," a woman says. I turn and see it's our waitress.

"She just went to the eye doctor," Jake says.

"Oh, that's too bad. But you do have such pretty eyes."

"Thanks," I mumble.

"I think a chocolate milkshake would cheer her up," Jake says. "And I'll have a coffee. Black."

"Coming right up."

I wait until after the waitress is gone to glare at Jake again, though it's a little difficult with my eyes dilated. "It's bad enough everyone else does that, but do you have to too?"

"What are you talking about?"

"Talking to me like I'm a kid."

"In case you haven't noticed, you are a kid. I'm just staying in character as your doting grandpa."

"Well maybe you could tone down the doting a little."

The waitress shows up with our drinks. She put a curly straw in my shake, to make it more fun I guess. "Here you go, sweetheart. Enjoy!"

I suck on the straw and watch the shake curl up it, into my mouth. It's been a while since I had a chocolate shake that wasn't a diet one. Jake just sits there; he gapes at me until I snap, "What?"

"Seeing you like this, so little, it just makes me think—"

His voice trails off, so I prod, "Think what?"

"I was just thinking it's too bad I'll never have any real grandkids."

"Oh," I say and look down at the table. I think of Jennifer, Jake's daughter who died four years earlier from cancer. His and Tess's only child, who died before she could have any kids of her own. "I'm sorry."

"It's all right," Jake says. Unable to think of anything that would be of comfort, I slurp down my shake while he watches.

After the shake, Jake buys us each a slice of pie—apple for him and chocolate for me. We don't say much until it's time to go back over to the eye doctor to get my glasses.

I walk out of the store in my new glasses. I keep Ming's in my pocket and hope someday I can give them back to her like Qiang wanted.

Chapter 19

With my eyes still affected by the eye drops, I doze for most of the cab ride home with my head against Jake's arm. I'm not sure at what point I actually fall asleep. One moment I'm up against Jake and the next I wake up to find him carrying me. When I begin to stir, he shushes me. "It's all right, kid. Go back to sleep."

I decide to give in to this suggestion. Before I drift back into unconsciousness, I hear Tess say, "Poor little dear is all tuckered out."

The next time I wake up, it's dark. I roll over and fumble around to find my glasses on the nightstand. I slip the glasses on, which allows me to see it's six-thirty. I've only been asleep for two hours, but it feels like much longer than that.

I crawl out of bed and grope around for the light switch. I have to remind myself it's not in the same place as it used to be because I'm not in the same place I used to be. I find the switch at last and keep my eyes closed as it flicks on.

I open my eyes slowly to see if those drops have worn off. The light doesn't sting quite so much this time. I blink a few times to make sure. Thank God that's over with.

My stomach begins to rumble as I smell Tess's pot roast. The table is already set in the dining room, which probably means she held dinner until I woke up. I follow my nose into the kitchen, where Tess stirs a bowl of mashed potatoes.

"Hello, sweetheart," she says. "Are you feeling better now?"

"Yes. Is dinner ready yet?"

"Almost. Why don't you go wait in the living room with Madison?"

I find Maddy on the couch; she clutches a pillow that's nearly as big as her chest. She stares intently at the cartoons on the screen. She barely seems to notice when I sit down beside her. "What are you watching?" I ask.

"*Spongebob*," she says.

"Is it any good?"

"It's OK." As the toy commercials come on, she finally turns to me. "Your glasses are pretty."

"Thanks."

"Was the eye doctor scary?"

"Not too bad. Just these drops he gave me were kind of annoying."

"When Jake carried you in, I thought maybe—" Her voice trails off and I see her face redden as if on the verge of tears.

"Hey, it's all right," I say. I pat her back. "No one hurt me. My eyes were just a little tired from the drops. That's all."

"If anything happened to you, I don't know what I'd do," she says. "I can't do this alone."

"You aren't going to have to do it alone. I'll help you through it. I promise."

She turns to the TV when her show comes back on. This time she leans against me the same way I leaned against Jake. I think about what Dr. Palmer said, how this is traumatizing Maddy. It is a big shock to her system, one she might never recover from.

When Tess calls us for dinner, Maddy hops off the couch in a heartbeat and races into the dining room as fast as her short legs can carry her. That is until she sees Tess has put a phone book down on Maddy's seat to help her reach the table. "I don't need to sit on anything," Maddy whines. "I'm not a baby."

"I just want to make sure you're comfortable, dear."

"No booster seats," Maddy says and then swipes the phone book to the floor.

"That wasn't very nice," Tess says, her voice hard enough that I flinch.

"Sorry." Maddy retrieves the phone book to hand it back to Tess, who tucks it under her arm.

"It's all right. Just sit down, dear."

Maddy can reach the table—barely. She has to be pushed in all the way and even then the table comes up to her chin. At least Tess doesn't try to put a bib around her neck, which would set Maddy off for sure.

I sit across from Maddy, the table not so high on me, but still not what I'm used to. To set a good example for Maddy, I sit calmly and wait for the adults to sit down. Jake comes in a minute later, still on the phone. "I'll call you back in about a half-hour," he says.

"Who was that?" I ask.

"Woods. They found that school where you were being held."

Tess clears her throat as she sits down. One of her rules is not to discuss business at the dinner table. "Now everyone, bow your heads and let's say grace."

I see Maddy's cheeks redden at that last word as she no doubt thinks of Grace. Her cheeks are still red all during the prayer, though she doesn't cry. But when Tess ladles some potatoes onto Maddy's plate, Maddy makes a disgusted face. "Yuck, potatoes."

"But you love mashed potatoes," Tess says.

"Do not."

"Well, what do you want?"

"Ice cream."

"That's for dessert, sweetheart. Eat your potatoes and then later you can have some ice cream."

"No! I want it now!" Maddy struggles to move her chair back and then hops down to the floor.

"Madison, you don't leave the table until you've eaten your dinner."

"I don't want dinner. I want ice cream!"

"Young lady, that is enough. Sit down right now or you won't get anything to eat at all."

"You can't tell me what to do! You're not my mommy!" Maddy scurries towards the kitchen, but she's not fast enough. Tess grabs her before she can reach the doorway and hefts Maddy into the air. Maddy's stubby legs kick futilely at the air. "Lemme go! I want ice cream."

I stare down at my plate, not sure what to do. As Maddy's father I should be the one to do what Tess is, but as a ten-year-old girl I don't have the authority to make Maddy sit down and eat her dinner. So I do nothing and feel lousy.

By the time she's seated again, Maddy's face is red and soaked with tears. "Go on and eat your dinner," Tess says. "Unless you want to go to your room for the night."

Maddy dips her spoon into the potatoes. She draws the spoon back towards her mouth. At the last second, she flings the spoonful of potatoes over Tess's shoulder, against the wall. Before Maddy can get another spoonful, Tess seizes her by the wrist. This sets Maddy into a full-fledged tantrum. She begins to shriek so loud I have to cover my ears.

"That's enough, young lady," Tess says. She starts to carry Maddy away, impervious to Maddy's thrashing.

I get up to follow them, but Jake grabs my wrist. "Let them go," he says.

"But—"

"Sit down and finish your supper. Tess can handle it."

I can hear Maddy's screams even from upstairs. It reminds me of Dr. Ling's lab, except nothing so sinister is going on here. It's just a tantrum, like the ones Maddy used to throw at my dinner table. Back then I carried her upstairs to her room and locked her in for the night. It didn't feel good then; it feels even less good now.

But when Jake lets my wrist go, I sit down to eat my dinner.

***

Jake, Tess, and I watch reruns of *The Golden Girls* until eight-thirty. Then Tess pats me on the back. "Time for you to get ready for bed."

"Already?"

Tess clucks her tongue. "Don't you start with me, young lady."

"Sorry."

"I want you to make sure you brush your teeth before you go to bed. We don't want you getting cavities in that beautiful smile."

"OK."

I start to trudge up the stairs. Tess calls after me, "I put a nightgown on the nightstand for you. Try not to wake Madison."

"I won't."

I ease open the bedroom door so I won't wake Maddy. As Tess promised, there's a nightgown on the nightstand. I leave the door open a crack to provide a little light while I change. The nightgown is a Garfield one that's a couple of sizes too big on me. I try not to trip over the hem of it as I shut the door and then crawl into bed.

After I've put my glasses on the nightstand, I hear Maddy stir. "Stace?"

"I'm here."

"I'm sorry."

"It's all right," I whisper. "I know what happened."

"You do?"

I slide across the bed to snuggle up against her. That will make it easier for us to talk without Tess or Jake being able to hear us. "Maddy, you can't let Grace go. You've got to hold on to that love. Then you'll always remember who you really are."

"What if I never see her again? Or if I do, what if I'm still a little kid?"

"Grace is always going to love you, no matter how old you are or what you look like."

Maddy sniffles and then says, "Sometimes I forget. I have to focus really, really hard to remember her face or her voice or her kiss—"

She turns her head to cry into her pillow. I rub her back and try to think of something to say. "Hey, you remember that picture you made in your cell?"

"Yes."

"Well, maybe you should make another one."

"That might work." She surprises me with a kiss on my cheek. "Thanks, Stace."

"You're welcome."

"G'night, Stace," she says with a yawn. Just like that she's out again.

Chapter 20

The next morning there's a knock on the door. "Girls, time to get up," Tess calls in a singsong voice. She opens the door a crack. "Rise and shine."

I groan as Tess turns on the light. After I scramble to find my glasses, I see it's eight o'clock in the morning. I've been asleep for almost eleven hours. I roll out of bed and nearly trip over the hem of my nightgown in the process. Tess is there to steady me before I can fall. "Don't worry, today we're going to buy you both some new clothes."

"Goody," I say, never much of a morning person. Tess, who got up early the majority of twelve years to see Jennifer off to school, is a lot more chipper.

"I had another accident," Maddy says, the shame evident in her voice.

"It's all right, dear. I'll clean it up later. First, it's time for you two to get a bath."

"A bath?" Maddy repeats. Her voice trembles. "Can't I take a shower?"

"I'm afraid you're too little for that."

"But—"

"No buts, young lady. Both of you march into the bathroom right now."

"Both of us?" I ask.

"You're not too big to take a bath with your little sister, are you?" Tess asks. She gives me a look to encourage me. I know what she wants from me, to set a good example for Madison.

"No, I'm not," I say. I hold out my hand to Maddy. "Come on, it'll be fun."

Maddy looks at Tess and then at me. "OK," she says.

I lead her down to the main bathroom. I hope Tess doesn't mind that I turn on the faucets to start filling the tub. She should know I have better sense than to let Maddy drown.

By the time I'm down to my underpants, Maddy still hasn't taken off so much as a sock. "Do you need help?" I ask.

"I don't want to," she says.

"Why not?"

"It's creepy."

She's got me there. Still, Tess is right that Maddy isn't big enough to use the shower. We can't trust her to bathe on her own either. This is for the best. Before I say anything, I remind myself I've talked criminals out of killing hostages; I should be able to handle this. "It's not so weird," I say. "You've seen girls naked before."

"But not you."

"How about you keep your eyes closed and I'll get in the water and then I'll close my eyes and you can get in the tub?"

"OK," Maddy says. "But you promise not to peek?"

"I promise." Maddy closes her eyes while I undress the rest of the way. Then I step into the back of the tub. I sink down in the warm water, to let it cover me. With my eyes closed, I say, "Your turn."

"I'm so fat," Maddy says. "It's gross."

"It's fine. You just haven't grown into your body yet."

"Maybe I never will." I hear her splash down in front of me. "You can look now."

Tess interrupts us. She kneels down beside the tub with a plastic bowl. "Who wants to go first? Stacey?"

"Sure," I say. That way Maddy will see it's not so bad. I close my eyes and let Tess pour the bowl of water over my head. I haven't had a bath like this in a good forty-two years. Back then it was my grandma who did it. I remember how long her fingernails were, how it felt like she would rip out all the hair on my head.

Tess is far gentler. It's more like a massage when she works the shampoo into my wet hair. I keep my eyes squeezed shut; I don't want to get anything into my already-bad eyes. She rinses my hair and then puts in some conditioner. After another rinse, Tess says, "You can open your eyes, dear."

I blink a few times. Maddy faces me to watch my reaction. I smile at her. "That wasn't so bad, was it?"

"No," Maddy says.

"Now it's your turn, sweetheart," Tess says. "Keep your eyes shut very tight."

"OK."

For once Maddy cooperates. She whimpers a little as Tess works in the shampoo, but she doesn't make a fuss. That's progress as far as I'm concerned. After Tess rinses the conditioner out, I pat Maddy on the back. "Good job."

The next step is to clean the rest of us. Tess rubs a bar of soap across my back and chest hard enough to scrape a couple layers of skin off. She even scrubs at my cheeks and of course behind my ears. There is one area she won't do. She blushes a little and then hands the soap to me. "I think you'd better handle the rest, dear."

"Sure," I say. I'm not as thorough on my lower half as Tess was on the upper half. In the last year I've gotten used to washing my girlish parts, but not with an audience. After a few token swipes with the soap, I hand it back to Tess. "All done."

"Thank you, dear."

She goes through the same routine with Maddy. Before she hands over the soap, Tess looks Maddy in the eye. "Can you handle this very big girl job?" she asks.

"Yes. I'm not a baby."

"Very good."

Despite what she says, Maddy is as half-hearted about it as I am. That will take time. For today, we're finished. Tess holds up a towel. "Up you go, sweetheart." I turn away as Maddy stands up. Tess is quick to wrap the towel around Maddy. She gives Maddy a quick hug. "You were very brave, dear."

"Thanks."

It's my turn then to get out of the tub. Tess wraps the towel around me, to let me dry myself off. We keep the towels around our bodies as Tess picks up a comb to work the tangles out of our hair.

This is the one time when Maddy is much better behaved than I am. Her hair isn't as long and thus not as snarled. Tess needs only a few strokes before Maddy's hair is smooth as black silk.

Mine requires a lot more effort. Tess has me sit down on the toilet to make it a little easier. Her first attempt to run the comb through gets a couple of inches before it snags. I cry out; it feels almost as bad as when Ling's goon yanked me backwards by the hair. Though I want to set a good example for Maddy, I can't keep tears out of my eyes as Tess continues to try to work the comb through my hair.

"Do you have to do it so hard?" I whine.

"I'm sorry, dear. We're almost done."

Someone takes my hand. Though I have my eyes closed tight, I know from the size of it that it's Maddy's hand. I squeeze it back to let her know I'm all right. It doesn't feel like it though as Tess finishes up; my scalp feels like someone's lit it on fire.

As I sniffle and wipe tears away, Tess pats my shoulder. "It's all right, Stacey. We're going to get it cut today so it won't be so bad next time."

"Thanks."

Then, clean and well-coiffed, we head back to the bedroom to change.

***

Jake reads the paper in the dining room when we come downstairs. "Well, look at that. Are those my two little grandchildren?"

"Yes," I say.

"I almost didn't recognize you now that you're not so grubby. And I didn't even hear any screaming."

"They were both very good," Tess says. "Especially Madison."

"It was just a bath," Maddy says, though she smiles about her accomplishment.

Maddy and I sit down at the table while Tess makes us some pancakes. Jake's already picked out the comics page to hand to Maddy. As she studies the comic strips, I see her mouth move as she works out some of the bigger words. I remember how unsteady her handwriting was too. Is that mental regression or something else? I should ask Dr. Palmer next time we see her. I hope that won't be too long.

"So what's on today's agenda?" Jake asks.

"Tess is going to take us clothes shopping," Maddy says. "And get Stacey a haircut."

"She sure could use it," Jake says. "That hair gets any longer and we'll have to start calling you Cousin It."

"It's not that long," I say.

"Here we go, girls," Tess says. She brings in a plate stacked high with pancakes. "Dig in."

Since she didn't eat last night, Maddy tears into the pancakes ravenously. I'm a little more reserved, though Tess does make excellent pancakes.

While she works on her pancakes, Maddy asks, "Where are we going to go?" I see a worried look flicker across her face. If Tess takes us to the garment district, then we might run into Grace, not to mention other people Maddy knows from around the neighborhood.

"I was thinking over to the Wal-Mart. I need to pick up a few groceries too. I didn't plan on cooking for two little girls, especially not one fussy eater."

"I'm sorry," Maddy says. "I didn't mean to be bad."

"It's all right, dear. Think nothing of it."

"Well, much as I'd love to accompany you three, I have to get to work. By now some of the forensics have come back from that school where he was keeping you."

Tess clears her throat. "I don't think the girls need to hear about that."

"I know." Jake gives his wife a chaste kiss. Before he can leave, Maddy runs over to hug his leg.

"Bye-bye Grandpa Jake."

My farewell to him is a lot more subdued. I wave and then turn back to my breakfast. I just hope those forensics from the school don't show that Qiang is dead.

***

There's a salon inside the Wal-Mart. Tess wheels us into it and then helps us out of the shopping cart. One of the stylists comes over and like the saleswoman at the eye doctor bends down with a phony smile. "I see two little girls who need a haircut," she says

"Especially this one," Tess says. She pats my head.

"I can see why. You're starting to look like Rapunzel."

"It's not that long," I say. My entire face turns warm out of embarrassment.

"Not yet. We're just in time." The stylist leads me over to a chair. I pout a little when I see the booster seat on it. I'm not *that* little; I'm not a toddler like Maddy. I look over at Maddy and Tess and remember how important it is for me to set a good example, so I climb onto the booster seat.

"Such long, pretty hair," the stylist says as she holds my long tresses up with one hand while she fastens the plastic smock around my neck with the other. "It's almost a shame to cut it."

"You don't have to." Much as I hated Tess's combing earlier, I really don't want to be in this chair, on the stupid booster seat.

"I don't think your mommy would like that."

"She's not my mommy. She's my grandma."

"Oh, I see. Where is your mommy?"

"Dead."

"I'm sorry."

I don't say anything. Tess would chide me for being so mean to this nice lady, but I'm tired of all the condescension.

The stylist runs the comb through my hair a few times, which is easier than when Tess did it. "So what do you want to do with it?"

"Can you give me a perm? And dye it red?" If she could do that, then at least I'd recognize a little something of myself.

"We'd have to ask your grandma about that."

Tess is across the salon to confer with another stylist about what to do with Maddy. She looks more comfortable on the booster seat, but then she's used to it from the car. "I think she would look really pretty with something short," the other stylist says. She holds a comb up to Maddy's jaw line. "About there."

"I don't want it short," Maddy whines. "I want it long and pretty, like Stacey's."

"Now, Madison—"

"It's my hair!"

Tess sighs. "I suppose a little bit longer. About shoulder-length."

"No," Maddy says.

"That's enough, young lady. You keep it up and you're going back to the car without any new clothes or anything."

Maddy pouts, but doesn't say anything, which is tacit approval for the stylist to go ahead. With that settled, Tess walks across the salon to me. "I think you can cut off about eight inches," Tess says.

"What about her bangs?" the stylist asks.

"Oh, I don't know. What do you think dear?"

"I don't care."

"I think she'd look really cute with bangs." The stylist combs my hair forward. Then she holds up the mirror. The heavy line of bangs has covered my entire forehead, right down to the tops of my eye sockets. My face looks different, smaller than before. This isn't the face of the little Chinese girl Dr. Ling tortured for weeks; this is someone new, someone innocent and cute with a whole new life ahead of her.

"I love it," I say.

"Then let's get to it," the stylist says.

My haircut doesn't take very long. Mostly the stylist has to snip those eight inches or so in the back. She has to trim a little along the sides as well to even it out. The worst part is when she trims my new bangs. Even with my terrible eyes I can see the scissors hover over my eyes; one false move and I'll need an eye patch. I whimper a little at that. The stylist puts a hand on my shoulder. "It'll be fine, sweetheart. Just stay still."

I do as she says and squeeze my eyes shut until she tells me to open them. She holds the mirror up again. I give my head a couple tosses and then smile at how much better it feels. I resist the urge to brush the bangs away; that's something I'll have to get used to.

Maddy's haircut takes a lot longer, mostly because she fidgets nonstop. The stylist gets one snip in before Maddy starts to wiggle in her seat. By the time I'm done, Maddy's is only done on one side. Her face is red and her eyes wet. "I wanna go home," she whines.

"Hi," I say.

"Hi. You look pretty."

"Thanks. You're looking pretty too."

"You think so?"

"Yes, but if you really want to look pretty, then you need to let the nice lady work."

"But the scissors are so sharp. She could cut me."

"She's not going to hurt you." I toss my hair for Maddy, so she can see I'm all right. "The lady didn't hurt me, did she?"

"No."

"Well then, why don't you be a big girl and let her work?"

"OK."

Tess and I stand back to let the stylist work. "That was very nice of you," Tess says. She runs her hand along my hair. "It is pretty."

"Better than I used to look?"

"I don't know. It's so different."

We sit not too far away from Maddy so we can watch. She has her eyes closed and from what I can tell, she's bitten down on her lip to hold down the fear.

Maddy stays calm until the stylist starts to clip by her ears. Then Maddy lets out a shriek they can probably hear at the back of the store. "Don't touch me!" she wails.

The stylist takes a step back, her face pale. She's probably seen tantrums in the chair before, but not like this. I bolt from my chair and hurry over to take Maddy's hand. She starts to sob openly now. "It's all right, Maddy. I'm here. No one will hurt you."

"Don't leave me, Stace."

"I won't."

"Promise?"

"I promise."

"OK."

I keep hold of Maddy's hand, which is hard when the stylist needs to get over to that side. We have to do a little dance around each other to clear the way. Through it all, Maddy cries silently, still haunted by visions of Dr. Ling's prison.

For all the trouble that's gone into it, the haircut looks nice. It's layered in front so she doesn't have bangs like me, while the back is long enough to touch her shoulders. The stylist's hand shakes a little as she holds the mirror up for Maddy. "See?" I tell her. "You look pretty. And no one hurt you."

"I do look pretty," she says. She tosses her hair a little. "Like a big girl."

"OK, girls, back into the cart," Tess says. She leaves us near the front of the salon while she talks to the stylists. I'm sure there will be a very large gratuity after all of this trouble.

Once she's paid, Tess returns to us. She strokes Maddy's shorter hair. "Do you want to go home now, sweetheart?"

"No," Maddy whispers. "I can do it."

Tess and I exchange uncertain looks, but then she pushes the cart past the cash registers, into the apparel section.

Chapter 21

It's not much fun to shop for clothes when you don't have credit cards with no limits and are confined to Wal-Mart's selection of cheap, sweat shop-made goods. As I browse the racks of little T-shirts, jeans, and hoodies, I don't get the same giddy thrill as I did when I shopped with Bobby Blades's credit cards a year ago. This is Tess and Jake's money now, their savings. That money should be for Jake's retirement, not to buy clothes for two little girls who aren't even his responsibility.

Once we've decided on all of our purchases, Tess loads them and Maddy into the cart. There's not enough room anymore for me to fit too, so I have to walk beside the cart as we make our way to the toy section. I stare at the rows of pink Barbie boxes and suppress a shiver. "You can each get one doll," Tess says.

"No thanks," I say.

"But we can't play if we don't both have one," Maddy says. "Pwease?"

I can't tell if she's being serious or not. I suppose she is. I roll my eyes. "Fine, but you can pick them both out."

Maddy stands up in the cart, which makes it easier for her to reach the shelves. She finds a doll with red hair like the one we had in Dr. Ling's dungeon and hands it to me.

The red hair is the wrong shade, I never had freckles, and my boobs were never that big, but I suppose it'll work.

The one Maddy picks out for herself is an actual Barbie in a pink business suit with a microphone and video camera. She's supposed to be a TV reporter. Maddy would rather be a print journalist, but they don't seem to have one of those so this will have to do. She stares at the doll; I'm sure she imagines herself as a grown-up in a business suit on camera.

Tess perhaps senses things are about to take a dark turn; she hurries us over to the stuffed toys. Again she says we can each have one toy. And again I decline. This time it's Tess who presses the issue. "Every little girl should at least have a teddy bear," she says. "Or how about a monkey? Isn't this one cute?" She holds out a hot pink monkey with a lighter pink belly.

It's my turn to throw a tantrum. I stamp my foot on the floor. "I don't want any stupid toys! Stop treating me like a little kid."

The last thing I expect is for Tess to cry. "I'm sorry, dear. You're absolutely right," she says. She tosses the monkey back into the bin. "I keep forgetting."

I know why she forgets: she looks at me and sees Jennifer, the daughter she lost four years ago. Tess had never tried to replace her daughter; it was only by chance I dropped into her lap. Even then I didn't need her in the same way, at least not after the first few days. I wasn't dependent on her the way Maddy and I are now. It was easy enough for both of us to think of her as an aunt, not my mommy, or my grandma. And then after three months without me, she gets all of this extra responsibility thrust upon her. It's not fair.

"I'm sorry, Grandma Tess," I say. I look down at my feet with shame. "I've been naughty."

"Don't think anything of it."

I retrieve the pink monkey from the bin. I hug it tight to my chest. "I like it," I say. "It's so soft."

"Thank you, dear."

Maddy picks out a pink bunny rabbit. She calls it Mrs. Hoppy after a similarly pink rabbit that used to be her favorite toy. I remember that Mrs. Hoppy because I bought it for her in the hospital gift shop the night she was born. The original is probably still in a box somewhere, in a storage unit or in a closet of Debbie's condo.

With a tired sigh, Tess says, "Well, I guess it's time for us to get moving."

***

Of course things can't be that simple. While Maddy and I study the candy bars in the checkout lane, I hear a woman's voice call Tess's name. My first thought is it's an employee to complain about the swath of destruction we've left in our wake across the store.

It's a lot worse than that. It's a hunchbacked old woman with glasses even thicker than mine. Her name is Minnie and she's the biggest gossip at Tess's church. I remember the first service I attended, how the old woman came up to Tess and Jake and asked, "And who is *this*?"

She does the same thing now after she exchanges pleasantries with Tess. "Are these adorable little girls yours?"

"For the moment," Tess says. Though Tess smiles, I can see the way her hands tighten around the handlebar of the cart. She probably hoped out here we wouldn't bump into anyone familiar. "This is Stacey and Madison."

"Stacey? Like the young woman who used to be staying with you?"

"Yes. One Stacey vanishes and another one falls into our laps," Tess says. "The Lord works in mysterious ways."

"I was so sorry to hear about that poor girl. Have they ever found her?"

"No, not yet. Jacob says the department is still looking, but there aren't any leads."

"Well, I'll keep praying for her."

"Thank you."

"So how did you happen to end up with these two cuties?"

"Oh, well, their parents died and there was no one to take care of them. Jacob and I couldn't bear the thought of them going to one of those dreadful group homes. We volunteered to take care of them until the state can find a good foster home. It helps fill the void with the other Stacey missing."

"I'm sure it does. You're such a generous woman. That's what I keep telling everyone: there's no one in the congregation more generous than Teresa Madigan."

"I'm nothing special. Just following what the Good Book says."

"Yes, of course. So will you be bringing Stacey and—"

"Madison."

"Stacey and Madison to services on Sunday? They are Christian, aren't they?"

"They are, but Jacob and I aren't sure they're ready for that yet. They only moved in a couple of days ago. It's been hectic for all of us."

"I imagine it would be."

An old bearded man who uses his cart like a walker shows up behind Minnie. He clears his throat. "Well, we've got to be off. It's good to see you, Teresa. And your two delightful new charges." The old woman waves to us. "I'm sure I'll see you both soon."

"I can hardly wait," I grumble after Minnie has toddled off with her husband.

"Who was that old witch?" Maddy asks.

"Never mind, dear. Are you all set to check out?"

"Yes," we say in unison.

"Good," Tess says. I couldn't agree more.

***

After our epic trip to Wal-Mart, there's nothing I'd rather do than collapse on my bed and sleep. There's just one problem: my bed is gone. I trudge up the stairs to find Jake in the bedroom, as he puts the finishing touches on a set of twin bunk beds. The lower bed is shaped like a race car while the rails for the upper one are metal the same red as my glasses.

"What's all this?" I ask. I drop my bags of clothes to the floor.

Jake turns and grins. "Ta-da," he says. "You remember Bob Wertz?"

"Young guy? Works in forensics?"

"That's right. We got talking and he mentioned he had these beds his kids weren't using anymore. I thought you two might like them so you won't have to share."

"But they're for *boys*," I say.

"You'd rather keep sleeping with Madison?"

"I don't know."

"Just try it for a couple of nights." He pats the ladder to the top bunk. "Go on, try it out. But no jumping around."

"I know. I'm not stupid."

As I climb up, Jake asks, "Tess get you two haircuts?"

"Yes. You like it?"

"It looks nice."

I swing myself onto the top bunk. From there I feel tall again. I look down at Jake. "You like the bangs?" I ask. I run a hand through them.

"Sure. You like the bed?"

"It's all right."

Tess leads Maddy into the room then. Maddy's reaction is the same as mine. "That's a *boy's* bed," she says with obvious revulsion.

"We could always repaint it," Jake says.

Maddy shrugs at this suggestion. Then she crawls onto the bed. As she does, I hear plastic crinkle. That's the other reason Jake brought the beds home, so Maddy's accidents won't ruin the other bed. I brace myself for Maddy to throw another tantrum at this. She doesn't. She doesn't say anything. I slide beneath the rails, out enough to see underneath my new bed. Maddy's fallen asleep. It's no surprise after the day we've had.

"I guess she likes it," Jake says.

"I guess so," I say and then I slide behind the rail again to take a little nap myself.

Chapter 22

For our big meeting with Dr. Macintosh, Tess has us in our best clothes, the ones we'll wear for church. Maddy's dress is pink with puffy sleeves while mine is dark blue with a white belt. We had to take another bath too, though this time when Tess combed my hair it didn't hurt so much. Maddy didn't complain either when Tess put her hair into cute little pigtails. She behaved herself all during the ride into the city too, which I take as a hopeful sign.

As we ride the elevator up, I don't realize my nervousness about meeting Dr. Macintosh is evident until Tess rubs my back. "Don't worry, dear. It won't be too bad. He just wants to talk."

"I know."

We get off on the fifth floor for his office. The last time I opened the door I could do it all by myself. I had been a grown woman back then with a job, friends, and perhaps a new career. It wasn't such a bad life. I didn't think so at the time, but now I'd give anything for that life back.

This time Jake holds open the door while Tess ushers me inside. Maddy clings to her koala-style; she's far more nervous than I am. I hope she doesn't throw a tantrum in the doctor's office. I don't think I could handle the embarrassment of it.

There are a bunch of kids and their parents in the waiting room, just like last time. I don't feel out of place among the kids, not now that I'm one of them. I don't want to get too close to them though, so I sit at the end, in a corner. Tess sits down next to me while Jake deals with the receptionist.

There's one person who looks out of place. He's a boy probably no more than the age Maddy used to be. With his longish brown hair and goatee, he looks more like he should be behind the counter of the Kozee Koffee. Is he another of Dr. Macintosh's special patients?

Next to him is the girl in the school uniform I saw the first time I came to this office. Like that first time, she plays with her phone. But before I can turn away, she looks up at me and smiles. I turn my gaze back to my feet, but it's too late. From the corner of my eye, I can see her come towards me.

She jiggles her phone. "Want to play?"

I force myself to look up at her. "Play what?"

"Angry Birds."

"Oh, no, that's OK."

Tess pats my arm. "It's all right, Stacey. Go play Angry Birds."

"I don't know. They might call our names—"

"Don't be shy," Tess says. "Play with your new friend."

I give Tess a look to plead with her, but she doesn't bail me out. The girl sits next to me. "I'm Stacey," I say.

"Jamie," she says. She points to the boy who was next to her. "That's my brother Caleb. And Travis. He's our babysitter."

"That's interesting."

She hands the phone to me. I stare at the screen, but have no idea what to do. I only ever used my cell phone to call Grace or Maddy, or to reply to their text messages. When it comes to all this new technology, I'm still an old man about it. "Um—"

"You haven't played Angry Birds before?"

"No. What do I do?"

"I'll show you." Jamie takes the phone back. I watch as she rams cartoon birds into various objects to kill pigs. It seems like a pretty stupid game to me. "Now you try."

My first attempts go pretty bad. My birds bypass everything to crash harmlessly into the ground. "Start them off a little higher," Jamie suggests.

I do that and have more success. I even get through the first two levels. As I play, Jamie asks, "Do you go to school around here?"

"Um, no. I just moved here."

"Me too. Our dad got a new job. He's a lawyer."

"My dad was a soldier," I say. I have to make up more of my cover story on the fly. "He died in Afghanistan."

"That sucks."

"I know. So I'm staying with my grandpa and grandma for a while."

We're interrupted by the receptionist when she calls Maddy's name. Tess goes with her, which leaves me with Jamie. As we continue to play, Jamie says, "You don't talk a lot, do you?"

"Not really."

"That's OK. I'm not all that chatty either."

She could have fooled me, but I say, "I guess we have a lot in common then."

"I guess so." We play for a while in silence. When I get stuck on a level, Jamie takes the phone from me to show me how to beat it. I look up at the clock; Maddy and Tess have been in there for a half-hour. At least there haven't been any screams from Dr. Macintosh's office.

"So what do you do when you aren't hanging around a shrink's office?" Jamie asks.

"Watch TV and stuff."

"Me too." She lists a bunch of shows I've never heard of.

"Yeah, those are pretty good," I say.

Jamie starts to talk about some cute boy in some show. I don't pay much attention since I'm still trying to destroy things on the screen with my angry birds. It makes me wonder how old Jamie is. She must be older than me if she's that interested in boys.

After an hour, Tess emerges from the room; she holds Maddy's hand. Maddy looks down at the floor; I'm not sure if she's crying or not. Tess stops for a moment to whisper something to Jake and then hustles Maddy out of the office. I hope Maddy just has to use the potty and nothing more serious.

"Stacey?" the receptionist says.

I hand the phone back to Jamie. "Thanks for letting me play."

"I'll call you later."

"OK."

"We can talk about the new *iCarly*."

"OK," I say again. I wonder what the hell an iCarly is.

Then I'm on my own.

***

Dr. Macintosh is already in one of the armchairs. He probably didn't get up from after Maddy and Tess left. He motions to the seat across from him. "Have a seat, Stacey," he says.

The office looks so much bigger now that I'm a foot-and-a-half shorter. My steps are tentative as I approach Dr. Macintosh. I want to turn and run away, back to Tess. I want to jump into her lap and cry while she comforts me, tells me everything will be all right—

No. That's what a scared ten-year-old girl would do. Maybe not even a ten-year-old. That's more what a toddler like Maddy would do. A big girl would sit down across from Dr. Macintosh. So that's what I force myself to do.

I throw myself onto the seat. My feet can't touch the floor now. I look down at them and study my shiny black shoes as if for the first time. I'm sure Dr. Macintosh already has a lot of material to write down in his notebook.

"Thank you, Stacey. Is that what you still want to be called? Would you prefer it if I called you Steve?"

"No. Jake is the only one who still calls me that."

"Jake is the man taking care of you?"

"Yes."

"He and his wife have been taking care of you for the last year?"

"Yes. But only for a few days like this."

"How long ago did this change happen?"

"A couple of months ago. It's hard to know exactly when. We didn't have a calendar in there."

"There being a converted school?"

"Yes. An elementary school. I guess he was being ironic or something."

"How long did it take you to become this age?"

"About five minutes." My eyes start to water as I remember the pain when I watched Maddy go through her change. "Five very long minutes."

"I see."

I look up at him for the first time. He's so damnably calm as he scribbles notes in his notebook. I want to punch him, not that it'd do anything but break my tiny fist. "No you don't! You don't have any idea what it was like!"

"Why don't you tell me?"

"You've seen a car crusher, right?"

"On television. Not in person."

"Imagine if you were the car, what that would feel like."

"It wouldn't be very pleasant, I imagine."

"Damned right." I put a hand to my mouth. "Sorry."

"It's all right. You can swear if you want. I want you to feel comfortable. Or as comfortable as you can under the circumstances."

"Thanks." I look back down at my feet. "Can I ask you a question?"

"Go ahead."

"Are you mad at me?"

"Do I seem mad at you?"

"Yes."

"Really?"

I make myself look up again, to meet his eyes. "You're acting too calm. Like you're trying to show you aren't mad at me. Which means you are mad at me." That's something I learned in my first career as a police officer. You have to be able to read people to break someone in interrogation.

"I'll admit I am a little miffed at you. I don't like when my patients lie to me. It's hard for therapy to succeed when the patient isn't being fully honest with her therapist." Dr. Macintosh smiles and then adds, "But I suppose it's like Clarita said: if you did tell me the truth I would have sent you to the psych ward for evaluation."

"You aren't now, though?"

"No. I wouldn't have believed something so crazy unless Clarita told me. She would never lie to me."

"Are you and Dr. Palmer—?" My voice trails off as I'm not sure how a ten-year-old would say *fucking*.

"An item? That's a little personal, don't you think?"

"That must be yes then."

Dr. Macintosh smiles again. "No. We had a fling when we worked at the same hospital when I was an intern. We decided to remain friends."

"Friends with benefits?"

"I see this hasn't changed your personality much."

"Meaning I'm still a pain?"

"That's one way to say it. I might have said, '*combative.*'"

"I'm sorry."

"You don't have to be sorry. It's who you are. There's nothing wrong with it."

"Some people would disagree."

The doctor nods. Then he puts down his pen. "Tell me Stacey, did you ever get to try the mirror exercise?"

"Once or twice."

"What did you come up with?"

"Not much."

He produces the hand mirror from between his side and the inside of the chair. He hands the mirror to me. "Go ahead and try it now. Describe what you see."

I hold the mirror up to my new face. I stare at the pudgy cheeks, tiny nose, thick bangs, and of course the slanted eyes behind the bright red glasses. My lower lip trembles a little. "A scared little girl."

"Is that how you see yourself? As a scared little girl?"

"Right now I do."

"What are you scared of?"

"That I'll have to stay like this. That I'll have to grow up again. That Maddy—" my voice chokes up. I put down the mirror and then try again. "That Maddy will forget about me."

"By 'me' you mean her father?"

"Yes."

"You still think you are her father?"

"I'll always be her father. No matter what I look like."

"Why do you think she'll forget about you?"

"Because she's regressing."

"What does that mean?"

"You're the doctor."

"I suppose I am. And I could give you some medical definitions and textbook cases and whatnot. That's not what you're interested in, though. To put it simply, you think her old life—as your daughter—is becoming like a dream to her. When she finally wakes up, it's all going to evaporate the way our dreams usually do."

"Yes. That's why Dr. Palmer wanted us to see you."

"That's one of the reasons."

"What other reason is there?"

Dr. Macintosh picks up his pen again. He flips back a few pages. "Your 'grandmother' Mrs. Madigan says Madison has been acting out. She's been throwing tantrums when she doesn't get her way. Clarita suggested the same thing. Would you say that's accurate?"

"Yes."

"So she's acting like a normal five-year-old?"

"Yes."

"And you think that's a bad thing?"

"It is when she's really twenty-three."

"There we are." Dr. Macintosh smiles at me. He leans forward in his chair; I lean back in mine as far as I can. "The other thing I want to help Madison with is to make the adjustment to this new life."

"Adjustment? But what if she doesn't stay like this?"

"Then we'll help her grow up again. In the meantime, for her sake and that of everyone else, she needs to learn how to be a little girl again."

"She does not!" I say and hate how childish I sound. "She's not a little girl."

"That's a matter of opinion. Right now Madison has the mind of an adult but the body of a little girl. Therefore as far as everyone else is concerned, she is a little girl."

"Not to me."

Dr. Macintosh makes an interested grunt as he checks his notes. "You did say you're still her father, right?"

"Yes."

"In my experience, most fathers always see their daughters as little girls, a child who needs protection. Like you're doing now."

My face turns warm. Once more Dr. Macintosh has used my own words against me. Jake and I could have used him in the interrogation room. "So you're saying I'm not objective?"

"I think that's a good description. I'll bet you remember when Maddy was born, don't you?"

"Yes."

"You remember holding her for the first time?"

"Yes," I say and start to tear up. "What's your point?"

"I'm only saying there's some part of you that will always see Madison as that newborn who needs your love and protection. It's that way for most parents I see in here."

"What about me? Am I a little girl?"

"You already said you were, didn't you?"

"In the mirror, yes."

"But that's not who you think you are?"

"No."

"Then who are you?" He motions to the mirror still in my hand. I hold it back up to my face. "Are you little Stacey Chang? Are you Stacey Chance, the girl who used to sit in that chair? Or are you Detective Steve Fischer?"

I stare into the mirror for a minute. When I can't stand to look at my adorable little face anymore, I put the mirror down. "I don't know!"

The doctor takes the mirror from me. Then he takes my hand and gives it a squeeze. "Stacey, let me suggest that you're all three."

"No. I can't be."

"Why not?"

"Because—" I need another minute to try to articulate what I'm feeling. "I can't be a girl. I was born a boy. I still remember everything." My face turns even warmer as I remember all the stuff I did that only boys can do, the kind of sex stuff a ten-year-old girl shouldn't know about.

"It's not our memories who determine who we are."

"It's not?"

"Let's try something else. Dr. Palmer said Stacey Chance was bright and a little shy. Is that how you would describe her?"

"I guess."

"What else would you say about her?"

I close my eyes and think back through my year as Stacey Chance. "She was sweet. People liked her. She was nice and polite most of the time. Sometimes she could be funny. And tough if she needed to be. She also had terrible taste in music."

"Those are all good things, aren't they?"

"Except for the music."

"OK, now tell me about Steve Fischer. What was he like?"

"He was tough. Honorable. *Combative*."

"Those are good things too, wouldn't you say?"

"Except combative."

"Even combative, in the right context."

"What's your point?"

"Do you remember what Lincoln said about the house divided against itself?"

"It couldn't stand."

"Right. I think you have a civil war going on inside you. Not just for the last couple of months since Stacey Chang entered the picture. I think it's been going on since you first woke up as a woman. Maybe even longer."

"What should I do? Fight myself?"

"I think you've been doing that already. That night at the karaoke bar, why did you run off the stage?"

"I got scared."

"Of what?"

"I don't remember."

"I think you do."

"Well I don't."

"It's not nice for a little girl to lie."

"I don't remember!"

"It was those boys, wasn't it?"

"I don't know who you're talking about."

"One of them yelled at you to take off your clothes. How did that make you feel?"

"I don't know."

"The last time we talked, you said you'd only been with women, isn't that right?"

"Yes."

"Are you attracted to boys?"

"Some," I say. I think of Seth and our disastrous date.

"Did you find those boys at the karaoke bar attractive?"

"I don't remember."

"How did it make you feel when they were ogling you?"

"I said I don't remember."

"Would you mind if I run a hypothesis by you?"

"Knock yourself out."

"I think Stacey got a kick out of those boys ogling her. She might have even found them attractive. But I think Steve didn't approve of that. I think it was Steve who made you run off that stage."

I know better than to mention that it wasn't until I thought of Dr. Macintosh coming backstage to kiss me that I ran away. "You make it sound like I'm schizophrenic."

"I don't think you are, yet."

"Yet?"

"In time, if you don't integrate your personalities, they could start manifesting themselves as separate entities."

"So that's what you want me to do? 'Integrate my personalities?'"

"Yes. I think you need to take the best of all three and merge them into one person."

"Who's that?"

"*You*. Whichever name you want to use for that." Dr. Macintosh gets up from his chair. I brace myself for him to give me a hug or something, but he doesn't. Instead, he walks over to his desk. I see him write something down. When he returns, he holds out a prescription to me.

His prescription is one word: Play.

"What does that mean?" I ask.

"Stacey Chang isn't as developed as your other personalities yet. I want you to go out and interact with kids her age. Then the next time I see you, we can talk a little more about who Stacey Chang is. Deal?"

"OK."

"I'll see you in a couple of days then. Have fun."

"I'll try."

I'm halfway to the door before Dr. Macintosh says, "I never got the chance to tell you before: I thought your singing was beautiful."

"Thanks, but my singing career is on hold for a while."

"It doesn't have to be."

"What do you mean?"

"Well, there's no bar that will let a ten-year-old sing in it, but there are other venues. I'm sure Mrs. Madigan will take you to church. You could join the choir."

"Maybe."

"You could even look into vocal lessons. I'm sure there are plenty of great teachers around here who would be happy to train a girl with a voice like yours."

"I'll think about it."

"Great. We can talk about it next time."

I nod and then walk out the door. At least I'm not crying this time.

Jamie and Caleb are still in the waiting room. Jamie touches my arm before I can hurry past. "How did it go?" she asks.

"OK."

"It gets easier," she says. Then the receptionist calls for her and Caleb to finally go in.

Chapter 23

A few hours later I lie on the couch with a Nancy Drew book. Maddy is upstairs to take a nap before dinner. So far I've enjoyed Nancy Drew more than I thought I would. To break it down like Dr. Macintosh would, Stacey Chang likes to see a girl solve mysteries the adults are too stupid to figure out. Stacey Chance feels a little nostalgic for being a teenager again. As for Steve Fischer, he'd just as soon throw the book into the fireplace. It's as bad as those shows on TV where they work out a crime from arriving at the scene to the trial in sixty minutes. As if any real case is ever that simple. Real cases take weeks or even months of work and the trial—if there is one—can take more than a year. The Staceys tell Steve to pipe down so they can enjoy the book.

As I start a new chapter, there's a knock on the door. I look up from the couch. Tess is in the kitchen, to make dinner. Jake is in his study to work on a case. He didn't want any help from me, the real-life Nancy Drew. I could always go fetch one of them, but I decide the big girl thing to do would be to answer the door. Besides, thanks to that old fart at Wal-Mart everyone knows about Maddy and I.

I open the door and nearly faint to see Dr. Macintosh. "Hello, Stacey. Are your grandparents home?"

"Yes. I'll go get them. You can sit down on the couch if you want."

"Thank you. I think I will."

I leave him to find the couch while I jog over to the door to Jake's study. I rap on the door. "Grandpa Jake, Dr. Macintosh is here to see you."

Jake opens the door a moment later. He looks over me, towards the couch. "Stacey, go up to your room."

"But Maddy's sleeping."

"So be quiet about it."

"What are you going to talk about?"

"Nothing important."

"It's about us, isn't it?"

"Maybe."

"Then I should be allowed to hear it too."

"Please, Steve. Just go upstairs and look after Maddy."

I stamp my foot. "No! It's not fair to talk about me behind my back."

"I'll carry you up there if I have to."

I flinch when I feel a hand touch my shoulder. I look up and see Dr. Macintosh behind me. "I think Stacey has a point, Mr. Madigan. She deserves to know what's going on. And I think she's mature enough to handle it."

Now that it's two against one—and one of the two is a doctor—Jake relents. "Fine, she can stay." He waves a finger at me. "But none of that whining or I'll drag you upstairs. Got it?"

"Yes."

"Go and fetch Tess then. If she'll leave the kitchen."

"I'm sorry I got here so early," Dr. Macintosh says. I don't hear the rest of the conversation as I run to the kitchen to get Tess.

As Jake figured, she's reluctant to leave her chicken untended, even for an important conversation with our shrink. She opens the oven to study the pieces of chicken. "I suppose they'll keep for a bit if I turn down the temperature." As she adjusts the temperature, she shakes her head. "I didn't make enough for five. I hope your doctor is a light eater."

"He probably is."

Tess takes my hand to follow me out to the living room. Jake sits in his old recliner while Dr. Macintosh is on an armchair. That leaves the couch for Tess and I. I climb up and snuggle close to Tess for protection.

"I'm glad you could see me on such short notice. Just so you know, I don't usually make house calls, but this is a special situation." Dr. Macintosh sets his briefcase on the coffee table.

From the briefcase he takes out some colored pamphlets. I peek around Tess's chest to see a dark blue cover with a coat of arms, complete with a lion on one side and a griffin on the other. '"St. Andrew's Academy?"' I read off the cover. "Is that some kind of special school for troubled girls?"

"Not at all. It is special, though," Dr. Macintosh says. "St. Andrew's is the most exclusive private school in the city."

"Oh dear," Tess says as she opens the brochure. There are pictures of tennis courts, swimming pools, and even a food court like the one in the mall. "I don't think we could afford anything like this."

"You don't have to worry about that. I've spoken with the headmaster and she's willing to take Stacey and Madison as scholarship students."

"You mean charity cases," I grumble. "The poor Chinese orphan girls. They'll probably have us pose for pictures so they can say how diverse they are."

"Don't look the gift horse in the mouth," Jake says.

Dr. Macintosh turns to me. "Stacey, do you remember what we talked about before you left?"

"My singing career?"

"Yes. St. Andrew's has a first-rate music department. My nephew's piano teacher used to play in the London Philharmonic. He's one of the foremost teachers in the world."

"So? I don't play the piano."

"Their other teachers have credentials just as exemplary. I'm sure they could help with your singing. If you'd be interested."

"Why do I have to go to school? I already graduated high school. I'm in college. So is Maddy. You want me to go back to fifth grade?"

"I was thinking fourth grade, but yes," Dr. Macintosh says.

Fourth grade, that's even worse. I shiver at the thought of sitting in a classroom with a bunch of spoiled rich kids as they talk about the ponies their parents bought them or whatever snobby kids yap about. "I don't think that's for me. Or Maddy."

"I think Madison especially would benefit from going to school. She needs to retrain her brain to read and write at a more advanced level."

I can't argue that point, not with the trouble Maddy has with words more than one syllable and how unsteady her handwriting is. "We could do that here. Tess could teach her and I could help."

"Do you think that's fair to Tess?" Dr. Macintosh asks. Before Tess can say anything, he adds, "I'm sure you wouldn't mind, Mrs. Madigan. I know how much you care for the girls. The fact remains, it's not fair to ask you to home school them along with everything else."

"I don't need to go to school anywhere," I say. "I can already read and write just fine."

Jake snorts. "I've seen your report cards. You could probably use a refresher course."

"That's not fair!" I say. "My grades are fine."

"They're average to below average," Jake says. "Not enough to get Harvard knocking on your door."

Tess puts an arm around me and glares at her husband. "Stacey was doing just fine in school, all things considered."

"What do you mean by that?" I ask.

"The way you were brought up, I'm sure it was difficult for you to focus on your studies—"

"I'm not dumb!" I shout.

"That's not what I mean, dear—"

"I know what you mean! You're saying I'm ignorant. Well I'm not. Maybe I just don't care about school as much as the rest of you do." I turn to give Dr. Macintosh a nasty look. "You don't need much education to be a singer anyway."

"That's a good point," Dr. Macintosh says and I hate him a little for being reasonable enough to agree with me. "I think if Madison goes to school, it would be much easier for her to have her big sister there, don't you think?"

"Maddy won't want to go to school either. She's happy here. So am I."

The doctor nods. "I think I see what's going on here. You're worried about interacting with other children.

That's perfectly normal. Most of the patients I see have some anxiety about that, especially those who have been through traumatic situations."

"I'm not scared!" I try to glare at the doctor, not that it seems to faze him. "I know what you're trying to do. You're trying to goad me into going to your school. It won't work."

"I'm sorry, Stacey. I should have known you were too smart to fall for that."

"Don't try buttering me up either."

"You shouldn't talk to the doctor like that, dear," Tess says. "He's trying to help you."

"I don't want to go!"

"Do you remember what else we talked about, Stacey? I think going to school would help you with those issues we discussed. It would allow you to interact with children your own age and in turn you might learn some things about yourself."

"I don't want to," I say again. I embarrass myself further when I bury my face against Tess the way Maddy does when she gets upset.

"I'll just leave the materials and let you four talk it over. My card is in there too if you need to get in touch with me," Dr. Macintosh says.

"I'll see you out," Jake says.

A minute or so later, Tess pats my head and then eases me back. She wipes the tears from my cheeks. "It's all right, dear. No one is going to make you go to school if you don't want to."

"But you want me to, don't you?"

"I think perhaps Dr. Macintosh is right. You can't sit here on the couch for the next eight years or however long it will take for Dr. Palmer to find a way to change you back. You should go play with children your own age."

I look down at the floor; my defenses weaken. "If I don't like it, can I stay with you again?"

"Of course, dear. And I'll be happy to have you around."

"Thanks, Grandma Tess," I say and then give her a hug.

***

Jake and Tess talk to Maddy about the school idea over dinner. As I expected, she's not thrilled with the idea. "I already went to school," she says. "I graduated high school."

"We know, sweetheart, but we think it's a good idea. You could learn how to read and write better, plus play with children your own age," Tess says.

"Can't I stay here and play with Stacey?"

"Stacey's going to be at school too," Jake says.

"She is?"

"Yes, dear. She'll be in the fourth grade."

"Where will I be? Kindygarden?"

"We were thinking first grade," Jake says.

Tess reaches over to take Maddy's hand. "Then you and Stacey can go to school and back together." The secondary benefit of this is Tess doesn't have to make another trip into the city or entertain Maddy for a few hours until I get out of school.

Maddy looks over at me and I force myself to smile. "It'll be fun," I tell her. "And since you've already been through it, you should be the smartest girl in class."

"You think so?" Maddy's always been an above-average student, but she isn't a valedictorian. Maybe this time she can be.

As Maddy thinks this over, the phone rings in the kitchen. Tess gets up to answer it. I straighten in my seat as I hear Tess say, "Yes, she's here. Who is this?" I know who it is before Tess says, "Stacey, there's a girl named Jamie on the phone for you?"

"Can I take it in your study, Grandpa?"

"Go ahead. Just don't mess up any papers in there."

"Thanks." As I run back to the study, my stomach flutters. I had hoped Jamie might not carry through on her promise to call me. Maybe I should tell her I'm sick. Or I could just tell her to mind her own damned business. That's what Steve Fischer would say, especially after a few whiskeys at Squiggy's.

I pick up the phone in Jake's study. I hear Jamie say, "We just moved here a couple months ago. We used to live in Miami."

"That must be quite a change for you," Tess says.

"It will be, especially in winter. I'm kind of looking forward to seeing snow."

"Yes, the snow is quite lovely just after it's fallen. It makes everything look so peaceful."

I jump in to say, "I've got it, Grandma."

"All right, dear. It's been nice talking with you, Jamie. Goodnight."

"Goodnight Mrs. Madigan." After we hear the soft click of Tess hanging up, Jamie says, "Your grandma is really nice."

"Yes, she is."

"Did you get a chance to watch *iCarly* tonight?" Before I can answer, she starts to talk about the episode. Since I haven't watched the show before, I have no idea what she means.

"It was really something," I say.

"You didn't see it?"

"Um, well, no."

"Oh, that's OK. They rerun these all the time. It'll probably be on tomorrow."

"That's good."

"Are you all right?"

"I'm fine."

"Am I bugging you? Maybe I shouldn't have called."

"No, it's all right. I'm just a little distracted."

"I get it now. I'll see you around Dr. Mac's office."

This is what I wanted, but now that I've gotten my wish, I don't want Jamie to go. "Please don't go! It's not you. I swear. It's my grandparents. We've kind of been fighting."

"Fighting? About what?"

"They want me to go to this fancy school. My sister and I could get a scholarship and it's supposed to be a really great school, but I don't know. I'm not really ready for school yet."

"Yeah, school sucks. My dad sends Caleb and I to this snobby school. Everyone there is like super rich. I mean, if your parents don't have a billion you're totally worthless," Jamie says and even over the phone I can hear her bitterness. "So what school is it they're trying to get you into?"

"St. Andrew's Academy."

There's a gasp on the other end, followed by a scream that prompts me to hold the receiver out a few inches. "O. M. G. Stacey, that's where I go to school! You so have to tell your grandparents you'll go."

"I don't know. We're kinda poor—"

"Don't worry about that. You'll have me to protect you. And Caleb, though he's not of much use. Maybe as bait or something."

Caleb must be nearby because I hear him shout, "Am not! I'm going to tell Daddy."

"Yeah, you go tell Daddy." Jamie snorts into the receiver. "What a little weasel. How soon are you going to enroll?"

"In a couple of days, I think. I'm not really sure."

"Well as soon as you get there, I can show you around. Just make sure you wear your uniform. They're kind of strict about that stuff."

"Oh, right. I guess they would be being a religious school and all."

Jamie snorts again. "Religious my ass. The only thing they worship is money. How do you think my dad got us in there? We're fucking Jewish."

"Really?"

"Well I'm half-Jewish. Dad is full Jew. Mom wasn't really anything. What about you?"

"My parents weren't big into religion. Grandma is going to start taking us to her church. It's Episcopalian."

"What's Episcopalian?"

"Some kind of Christian. I'm not sure what the difference is." I was brought up as a Presbyterian by my parents. There's not a whole lot of difference, just some minor ones people like to make seem like a big deal.

"Maybe I'll have to switch. After my bat mitzvah, though. That way I can bleed all my relatives dry first."

I giggle at this. To talk to Jamie makes me miss the time I spent with Maddy and Grace. "Maybe I'll convert so I can do that too," I say.

"Great idea. We could have a joint party." Jamie sighs into the receiver. "Daddy wants me to get off the phone. In a minute, Daddy. Let me say goodbye to Stacey first."

"Who's Stacey?" I hear her dad ask.

"My new friend." My cheeks turn warm at this. "I've got to go. Are you on Facebook?"

"No. My grandparents don't even have a computer."

"That is so lame. Guess I'll have to call tomorrow."

"Talk to you tomorrow. Bye."

"Bye." I hang up the phone and then sigh. Stacey Chang has her first friend.

Part 4
School Days

Chapter 24

The next Monday, Tess pulls up to the gates of St. Andrew's. It is the kind of school that has gates to keep out the riffraff. It's also an elementary/middle school with a campus bigger than the community college I should still attend.

I lean closer to the window so I can get a better look at the lush green lawn. There's even a marble fountain out front surrounded by a brick patio, on which is inlayed the school's crest. Jamie said students aren't allowed out on the lawn or near the fountain; it's just to impress visitors like us. "Stacey, you're in the way!" Maddy whines. I slide back so she can see the school we'll attend for the time being.

I turn forward to look over Tess's shoulder. The administration building is up ahead. It looks like an old colonial mansion made from red bricks. Beyond the admin building I can see a couple of newer brick structures with ivy climbing up the walls.

Tess stops on the circular drive in front of the administration building. My hopes that Jamie will be there are dashed when I see a blond boy next to a similarly blond middle-aged woman. The woman I know from the brochures is the headmaster, Dr. Lynne Armey. I don't know who the boy is; probably some poor sap assigned to show Maddy and I around.

"Here we are, girls," Tess says. While she tries to sound cheerful, there's a quiver in her voice. She's just as nervous as we are. She probably expects someone to run us out of here for not having enough net worth.

I run my hands over my blue jacket emblazoned with the same crest as out front. Then I try to arrange my plaid skirt so it doesn't bunch up when I get out of the car. The last thing I want is to look like some poor, ignorant country cousin in front of the headmaster.

Tess opens the door and then offers a hand to help me out. While Tess unbuckles Maddy, I toss my backpack over my shoulder. Tess carries Maddy out of the car and sets her next to me. Like me, Maddy takes a moment to smooth down the plaid jumper the younger girls wear. Maddy still tries to work out a stubborn wrinkle as Tess takes us both by the shoulder to guide us over to the headmaster.

Dr. Armey extends a hand for Tess to shake. "Welcome to St. Andrew's Academy, Mrs. Madigan. It's so good to meet you, Stacey, and Madison."

"Thank you. We're very glad you were able to take us on such short notice."

"We don't ordinarily take students after the semester has begun, but you come highly recommended from Dr. Macintosh." I'm sure there was a sizable donation involved as well, but I don't say anything.

"Now then, young ladies, I'll be taking your grandmother away to finish some paperwork. I'll leave you in the capable hands of my son, Vincent. He will show you around the campus and to your homerooms."

Before we're separated, Tess bends down to kiss us both on the cheek. "I'll see you at three o'clock," she says. She leans closer to me and brushes hair from my ear so she can whisper, "Take good care of your sister."

I nod to her to silently promise to look after my little sister. Then Tess follows Dr. Armey up the stairs, to leave us with her son. Vincent Armey stares at us sullenly for a moment before he points to the steps. "Come on, let's go," he says.

I take Maddy's hand and give it a squeeze as he ascends the stairs to begin our tour.

***

Vincent isn't much of a tour guide. His idea of a tour is to plod along, shoulders slouched, and hands in pockets. He occasionally takes one hand out of a pocket to point at something. It's a good thing most of the doors are labeled or I'd have no clue what he means.

We leave the admin building after a tour of about two minutes and then trudge over to the library. "This is the library," Vincent mumbles. At least I think he says that. Even if he didn't, it's pretty obvious from all the books where we are.

The third floor of the library is mostly reserved for study areas. I see some of my fellow students in the cubicles. Most of them are hunched forward as they play Angry Birds or Tweet or something like that on their phones instead of actually studying. I hope to see Jamie there, but she's not.

To my surprise and relief, we find her outside the library. She then falls into step with us. Before I can say anything, Jamie taps Vincent on the shoulder. "I'll take over from here," she says.

"But if Mom finds out—"

"She won't find out." Jamie turns to us. "You guys aren't going to tell, are you?"

"No," I say and Maddy shakes her head in agreement.

"See?"

"But—"

"Wouldn't you rather go smoke a cig in the bathroom than lead around two little kids?"

"Yeah, I guess," Vincent says. "You'd better not get me in trouble."

"If anyone asks, say you got sick and asked me to take over," Jamie says. Vincent considers this for a moment and then nods. He plods away, presumably to go smoke in the bathroom as Jamie suggested.

She claps her hands and then turns to us. "Now that he's gone I can give you a real tour of the place."

"Shouldn't you be in class?" I ask.

"I told Mr. Dumbowski I needed to see the nurse."

"Aren't you going to get in trouble?"

"Nah. He doesn't care."

"Well, OK," I say.

"I already had to go through the craptacular Vincent Armey Tour. You're not going to be missing much." She gives me a friendly slap on the arm. "We'll start by dropping the kid off at kindergarten."

"I'm not in kindygarden!" Maddy shouts. She stamps her foot and adds, "I'm in first grade!"

"Sorry, kid," Jamie says. She pinches Maddy's cheek, which only makes Maddy angrier. "You're a short little rugrat for first grade."

"I'm not short!"

"You are a little short," I say.

"Am not," Maddy says. "I'm big enough to see the school too."

"Fine," Jamie says. "I guess you guys already saw the library, right? The third floor is great if you just want to hang out for a while. Your grandma still hasn't bought you a phone, has she?"

"No," I say. "She doesn't even have one. My grandpa just uses his for work."

"Too bad. Then we could text during class and stuff."

"Yeah, too bad." Probably just as well for me, the Luddite.

Jamie motions for us to follow her down the sidewalk. She points to the roughly rectangular courtyard between the buildings. "That's the quad, where you can go to hang out during lunch and recess and stuff. Your sister should stay away from there. It's mostly for the older kids."

"I'm not a baby," Maddy protests.

Jamie stops and then turns to Maddy with an evil grin. "What the older kids like to do with a firsty who shows up there is pull that cute little jumper right over your head backwards so your undies show."

"That's mean."

"That's getting off easy." Jamie turns to me. "You should be careful there too. They aren't a lot nicer to fourthies."

"What about fifthies?"

"Basically all the elementary kids stay away from there."

"Where do we go then?" Maddy asks.

"The playground is over by the gym. You got to give the gym a wide berth, though. That's where the jocks hang out."

"I thought this was a nice school," Maddy says.

"Hate to break it to you, kid, but most people here are jerks. That's how most rich kids are. Except a few of us."

"We're not rich," Maddy says.

"You'd better keep that to yourselves. Though I'm pretty sure the word's already out about a couple of scholarship kids. Fresh meat."

"I don't want to be fresh meat," Maddy whines.

Jamie tousles Maddy's hair. "Don't worry, you just got to stick with me and your sister."

"OK."

"You're stuck with Mrs. Ellsbury," Jamie tells Maddy.

"Is she mean?" Maddy asks.

"Only when she's sober. Lucky for you kids that's not often."

I put a hand on Maddy's shoulder as she whimpers. "I'm sure it's not that bad," I say. I glare at Jamie. "Don't scare her so much."

"It's the truth. I swear it on the Torah."

"Don't listen to her," I tell Maddy. "It'll be fine."

"I hope so."

I missed Maddy's first day of school the first time around. This time I get to watch as Jamie ushers her through the door. I can tell right away Jamie hadn't lied about Mrs. Ellsbury; the woman has the red nose and bleary eyes of a drinker. I know because that was my face often enough when I was still Steve Fischer.

The old woman reaches out with a wrinkled claw to take Maddy from Jamie. "This must be Madison." Maddy looks back at me. I smile and nod to her. She turns to nod at her new teacher. "You can have a seat right over there."

Maddy gives me a wave and then trudges over to her desk to sit down beside a girl with brown pigtails. Jamie closes the door behind her on the way out. I'd like to stay and watch Maddy for a while to make sure she's all right, but I have to get to my own homeroom soon.

***

We take a little detour so Jamie can show me the gym. From the banners that hang from the ceiling, I learn the school colors are blue and gold and the mascot a bulldog. "It used to be the Braves," Jamie says. "They had an Indian in war paint and all that shit. Then there were all these protests and they changed it."

"That's good."

We sit down on the top row of the bleachers to watch some older boys play dodgeball. Jamie giggles and then says, "Too bad it's not shirts against skins, huh?"

"Yeah, too bad," I say. The sweaty boys in their T-shirts and shorts don't do anything for me, but then I'm only ten years old on the outside and a lot different from that on the inside.

Finally Jamie takes me to my homeroom. "You've got Ms. Lowry. She's not too bad from what I hear. I hear she's been making friends with Mr. Delmore the gym teacher, if you know what I mean."

"Gross," I say with childish revulsion.

In the hallway, Jamie stops me in front of the door to my homeroom. "The important thing is not to let any of these jerks get under your skin. You don't have to take any shit from them just because their parents are loaded and yours weren't. Got it?"

"I got it."

"You don't seem like the fighting type to me, so just ignore them if they say something."

"I'll try."

Jamie opens the door for me. "Here you go, kid. I'll see you at lunch."

With that I'm on my own.

Chapter 25

When I step into the classroom, I shudder. Not because of the teacher or the fifteen other kids in the room. It's the room itself. It looks almost identical to the one Dr. Ling kept me in, except it's cleaner and populated with desks. There's the chalkboard on one wall and the cursive letters posted up by the ceiling. Even the windows are in the same locations, though not boarded up. Before my eyes the desks, students, and teacher disappear and I'm back in that grimy room, where the only light comes from cracks between the boards over the window.

"Are you all right?" a woman asks. I think at first it's Qiang. Then I remember Qiang is dead. She died to get Maddy and me out of that awful place.

I blink a couple of times and see a white woman with curly brown hair. Her glasses are the same shape as mine, only a more fashionable black. She wears a turtleneck sweater and a long skirt that seems old-fashioned, like something one of my teachers back in the '60s would wear. This woman is definitely not Qiang. "I'm fine," I mumble.

She takes me by the shoulders to steer me into the center of the room and then turns me so I can face my new classmates. Most of them are white, with one black girl and two Middle Eastern boys. With an Asian girl in me, my class has most of the diversity rainbow covered.

My new teacher bends down to say in my ear, "I'll bet you're our new student, Stacey, aren't you?" The perky way she says this is with the same condescension as the saleswoman at the glasses store.

"Yes," I say and look down at the floor.

"OK, Stacey, why don't you tell the class a little about yourself?"

Much as I don't want to, I'm sure I don't have a choice in the matter. "My name is Stacey Chang—" my voice falters as I hear a couple of girls giggle in the back of the room at this.

I'm pretty sure I hear one of them whisper, "Look at those glasses." That's accompanied by another round of giggles.

I force myself to go on. "My sister and I just moved here a couple weeks ago to live with our grandparents. We used to live in California with our parents, but they're dead now."

That ought to shut up the gigglers in the back. Ms. Lowry gives my shoulders a squeeze. "That's very sad, Stacey, but I think you'll be very happy here and make lots of new friends."

"Uh-huh," I mumble.

"Now, go take your seat. You can have the open one next to Darren."

She points to a seat next to a dark-haired boy with glasses who doodles in a notebook. I've seen his face before. I'm not sure where, though. There's not any time to figure it out. I open my backpack and get out my supplies. It's time to learn.

***

As a white, middle-class boy who was big for his age, I never faced any discrimination in school. I was usually the one to dish out the discrimination to my classmates. In third grade I beat up a Puerto Rican boy who joined our class; I left him with a black eye and his lunch money in my pockets. Now days I would have been prosecuted for a hate crime, but back then I just got suspended for a day and a stern lecture from my parents, not that it did any good.

It's not long before I get my first taste of discrimination as an orphaned little Chinese girl. At first it might be unintentional. Maybe Ms. Lowry even means to be helpful when she points to the math problems on the board. "Stacey, why don't you give it a try?"

The nice explanation is that Ms. Lowry called on me to do math problems because I'm the new girl and she wants to see how much I've learned. The other explanation is that she thinks because I'm Asian I'm great at math. I try not to think about that too hard as I trudge up to the front of the room.

The first couple of problems are easy. I only have to multiply single numbers. I don't remember a lot from elementary school, but I do remember my multiplication table. I breeze through the top row of five problems.

It gets a lot harder on the second row when I get to double-digit numbers. If I only had to multiply by ten that would be easy enough, but Ms. Lowry wants to know what 96 times 64 equals. I stare at the numbers for a moment as I try to think about it. Too bad I don't have a calculator up here with me.

"I can do it!" another girl calls out. "Let me do it, Ms. Lowry."

"Not yet, Keshia. Give Stacey a chance."

I try to remember what my first fourth grade teacher told us to do. I remember something about writing the answer out in two rows. So to start I multiply 96 by 4. It starts to come back to me as I work on the answer. I step back and turn to Ms. Lowry.

"That's a nice try, Stacey, but you forgot the zero in the second row," she says.

"I did?" I turn back to the problem on the board. Damn it, I did forget the zero in the second row. I hear someone snicker behind me, probably that Keshia girl.

"Keshia, why don't you come up and help Stacey out?"

It turns out Keshia is the lone black girl in class. She's taller than me by about a foot and from the way she brushes me away from the board, I know she's a lot stronger too. With a smug grin she erases my attempt from the board. "This is how you do it," she says, just as smug about it.

I have no choice but to stand there and watch her work, though I'd like to slink back to my seat and slouch down the way I did in most of my college classes. Instead I have to endure the humiliation as Keshia solves all five problems in the time it took me to get one wrong.

"Very good, Keshia. Take a seat." Ms. Lowry looks down at me and smiles. Her voice is so obnoxiously saccharine as she says, "That was a very good first try, Stacey. Go and take your seat."

"Yes, ma'am," I mumble.

Once I'm back in my seat, Ms. Lowry says, "I haven't got your books yet, Stacey, so you'll have to share with Darren until after lunch."

Darren continues to doodle in his notebook. He doesn't look up until I bump his desk with mine. Then he turns and stares at me for the first time. When I get a close look at him, it finally clicks where I've seen him before: the picture on Dr. Macintosh's desk. He's my therapist's nephew. What a small world. Or maybe not. I remember how they insisted I go to the fourth grade; this must be why.

Without a word, he shoves his book over so I can see it. He doesn't seem very interested in reading it. He doesn't seem interested in anything, except whatever is in that notebook. Must be the artistic type.

We go through math problems for another forty-five minutes. Keshia is the type of suck-up who raises her hand first to every question. If Ms. Lowry doesn't look her way, Keshia starts to wave frantically. When she answers a question right—which is every question she gets to answer—she glances over at me with that smug grin. Apparently there's some kind of rivalry between us, despite that I've only been here for an hour.

Halfway through math, Darren stops drawing. He's filled the page. I sneak a glance at the page as he turns it over. The lines of his college-ruled paper are riddled with music notes. He must notice I've seen part of his opus as his cheeks redden. He hides the notebook in his backpack so I can't see any more of it.

After math is English. Keshia's an expert on this subject too. They've been reading *Huckleberry Finn*, which I read nearly forty years ago. As the new girl I don't get called on during this part of class.

Then it's time for spelling. Though I've hunkered down, Ms. Lowry still sees me. "Stacey, can you spell 'Magnificent?'"

"Um—"

"She doesn't know," Keshia says. "She probably doesn't even know English."

"I do so," I say.

"That's enough, girls," Ms. Lowry says. "Keshia, let Stacey try to answer the question."

My nemesis crosses her arms over her chest, but she's still wearing that smug grin, secure in the knowledge I can't spell the word. I can't wait to prove her wrong. Then I can grin smugly at her for a change.

"Magnificent: M-A-G-N-I-F-I-C-A-N-T."

"That's very close, Stacey, but incorrect. Would anyone else like to try?" Ms. Lowry looks around the room. I can see her swallow a groan before she says, "Go ahead Keshia."

"Magnificent: M-A-G-N-I-F-I-C-E-N-T." Keshia stops just short of sticking out her tongue at me as she finishes.

"Very good, Keshia."

I slide down a little more in my seat and wish I could disappear through the floor. I'm saved when Ms. Lowry says, "Time for lunch. Darren, would you escort Stacey to the cafeteria?"

"Yes, ma'am," he says. He sounds as happy to be my tour guide as Vincent Armey.

***

I try to strike up a conversation with Darren on our way to the cafeteria as much to keep Keshia away from me as to make a new friend. "So you write music?" I ask.

"Sometimes."

"What kind of music?" He shrugs. Clearly he doesn't want to talk about it. "I know your uncle," I finally say.

"That's good."

"He says I have a great singing voice."

"Uh-huh."

"Maybe I could sing one of your songs?"

"I don't write songs," he says.

"Oh. Sorry."

As shown in the brochures, the cafeteria is more like a mall food court than a traditional school cafeteria. Darren and I part company; he's brought his own lunch. Tess would have packed lunches for Maddy and me, but she thought it would be more of a treat for us to sample the school's food.

My stomach is too nervous for me to be all that hungry. I especially don't want any of the greasy pizza, burgers, or tacos in some of the food court shops. There's one that specializes in salads and sandwiches. I get a garden salad with ranch dressing. It costs four times what I'd pay for the same at a diner a mile or two off the grounds.

Once I have my salad, I have to find somewhere to sit. I remember from my last time at school how everything is subdivided based on social status. There are the jocks and the nerds, each divided then by class.

I stop by the table of two blond girls from my class. "Can I sit here?" I ask and motion to an empty seat.

"No, we're saving that," one girl says.

They probably aren't saving it; they just don't want me around. They'd be the uncoolest girls in school if they let me hang around with them. "OK," I mumble.

I'm still in search of a seat when I hear Jamie call my name. I turn and see her at a table in a corner, all by herself. She waves about as frantically as Keshia to get my attention.

Intent on reaching Jamie, I don't notice my enemy until it's too late. One moment I'm walking along and the next I trip forward; the salad tumbles from my hands. I land face-first next to the overturned salad bowl. When I lift my head, there's a piece of lettuce stuck to my face. The whole cafeteria explodes with laughter at that. Some point their phones at me, probably so they can upload my picture onto the Internet.

"Better watch where you're going, Chopsticks," Keshia growls and then saunters off; she hums a jaunty victory tune. Chopsticks? As far as mean nicknames go, it's pretty weak. She should at least make fun of my glasses or maybe my shortness. Still, my eyes water at the hurtful remark, plus the humiliation of falling on my face in front of everyone.

As I try to pick up my lunch, Jamie squats down beside me. She helps me clean up the mess and then pats my shoulder. "Don't mind her. She's just worried she'll stop being the princess around here."

"I don't think she has much to worry about," I say.

I dispose of my salad. I don't have much money left from what Tess gave me. Jamie offers to buy me a new salad. "Thanks," I say, "but are you sure you want to be seen with me?"

"I'm not scared of her," Jamie says.

With a new salad and Jamie to escort me, I make it to the back corner of the cafeteria. No one sits within five rows of us. I start to wonder if it's me, but then I remember Jamie was already over here. Maybe she's an outcast in her own right.

Someone else is also alone: Darren. He's got his notebook out and while he eats his lunch, he continues to scribble in it. "What's the story with him?" I ask.

"Him? I don't know. He's pretty weird. At recess he hangs out under the slide with that notebook. It's like his best friend. I don't know what the hell is in it. He won't show anyone."

"He's writing music," I say. "I saw some of it."

"Music? He trying to be Justin Bieber or something?"

"More like Mozart I think," I say.

"Gross," Jamie says. She wrinkles her nose. "Is that what you listen to?"

"No! Of course not," I say. I know better than to mention my fondness for Creedence Clearwater Revival, who topped the charts when Jamie's dad was probably still in diapers. I try to think of the music Maddy listened to. "I really like Lady Gaga."

"Me too! She's so ultra-cool." Jamie starts to talk about her songs and I pretend I know what she means, just like when I used to talk to Maddy at the Kozee Koffee. Eventually the subject turns back to school. "How's it going? Other than Little Miss Perfect hassling you."

"It's all right. Ms. Lowry is nice."

"Just wait until Mr. Delmore dumps her."

"Maybe he won't," I say. I hope that doesn't happen at least until I'm out of fourth grade.

"You better hope so."

Lunch is over far too soon. When I get back to class, I find Ms. Lowry with a stack of textbooks. "Here you go," she says. With the books are a stack of forms I have to fill out to take possession of them and to promise I'll return them in good condition. My hand gets sore by the time I'm done; I didn't have to do this much paperwork to book a murderer when I was still a police detective.

After I finish, I take my books back to my desk; my arms wobble from the weight. I find a note on my desk. When I open it, I see it's a love note from Keshia. She's drawn a girl with enormous glasses and slanted eyes. Her tongue sticks out to give her a dumb look. The caricature holds a bowl I assume is supposed to be full of rice. She has a set of chopsticks in her other hand. At the bottom are the words, "Stacey Chopsticks."

I don't give Keshia the satisfaction of getting angry about this. Instead I tuck it into my math textbook. Then I slouch down in my seat and wish again I could disappear.

***

Recess is an uneventful hour later. I follow the other kids out to the playground. I look around for Jamie, but she's not around, at least not yet. There is a familiar face, though: Maddy sits on the sidewalk and stares at the other kids.

I sit down next to her. "How's it going?" I ask.

"I wanna go home," she whimpers.

"So do I, but we got to stick it out."

"These girls are mean," Maddy says. From the redness of her cheeks, I'm sure she's barely holding back tears; she doesn't want to cry in front of the other kids. "One of them called me 'Fatty Maddy.'"

"You're not fat," I lie.

"Am too," she says. She grabs a roll of fat with one hand and tries to yank it off. "I'm a fat baby. That's what they said."

"Who?" I ask. I look around the playground, to search for the girls who said that to my daughter.

"Some kids."

"Did you tell the teacher?"

"No. Then they'd really hate me."

Maddy isn't so old as to have forgotten the code of the playground. If there's someone kids hate more than a bully it's a tattler. For most people that doesn't change much as they get older. In some neighborhoods you'd as soon find Bigfoot as someone who will snitch on the gangs or dope peddlers.

"That's a good point," I say. "You want to swing or something?"

"No."

"Come on, Maddy, try to have some fun."

"I don't wanna."

Come to think of it, I don't want to swing either. I wish I could call Tess and ask her to pick us up. She would do it, but then we'd have to answer a bunch of questions about why we want to leave. After all the effort to get us in here, we can't leave so soon.

"Just give them a few days to warm to you," I tell Maddy.

"OK."

"Then they'll see how smart you are and they'll all want to be your friend."

"I'm not that smart," she says. "Not as smart as some of the kids."

"Give it time," I say. "It's been a while since you were in the first grade."

"I guess."

We sit there through the rest of recess, until Mrs. Ellsbury calls for the first graders to get back to class. I help Maddy up and then, unconcerned if anyone sees, I give her a hug. "It'll be all right," I tell her, as much for myself as her.

Chapter 26

Two days later, Maddy and I don't go to school. At least we won't until the afternoon. We sit in the waiting room of Dr. Macintosh's office instead. Jamie's appointment isn't until later, so she and Caleb aren't around. That leaves me alone with Tess while Maddy goes inside to talk with the doctor.

"I'm sure she'll be all right by herself," Tess says.

"I'm sure."

"Does she like school so far?"

"It's a little hard fitting in."

"I suppose it would be," Tess says. "Have the kids been giving her a hard time?"

"Not too much," I say. I don't want to worry Tess more than I have to.

"How about you, dear? Any kids giving you a hard time?"

"No," I lie.

"That's good. Just remember it's all right to be different. God makes us in all shapes, sizes, and colors so we can appreciate our differences and our similarities."

"Right," I say, though God had nothing to do with my differences; that would be first Artie Luther and then Dr. Ling.

We don't say much for the rest of the hour, until Maddy emerges from the office. "Bye-bye, Dr. Mac!"

The doctor calls me in for my session. "Have a seat," he says. He motions to one of the armchairs. He doesn't sit down right away, though. Instead he goes to his desk to fetch something.

When he turns to face me, he wears a plastic silver tiara and a pink boa. I put both hands over my mouth so I won't laugh. He walks nonchalantly over to the desk, seemingly oblivious to the tiara and boa. He takes out his notebook and pen and then stares at me. "You find something funny?"

"Yes."

"This old thing?" he asks. He flourishes the boa.

"Yes."

"What's so funny about it?"

"I don't know."

"Because it's for girls, right?"

"I guess."

"And you'd say the tiara is for girls too, right?"

"Yes."

He nods and then takes both off. He holds them out to me. "Don't you want these?"

"No thanks."

"Why not?" he asks.

"I'd look silly," I say.

"Really? Why would that be? After all, you're a girl. It's perfectly natural for girls your age to wear these."

"Maybe, but I don't want to."

"Because you still don't see yourself as a girl?"

"I don't know. Maybe."

"Stacey, I want you to go ahead and put these on, just for this session."

"Why?"

"To help you feel more comfortable in your own skin."

"Fine," I say. I snatch the tiara and set it atop my head. Then I wrap the pink boa around my neck. Dr. Macintosh produces the mirror so I can see myself. The tiara is crooked; I adjust it to sit level on my head. In the mirror my cheeks redden. I look ridiculous, like a little girl playing dress-up. I suppose that's the point. "Happy now?"

"The real question is: are you happy now?"

"No. I feel stupid."

"Why's that?"

"I look like a little kid."

"Isn't Stacey Chang a little kid?"

"I suppose."

"How have things been going for Stacey Chang at school?"

"Maybe you should ask your nephew. He sits next to me. Is that on purpose?"

"I don't control Ms. Lowry's seating chart."

"Seems a little convenient, though, doesn't it?"

"Perhaps it's just fate."

"Sure."

"Have you and Darren been getting along?"

"He doesn't say much. Jamie says he's weird."

"Who's Jamie?"

"My friend. She's a patient here too."

"You must mean Jamie Borstein. I suppose it's not a surprise you two would hit it off."

"Why would you say that?"

"You're close together in age, you have similar backgrounds, and you're both terribly lonely."

"I'm not lonely."

"You're not?"

"No. I have my sister, remember?"

"But that's not the same, is it?"

"I don't know."

"So what do you and Jamie talk about?"

"TV, music, boys."

"I see. Do you like talking about boys?"

"No."

"Why not?"

"I'm only ten. I'm too little for boys."

"That's debatable."

"Everything's debatable with you."

"I only want to try to help you see the truth."

"That I still think I'm a boy?"

"That's part of the truth. Do you still think you're a boy?"

"Sometimes."

"What about right now?"

I wave the boa at him. "Not so much."

"That's good. We're making progress."

"I can't forget about being a boy," I say. "I was a boy for fifty years."

"You don't have to forget that time of your life. You just need to feel comfortable within your body—as Stacey. That's a lot harder to do if you still see yourself as Steve."

"Maybe I don't want to see myself as Stacey Chang."

"Why not?"

"Because she's little. She's weak."

"In what sense?"

"Every sense." I take a deep breath and then tell Dr. Macintosh about Keshia. She kept it up my second day, though I was smart enough not to let her trip me. Still, every time she answered a question she would look at me, as if to shove her knowledge in my face.

When I finish, the doctor nods. "Sounds like this Keshia has problems of her own."

"She's a bitch," I say. "That's her problem."

"I suspect it's deeper than that."

"You would."

"I suspect Keshia is focusing on you because you threaten her role."

"What role?"

"The successful minority student. I suspect her parents have been pushing her all her life to prove herself to be equal to her white peers. That's driven her to be the best in her class. The last thing she wants is for someone to usurp that."

"She doesn't have anything to worry about. I'm still not very bright."

"Maybe you're not trying hard enough. Do you want to succeed at school?"

"Yes."

"If you have to remain Stacey Chang indefinitely, then I think it would behoove you to do well in your studies."

"Behoove me?"

"It would benefit you."

"Oh," I say. "See, I'm not smart. I can't even spell 'Magnificent.'"

"How old is Stacey Chang?"

"Ten."

"Then you have plenty of time to learn."

"Maybe I'm just not that smart. Maybe I'll always be dumb."

"Do you think Steve Fischer was dumb?"

"Ask his coworkers."

"I'm more interested in what you think."

"I wound up here, didn't I? That wasn't very smart."

"So you blame yourself for what happened?"

"I went into that lab without any backup. Wouldn't you say that's pretty stupid?"

"Maybe, but you could also say it was pretty brave."

"Yeah, well, maybe I was brave because I was dumb."

"True courage is being smart enough to see the danger and throwing yourself into the fray anyway," Dr. Macintosh says.

"Whatever."

"Don't shut down on me, Stacey," he says. He waits a moment, but I don't say anything. "Even if Steve wasn't a straight-A student, that doesn't mean Stacey couldn't be, if she works hard at it."

"Why? I never needed to be smart before."

"You liked being a police officer?"

"Yes. It was all I ever wanted to be."

"What about working as a salesgirl at your friend's clothes shop?"

"It was all right."

"But not really a career, was it?" Dr. Macintosh smirks at me. "Did you get much satisfaction out of working there?"

"Some."

"Not the same as being a police officer?"

"I don't know. They're totally different things."

"Are they?"

"Yes." The way he stares at me, he expects me to say more. "One is putting dangerous criminals in jail. The other is selling old clothes to hipsters."

"I see. Then why did you keep working for Grace?"

"She's my friend. And it let me see Maddy."

"Are those the only reasons?"

"I guess."

"You guess or you're sure?"

"I don't know. It was kind of nice not being in life-or-death situations all the time. You know, if someone buys an ugly T-shirt you aren't going to get a bullet in the head."

"I see. So you enjoyed the ease of the job?"

"A little. Does that make me a slacker?"

Dr. Macintosh smiles and shakes his head. "Not at all. I read Steve Fischer's obituary. He sounded like quite a good cop. All those commendations and medals."

"Yeah, he was a real hero."

"After all that, maybe he needed a break."

"I'm real lucky Artie Luther helped me out with that then."

"Don't hide behind sarcasm," Dr. Macintosh chides me. "Had you given any thought to your retirement?"

"Not really. I always assumed I wouldn't make it. Or else my liver would give out."

"I see. Do you think Steve had a death wish?"

"What?"

"Do you think he worked those long hours, drove himself so hard, because he wanted to die?"

"No."

"But you assumed you would die in the line of duty, right?"

"In this city the odds are pretty good."

"What about your partner, Jake? Do you think he plans to die in the line of duty?"

"I don't know. I hope not for Tess's sake."

"I see. Your friend has something to live for. And you didn't."

"That's not what I meant."

"I've seen cases like that before: a man takes a lot of stupid risks because he wants to die but can't bring himself to commit suicide because that would be cowardly. Do you think that would describe Steve Fischer?"

"No."

"Why not?"

"I didn't want to die!" I snap.

"You said you spent a lot of time drinking and clearly you took a lot of stupid risks. How would you describe that behavior?"

"Stupid."

"That's a good ten-year-old way to put it. But when you became Stacey you didn't do that anymore, did you?"

"No," I say. In truth I did engage in some risky behavior as Stacey Chance, behavior that got me shot twice, once by Artie Luther's favorite assassin the Tall Man and the second time by Jake when he betrayed me to Luther, but that was so I could become Steve again.

"As Stacey, would you say you're more passive than you were as Steve?"

"Maybe."

"Why is that?"

"Stacey is smaller. And weaker. She can't brawl like Steve could."

"That's a pretty good explanation, though I don't think size is that important. Plenty of short people have been good at fighting."

"Maybe."

"If you felt weak, you could always go to the gym. You could learn karate or some other martial art."

"That takes a lot of time and money."

"I suppose it does. Did you ever think about buying some weights? Maybe go jogging?"

"Are you saying I'm fat?"

"You are a little pear-shaped."

"Pear-shaped? I'm only ten."

"Childhood obesity is a serious problem."

"I guess."

"But I think we've gotten off the issue here. Do you think it might be accurate to say Stacey didn't engage in risky behavior because she had more to lose?"

"I don't know."

"Stacey had her guardians, the Madigans. Then of course she had her friends, Grace and Madison. Who did Steve Fischer have to lose?"

"Stop it!" I shout. I curl up in the chair and bury my face in one arm of it while I sob.

I feel Dr. Macintosh pat my back. "It's all right. You should focus on the positive. You were given a magnificent gift: a second chance. It's important to make the most of it. Apply yourself to your studies. Stacey Chang can be whatever she wants to be."

"All right." With another sniffle I uncurl myself. I wipe at my eyes with the pink boa.

As I start to take the boa off, Dr. Macintosh says, "You can keep that. You earned it."

"Gee, thanks," I grumble.

I still have the stupid boa and tiara on when I go out into the waiting room. Maddy runs over to me and almost bowls me over. "You look pretty," she says.

"Thanks," I say. I look back at Dr. Macintosh, who nods to me. Then I put the tiara on Maddy's head and the boa around her neck. "Now you look pretty."

Chapter 27

When I get to class it's after lunch. Tess took us to McDonald's on the way to school. I remembered how Dr. Macintosh described me as "pear-shaped" and ordered a salad. Tess gave me a concerned look, but didn't say anything.

Keshia gives me a look too, an angry look that suggests I should have stayed away. I take my seat and make sure not to look at her. When I open my history textbook, I study the words intently to try to absorb the knowledge. I stare at it so hard, I don't hear Ms. Lowry when she says, "Stacey?"

"Huh?" Keshia leads some of the other girls in snickering.

"I asked you a question."

"What question?"

"I know!" Keshia says.

Ms. Lowry ignores her to glare at me. Maybe she and Mr. Delmore had a rough night. "Young lady, you need to pay attention."

"Yes, ma'am."

"Now, as I was saying, this year is St. Andrew's sesquicentennial. Do you know what that means, Stacey?"

I think about it for a few moments. I'm old enough to remember the bicentennial in 1976. That meant two hundred years. A centennial is one hundred years. Since I doubt the school is older than two hundred years, I guess, "A hundred fifty years?"

"Very good, Stacey. St. Andrews is turning one hundred fifty years old. To celebrate, Headmaster Armey has decided all grades from kindergarten to sixth grade will put on a presentation for the parents and alumni."

Everyone but Keshia groans at this. "Our grade has been assigned to do a presentation on the arts in the last one hundred fifty years." There's another groan at this. "Since there are sixteen of you, I want everyone to pair up. Each pair will be assigned two decades to present for the parents and alumni."

"Do you mean like an essay?" Keshia asks.

"It can be an essay. You could also do a skit or a slideshow or something similar. Dr. Armey is encouraging us to be creative."

I glance over at Keshia and can see the wheels in her mind start to turn. The good thing about being her partner is you wouldn't have to do any work; she's the type who would do everything herself. At most you might have to do some manual labor for whatever she comes up with.

But of course she doesn't want to be partners with me. No one does. I watch helplessly as the other kids push their desks together; no one so much as looks at me. It's like a game of musical chairs and I'm the one left standing.

Except thanks to our even numbers, I'm not the only one left. Darren mumbles, "You want to be my partner?"

"I guess so," I say. I force myself to smile. "It's not like I have a choice."

"Yeah," he says to indicate I'm not his ideal partner either. He'd probably rather not have any partner.

After we've partnered up, Ms. Lowry walks around the room and hands out slips of paper. I cross my fingers and hope she'll give Darren and I something contemporary; the 60s and 70s would be right up my alley. I wouldn't even have to do any research; I could just go from personal experience.

I'm not that lucky. Instead of my era, I get my grandpa's era: 1930-1950. I suppose it's better than the 1890s. At least I have a vague idea of the arts during the Depression and World War II era. I turn to Darren. "So what should we do?"

"I don't know."

"That's not very helpful." I see his notebook on his desk. "You like music. Maybe we could do something with that."

"I guess."

"Come on, you must know something about music from back then."

"Not really."

"My grandpa has some jazz records and stuff. That might help."

"Maybe."

"What about your uncle? What kind of music does he listen to?"

"I don't know."

I shake my head. I can see I'll have to do the lion's share of the work on this project. I guess it'll let me show Darren's uncle how smart I really am. "Well, it shouldn't be too hard to find out. We could go look for some books in the library and stuff."

"I guess."

"Do you have a computer? Or one of those phones?"

"Yes."

"With you?"

"Yeah." He reluctantly takes out a phone like Jamie's. I wonder if he has Angry Birds on it? Darren doesn't seem the type for that. He pushes a few buttons to bring up Google and then Wikipedia.

"Let's start with jazz," I say. Darren punches that in. From what the article says, jazz is more associated with the Roaring Twenties than the 30s. "What was that other stuff? Like Glen Miller or whoever."

Darren types in Glen Miller and brings up the article on him. Big band music, that was the stuff my grandparents listened to. I remember when I sat in the back of their station wagon and whined like Maddy about my Creedence.

"Now we're getting somewhere," I say. I hope to engage Darren. He doesn't take the bait. It wasn't this bad for Grace and Maddy to deal with me as Stacey Chance, was it? Did they have to pry words out of me with a pair of pliers?

"What about Frank Sinatra?" I ask. "I think he was from around that time." Darren looks up Old Blue Eyes, who was a favorite of my dad. I had my dad's record collection, but it got burned up with the rest of Steve Fischer's stuff thanks to one of Artie Luther's goons. "There we go, a couple of leads. You can research one and I'll look up the other, OK?"

"OK."

"Which one do you want?"

"Doesn't matter."

"Come on, Darren. Work with me here."

He thinks about it for a long time, as if it's a life-or-death choice. Then he says, "I'll take Miller."

"Fine. I'll take Sinatra. We can read about them, listen to a few songs, and then tomorrow come up with some ideas about what to do. Right?"

"Sure."

I raise my hand to bring Ms. Lowry over. "Can we go to the library, Ms. Lowry? We have a couple of ideas to research."

"She doesn't even have a phone," Keshia stage whispers to a couple other girls. They laugh along with her. Now that I look around, I see everyone else does have a smartphone of some sort. Most of them the latest iPhones. A few of the less wealthy have other brands. In my day the closest we had to a portable phone was two paper cups tied together with string.

"Very well," Ms. Lowry says. "I'll write you a pass."

"Thanks."

I take the note and then turn to Darren. "Are you coming?"

"No. I'll use my phone."

"Fine. See you later."

***

I look around the library for Jamie, but she's not there. I go up to the biographies to find one on Sinatra. I also get a couple on the Rat Pack. Then I sit in a cubicle to read, though mostly I look at the pictures. I remember some of those old movies with Sinatra and Sammy Davis Jr. We didn't have VCRs back then, but they showed those on TV sometimes. Dad could do a pretty decent impression of Sammy. That was about the only time when he kidded around with me. Back then dads were supposed to be the pillars of strength and virtue to their kids.

I sigh at this thought. I tried to be that for Maddy, but times had changed. Other fathers were more touchy-feely, into all that sensitivity bullshit. They'd want to talk about their feelings, like women. I sigh again and know what Dr. Macintosh would say about this line of thought, that I shouldn't be so gender-biased. Then again he is one of those touchy-feely types too.

I force myself to study. I jot down a few notes on songs I can look up later. Maybe Tess can take me to the library to get some CDs. This would be so much easier if I had a computer or one of those fancy phones. I ought to ask Jake about one of those, but I know Jake and Tess are close to the edge as it is now that they have two extra mouths to feed.

I'm still in the cubicle an hour later when someone taps me on the shoulder. I expect the librarian or Ms. Lowry, but it's Jamie. "Hi," she says. "You weren't at recess. I asked your sister if you were here and she said you were. Then I asked that weird kid Darren and he said you went to the library. What gives?"

"I was just studying," I say. "For our presentation."

"Oh yeah, that thing. What did you guys get?"

"Art."

"We got 'Significant Events.' Whatever that means. The thirdies lucked out; they got Sports. I hear the sixthies got Fashion."

"What about the firsties?"

"Presidents."

"That's not so bad," I say. I think of Madison, whose first name is the last name of a president, not that Debbie and I considered that when she was born.

"So what are you doing?" Before I can say anything, Jamie snatches my biography of Sinatra away. She sticks a finger down her throat. "Yuck. That's like the shit my grandpa plays in the car."

"Yeah, I know. Gag."

"Where's the rest of your group?"

"You already talked to him."

"That kid?" She pats my arm. "No wonder you came up here."

"Actually it's because I don't have a phone like everyone else to look stuff up."

"Oh, right." Jamie smiles. "How about you come over to my place after school? You can use my computer."

"I don't think my grandma would go for that. She wouldn't want to wait around—"

"Daddy can take you home after we're done. Or we can call a cab."

"I don't know—"

Jamie presses a few buttons. A couple moments later she's on the phone with Tess. "Hi, Mrs. Madigan. It's Jamie, Stacey's friend. Yeah. No, nothing's happened. She's fine. She was just wondering if she could come over to my house to do a little homework. What? Oh, that's what she said. My father would be happy to drive her home when we're done. We should be done by seven. What? She's right here."

Jamie stops and then holds out the phone to me. "Hi, Grandma."

"Hello, dear. Are you sure you want to go with your friend after school?"

"Yes."

Tess sighs into the phone. "I suppose it will be fine. I'll keep some dinner warm for you when you get back.

Just don't be out too late, understand? I still want you in bed by eight-thirty."

"Yes, Grandma Tess."

"Good. Tell your friend goodbye for me, dear."

I hand the phone back to Jamie. "She said it was OK."

"Great. We can meet out front after school."

"All right."

Jamie pats me on the shoulder. "I'll let you get back to work."

I wait until I see her go down the stairs before I turn back to my stack of old books. If nothing else, I'd really like to do well on this to prove to that little snot Keshia I'm not an idiot. That would serve her right. With that in mind I get back to work.

Chapter 28

From TV and movies I expect a stretch limo to show up for Jamie and Caleb with a driver in a black suit with a little hat. Instead it's an ordinary silver Mercedes. The driver wears a dark suit, but no hat. He does open the back door so we can climb inside.

I sit in the middle, so that I'm between Jamie and her little brother. Caleb hasn't said anything since he joined us on the front steps of the admin building.

"It's great your grandma finally let you come over," Jamie says. "We haven't had anyone over since we moved here."

"It's hard making friends," I say.

"Yeah, especially at a place like that." Jamie's phone beeps. She checks the screen. "I'm getting an update from one of my friends back in Miami," she says. She lets me see the screen. It's her Facebook account. Jamie has over five hundred friends on Facebook, but apparently none in the city who can hang out with her.

With the afternoon traffic it takes about forty-five minutes to reach the glass tower Jamie and Caleb call home. From the look of it, it's about as tall as the headquarters for Lennox Pharmaceuticals. There's a lobby that's just as opulent, complete with its own fountain that puts the one at St. Andrew's to shame.

"Some night I'd really like to go swimming in there," Jamie says.

"That sounds like fun," I lie.

Caleb has already trotted over to the elevators and pushed the button. When one of the elevators shows up, Jamie and I have to hurry in order to make it before the doors close. On the way up to the sixteenth floor, Jamie swats Caleb on the back of the head. "The little weasel is always doing that," she says.

"Do not," he says.

"You do so." She sighs. "Is your little sister this annoying?"

"No. Maddy is nice."

"Lucky you."

There's a corridor inlaid with brown marble and gold. There are only three doors; Caleb races Jamie to the one at the far end of the hallway. "I win!" he shouts.

"Only because you cheat," she says.

The door opens on its own. I recognize the young man from Dr. Macintosh's office. "This is my friend Stacey," Jamie says. "We're going to do homework."

"Whatever," he says.

The condo is easily bigger than Jake's entire house. Caleb runs over to the leather couch in the living room and turns the sixty-inch plasma TV to cartoons. Jamie takes my hand and leads me into the kitchen. There's an old Hispanic woman in there to cook dinner. Jamie ignores her and opens the fridge. She takes out two bottles of Coke, one for each of us.

"Come on, you got to see my room."

Her room is somewhat of a disappointment. It's bigger than the one I share with Maddy, but it's not that different from any little girl's bedroom. The walls are pink and covered with posters for her favorite singers and bands. There are also posters of older boys, probably from the shows she tells me about. "You can leave your bag on the bed."

It's a canopy bed with a pink comforter. It's made up neatly, no doubt thanks to a servant. Though Jamie says her father isn't that rich, he must do well to afford this spread. It's a lot better than I could ever hope to do, no matter how smart I am.

Jamie drops her bag on the floor and then flops into an office chair. She opens a pink laptop. While it boots up, she takes off her uniform jacket and shakes out her ponytail. I decide to take my coat off too.

I hope to get to work, but Jamie has other things in mind. She logs on to Facebook, and browses through the messages her digital friends have posted on her wall. Some of these messages include links to videos. It seems every video is either about a hot boy or a cute cat.

The former seem to interest her a lot more. "I can't wait until that comes out," she says after she watches a movie trailer someone linked to her wall. "I hope he takes his shirt off."

"Yeah, that'd be great," I say.

I sit next to Jamie and fidget in my seat. I didn't come here to watch her answer her messages. An hour goes by before she says, "OK, got all that out of the way. Now I guess we should get down to business."

"Good idea." I tell her some of the albums I want to look up. She goes to a website where we can listen to the albums for free. Two minutes into the first track, Jamie starts to make gagging gestures. I giggle at this. "I know. It's so lame."

"I don't know how old people can listen to such garbage," she says.

"It's weird," I say, though I know it's because the "old people" grew up with that music and don't think it's shit, like me with my Creedence.

Jamie retreats to her bed so she can play Angry Birds while I do some research. The music continues to play in the background as I track down links to music from the '30s and '40s. I find some Glen Miller stuff too, since I figure Darren won't do anything.

Another hour later there's a knock on the door. Travis the male nanny opens the door. "Esmerelda says five minutes to dinner," he says. "Make sure you and your friend wash up first."

"We will," Jamie says. She sounds much sweeter than usual. After the door closes, she tosses her phone aside and sighs. "God, he is so hot."

"Yeah, he is," I say. Even if I were a grown woman I wouldn't go out with Travis. I'm not into the hairy hipster type. For Jamie I doubt it matters a whole lot.

"Did I ever tell you about the time I opened the bathroom door and he was in there shaving? He had his shirt off and everything."

"Wow," I mumble, though I imagine Travis's chest is pale, scrawny, and hairless.

"I could have just died from embarrassment," she says. Then she adds, "I just wish I'd had my phone with me so I could get a picture."

"That would have been great," I say.

She gets up from the bed. "We'd better go wash up."

She leads me to the bathroom. It has a tub that could have easily fit me when I was still six-three and over two hundred pounds. The tub has whirlpool jets too. My face warms as I remember the hot tub upstate where I masturbated for the first time as a woman while I thought of Grace, my daughter's lover.

I come back to reality as Jamie snaps her fingers in front of my eyes. "Hey," she says. "You in a trance or something?"

"What? No. I was just thinking of something."

"Must be something pretty interesting to get your face all red."

"It's nothing important." I turn to the sink to wash my hands. When I look up at the mirror, I see what Jamie meant; my face is still red from when I thought about Grace. I splash a little cold water on my cheeks. That doesn't help a whole lot. "Maybe I should go home," I say.

"You can't yet. Daddy's not home."

"Oh. Well, I guess I can stick around." Since I'm only ten I can't just hop on a train like I used to do. I could, but Tess would have a fit; she didn't like me to go out by myself when I was eighteen.

Jamie practically skips out to the dining room. The table is already set. Caleb slouches in one chair, probably annoyed to be dragged away from the TV. Jamie and I sit on the opposite side of the table from him.

The Hispanic woman from the kitchen brings in a tray loaded with tiny chickens. Game hens, I think they're called. "Thank you Esmerelda," Jamie says. Esmerelda puts a chicken down on my plate. It's got some kind of stuffing in it. I poke at the thing with my fork. "It's great," Jamie tells me.

I take a cautious bite. As the old saying goes, it tastes like chicken. It makes me think of the chickens I used to barbecue in the backyard for Debbie and Maddy. They usually complained my chicken was dry, but this stuff is pretty juicy.

Besides the chicken we have mushrooms in some kind of sauce. I don't usually eat mushrooms even on pizza, but these are delicious. While I scarf down my meal, Jamie talks more on her favorite subject: boys. There's one boy in sixth grade she's particularly fascinated with who has the unlikely name of Thurston. He's captain of the JV lacrosse team. "I didn't even know what lacrosse was until I saw him," she says. I share in a giggle with her.

We eat carrot cake for dessert, which is Jamie's favorite, when her father gets home. As if she's still a toddler, she bolts from the table to meet him at the door. "Daddy!" she cries out and hugs him around the waist. He's only about six inches taller than her, maybe five-seven at most. He's mostly bald with a fringe of black hair left. His glasses are about as thick as mine, which is more an indictment of my bad eyes than his.

He kisses her on the top of the head. "Hello, sweetheart," he says in a gruff voice that sounds like it could use a throat lozenge.

"Come on, Daddy, Stacey's here!"

"Who's Stacey?"

"My friend." Jamie's voice loses its little girlish quality. "I've been talking about her for over a week now. We met at the doctor, remember?"

"Oh, that Stacey," he says. He follows Jamie into the dining room. His eyes narrow at me, to size me up. My face reddens again under his gaze. "This must be the famous Stacey. I'm Gary Borstein, Jamie's dad."

I take his proffered hand to give it a slight shake. "Stacey Chang."

"So you go to school with Jamie?"

"Yes, Daddy," Jamie says, "but she's a grade below me."

"Oh, I see. How old are you, Stacey?"

"Ten."

"That's a good age," he says.

"I guess," I say.

"Jamie turned eleven two months ago."

"Six months ago, Daddy."

"Oh, right. Sorry, sweetheart."

Jamie's father sits down at the head of the table. Esmerelda has already fetched his dinner from the kitchen. He starts to dig in. "So you two met at Dr. Macintosh's?" he asks.

"Yes."

"That's great. Jamie needs friends."

"I *had* plenty of friends, Daddy."

"I know, honey." He takes a bite of his chicken. Then he asks me, "What do your parents do?"

"I live with my grandparents."

"Her parents died."

"Oh, that's too bad. It's good of your grandparents to take you in."

"Yes. They're very nice."

"Her grandma is super-duper nice," Jamie says.

"Yeah, she is," I say. "My grandpa is nice too. He's a cop."

"Really? Maybe I ran into him at court," Jamie's father says.

"Dad-dy," Jamie says. She stretches the word out. "Stacey doesn't care about that. She's just a kid."

If Maddy had talked to me like that I would have sent her to her room. That was a lot more of a punishment fifteen years ago, before there was the Internet and smartphones everywhere. Jamie's father must not mind because he says, "I suppose you're right, sweetheart."

Jamie takes my hand and pulls me from the chair. "Come on, let's go back to my room."

Once inside, Jamie plops on her bed and sighs. "Daddy is such a nerd sometimes."

"He seems nice."

"He's always nice to company. Too nice really. He starts trying to butter up everyone like they're a client."

"I guess so," I say. I don't want to press the issue.

Jamie rolls over. I think at first she must be mad at me, but then she opens the drawer to her nightstand. From this she takes out a smartphone. She tosses it to me; I fumble the catch so the phone lands on the floor. "That's only an iPhone 3, but it should still work."

"Wow," I say as I pick the phone up. "This is so expensive. I can't accept a gift like that."

Jamie snorts. "Oh please, that's like two generations old already. You could probably buy one for ten bucks on eBay."

"I hadn't thought of that," I say. The catch-22 is I would have to have Internet access to buy a phone like this online. This I suppose is much easier. Then Keshia and her cronies won't have any reason to make fun of me. "Thank you so much."

Jamie shows me how to turn the phone on and how to access the Internet. She brings up her Facebook page. "You should get one of these and then you can friend me."

"I'm already your friend."

"Well duh, but then we can share messages and pictures and stuff like that."

"I don't think my grandparents would like that."

"Why? It's not like you're going to be using it to talk to pedophiles. Are you?" She gives me a wink and then slaps my arm. "I'm just kidding."

"I'll ask them."

"Why do you have to ask them? It's not their phone. My dad is paying for it."

I don't want to keep secrets from Jake and Tess—or any more than I already keep from Tess—but what Jamie says makes sense. It's not their phone or their money. Besides, they aren't my real grandparents and I'm not really ten years old. I can take care of myself. "I'll do it," I say. I turn the phone off and then slip it into my backpack.

I see on the clock it's after six. "I should be getting home. I promised to be back by seven."

Jamie rolls your eyes. "You're such a goody-goody."

"I don't want to worry them. They've been really nice to me."

"I'm just teasing," Jamie says. "Hey, do you think your grandma would let you sleep over this weekend?"

"I don't know. Maybe. Is your father going to be home?"

"Most of the time. Travis will be around too."

"Does he live here?"

"I wish," Jamie says and sighs like a romance book heroine. "He has some grubby little place in the garment district. He lives with these two stupid girls. They're actresses or something stupid like that."

From the way Jamie says the latter part, I know she's jealous. She would give anything to share an apartment with Travis, not that she would know what to do with him once they were alone. To some extent it was the same way for me when I was a boy; my friends and I would stare at *Playboy* centerfolds though we wouldn't have had a clue what to do if the model on the page had sprung to life and asked us to fuck her.

"I'll ask her about the sleepover when I get back," I tell Jamie. We share a brief hug and then she takes me out to the dining room, where her father works on his carrot cake.

"Daddy, Stacey needs to go home."

"Where does she live?"

"In the suburbs," Jamie says.

I give him the address and he winces. He knows it'll be probably ninety minutes round trip at a minimum. "All right," he says. He pats me on the head. "Let me get my keys."

***

I'm surprised Mr. Borstein drives himself. He has a silver Audi sedan with a vanity plate that reads, "BORSTEN1" in an underground garage. I sit in the backseat, on the passenger's side to make it easy for him to see me. This is the first time I'm really alone with an adult stranger since I became little; I'm not sure how to act. So I stare out the window and watch the scenery as we make our way towards the suburbs.

We're stuck on the bridge off the island when he says, "I was really glad to see you were real. The last 'friend' Jamie had turned out to be some seventy-year-old retiree in Boca Raton she'd been chatting with online."

"Gross."

"My Jamie's a good girl. She's just headstrong. That's why it's hard for her to make friends."

"She had some in Miami, didn't she?"

"A few. It broke my heart to have to move her and Cal up here. There wasn't much choice. Someone made me an offer I couldn't refuse." Mr. Borstein shakes his head. "You're too young to know what that means."

I wonder if that means he was run out of Miami or someone up here offered him a really good job? Either way, it's clear his children aren't happy about it. "I'm glad you did," I say. "I'm new here too. We used to live in California."

"Oh yeah? Whereabouts?"

"San Francisco."

"That's a good town. The wife and I went there on our honeymoon."

"That's nice." I clear my throat and then ask, "What happened to your wife?"

"She passed on. Cancer," he says.

"I'm sorry."

"To be honest, that's part of why we had to get out of Miami. Her ghost was still there." He turns his head to look back at me. "Not a scary real ghost. More like her presence, if you know what I mean."

"I know. I felt that when my parents died," I say. In truth my parents and I never had much of a relationship. I think instead of Maddy after the divorce, how her presence had always lingered, especially on my anniversary. "I was glad when they sent us to live with Grandma and Grandpa. Sometimes I can still feel them, when I see something of theirs, like the doll Daddy bought me or the necklace Mommy gave me. Sometimes I like to be reminded of them, but other times it's too sad, you know?"

Mr. Borstein smiles at me. "You're a pretty special kid, Stacey Chang."

"Thanks."

He turns back to the steering wheel. We don't say much more until I get home. Before I get out, he says, "You come over whenever you like, all right? Just as long as it's OK with your grandparents."

"Thanks, Mr. Borstein." I decide to reward his kindness with a kiss on the cheek. Then I grab my backpack and run inside.

Chapter 29

When I see Darren the next day, I say, "My grandma said it's OK if I come over today."

"OK. My uncle usually picks me up around four," he says. "I stay in the library until then."

He turns back to his notebook. I can see I won't get anywhere with him, so I work on some homework I should have done last night.

The rest of the day goes by slowly. At recess, Maddy sits down next to me. "Hi," she says.

"Hi," I say. "Something wrong?"

"Mrs. Ellsbury is making us do this stupid play for the sequicennial," Maddy says. She mangles the word. "She cast me as Eleanor Roosevelt."

"That's good. Isn't it?"

"Can you help me with my lines tonight?"

"I can't tonight. I'm meeting Darren to work on our project."

To my surprise, Maddy starts to cry. "It's not fair!" she shouts. "You're never around anymore. You're always playing with your friends. You promised to be there for me, but you're not! You don't care about me."

"Maddy, of course I still care about you. You're my baby sister."

"I'm not a baby!"

"Fine, you're my younger sister." I put a hand around her shoulder to pull her close. Some other kids probably see us, but I don't care. "You're still my best friend too."

"What about Jamie?"

"She's my other best friend."

"You can't have two best friends."

"OK, you're my bestest friend."

"Then why do you play with her and not me? Because she's a big girl?"

"I'm just doing what Dr. Mac said to do. I'm trying to fit in." I give her a squeeze. "You should try to make some friends your age. Aren't there any nice kids in your class?"

"No."

"Really?"

"Really."

"Well, is there at least one who's less mean than the others?"

"I don't know."

I survey the playground. There's a girl with brown pigtails similar to Maddy's who sits by herself under a tree. She reads a book, though I can't tell what it is. "What about her?" I ask.

"That's Marcy."

"What's wrong with her?"

"She talks funny. She's from Switzerland."

"She speaks English, doesn't she?"

"Yes, but it sounds funny. Like that German guy in that old TV show."

Maddy must mean Colonel Klink on *Hogan's Heroes*. "You know it's not nice to judge people by how they talk or look. Do you like it when people make fun of you for being chubby?"

"No."

"Well then, why don't you go over there and ask her to play?"

"OK."

Maddy trudges across the playground and sits down next to Marcy beneath the tree. I watch them exchange a few words. Whatever Maddy says is effective; Marcy closes her book and then they skip over to the swings.

I watch this with a smile. My little sister has made her first friend.

***

I find Darren on the third floor of the library after school. "Hi," I say. "You almost ready to go?"

It's not that I'm anxious to go to Dr. Macintosh's house—far from it. I just want to get it over with. Then I can go home and text with Jamie. She'll probably want to know all about Dr. Macintosh's house, if it's as weird as his nephew.

We don't say anything as we go downstairs. He clutches his backpack to his chest like it's a pillow as we cross the quad to the admin building. I see one car out front, a Lexus SUV. I thought Dr. Macintosh the type who would have a Prius or Volt or something fuel-efficient like that. Maybe I should ask him about that in our next session.

Unlike when I ride with Jamie, no one opens the door for us. As we climb into the back of the SUV, Dr. Macintosh says, "That's not so bad, is it?"

At first I think he said that to me; then I see the Bluetooth receiver on his ear. "She's just expressing herself," he says. "Try to explain why it's wrong in a calm, rational way. If that doesn't work, then discipline her. No, don't raise your hand to her. Send her to a corner to think about her actions. Let me know how that works out. Bye."

He finally turns back to us. "Sorry about that, kids. One of my patients has been smearing spaghetti sauce on the walls."

"Gross," I say.

"You two have your seatbelts on?" Dr. Macintosh asks.

"Yes," Darren and I say in unison.

"Great. Here we go then." He shifts the SUV into drive. The traffic is worse than it usually is when I go to Jamie's house. We're into rush hour, which lasts for about four hours in this city as the businesspeople flee to the suburbs.

Dr. Macintosh takes advantage of this to ask me about the project. "Darren says you're studying art of the '30s and '40s?"

"Yes. We're focusing on music mostly," I say.

"Why's that?"

"Well, because we both like music," I say.

"That's a valid reason."

"But not a good one?"

"There was a lot more to art than music back then. There were a lot of great painters. Some tremendous writers too like Hemingway and Faulkner. Are you going to leave them out?"

"We only get five minutes at most," I say.

"I see. So you're hoping to use music symbolically?"

"Maybe," I say, not entirely sure what he means by that.

"That could work. I'll be happy to help you and Darren out as much as I can."

"What do you know about the '30s and '40s?" I ask. "You're not that old."

"You don't think so? Darren, how old do you think I am?"

"Thirty-six," Darren says.

"Cheater," Dr. Macintosh says with a smile. "I have quite a collection of Cole Porter albums. Do you know who he is?"

"Not really," I say.

Dr. Macintosh clucks his tongue and shakes his head at the same time. "He's only the greatest singer/songwriter in the history of America. You kids today think everything started with Lady Gaga. There was a lot of music before then. Centuries of it."

"We only have to cover twenty years," I say.

"Well you're in luck because Mr. Porter is in that period."

Dr. Macintosh doesn't live in as nice of a place as the Borsteins. His house is about what I expected, an old brownstone that's still in cherry condition. He opens the car door to help me down. Before I can say anything, he takes my backpack from me. He exaggerates a grunt and bends forward. "That's so heavy. What do you have in there, lead weights?"

I glare at him behind my glasses. "I wouldn't be so pear-shaped then, would I?"

He straightens up, chastised. "I'm sorry, Stacey. I was just goofing around." He sighs. "I thought maybe we could be friends, not just doctor-patient."

"I'm only here because the teacher made Darren and I work together," I say with a huff. Then I stomp up the steps. Darren's already got the door open. He's in the living room, his backpack tossed on top of a grand piano. Darren sits at the piano's bench and flexes his fingers. "You play the piano?"

"Yes."

"Darren's mom was a virtuoso," Dr. Macintosh says with a hint of sadness. "She played Carnegie Hall when she was thirteen."

"Wow, that's good," I say. I glance at Darren. "Are you going to play there?"

"I don't know."

Dr. Macintosh tries to brighten the mood. "Darren, why don't you play some Porter for Stacey? I'm sure she'd love to hear it."

I really don't want to hear more old music from my grandpa's generation, but I nod anyway. Darren plays the scales to warm up his fingers. Then he starts in on the song. I have no idea what it is. I don't really care either. I'm more interested in Darren. As he plays his face takes on a look of tranquility I've never seen before. As the song reaches its climax, he thumps the keys with authority.

When he finishes, I applaud. "That was beautiful," I say.

Darren's face reverts back to its unreadable mask. "Thanks."

Dr. Macintosh claps me on the shoulder. "Stacey here is quite an accomplished singer. Maybe you two could do a duet."

"I don't know the words," I say.

"No problem. I've got the lyrics right here." Dr. Macintosh presses sheets of music into my hands. I don't know what any of the funny symbols on the lines mean, but I can read the words. "Darren, why don't you play it through once and then Stacey can jump in the next time?"

"OK," Darren says. As he plays, I follow along on the paper to try to get a feel for the music. This is a lot easier in the karaoke bar.

During the song, I tug on Dr. Macintosh's shirt. He bends down so I can whisper in his ear, "What if I can't sing anymore?"

"I'm sure you can. I doubt it changed your vocal chords that much." I hate him a little when he tousles my hair. "Just give it a try."

So I do. My voice sounds higher, thinner. It's a little girl's voice, not a woman's voice like at the karaoke bar. I keep my eyes on the paper so I don't get lost. Darren is such a smooth player that he can cover up when I miss a word and circle back so I can pick it up.

As we finish, Dr. Macintosh applauds. "That was wonderful," he says.

"You're just saying that," I say.

"Lightning strike me if I'm lying." He waits theatrically, but no lightning hits him, much as I want it to. "See?"

Darren addresses his feet as he says, "You were good."

"So were you," I say. I look down at my feet too.

"Now kids, I don't mean to tell you your business—"

"That's all you do," I grumble.

"Maybe, but I think this is how you should do your presentation."

Darren and I go pale at the same time. "You want us to perform? In front of everyone?" he asks.

"Why not? You're both very talented. It would be a shame to waste that by reading an essay and playing MP3 clips."

"I don't know," I say. I remember that night in the karaoke bar. Though now no one should demand I take off my top. "It might work."

"Of course it will work. You just need to practice." Dr. Macintosh pats me on the back. "You're welcome to come over whenever you want. Right, Darren?"

"I guess," Darren says.

I tug on Dr. Macintosh's sleeve. "Can I talk to you in the kitchen?"

"Of course."

The kitchen is full of stainless steel appliances that look almost new. I doubt Dr. Macintosh cooks much. I sit on a stool at the island so I can more easily look him in the eye. "I know what you're doing," I hiss.

"What am I doing?"

"You're trying to hook me up with your nephew."

"By 'hook you up' you mean what exactly?"

"You want us to be friends because you think we're both shy little outcasts." I cross my arms. "I already have a friend."

"I see. So you think I have purely selfish motives here?"

"Yes. Isn't that against whatever oath you take?"

"I don't think it's compromising my ethics to encourage two shy children to be friends. Especially not when they've already been assigned to work together."

"And you want us to perform in public."

"Which you find scary after what happened at the karaoke bar, right?"

"Maybe."

He puts a hand on my shoulder again. "Stacey, you truly do have a beautiful voice. And Darren is every bit the player Mary Anne was."

"Mary Anne is your sister?"

"Yes."

"I thought she joined the Peace Corps and got knocked up?"

"She couldn't handle the pressure of her talent, so she joined the Peace Corps."

"Aren't you afraid Darren might crack up the same way?"

"I think it's more important to confront his fear of performing in public. Who better to help him than the most talented little singer I know?"

"You can't butter me up like that."

"I'm sorry. I forget you don't like me to praise your talent. You'd rather I said you're no good?"

"Maybe."

"That's too bad, because that would be a lie." He gives my shoulder a little shake. "Stacey, you said before you're not sure what you want to do with your life. Maybe this is the answer. Shouldn't you at least explore the option?"

"I don't know."

"It's just one school presentation. It'll be less than five minutes. Can't you give it a try?"

I sigh. I hate the way Dr. Macintosh makes things I don't want to do seem so reasonable. "I'll try," I say.

"Good." He helps me off the stool. "There are some other songs you two can try as well. Or if you want to try someone else, we can. Darren is good at playing by ear."

He leads me back to the living room and then we get started.

Chapter 30

I survive my first week of the fourth grade as Stacey Chang. To celebrate, I have my first real sleepover at Jamie's house. All Friday afternoon I check the clock and watch the minutes tick away. The closer the end of school gets, the less I can concentrate on my project with Darren. If he notices my agitation he doesn't say anything, which isn't unusual.

The bell finally rings to signal it's three o'clock. We have to wait until Ms. Lowry says, "Class dismissed. Have a good weekend, children." Then I can grab my backpack and dart out the door. I try to be quick so I can avoid Keshia.

I'm not quick enough. Just like in the cafeteria, one moment I walk under my own power and the next I fall forward. I put out my hands to break my fall, which only sends pain through both wrists as I hit the floor. My glasses bounce off my face to skitter a few inches away. I reach out to grab them, but they're enveloped by a dark brown blob.

"You lose something, Chopsticks?" Keshia says.

"Give back my glasses," I say. I scramble to my feet. Even at close range it's hard for me to see where Keshia has them. I flail at her, but she easily holds the glasses over my head. "Give them back! I need them."

I don't see her hand until it shoves me against the wall. "What are you going to do about it?" she growls.

There's not much I can do. Keshia is bigger, stronger, and she can see. All I can do is cry pathetically. "Give them back," I whine. I hate myself when I say, "I'll tell Ms. Lowry."

"Ooh, I'm so scared," Keshia says. "You think she's going to believe some dumb scholarship kid over the best student here?"

I can't see much around me, but I hear snickers accompany this. Apparently we've drawn a crowd. If they came to watch a fight they're going to be sorely disappointed because even if I do throw a punch it won't be much of a fight.

I'm saved by Ms. Lowry. "What is going on here?"

"Nothing, Ms. Lowry," Keshia says. "Stacey dropped her glasses. I was giving them back."

She presses the glasses into my hands. I put them on in time to see Keshia grin evilly at me, to dare me to tell Ms. Lowry. Much as I want to, I know that will only make my situation worse. "Thank you," I mumble.

"You should be more careful. Someone might break them next time," Keshia says. She tousles my hair like I'm a kindergartner and then saunters away with her cronies in tow.

I grab my backpack and then race out the door. I run across the quad, ignoring the taunts of older students, and then past the admin building. Maddy has just gotten into Tess's station wagon. I'm out of breath by the time I reach the car.

"Stacey! There you are. Are you all right, dear?" Tess asks.

"I'm...fine," I say. "Got a little...tied up."

Tess gets out of the car so she can unlock the tailgate. Inside is a pink Power Puff Girls sleeping bag and a pastel suitcase with flowers printed on it. Both of these belonged to Tess's daughter Jenny when she was my age. There's also my pink monkey, which Tess drapes over my neck. "Do you want me to take your backpack home?" she asks.

"I'll keep it," I say. I probably shouldn't because after Tess passes the sleeping bag and suitcase to me, I'm doubled over from the weight.

"Have a good time, dear. We'll see you on Sunday morning. If there are any problems at all, just call and we can come get you."

"Thanks," I say. I hope that won't be necessary. I take a few steps back then and hope Keshia doesn't show up again to trip me. Not that she'd be so stupid to do it in front of an adult.

I watch Tess drive away. Maddy turns to wave at me. I'd like to wave back, but my hands are too full. I hope she'll be all right by herself tonight. She seems to be fine, but you never can tell when the next tantrum will happen.

I feel a hand on my shoulder and cry out. It's not Keshia, this time. "Not exactly a light packer, are you?" Jamie says.

"My grandma packed for me."

Jamie takes the sleeping bag from me and then leads me to the car. The driver gets out to take my suitcase. He puts it in the trunk and then we're on our way.

***

Once we get back to Jamie's place, we go back to her bedroom like before. This time she has a surprise for me.

It's a digital camera that she picks up from her desk to aim at me. "What's that for?" I ask.

"So we can get some glamour shots of you," she says. She motions me over to her desk. She opens her laptop and then brings up Facebook. Only it's not for her account—it's a page for Stacey Chang. The wall is blank at the moment and there's a generic avatar instead of a picture. I already have one friend in Jamie. "You don't mind, do you? I thought it'd be easier to do it here without your grandparents around."

"That's cool," I say, though inside I feel a nervous flutter. I really don't want to be on Facebook, where any stranger in the world can see me. Dr. Ling might be dead, but there are still plenty of creeps out there who might want to do nasty things to a little girl. Still, I know how much it would hurt Jamie if I don't do it; like most girls her age she practically lives on Facebook.

So for the next hour I let Jamie stage a photo shoot for me. First she brings out a case full of cosmetics. "These were my mom's," Jamie says with a note of sadness. Then she starts to slather on rouge and eyeshadow. Like most girls her age she puts too much on, so I look like a cheap whore. When Jamie goes to the bathroom, I wipe some of it off with a tissue so it's a little more subtle.

When we get to the actual pictures, she makes me sit on the bed. "You should take the glasses off," she says.

"I like the glasses."

"People will think you're a geek."

"You don't think I'm a geek, do you?"

"Me? I think you're a total geek," Jamie says with a smile.

I throw my pink monkey at her, but it sails wide to hit the wall. "Just hurry up and take the pictures." We take a couple normal ones. Then she asks me to make some funny faces. I haven't made funny faces into a camera in forty years, at least sober. All I can think to do is stick my tongue out.

"Come on, you can do more than that."

"Like what?"

She crosses her eyes and folds her tongue in half like a slice of pizza. "Gross!" I shout. "I can't do that."

"Try it. It's totally not hard."

I stick my tongue out again and try to fold it the way she did. My tongue wobbles but stays flat. Jamie shakes her head. She steps over to the bed and grabs my tongue with one hand to fold it in half. "Like that."

Try as I might, I can't get it right. "You're hopeless," she says with a sigh.

I try something I used to do back when I was a little boy. I roll my eyes back until I can't see anything. "Oh my God, that is so gross!" Jamie shouts. "I love it!" She takes a few pictures of me like that.

For the last batch she puts the camera on the desk and then sets the timer. We squeeze together in front of the camera and smile broadly. In a couple of other ones she does the thing with her tongue and I do the thing with my eyes. We wind up in a giggling heap on the floor.

"Those are going to be so awesome," she says.

"You think so?"

"Trust me," she says with a laugh. I watch as she connects the camera to the computer so she can transfer the pictures. It's a lot easier than in my day where you had to go to a store and wait hours or even days to have the film developed unless you were lucky enough to have a Polaroid.

In minutes I can see the pictures blown up on the screen. My face turns warmer as I see how adorable I look, even when my slanted eyes are rolled back to show just the whites. There's the surreal moment where I have to remind myself that's my face on the screen, me with the red-framed glasses, thick bangs, and shy smile.

"Are you all right?" Jamie asks. "You aren't going to puke, are you?"

"What? No," I say and force myself to smile. "I'm just surprised how good these are."

"I told you I know what I'm doing," she says.

I think about calling home, but I know Jamie would take that as an affront, as if I don't want to be here. So I try to relax while she starts to set up my Facebook page. She wants to use one of the goofy pictures of me as my avatar. "Don't you dare!" I shout.

"Come on, it'll be funny," she says. As she pushes the button, I roll over on the bed; I don't want to see it. Everyone will think I'm a freak. "OK, here it is."

I look up. To the left I see one of my nice pictures. Beside that is my name and location. Before I can say anything, Jamie snaps a picture of me. Thirty seconds later I can see how I look, a mixture of horror and relief on my face. I give her a playful slap on the arm. "Don't scare me like that!"

"All right," Jamie says, "now it's time to make some friends."

***

By dinner I have thirty friends on Facebook. They're Jamie's friends who only accept my request because I'm her friend. My wall has a few standard greetings from these new friends; they welcome me and hope to see me around. As stupid as it is, I feel some satisfaction with this. Maybe I don't know these people for real, but at least they know I exist.

"So what do you want to say?" Jamie asks.

"I don't know. What am I supposed to say?"

"Whatever you want."

She slides over so I can use the keyboard. What do I say to all of my new friends? I should try to say something funny, something to endear them to me. I can't think of anything. As Steve and Stacey, no one's ever said I'm a laugh riot. So I just type, "Hi everyone! It's great to meet you!" The exclamation points are a bit much, but they make it sound perkier than a period, or at least that's what I think.

"That's it?" Jamie says.

"What else should I say?"

"Here, slide over." I do so and watch Jamie type in a message that's ostensibly from me. It says, "I'm sleeping over with Jamie Borstein tonight. We're gonna eat sooooo much popcorn, LOL." She posts it and then says, "It's not great, but it's a start."

"Is that what we're doing tonight?"

"Maybe. You're not allergic to popcorn, are you?"

"No."

"Caleb is allergic to peanuts. His face gets all puffy and red if he eats something that even touched a peanut. It's pretty gross." Jamie smiles evilly at me. "We should totally give him a peanut and then take pictures."

"What? No! That's gross!"

"I'm just teasing. You are soooo gullible."

"Am not."

"Here, I'm going to type that in. 'I am so gullible I believe whatever Jamie tells me.'"

"Don't!"

Jamie starts to laugh. "Got you again!" She rubs her hands together with glee. "We are going to have so much fun tonight!"

"Gee, I can hardly wait."

***

Though I'm not hungry after dinner, Jamie insists we have a big bowl of popcorn while we watch movies in the living room. About a year ago Maddy and I had a sleepover that ended when Grace came over so they could reconcile while I stupidly snuck out to finish off Artie Luther. Before that happened, Maddy and I watched *Twilight* in the same way Jamie and I watch TV now, on the floor in sleeping bags. The only difference is Jamie is partial to *Harry Potter* movies.

Not for the eponymous character, as it turns out. She likes the redheaded boy, Ron Weasley. Whenever he comes on the screen, she gives a little sigh. "It's too bad they aren't making any more of these," Jamie says. "I wish they could go on forever."

"That would be great," I say, though I've never seen any of the movies.

Jamie picks up on this. "Have you even seen these before?"

"Not really."

"Oh my God! You cannot be serious. These are the best! The books are even better. You haven't read those either, have you?"

"No."

She shakes her head sadly, to pity me. "What do you like?"

"I mostly read Nancy Drew books."

"Nancy Drew? Seriously?" Jamie smiles at me. "That is so retro. You probably still play with Barbies too."

"No," I say. Then I add, "Well, sometimes. If Maddy asks me."

"No way!" Jamie shakes her head again. "I forget sometimes you're only ten."

"I'm not a baby!" I say and sound just like Maddy.

"Stay here a second." Jamie scrambles out of her sleeping bag to run back to her room. I assume she's gone to get her phone so we can play on Facebook or something. Instead she returns with a book: *Harry Potter and the Philosopher's Stone*. "This is a first edition, from England. Mom got it when she went over there for a conference or something. She bought the first five because the others weren't out yet. I couldn't read them on my own so she read them to me at bedtime."

"That's so sweet," I say.

"Yeah, she was really sweet." Jamie's eyes water, but then she forces herself to smile. "I'll read a little to you tonight, but then you're on your own, OK?"

"OK." I snuggle closer to her in my sleeping bag and then listen while she reads to me from the book.

I'm not sure when I fall asleep, but the next thing I know, someone shakes me. Jamie whispers, "Come on, Stacey. You can't go to sleep yet. It's not even midnight."

"It's not?" It feels to me like it should be two in the morning, but maybe that's what happens when you start to go to bed at eight-thirty instead of midnight. "How long was I asleep?"

"Long enough to start snoring."

"I don't snore!"

"Do so. You sound like a chainsaw." She imitates my snoring, which sounds like a pig as it chokes on something.

"I don't sound like that!"

She ignores this and pulls her phone out from her sleeping bag. "I wanted to show you something. I found this really cool app the other day." She pushes a few buttons on the phone and then turns the phone lengthwise.

When she shows me the screen, I see a Ouija board, like the kind kids played with in my day to predict stuff, only this one is all digital. "A Ouija board?" I say.

"Yeah, it's cool. You ask it a question about the future and it gives you an answer."

"Don't you need to be psychic or something to make that work? I mean, how can a computer tell you the future?"

"Maybe it's a psychic computer. We don't have to play if you're scared."

"I'm not scared. I just don't think a computer can tell the future."

"Then what's it going to hurt to play?"

She has me there. I sigh and say, "Fine. What do we ask it?"

Jamie thinks for a moment and then starts to type. "What is the first name of my first boyfriend," she says as she types.

We watch as the cursor begins to tremble and then move around the digital board. The first letter is 'E.' Then comes 'R,' followed by 'I' and 'C.' The cursor comes to rest. "Eric," Jamie says. "I wonder if it means Eric Jules?"

"Who?"

"He's on the JV basketball team. Oh my God, he is so cute. He's got curly blond hair and this really cute little scar on his left cheek from when he fell on the steps when he was a kid."

"How do you know so much about him? Haven't you only been here like two months?"

"One of my friends is a friend of his on Facebook. I sent him a friend request but he didn't answer it. Jerk."

"And he's going to be your boyfriend?"

"I hope so." Jamie sighs just like when she sees Ron Weasley on the screen. "I think I'll start getting the wedding invitations printed. Mrs. Jamie Jules."

I giggle at this. "That sounds silly."

"Shut up." She taps the phone. "Let's see who it picks for you. It probably won't do anything because you're too little to even like boys."

"I am not! I like boys."

"Who do you like, then?"

"Lots of them."

"That's what I thought," she says and then sticks out her tongue.

I slide away from her. "This game is stupid," I complain.

"Come on, Stacey. We can ask it something else if you're too scared to play."

"I don't care."

"Fine. Let's see—" her voice trails off and then she begins to type. "Who is going to be Stacey's first kiss?"

"Don't ask it that!" I shout. If this thing is any kind of psychic at all, it'll bring up a girl's name. I can only imagine the grief Jamie will give me for that.

I'm too late to stop her; she's already hit the button. There's nothing to do as the cursor moves around. As it does, I start to feel sick to my stomach. After a minute the cursor finally stops. D-A-R-R-E-N. Darren is my first kiss.

"Who's Darren?" Jamie says.

"I don't know," I say, a little too quickly.

Jamie stares at me and then starts to laugh. "Oh my God! The weird kid under the slide! He's your first kiss."

"Shut up!" I shout. "I don't even like him. We're just working on the project together."

"Stacey and Darren sitting in a tree—"

She has to stop when I hit her in the jaw with my pillow. This isn't a playful pillow fight blow, but one intended to hurt. Her taunting rhyme ends with a cry of pain. "Ouch! You little brat! I bit my tongue."

She grabs her pillow and hits me in the side of the head hard enough to make me tumble onto my side. Before I can sit up, she's on top of me to pin my arms down. We're wrestling like this when Mr. Borstein shouts, "What the hell is going on in here?"

Jamie slides off of me. Her face turns red as she faces her father. "We were just playing, Daddy," she says.

"That didn't look like playing to me."

Being the youngest one in the room, I'm the one who breaks first. Though I don't want to, I start to cry. "I'm sorry, Mr. Borstein. It's my fault. Jamie and I were playing and I got mad and I hit her with a pillow." I sniffle and then add, "I'll call my grandpa to pick me up."

Jamie's father tousles my hair. "You don't have to do that, sweetheart. I'm sure Jamie is as much at fault as you are. Aren't you?"

"Yes, Daddy," Jamie says, sincere enough that I believe her. She pulls me into a hug. "I'm sorry, Stacey. It was a stupid game anyway."

"I'm sorry too."

"That's good, girls. Now clean up this mess and then get to bed, all right?"

"Yes, Daddy," Jamie says.

"Thank you, Mr. Borstein," I say.

He tousles my hair again. "It's all right."

Then he leaves us to clean up spilled popcorn and the rest of our mess. While I clean, I make sure to tap a button on Jamie's phone to shut down the Ouija app that still showed Darren's name on it.

***

I asked Tess for a sleeping bag because I figured Jamie and I would sleep in the living room. After we clean up, she starts back to the bedroom. "Where are you going?"

"To bed. Where else?"

"Oh." I follow her to the bedroom and drag my sleeping bag with me. Jamie's room is big enough that there's plenty of room on the floor for me to stretch out.

As I smooth out the sleeping bag on the floor, Jamie asks, "What are you doing?"

"What's it look like? Going to bed."

"You don't have to sleep on the floor." She pats the mattress of her bed. "You can sleep with me. Unless you think I have cooties or something."

"No," I say. The bed is a queen size, with more than enough room for two little girls. As I climb on the bed, I tell myself that Jamie and I aren't going to "sleep together" in the sense that Grace and I slept together. It'll be like when Maddy and I share a bed as sisters.

I make sure to keep my pink monkey between us. Jamie has an ordinary brown teddy bear she clutches to her chest. "You got enough covers?"

"I'm fine," I say.

With a yawn she says, "G'night, Stacey."

"Goodnight, Jamie."

Chapter 31

The next day is the most fun I've had as Stacey Chang. A Mercedes sedan waits to drive us around after breakfast. Travis sits in the front seat, which leaves us kids to squeeze into the back. I sit in the middle again, Jamie leans close to me, and Caleb presses against the door to look out the window.

Jamie instructs the driver to take us to the downtown shopping district. Along the way, Jamie and I play against each other in a Facebook trivia game. She of course trounces me. Then she gloats about it to all of our online friends. "You're just a lot faster ringing in," I say, which is true. I couldn't remember which button on the phone to hit ninety percent of the time.

"You snooze, you lose," she says and then sticks out her tongue at me.

"Yeah, well, we'll see about that."

The next game doesn't go any better than the first. I'm still too slow for Jamie and a lot of the pop culture questions are more tween-oriented. I manage to get twenty points more than last time, not that it matters since Jamie scores even higher.

I'm grateful we pull up to Macy's then. The driver lets us out by the sidewalk so we just have to walk inside.

It's still difficult because we have to fight through the crowds on the sidewalk. Jamie takes my hand so we don't get lost as we snake our way through the throng.

I haven't been inside the department store in twelve years. Back then I was a thirty-nine-year-old man who wanted an expensive piece of jewelry that might save his marriage. With only a policeman's salary, I had to buy a pair of diamond earrings. Debbie liked them, but it was too little, too late to salvage things between us.

This time I can barely see over the jewelry counter. I have even less money, so I just stand back while Jamie studies the necklaces. She finds something she wants and then starts to bark at the salesgirl like an old pro. "Don't bother gift wrapping it," Jamie says. "We'll wear it out."

I assume she meant the royal we until she turns to me and presents me with a red cardboard box. "What's this?"

"Open it and find out, dummy," she says.

I open the box and see a silver necklace. It's one of those half-heart necklaces. My half says, "ST ENDS EVER." Jamie has the other half of the heart. When we put them together, they spell out the full message: BEST FRIENDS FOREVER. Though there are millions of similar necklaces around the city, my eyes still tear up. "This is so sweet," I say. "No one's ever done something like this for me before."

For the first time, Jamie acts shy; her cheeks redden. "I thought we should make it official," she says.

We share a hug. Then we put the necklaces on each other's necks. Now in a small way we're bonded. As we skip away from the jewelry counter to show the necklaces off to Travis and Caleb, I wonder why Maddy, Grace, and I hadn't ever done anything like this. If Maddy and I ever do get back to being ourselves again, I'll have to buy her a necklace so she'll know how important she is to me.

***

It's a lot different to shop with Jamie than with Maddy and Grace. It's not just that we shop in a different section of the store. The stores we visit are different too. Jamie is too young for liberal guilt, so she shops at the Gap, Old Navy, and similarly commercial stores instead of vintage shops.

Jamie takes it upon herself to update my wardrobe. When I try to resist and say I don't have the money, she says, "Daddy won't mind."

"Are you sure?"

"He doesn't care, so long as I don't try to buy a Ferrari or something."

"What if you did?"

"I'd be paying for it out of my allowance for a long, long time." We laugh at this and then Jamie takes a T-shirt off the rack. It's pink, which to this point I've always avoided. When she holds it up against me, I shift uncomfortably. "I think that would look great on you."

"It's a little girly," I say.

"Well, duh. You're a girl."

"That's true." In the end I let her buy the shirt. I don't want to offend her. Besides, nothing says I actually have to wear it. Maybe I'll have to wear it once so Jamie can see me in it.

"We should get something really cute for the presentation," she says.

She finds a red dress I'm sure Tess would not approve of. The skirt barely touches my knees and the neck dips to the point it would show off my cleavage if I had any. "Hey, it matches your glasses," Jamie says.

She's right about that. That makes me love the dress. "I guess I'll try it on," I say. In the mirror I see it's just as short and revealing as I thought. I smooth the red fabric over my potbelly; maybe I can lose a few pounds before the presentation. I step out of the dressing room so Jamie can see me in it. "You think it's too short?"

"You look great. But you need some pretty shoes to go with it."

I feel an icy hand grip my stomach. It took me a while to walk in heels as a grown-up; I don't want to try it as a kid. My fears are assuaged when Jamie picks out a pair of red flats. "Wow, you look awesome," she says.

"You think so?"

"Oh yeah. Keshia is going to be so jealous."

"I hope not. She'll probably try to beat me up again."

"You'll be fine." Jamie grins at me. "You want to look good for Darren, don't you? Then he'll kiss you for sure."

I slap her on the arm. "Shut up!"

Jamie gets a dress similar to mine, only it's light blue. We have both of them boxed up so we don't get them wrinkled before our big night. I feel like Princess Stacey again as the driver takes our purchases and loads them into the trunk.

Caleb didn't go with us into the clothes stores. Travis took him to the arcade so he could blow a few dollars on the machines there while he waited for us. "What took so long?" he whines.

"None of your business," Jamie snaps.

From there we go to the movie theater. After some negotiation between Jamie and Caleb, they agree to *Dolphin Tale*, in 2D because Jamie claims the 3D glasses give her a headache. "They don't make prescription ones for Stacey either," she says and then sticks her tongue out at me.

Jamie and I get a tub of popcorn to share, along with two sodas and a box of Sno Caps. Caleb just gets candy and soda, enough that I'm sure he'll be bouncing off the walls before the movie is half over. We find seats in the middle of the theater. Jamie insists I sit on the aisle next to her.

We munch our snacks and sip our sodas while the previews play. I think of my date with Seth that seems like a million years ago. How long will it be before I can go on another date with a boy? It might be years unless Dr. Palmer can change Maddy and I back.

About ten minutes into the movie, Jamie bumps her soda in the cupholder between us. The soda topples over to splash onto my jeans. I cry out and leap to my feet. "I'm so sorry," Jamie says. She takes my hand while people begin to hiss for us to be quiet and get out of the way. "I'll help her clean up," she whispers to Travis.

I wait until we're out of the theater to ask, "Why did you do that?"

"It was an accident."

"Was not. You did it on purpose."

"I did not!"

"I saw you." I start to tear up as I reach for my necklace. "I thought we were friends."

"We are," Jamie says. She leans close to me and then whispers, "I needed something to get us out of there."

"What?"

Jamie pulls me towards another theater a couple doors down. The digital sign over the door indicates this theater is for *Dream House*. She puts a finger to her lips to keep me quiet as we slip through the door.

In my day it was a lot harder to sneak into a movie. The theaters had ushers to make sure no one got unruly. You also had employees who gave a shit. Now it's so easy that the only difficulty will be to get the soda stain off my jeans. No one stops us or even questions us as we take seats near the back of the theater.

Jamie can't resist a triumphant snicker. "You get it now?" she asks.

"Won't Travis figure it out?"

"He won't care."

We slouch down into our seats just to make sure no do-gooder adult tattles on us. I can't help but feel a giddy thrill at this act of rebellion. It's been a long time since I did anything like this.

The movie follows most of the standard horror movie formula. A lot of things go bump in the night. While I've seen a lot worse than anything in the movie in my police career, I still feel a nervous tremor. As the movie goes on, I begin to curl up tighter and tighter in my seat. I glance over at Jamie, who is just as nervous.

By the end I peek over my arm until something scary happens. Then I cover my face and whimper. I keep my face covered for probably the last fifteen minutes and during the credits. Even as the lights go on I'm scared to look up, afraid of what I might see.

When someone touches my shoulder, I scream. "It's over now, girls," an old woman says. She sounds a lot like Tess, but I know Tess couldn't be here. I finally look up to see the old woman wears a theater uniform.

I expect Jamie to make fun of me, but her face is pale and she trembles as she uncurls from her chair. "Is it over?" she asks, her voice tiny.

"It's over," the woman repeats. "You two should go before you get in trouble."

I take Jamie's hand and lead her up the aisle. Back in the safety of the lobby, Jamie sighs with relief. "Oh my God, that was soooo scary," she says. "I almost wet my pants."

"Me too."

We find Travis and Caleb in the lobby. Caleb plays with his phone on a bench, oblivious. "You guys done?" Travis asks. I take it from his reaction he knows we snuck into a different movie, but won't bust us for it. Jamie probably does this all the time.

"We're done," Jamie says.

***

The cook has the night off, so we have a couple of pizzas delivered. Caleb refuses to eat any toppings or to pick them off, so he gets a cheese pizza. Jamie and I eat a Hawaiian one with pineapple, ham, and bacon despite that her father's half-assed Judaism prohibited pork. "He won't find out if we eat it all," Jamie says with a sly grin.

I'm not all that hungry after the movie, but I pitch in to do my part. There's a special *iCarly* on, so we sit in front of the sixty-inch TV to watch that. It's better with Jamie right here instead of texting me a thousand times while I try to watch.

"I want a loft like that when I get older," Jamie says. "We can share it."

"That would be great," I say and mean it. If I have to grow up again, it wouldn't be so bad if Jamie and I could be roommates. "Here or back in Miami?"

"Here, I suppose. Though Seattle might be cool too." Jamie says that's where *iCarly* takes place.

"I've heard it rains a lot there," I say. Although this is a hypothetical scenario I wouldn't want to move too far from the city, not unless Maddy comes with us.

"That's true. But we won't be outside that much. We'll be inside, kissing boys. Me and Eric and you and Darren."

"Shut up!" I squeal. I grab a couch pillow to give her a little tap on the shoulder. "I don't like Darren. He's weird."

"Sure, that's why you went over to his house."

"That was just for the project."

"Whatever you say." In a more ominous tone she adds, "The Ouija board never lies."

I've forgotten about the scary movie, at least until it's time for bed. It's been a long, long time since I was scared of the dark, yet as soon as Jamie turns off the light, I shiver. At any moment I expect something to burst out of the closet or from under the bed.

"Jamie?"

"Huh?"

"Do you think maybe we could leave the light on tonight?"

"I guess," she says. From the way she doesn't chide me about being a scared little baby, I know she's rattled too. She hops out of bed to turn the light back on. Then we go to sleep and cling to each other for protection from monsters.

Chapter 32

Jamie's father must not work on Sunday mornings, as he's the one who takes me back to Jake's house. Jamie comes along to keep me company. After breakfast we showed him our necklaces and the new clothes we bought. He's especially impressed when we come out in our new dresses. "Where'd my daughter and her friend Stacey go? All I see are these two little beauty queens," he says.

"Dad-dy, don't be silly," Jamie says, but she smiles at the compliment anyway.

As we pull up to Jake's house, Jamie says, "I'll text you later so you can tell me how your grandma freaks out when she sees that dress."

"She's not going to freak out that much," I say, or at least I hope she doesn't.

We hug and then I get out of the car. Mr. Borstein takes my packages, as well as my sleeping bag and suitcase. I take my backpack and my pink monkey. To my relief, Tess is there to greet us at the door. She doesn't look any worse for wear either.

She just about knocks the monkey out of my hand as she squeezes me in a hug. "Hello, dear. How was your sleepover?"

I try to answer, but my mouth is muffled by her chest. I'm saved by Mr. Borstein. He sets down the suitcase so he can shake Tess's hand. "Hello, Mrs. Madigan. I'm Gary Borstein, Jamie's father."

"It's good to meet you. I hope Stacey hasn't been too much trouble."

"Oh this one is nothing but trouble," Mr. Borstein says. He gives me a playful wink. "But seriously, Stacey is a wonderful girl. You must be so proud."

"We certainly are."

I sneak into the house, eager to find Maddy. She's not in the living room, despite that cartoons are still on the TV. I hurry up to the bedroom, where I find her in front of the vanity, as she brushes out her damp hair. She only wears a towel around her midsection. I say, "Hi."

She turns to me and smiles. "Hi!" Maddy gives me a hug that's not as tight as Tess's, but still pretty firm. The towel miraculously stays on throughout this. "You're just in time. We were going to leave for church in a few minutes."

"You were?"

"Yes. Grandma said we should go to the later service in case you showed up."

"That's great," I say, though I'm not really in the mood to get dressed up and go to church.

"It is. Then you can meet my new friends."

"New friends?" I say. I wonder if she'll show me a couple of stuffed toys.

"Margarita and Anita. They're both really nice and they have a playhouse in their backyard for tea parties and stuff and they've got a doggy named Amarillo because he's yellow."

I think of the dog Maddy used to own, a golden retriever named Max. It makes sense she would like kids who have a similar dog. If they're real and not her imagination. She might have made them up just to get even with me for sleeping over at Jamie's house this weekend.

I change into my church dress and then run a comb through my hair. My eyes are a little red from a lack of sleep, but I look presentable. Maddy looks much better, her hair smooth after the brushing she gave it; her cheeks glow with excitement.

Jamie and her father are gone by the time I get back downstairs. Tess waits down in the living room. She smooths my hair and dress. "So what all did you and your new friend do?" she asks.

"We went shopping and saw a movie and Jamie bought this for me. She has the other half so we'll always know we're best friends," I say in one childish gush. I fish my necklace from under my dress so Tess can see it

"That's very nice, dear," she says, but her face clouds with sadness.

"What's wrong, Grandma?"

"Nothing, dear. It's a very pretty necklace."

Then it hits me: Jenny had a necklace like this when she was a kid. Maddy, as Jenny's best friend, had the other half. I hide the necklace under my dress again. "I'm sorry, Grandma."

"Don't be, dear. You didn't do anything wrong."

I give her a hug anyway. Then she says, "I should go check on your sister."

Maddy bounds down the steps a minute later. "Do I look all right, Grandma?"

"You're very pretty, dear."

"Margarita and Anita will be there, won't they?"

"I'm not sure, dear. They might not go to the same church."

"But they have to. I want to show them my dress."

Maddy's face starts to redden as if she's about to throw a tantrum. Tess is quick to defuse it; she puts an arm around Maddy. "If they aren't there, we can go over to visit them later, so long as it's all right with their mother."

"OK."

Jake, with a good sense of timing, stays in his study until then. "The prodigal granddaughter returns," he says.

"I wasn't prodigal. It wasn't even two days."

"I'm just teasing." He makes an exaggerated groan as he scoops Maddy from off the floor. "All right, time for you little heathens to go to church."

***

The church is built in the colonial New England style, complete with a white steeple. I've been inside a few times, most notably for Jake's wedding. Jake was brought up as a Methodist, but converted for Tess once they got serious. Not that it was that big of a conversion, just a few different rituals to learn.

As senior members of the congregation, Jake and Tess have seats in the second row. They aren't explicitly reserved, but everyone knows to leave them vacant. For a while I sat in that row as their adopted daughter; I leaned against the end of the pew while I tried not to fall asleep.

The first time I came here as Stacey Chance, I heard murmurs among the parishioners as they wondered who was this pale, skinny girl with the Madigans. The reverend eventually cleared it up when he announced Jake and Tess had taken me in as foster parents. Though I went to the church for a year, I never did feel like part of the congregation.

Everything is amplified as we enter the church; I hold Tess's hand and Jake holds Maddy's. The whispers are even more insistent and heads turn to catch glimpses of us. Needless to say there aren't any other Chinese girls in the congregation.

Not quite as out of place is a Hispanic woman and two little girls. One is a couple years younger but has her hair done just like mine and wears glasses that aren't as thick. The other girl is closer to Maddy's age, her hair in pigtails with ribbons that match her yellow dress. Maddy waves to them and they wave back. Maddy tries to pull away from Jake, but he keeps a tight grip on her hand.

"Can't we sit with them?" she asks.

"Not today," Jake says.

"But—"

"You can see them after the service."

I worry Maddy will have another tantrum in the church, but she doesn't. "OK," she says and then lets Jake steer her to the second row. I take my usual seat with Tess beside me. Maddy is on the far side, next to Jake. That way we can't get into any mischief.

As probably the most senior member of the church, Minnie has a seat in the front row. She turns to give us a big grin. "Such adorable children," she says. "Let's see, it was Stacey and Morgan?"

"Madison," Maddy says.

"Oh, dear me, I'm sorry. You look very pretty, Madison."

"Tank you," she says in her cute lisp.

"Stacey looks very cute too."

"Thank you," I say out of obligation.

"Stacey is a little shy," Tess says.

Like before, there comes the awkward moment when the reverend says, "And we'd like to take a moment to welcome some very special guests. Jacob and Teresa Madigan have opened their hearts once again to take in two precious little girls: Stacey and Madison." I want to slouch down in my seat, but Tess has a hand on my back. My cheeks burn with embarrassment to have a hundred people stare at me. "Now, let's bow our heads and pray."

***

Maddy's new friends wait for her outside. Before we can meet them, we have to endure more attention from the reverend. He bends down so he's eye level with us and then shakes each of our hands in turn. "Welcome, Stacey. Welcome, Madison. I hope you enjoyed today's service."

"Yes," we say together.

He mercifully turns his attention to Tess and Jake then. While Jake answers how we came to live with him, Maddy tugs on Tess's sleeve. "Can I go see Margarita and Anita, Grandma?"

"Very well, dear, but stay where I can see you. Stacey, go with her."

"Yes, ma'am," I say. Maddy breaks into a run, to rush over to her new friends. They bounce up and down a little with excitement to see each other again.

Maddy nods to me and says, "This is my big sister, Stacey. She's ten."

"Hi," I say.

"You guys want to play tag?" Maddy asks. Then she slaps my arm. "Stacey is it!"

The girls scatter in three different directions. I jog along the front lawn of the church while Maddy and her friends dart between groups of milling parishioners. They scream like banshees as they run, especially if I get anywhere near them.

I finally catch Margarita and tap her on the shoulder. "You're it," I say. Then it's my turn to run.

Margarita catches her sister Anita, who takes losing as gracefully as Maddy would. "No fair!" Anita shouts. "You cheated!"

"Did not!"

They squabble for a minute, until Maddy takes charge. "No one cheated," she says with authority despite her small size. "You're it, Anita."

"I don't wanna be it."

"Too bad." Maddy glares at Anita, to dare the other girl to challenge her. Anita doesn't. "You gotta wait ten seconds for us to get a head start."

"OK," Anita says, chastised.

We play until Margarita and Anita's mother comes to collect them. Tess isn't far behind. "Grandma, can I go over to play with Margarita and Anita later?" Maddy asks.

"Have you finished all your homework?"

"Yes."

"Then you may if it's all right with Mrs. Vasquez."

It is all right with Mrs. Vasquez. Maddy and her new friends say goodbye; they promise to see each other soon. I feel like the fifth wheel as I stand off to the side throughout all this.

On the way home, Maddy nudges me in the ribs. She hisses, "You're not the only one who can make friends."

Chapter 33

Jamie isn't at recess on Monday. She and Caleb have their appointments with Dr. Macintosh in the afternoon. Maddy, motivated to add even more friends than the Vasquez sisters, attempts to teach Marcy the Swiss girl how to jump rope. The way Maddy barks at Marcy, I doubt their friendship will ever blossom. Next time I see Dr. Macintosh I should probably mention the bossiness that's accompanied Maddy's push to make friends. It's good, though, to see her with some of her old confidence back.

With nothing else to do, I sit on the lawn and play with my phone. There are always messages to read and links to click on, despite that most of my two hundred "friends" should be in school right now. This gets boring after a few minutes, so I decide to look for something else to do.

I see Darren in his usual place under the slide. He scribbles something in his notebook, probably more music. Is he writing a symphony? Maybe an opera. I bet Darren is the type who would like opera, though to me it sounds like someone running a bag of cats through a wood chipper. After a week as partners, he shouldn't hide his music from me. We've sung Cole Porter songs at his uncle's house, so what's the big deal if I see his magna opus?

I borrow a little of Maddy's attitude as I stomp over to the slide. Without permission, I sit down next to him. "How's it going?" I ask.

"Fine."

"Is that the same thing you were working on last week?"

"No. It's something else."

"Really? What?"

I try to peek over his shoulder, but he blocks me with his body. "Leave me alone!" he shouts.

"I'm just curious. Come on, we're partners. Can't we be friends too? Don't you like me?"

"Yes."

"You do?"

"Yes," he says again. It's hard to hear him; his voice sounds like someone's got a vise around his windpipe. "I do like you."

"I like you too, Darren. So why can't I see what you're doing?"

"It's not finished yet," he says.

"I don't care about that."

"I can't show it to anyone until it's done."

"That's stupid."

"Is not."

"Is too."

"Is not."

I sigh and shake my head. It's like when I argue with Maddy. "Fine, be that way. I don't want to see your stupid symphony anyway." That's an old interrogation trick, to supply an answer and hope the perp corrects you with the right one. Darren doesn't fall for it.

I take out my phone and feign like I'm checking messages. I even give a fake laugh as if I see something funny. Darren finally relaxes a little; he doesn't shield the notebook from me quite so much. While I still pretend to text message on the phone, I shift it to my left hand. With my right, I go for the notebook.

I snatch it off his lap before he can stop me. He is quick, though; he grabs one end of it with his hand. He tries to tug it out of my grasp. "Stop it!" he yells. "You're going to rip it!"

"Am not!" We play tug-of-war with the notebook for a minute, until finally it shoots out of both of our hands. Darren is taller than me, but I'm faster than him. I catch the notebook in midair and then roll onto my side. He actually falls over me as he tries to grab it away from me.

Finally I can see what he's so embarrassed about. It's a song, a song about *me*:

Stacey, you brighten my days;
Like a summer sun's warm rays;
When I see you I don't know what to say;
Except, "I hope you'll stay."

There's more, but by then my eyes are already too watery to read. Maybe Darren isn't John Fogerty yet, but it's a good start. An even better start because he wrote it about me. "Oh my God," I whisper.

"It's stupid, I know," he says. He tries to take the notebook back, but I won't let him. He gives one last feeble tug before he gives up. "I was still working on the bridge."

"No one's ever done anything like this for me before," I say. This goes beyond the necklace Jamie bought for me;

this is something Darren made from his heart for me. Never had I dreamed someone could think me worthy of a song, not me with my glasses, potbelly, and terminal shyness. "You really wrote this for me?"

He looks down at the ground. "Yes."

We're drawn as if by a magnet towards each other. It's not a seamless merger; we bang our upper teeth together. Our cheeks turn red at the same moment. "Sorry," we say in unison. Then we try it again.

My first kiss as a little girl is what you'd expect: dry and brief, little more than a peck. Yet when we pull back, I sigh as if he's just ravished me. I stare at him and see him in a new light: Darren, my adorable troubadour. Why didn't I ever notice before how cute he is, even with the glasses? Or what a perfect couple we make: him at the piano and me singing his words?

Just like that I have my first boyfriend. Never doubt the power of the Ouija board.

Part 5
Childhood's End

Chapter 34

Dr. Palmer could hear them long before she saw the girls. Half the pediatric ward could hear them squabble. "That's mine, give it back!" Madison shouts.

"Is not! Grandma bought it for me," Stacey shoots back.

"You don't even play with it."

"I am now."

"Gramma!" Madison wails.

Even from down the hallway and through a door, Dr. Palmer can hear the exasperation in Tess's voice as she says, "That's enough, children. Put the toys away or I'll take them from you."

"No fair," Madison says with a whimper.

Tess must not realize how loud the kids are and how shitty the hospital's soundproofing is, as she says, "I want you both to be on your best behavior for the doctor. If you're very good, Grandma will take you for ice cream."

The girls cheer at this. Dr. Palmer shakes her head. It's hard to believe five months ago these were two young women, one nineteen and the other twenty-three. Even harder to believe eighteen months ago one used to be a fifty-year-old man.

Now that the girls have been sufficiently bribed, Tess finally opens the door. She looks as tired as she sounds, her skin gray and hair dull, the effects of chasing after two little girls every day. Still, Tess forces a smile to her face. Dr. Palmer can't be positive, but she's fairly sure the lines on Tess's face have deepened. She looks more like a grandmother all the time.

"Hello, Doctor. I've brought your two little patients."

"Mr. Madigan couldn't make it?"

"He's working some overtime," Tess says with a sigh. It isn't cheap to raise two little girls. Dr. Palmer has offered to help the Madigans out, but they refuse to take any money. Mac has met similar resistance, though they both have money to spare.

It's obvious how much the girls have regressed mentally by the way they shy away from Dr. Palmer and stay close to their grandmother. Madison actually clings to Tess with one arm while the other clutches a stuffed rabbit. This despite that they've met Dr. Palmer several times in the last three months to monitor their health.

"Hello, girls," Dr. Palmer says. She smiles as wide as she can, but that only causes them to whimper in unison. "I'm not going to hurt you. I just want to make sure you're still feeling all right."

"You'll be fine, children," Tess says. "Dr. Palmer hasn't hurt you before, has she?"

They shake their heads, but don't say anything. Dr. Palmer turns to Stacey. "Why don't you go first? Hop up here on the table."

"I don't wanna," Stacey says.

"I promise it's not going to hurt," Dr. Palmer says.

"Is too," Stacey says.

"Go on, dear," Tess says. "Be a big girl and get on the table. Otherwise you're not going to get any ice cream."

The challenge to her pride at being a big girl and promise of ice cream is enough to prompt Stacey to hop up on the table. She turns her head away to face the wall while she sticks out her right arm. It's hard to believe this little girl scared of a needle used to be a decorated police officer. Dr. Palmer pats Stacey on the arm. "It's all right," she coos. "I've got something new that isn't going to hurt at all. You'll feel just a tiny little prick."

It took her staff weeks to reverse-engineer Dr. Ling's device to measure cellular decay. Once they did, they figured out how to apply the same concepts to one of the newer style diabetes monitors. The end result is about the size of a credit card, with a tapered end that goes into the patient's skin to extract the needed cells. Much less painful and messy than the old meat thermometer design of Dr. Ling.

It's so much better, Stacey doesn't even flinch until Dr. Palmer has a Snoopy Band-Aid over the area just in case it bleeds a little. "Is it over?" Stacey asks.

"It's over. You were very good."

The monitor beeps a few seconds later. The digital numbers come back with the reading: 10.8. That's higher than Dr. Palmer expected. Since Stacey said the first reading came back at exactly ten about five months ago, this reading should be 10.4 if Stacey is aging normally. The higher reading means she's aged faster than normal, if only by a small amount, not enough to be noticeable.

"You can sit up now. I just want to check and make sure your heart and breathing are in tip top shape."

"OK," Stacey mumbles. She flinches a little as Dr. Palmer presses the stethoscope to her back. "It's cold."

"I'm sorry." Everything seems all right. No signs of asthma. Heartbeat is strong and regular. That's something to be concerned about with as much as Stacey's body has been through in its lifetimes. "How are your eyes? Glasses still working for you?"

"Yes."

"Anything else? Any tummy aches from eating too many cookies," Dr. Palmer says. She gives Stacey a playful poke to the belly, but the little girl doesn't react.

"I'm fine," Stacey says. "Can I go now? I promised Jamie I'd call her."

"You can go," Dr. Palmer says. "If I had any lollypops I'd give you one."

"Grandma, can I go call Jamie now? I promised to call."

"I suppose, but don't go too far. And don't get underfoot."

"I won't." Stacey leaves the room with her phone pressed to her ear. Her voice cranks up in excitement as she says, "Hi, it's me!"

Dr. Palmer pats the exam table. "OK, Madison. You're next."

"I don't wanna," Madison says and her face reddens. Dr. Palmer knows from experience the toddler is about to throw a tantrum.

Tess bends down to look Madison in the eyes. "Now, sweetheart, you saw what happened with Stacey. She wasn't hurt at all. Don't you want to be a big girl like her?"

"I am a big girl," Madison says. To prove it she climbs up the steps to the top of the exam table. Dr. Palmer notes a brown roll of fat becomes visible as Madison climbs up. "See? I did it all by myself."

"You sure did," Dr. Palmer says. She holds up the monitor. "Now, hold out your arm. It's just going to be a tiny poke."

"I don't wanna be poked."

Dr. Palmer pats the head of Madison's stuffed rabbit. "I bet your bunny wouldn't mind, would she?"

"She's stuffed," Madison says. She gives Dr. Palmer a pitying look.

"You're not afraid, are you? This didn't hurt Stacey and she's not a big tough girl like you are."

Madison thinks it over. Then she sticks out her arm. Like Stacey she turns her head away. At the same time she clutches the rabbit hard enough that her knuckles turn white. Dr. Palmer expects the rabbit's seams to burst at any second.

A few seconds later it's done. Dr. Palmer puts a Band-Aid over the barely visible hole and then pats Madison on the head. "It's all over. You were very brave."

"Tanks."

The monitor beeps a few seconds later; it comes back with a reading of 5.9. No wonder Madison's clothes are tight: she's aged a year in about five months. Could it be the aging rates are because of the difference in the girls's ages or is it because of the different serums Dr. Ling gave them? She makes a mental note to look into it later.

After she makes sure Madison is a healthy almost six-year-old, Dr. Palmer says, "Why don't you go find your sister while I talk to Grandma for a minute?"

"Do I have to, Gramma?"

"Yes, dear," Tess says.

"OK." Madison trudges from the room.

Dr. Palmer closes the door. Then she pats Tess's shoulder. "I think I'd better check out Grandma too."

"I'm fine. Just a bit tired."

"Those two keep you busy, don't they?"

"They certainly do." Despite her protests, Tess sits down on the exam table. From the look of it, she would like nothing more than to lie down and sleep for a while. "I forgot what a handful little girls can be. It was hard enough with Jennifer. Having two of them—"

"I imagine it's got to be difficult," Dr. Palmer says. She puts the stethoscope to Tess's back to listen for any wheezing that might indicate respiratory problems. "I bet they're both pretty strong-willed, aren't they?"

"They are both headstrong little things when they want," Tess says. Then she sighs and adds, "But they're so sweet too. Just this morning Stacey let Madison have the last bowl of cereal."

"That's really considerate of her."

"They have such good hearts," Tess says. And then she breaks down. She starts to sob like one of her little charges.

Dr. Palmer isn't prepared for this. She takes a couple of tissues from a dispenser on the counter. Tess takes these and wipes futilely at her eyes. "It's all right," Dr. Palmer says.

Tess needs a few minutes to collect herself. Once her tears have mostly dried, she forces another smile to her face. "I'm sorry. I don't know what came over me."

"It's fine," Dr. Palmer says. "I see those girls and sometimes I want to cry too. What happened to them isn't something anyone should have to endure. But it's good they have someone like you to help them through it."

"Thank you, dear," Tess says.

"Look, if you and Jake can manage to find a sitter for the kids, I've got something to show you at the lab. We've made some great headway on the problem."

"You have a cure?"

"Not yet, but we're getting close."

"That's wonderful," Tess says, but a moment later she frowns. "What happens if you can change their bodies back? They'll still be children inside."

"I know, but maybe seeing themselves grown up will unearth the old memories. Dr. Macintosh thinks the regression isn't permanent. He says it's more like a wall their subconscious is putting up to help them adapt to their surroundings. Once their bodies are restored, those walls will get knocked down."

"But still, what about their new friends? Stacey and Jamie have become so close. It will hurt them both terribly. Madison has her own little friends too. She's quite popular at school and in the neighborhood."

"Kids are resilient. They'll make new friends."

"I hope so." Tess shakes her head. "Everything has become such a mess. It makes me wonder why God allows these things to happen."

Dr. Palmer has never been much into religion, so she can only shrug. "They say he works in mysterious ways."

"Very mysterious sometimes. The way those poor girls have suffered...it makes me lose faith sometimes."

"I'm sure everything will work out in the end. You have to hang in there."

"I suppose so."

"In the meantime, there's something else I should mention." She tells Tess the results from the monitor. "Right now there's not much outward change, but we could have some problems in a few months, especially with Madison."

"What do you suggest?"

"There's nothing we can do right now. We'll just have to keep an eye on things. I might want to see them more often to keep tabs on them. I can stop by your house in a couple of weeks to make it easier."

"They're usually home by six-thirty. I try to put Madison to bed by seven-thirty, though sometimes that's difficult."

"I imagine it would be. Madison is a pretty spunky girl."

"She certainly is."

Before Tess can leave, Dr. Palmer puts a hand on her shoulder again. She looks into the older woman's eyes. "How much sleep are you getting?"

"Six hours or so, depending on if they have any nightmares."

"You should try to get a few hours more. I can prescribe something—"

"That won't be necessary. I'll be fine."

"What about your husband? How's he holding up?"

"He's been working himself hard these days. Some days I don't see him until he climbs into bed after midnight."

"I really wish you'd let me help you out."

"We can manage."

Dr. Palmer wants to argue, but she knows it won't do any good with a woman like Tess. A woman like her would never accept charity, not so long as she has a choice about it. She's too proud for that. "Maybe the next time Madison needs some new clothes I can take her shopping."

"That's very generous of you. I'll talk to Jacob about it."

"Good." Dr. Palmer shakes Tess's hand. "I'll see you guys in a few days then."

She just hopes the news is as good as she's made it sound.

***

It's been really hard to keep a secret like her boyfriend from Jamie. Stacey hates how they have to sneak around at lunch and recess to find a private place. Most of the time she and Darren go to the supply closet on the third floor. There they can manage to kiss and hold hands for a few minutes without the need to worry someone will see them.

The situation isn't much better at Dr. Mac's house. Darren's uncle is always around to give them advice on their presentation or offer them snacks or something. The only way they can be alone is for Stacey to pretend she has to use the bathroom and then wait for Darren to make an excuse to get away from his uncle so he can slip into the bathroom with her.

The best times are when Jamie has her appointments with Dr. Mac. Then at recess Stacey and Darren can sit under the slide and talk. They plan out their whole lives: they'll get a loft somewhere in the city for their home base. They'll travel all over the world and perform on stage with Darren playing the piano and Stacey singing. They'll be richer and more famous than Lady Gaga and Justin Bieber combined. Stacey will have her own horse, maybe even a stable of them, and Darren will have the biggest stereo ever so he can listen to music all the time. Eventually they'll have two kids: a boy and a girl named Darren Jr. and Qiang after Stacey's mommy.

Darren hasn't asked if she wants to go public yet. She's glad about that because she doesn't want to have to explain. Mostly Stacey doesn't want that big meanie Keshia to find out because then she'll try to steal Darren away. Stacey doesn't know what she'll do if that happens, not after she and Darren have planned to grow old together—or at least she's planned to grow old with him. She has a whole page in her diary to practice her signature as Mrs. Darren Macintosh. Sometimes she just stares at that page for a while and imagines what it will be like, how awesome it will be.

Her phone beeps. There's a text from Jamie. "Where are you?" Jamie asks.

"At Dr. Mac's," Stacey types back. She hates to see both of her doctors a day apart. It's so unfair.

They talk about last night's *X Factor*, which is Stacey's favorite show after *iCarly*. Jamie says Stacey should try out in a few years. She would win for sure. That's what Stacey thinks too. She has to wait for the right time to ask Grandma and Grandpa about it. She knows they won't be all that enthusiastic about it. They'd never let her go to Hollywood, at least not alone.

The receptionist calls Stacey's name. She signs off and leaves the phone with Grandma so it can't interrupt her session with Dr. Mac. Even though they see each other most every day, Dr. Mac still acts like he barely knows her. "Hello, Stacey. Have a seat."

She takes her seat across from him. She doesn't know why she has to come here. She's fine now. Sometimes she can't even remember what Mommy and Daddy look like. That makes her feel sad until she remembers they're up in Heaven to watch over her and Maddy.

What she does like is to see the picture of Darren on Dr. Mac's desk. She tries not to stare too hard at it, but the picture makes her feel like he's here with them. She sneaks a glimpse at the picture as she sits down and hopes nothing gives her away to Darren's uncle.

"So how is everything going?" Dr. Macintosh asks.

"Fine."

"No problems with Keshia?"

"No."

"Homework not too difficult?"

"No."

"Project coming along?"

"You know it is. We practice in your house."

"You think you'll be ready for it on Friday?"

"Yes."

"Are you excited?"

"A little."

"Not a lot?"

"It's just a couple of minutes. It's not like being in Hollywood or anything."

"I see. You want to sing in Hollywood?"

"Maybe someday. When I get bigger."

"That's probably a wise decision. So you want to be a singer when you grow up?"

"Or maybe a veterinarian," she says to throw him off. Grandma Tess says it's not nice to lie, but sometimes Stacey has to so Dr. Mac won't find out about her and Darren.

"You like animals?"

"Some."

"Cats?"

"Yes."

"Dogs?"

"A little."

"Horses, I bet. All little girls love horses."

"They're OK."

"Have you ever thought about being a police officer?"

Stacey shakes her head. "That's for boys."

"There are a lot of policewomen these days."

"So? I don't want to wear some ugly uniform."

"I see. You want to look pretty?"

"Duh. Girls are supposed to be pretty."

"Is that a fact?"

"Most girls anyway."

"Not like Keshia, I bet."

"She's not pretty."

"What about Madison? Is she pretty?"

"I don't know. She's a baby."

"I'm sure she would take issue with that."

"So? She is a baby. A big fat baby."

"Do you think your sister is overweight?"

"Duh," Stacey says again. "Her clothes hardly even fit anymore. Grandma says if Maddy gets any bigger, she'll need a whole new wardrobe."

"And does that make her ugly?"

"I don't know."

"Why not? It's a simple question."

Stacey squirms in her seat. She hates when Dr. Mac does this to her. She always feels trapped. She glances at the picture of Darren and wishes he were here to hold her hand. "She's my sister."

"I see. That means you can't judge her like kids in your own class."

Stacey squirms a little more. It's hard for her to admit it, but she says, "Maddy is cute. For a baby."

"That's good." Dr. Mac taps his notebook with his pen. That always means he's about to ask her something hard. "What about you? Are you pretty?"

She thinks about that one. She knows what Darren thinks. He's said a bunch of times that she's the prettiest girl at school. But when she looks in the mirror, she isn't so sure. Other girls don't have glasses like she does. Their eyes aren't shaped like footballs either. Except for a few like Keshia, their skin isn't so brown either. She's *different* from the other girls. All the stories they read say being different is good, but she isn't sure about that either. No one makes fun of you if you're the same as them, only if you're different. "I guess so," she finally says.

"You guess? Shouldn't you know?"

"Maybe."

"Do other girls besides Keshia give you a hard time at school?"

"A couple."

"Do they think you're pretty?"

"No. They think I'm ugly."

"Why would they think that?"

"Because I'm different."

"What makes you different?"

She repeats the list she already went through in her own mind. As she does, Dr. Macintosh nods along, to confirm everything. She decides to turn the tables on him. "Do you think I'm ugly?"

"Of course not."

"You're just saying that."

"Why would I do that?"

"To be nice. That's what grown-ups do. They tell fibs all the time."

"Do your grandparents fib?"

"Sometimes."

"What do they fib about?"

"That we aren't poor."

"Why do you think they lie about that?"

"So they won't make us feel bad."

"Does it make you feel bad to think you're poor?"

"Sometimes," Stacey admits. "Sometimes I wish we could afford lots of nice things like you and Jamie have. And if we had more money Grandpa wouldn't have to work so hard."

"Does he work too hard?"

"I hardly see him anymore. He's always in his study or at work. He's not even around to tuck Maddy in at night."

"What about your grandma?"

"She works hard too. Especially when Maddy is being a brat."

"And I'm sure you're never a brat, right?"

Stacey looks down at her feet. She hates the way Dr. Mac does this to her, to make her feel bad about things she hardly thinks about. "Sometimes. But most of the time it's Maddy's fault. Like the other day I wanted to watch *iCarly* and she wouldn't change the channel."

"And then what happened?"

"I took the remote. The stupid baby went and told Grandma and she sent us both to bed."

"Did that make you angry?"

"A little. I watched it the next day at Jamie's house so it was OK."

"Did Madison get to watch her program?"

"I don't know."

"You didn't care?"

"She probably didn't want to watch it anyway. She just didn't want me to watch my show."

"Why would she do that?"

"Because she's a brat, like I said."

"I see. Do you love her?"

"What?"

"Your sister. Do you love her even though she is a brat?"

"Yes," Stacey admits. "Can I go now?"

"Almost." He reaches beside him to take out a hand mirror. He passes it over to her. "What do you see in the mirror?"

"Me."

"I see. Let's pretend for a moment. Let's pretend we're strangers. How would you describe yourself to me?"

"Um, well, I'm four feet tall and I've got black hair—"

"That's your physical appearance. I can see all that. Describe what I can't see."

"Oh." Stacey stares harder at the mirror. As she stares into her eyes, something weird happens: they turn blue. Not just blue, but round as well, like the other kid's eyes. Like in a nightmare her whole face changes: her skin turns pale white and her hair goes from black to a dark red that's curly and pretty. Her cheeks turn slimmer while her nose gets longer. This face is older than hers, a grown-up's face.

She yelps and then tosses the mirror into Dr. Mac's lap. She curls up in the chair and whimpers like Maddy. She feels his hand on her shoulder. "Stacey? What happened? What did you see?"

"Nothing," Stacey mumbles into the cushions.

"It wasn't nothing," he says. "Let's talk about it."

"No."
"Why not?"
"I don't wanna."
"Stacey, that's not a big girl answer, is it?"
"I don't care."

Dr. Mac sounds more like Grandpa as he says, "Young lady, sit up right now."

Though she doesn't want to, Stacey obeys. She won't look at the doctor; she stares down at the floor. He hands her a tissue to wipe at her eyes with. "Thanks."

"Now let's talk about it. What did you see?"
"You won't believe me."
"Try me."

Stacey gathers her courage. Dr. Mac will think she's gone crazy. "At first it was me. Then my face started to change."

"How?"
"My eyes turned blue and my hair turned red."
"I see. Go on."

"And then I looked in the mirror and there was this pretty lady instead of me."

"Do you know who it was?"
"No. I never saw her before."
"You say she had blue eyes and red hair?"
"Yes."
"What else do you remember about her?"

"Her hair was curly and really pretty. Her skin was white. She didn't have stupid glasses either."

"And she wasn't a little girl like you?"

"No. She was a grown-up." Stacey looks up at Dr. Macintosh. He writes in his notebook, probably that she's crazy and needs to go to the hospital. "Do you know her?"

"No, I don't." He leans forward in his chair. "But I bet if you think hard enough you'll know who she is."

They end the session like that. Stacey goes out to Grandma Tess. She hugs her grandma; she needs to feel the warmth of someone's body at the moment. Grandma strokes Stacey's hair and asks, "What's wrong, dear?"

"Nothing," she says. She pulls away from Grandma and then waits for Maddy to end her session; she counts the moments until she can hug Darren again.

Chapter 35

The company doesn't like Dr. Palmer to bring outsiders into the lab. They especially don't like her to bring a cop like Jake Madigan in. Lennox Pharmaceuticals has a code of ethics, but adherence to that is optional. It's more important to get results.

Dr. Palmer doesn't care if she offends the Lennox big shots, not for the Madigans. It was a Lennox project that had put them into this bizarre situation, so they have a right to know what's going on. When the big shots balked to give Jake and Tess access to the lab, she had gone to them and said they could let the Madigans in or else she would go to the media to tell them how over a year ago the company had tried to buy back its own formula from a notorious gangster.

She doesn't feel bad about that as she ushers them inside. Jake looks just as frazzled as Tess, both of them in dire need of a vacation. "When was the last time you got a good night's sleep?" she asks him.

"Probably during the Carter administration," Jake says. "I'll be fine once the coffee kicks in."

Dr. Palmer doesn't say anything to that. She's not Jake's doctor. If she were, she would tell him that he's not a young man anymore; if he wants to live to see the girls grow up, he'd better start to take care of himself.

She ushers them through the last security checkpoint. Dr. Palmer has tried to tighten security since she learned someone had given away Lennox secrets to Dr. Ling. The company did full background checks on everyone—including her—and doubled the number of cameras in the building. There's also a new digital security system on the computers to prevent someone from hacking into the network. It might be a lot of wasted effort since Ling died, but even with Ling dead, there are still plenty of competitors who would pay a lot of money to find out what goes on in the lab.

The lab hasn't changed much since the security upgrades. There are more cameras, but the equipment is all still the same. She motions Jake and Tess to stools by a counter in the center of the room. She made sure someone cleared off the counter before she brought the Madigans up here; no sense to show them things they don't need to see.

"OK, before I show you our big breakthrough, I want to give you a little background first. There are certain diseases that can cause the body to age at a more advanced rate. That's what we've been looking into in order to help the girls."

"You're going to give them a disease?" Tess asks.

"In a way. We're going to trigger the same reaction the disease does. The main difference is we'll be able to stop the reaction, kind of like flicking a light switch."

"That sounds pretty fantastic," Jake says.

"I thought you might be skeptical. That's why I arranged to have the proof brought in here." She goes over to another counter, where there's an object covered with a towel. Like a magician, Dr. Palmer pulls the towel away to reveal a white rabbit.

"That's going to change the girls back?"

Dr. Palmer brings the rabbit's cage over to the counter and sets it down in front of the Madigans. For its part, the rabbit shuffles around the cage; its ears and nose twitch. "As you can see, this is a fully grown, adult rabbit."

"That's very nice, dear," Tess says. She sounds like Dr. Palmer is one of her girls showing her a pretty picture she colored.

"Now here's the thing: this rabbit was born two weeks ago."

That finally gets their attention. Their eyes go wide as they look to her and then the rabbit. "You can't be serious," Jake says. "Is this some kind of trick?"

"I have the pictures right here," Dr. Palmer says. She opens an envelope on the counter so they can see the sequence of photos that show first a hairless newborn; it gets larger and furrier with each photograph until it looks exactly like the one in the cage. "Before you say anything, note the tattoo we put on the bunny's rump. That's so you know we didn't switch them."

"That's amazing," Tess says. She leans closer to the cage, to study the rabbit. "And you think you can do the same for the girls?"

"I hope so. We still have to run a few more tests. We'll try it on primates next. If the results are good, then we can try it on humans."

"How long will that take?"

"We're working on the primate serum now. It should be two weeks to administer it. Then if the results are the same as with our friend here, we can try it on one of the girls in a month."

"One of them?" Jake asks. "Not both?"

"Even if this does work on animals, it's always dangerous trying a new drug on a human. There could be side-effects."

"They could die?" Tess says.

"It's a possibility."

Tess shakes her head. "How could we ever make that kind of choice?"

"I don't think there's much of a choice to make," Jake says. "We try it on Stacey first. She's the oldest. She'll want to protect her little sister."

Jake gives Dr. Palmer a look. She nods to him. The real reason they would try it on Stacey first is that she's Madison's father. As such, she wouldn't want to put her daughter in harm's way.

"I don't know," Tess says. "It seems like we're playing God."

"We're just trying to fix the damage Ling did with his experiments," Dr. Palmer says. "We can save them the pain of growing up again. Isn't that what you want?"

"I suppose so," Tess says. She looks into one of the rabbit's eyes. "Thank you, Doctor."

"I'll keep you posted on what's happening," Dr. Palmer says. "In the meantime, don't say anything to them. There's no point confusing them about who they are until we have to."

She shakes hands with the Madigans and then shows them out. Once they've gone, Dr. Palmer checks on her test subject again. She kept from the Madigans that this rabbit was their fifth test subject. "Don't *you* die on me," she says to the rabbit in the cage.

***

Today is their last rehearsal at Darren's house. Tomorrow they have the dress rehearsal at school. She listens to Darren explain the intricacies of how to tune a piano; she doesn't hear the words so much as his passion. She loves to listen to Darren like this, when he talks to her instead of mumbles like he usually does. "You know so much about pianos," she says.

Then his face reddens and the mumbling returns. "Well, I've been playing them pretty much my whole life."

"You must really love them."

"I guess." He fiddles with the keys. "Let's try it again from the top. You were a little late on the second part."

"Was not! You were early." But as she always does, she acquiesces to his judgment about music. She runs through her scales the way Mr. Lewis, her music teacher, taught her to warm up her voice. Once she's ready, she signals for Darren to begin.

They're halfway through when Darren's uncle comes into the room. He's on the phone, saying, "Thank you so much, Mrs. Madigan. I'm sorry about the short notice. No, I don't think it's too serious. Thanks. I'll pass that along."

By the time he hangs up, Darren has already stopped; he senses something is wrong. "I'm sorry, kids, I have to go. One of my patients is in trouble." He fixes them with a serious look. "Can I trust you guys alone for a little bit?"

"How long?" Darren asks.

"Just until Stacey's grandma gets here. An hour maybe. She'll look after you until I get back."

"We can do it," Stacey says. She hopes she looks sincere, though inside she wants to scream for joy. A whole hour alone with Darren!

"Thanks, kids." Before he goes, Dr. Macintosh kisses Darren on the top of the head. "I'll see you in a couple of hours." He doesn't kiss Stacey; he just tousles her hair. "I'm trusting you to behave."

"We'll be good," she says.

"I know you will."

Then he's gone. Stacey sighs and then leans against the piano. "So what do you want to do now?"

"I don't know. We should probably practice again."

Stacey shakes her head. She sits next to him on the bench. "Dar-ren, we have a whole hour. *Alone.*" She takes his hand and gives it a squeeze. "Isn't there anything you want to do?"

"Oh," he says. His face lights up with a smile as the realization kicks in. "I see what you mean."

They kiss once on the piano bench. Then she pulls him to his feet. They go upstairs to Darren's bedroom. She's worried it'll be gross, with dirty clothes all over. It's not. Everything is nice and neat. The posters on the wall are of Mozart, Beethoven, and Chopin, not athletes or superheroes like most stupid boys would have. Even the comforter on his bed has piano keys on it.

"You are such a geek," she says.

"Sorry," he says.

She slaps him on the arm. "Oh my God, I'm kidding!"

"Sorry," he says again.

They lie down on the bed. They kiss again, this time a little longer. Stacey runs her hand through Darren's hair afterwards and thinks of what to do next.

"What do we do now?" he asks.

"We should take our shirts off," she says.

"We should?"

"That's what they do on TV."

"OK." It's easy for Darren to take his shirt off since he has on a T-shirt. His chest is pale and skinny, not like the boys in pictures Jamie has shown her. Too bad she can't tell Jamie she got to see a real boy with his shirt off.

She's still in her school uniform, so she has to unbutton her blouse. Her fingers begin to tremble about halfway down as Darren stares at her. "You need help?"

"I can do it," she snaps. She doesn't need help from a *boy*, even if that boy is Darren. She finishes unbuttoning the shirt and exposes her naked tummy to him. She thinks back to her last appointment with Dr. Macintosh. "Darren, do you think I'm pretty?"

"Yes."

"Really? As pretty as the other girls in class?"

"You're way prettier than them," he says. He tries to kiss her again, but she pushes him away. "What is it?"

"I mean, am I prettier than Lacy Doubletree?" she asks. Lacy is a girl in their class who already has a contract with a modeling agency.

"Are you kidding? You're much prettier than Lacy."

"But she doesn't have stupid glasses and her hair is blond and her eyes are blue. I mean, she's like a total Barbie doll."

"I don't want a Barbie doll," he says. He brushes hair away from her face. "I want you."

"Oh, Darren," she says and starts to cry. They kiss again, this time until they both gasp for air. Afterwards they lie on the bed and hug each other.

That's how Grandma Tess finds them. Stacey is roused from sleep when Grandma shouts, "What is the meaning of this?"

Stacey sits up. She tries to find something to cover up with, but her clothes are on the floor. She grabs one of Darren's pillows to put over her chest. "I'm sorry, Grandma," she says. "We were just taking a nap."

"Where are your clothes?"

"On the floor."

"Put them on this instant, young lady."

"Yes, Grandma."

Stacey rolls off the bed to gather up her shirt, jacket, and shoes. While Stacey puts these on, Grandma starts to lay into Darren. "You! How could you do that to my granddaughter? I thought you were a nice boy."

"I'm sorry." Stacey loves Darren more than ever when he says, "It's all my fault. I asked Stacey to take off her clothes, like they do on TV."

He hasn't bothered to cover himself. Grandma picks up his shirt and throws it at him. Stacey cringes at this; she's never seen Grandma Tess this angry before. Will she hurt Darren? "Grandma—"

"Go into the living room to wait for me, young lady. I'll deal with you in a few minutes."

Stacey wants to stay and help Darren, but she doesn't. She puts her head down and then hurries into the living room. She puts on the rest of her clothes and then throws herself on the couch to sob into the cushions.

A few minutes later she feels a hand on her back. Stacey turns to see Grandma Tess on the edge of the couch; she still looks mad. "Did you hurt Darren?" Stacey asks.

"Of course not. We just talked." Grandma pats Stacey's back. "Come on, dear, sit up. We need to have a talk too."

Stacey sits up. She clutches one of the throw pillows to her chest but wishes it were Darren. "It's not his fault," she says. "I'm the one who said we should take off our clothes."

"Why did you do that?"

"That's what people who love each other do on TV. They go to the bedroom and kiss and take off their clothes and then they hug."

"Is that all you and Darren did?"

"Yes," Stacey says. She wonders what else there is.

Grandma smiles a little, though Stacey can still see she's mad. "That was a very naughty thing to do, Stacey. You're much too young for that."

"Am not. I'm ten."

"That's not the kind of thing you should do until you're married, like your grandfather and me."

"But Darren and I are going to get married."

"You are?"

"When we're big enough. We're going to get married and buy a house and we'll have babies."

"Oh, I see. You have it all planned out, don't you?"

"Uh-huh."

Grandma Tess sighs and then shakes her head. "Oh, sweetheart, that's a long time away. I know you and Darren think you're grown up, but you're still just children."

"We are not!"

"Stacey, please, listen to me. You're just a little girl. Much too little to be playing with boys like this."

"We weren't playing. We love each other." Stacey starts to cry again. "You don't understand anything! You're just a mean old lady."

"Don't talk to your elders like that, young lady, or I'll wash your mouth out with soap."

"Sorry," Stacey says, though she isn't.

"After this project is done, I think it would be best if you and Darren didn't spend so much time together."

"But Grandma—"

"No buts," Grandma says. "You're not to do anything like this with a boy again, not until you're older."

"How old?"

"Eighteen at least, when you're grown up."

"That's not fair!"

"I'm sorry, dear, but that's final."

"No, you can't do this. We love each other!"

She begins to sob. Grandma Tess pulls her close for a hug. Stacey tries to resist, but she can't. She's too little. Someday I'll be big enough, she tells herself.

They sit on the couch for a while, until Dr. Mac returns. He sees them and right away he frowns. "What happened?" he asks.

Grandma gives Stacey a little push to get her off the couch. "Go say goodbye to Darren, sweetheart. But keep the door open."

"Yes, ma'am."

Stacey trudges back to Darren's room, where she finds him on the bed; he scribbles in the notebook. He's fully dressed now, knees tucked up beneath his chin. "Hi," she says.

"Hi."

She looks down at the floor. "I'm sorry."

"It's my fault too," he says.

"Grandma says we can't play together anymore."

"What about the presentation?"

"There's still that, but I can't come over here anymore."

"Oh." He puts down the notebook. "It's not fair."

"I know. It sucks." She sits on the edge of the bed and puts one hand on his foot. "We can still see each other at recess."

"Only when Jamie isn't around, right?"

"I don't know." Stacey sighs. "We can still go to the closet."

"I guess."

"It'll be fine. We'll find a way."

"OK."

"Stacey! Time to go," Grandma calls out.

"Coming, Grandma." Stacey gets off the bed. Before she goes, she kisses Darren on the lips, maybe for the last time. "See you tomorrow."

"See you."

And then she has to go.

Chapter 36

The next day at school, Darren isn't there. Ms. Lowry says he's sick. Stacey knows that's not true. He stayed home so he doesn't have to see her. Was it his idea or Dr. Macintosh's? While she sits alone and the rest of the class works on their projects for tonight's presentation, Stacey starts to hate them both.

Of course Keshia can't resist the chance to make Stacey feel even worse. Keshia whispers loud enough so everyone can hear, "Even the weird kid can't stand her."

Stacey puts her head down on her desk for a few minutes, until Ms. Lowry puts a hand on her back. "Are you feeling sick, Stacey?" Ms. Lowry asks.

"No." She wipes at her eyes so no one else will see her cry. Then she lifts her head enough to ask, "Can I work in the library?"

"All right," Ms. Lowry says. "I'll write you a pass."

Stacey goes up to the third floor of the library, where she can be alone. Except she isn't alone for long until she feels another hand on her back. She figures it's Mrs. Brown the librarian to scold her, but it's Jamie. "Stacey, what's wrong? Did that bitch Keshia do something?"

"No."

Jamie pulls up a chair to sit beside Stacey. "Then what happened?"

"Grandma says I can't see Darren anymore."

"Why would she say that? I know he's weird—"

"He is not!" Stacey shouts loud enough that the other kids in the library turn to stare at her. In a lower voice she says, "I love Darren and he loves me. We kissed a whole bunch of times and then when his uncle had to go, we went back to his room and we kissed and hugged without our shirts on."

"Oh my God," Jamie says. "The Ouija board was right."

"But Grandma Tess saw us and now she won't let me see him anymore. He didn't come to school today and the presentation is tonight." Stacey starts to cry again. "It's not fair!"

"How long has this been going on?"

"A month or so."

"Why didn't you tell me?"

"I don't know."

"I thought we were friends. I've told you everything."

"I'm sorry. You're always saying Darren is weird. But he's not. He's nice. He wrote a song for me."

"He did?"

"Yes." Stacey clears her throat. She keeps her voice low so no one else will hear as she sings the song Darren wrote for her.

Long before Stacey finishes, she and Jamie are both in tears. "That is so amazing," Jamie says. "He wrote that for you?"

"Yes."

"Wow. I'm sorry I said he's weird."

"I'm sorry I didn't tell you."

They hug and then Jamie pulls out her phone. As she types, she says, "I can't wait to tell everyone about this. Stacey and Darren sitting in a tree—"

"Jamie, don't!"

Jamie laughs and then grins at her. "Got you." She holds up the screen to show a bunch of random text. "You are so gullible."

They laugh and hug again, still best friends forever.

***

Stacey goes home with Grandma Tess and Maddy after school. She hopes Darren shows up for the presentation tonight. If he doesn't she'll have to go on alone. She supposes someone else could play the piano or she could sing without music, but she doesn't want it to come to that. They worked so hard on this together, they should finish it together.

Maddy can't sit still the whole way. She bounces up and down in her seat and chirps excitedly about the pageant tonight. "I'm going to be the best one!" she says.

"Good for you," Stacey grumbles.

"Grandma, Stacey's being mean."

"Tattletale."

"Am not."

"Are too!"

"Quiet down, girls, or neither of you is going anywhere tonight."

"But Grandma—"

"That's enough, Madison."

Maddy crosses her arms and pouts. She still fidgets in her booster seat and mumbles her lines for the pageant. Stacey shakes her head. The stupid baby only has two lines. She won't be on stage more than a minute. Stacey has to do five whole minutes, maybe by herself.

Grandpa is home before they are for once. He's back in his study, still at work. As soon as they're in the house, Maddy races towards the stairs. "Don't get dressed yet, dear," Grandma says. "Not until after dinner."

"But Gramma—"

"Just go practice for a little while, dear."

"Fine." Maddy walks up the stairs and then slams the door.

Stacey throws herself on the couch to watch TV. Maybe she should practice a little, but she'd rather save her voice for tonight. If she needs it.

Maddy is still upstairs, Grandpa in his study, and Grandma in the kitchen when the doorbell rings. Stacey slides off the couch and wonders if maybe it's Darren to see her. Maybe it's Dr. Macintosh to apologize.

It's neither. At the door is a woman who's very pale and so skinny she looks almost like a skeleton. Her hair is long and brown, but it looks all mussed and tangled like she hasn't combed it in a while. Despite all that, the woman's face brightens with a smile. "Hi there," she says. "Is this the Madigan house?"

"Yes," Stacey says, unsure what to do. In school they said not to talk to strangers. This woman is obviously a stranger, but Stacey can't just slam the door, can she? That would be rude. "I'll go get Grandpa."

"OK. I'll wait right here."

Stacey shuts the door softly. Then she runs to Grandpa's study. He says she's not supposed to go in there without knocking, so she taps on the door. "Grandpa? There's a stranger at the door."

The door opens a minute later. "A stranger? Did she say what her name is?"

"No." Stacey's face turns warm. "I forgot to ask."

"Did she say what she wants?"

"No."

"I see." Grandpa pats Stacey's back. "You go watch TV. I'll take care of this."

Stacey gallops over to the couch and lies down as if she's going to watch TV again. But after Grandpa answers the door, Stacey rolls off the couch. She creeps towards the door and hides herself with the curtains.

"I'm sorry to show up here like this," the woman says.

"You could have called the office," Grandpa says.

"I've called the office! I've called and called. No one will tell me anything. It's been five months now. Do you have any leads at all?"

"I'm afraid not," Grandpa says. "We really should talk about this later. Stop by the precinct tomorrow—"

"I don't want to wait until tomorrow!" the woman shouts. Stacey presses herself closer to the wall. Is this lady crazy?

"I'm sorry, Grace. I wish there were more I could do."

"Her mom's going to have her declared dead soon, did you know that?" Stacey peeks out from behind the curtain. She can see the lady's face, her hollow cheeks wet with tears. Stacey starts to feel bad for the crazy lady. She's not crazy; she's just sad.

"I hadn't heard that, no. I'm sorry," Grandpa says, though he doesn't seem sorry. He looks mad. Why is Grandpa mad at this poor lady?

"I know she's not dead. In my heart, I know. If Madison were dead, I would feel it—"

Stacey bursts out from the curtains. "Madison's not dead!" she shouts. "She's upstairs."

"What's she talking about?" Grace asks. "Madison's here?"

Grandpa turns to Stacey, his face red. A vein pulses on his forehead, which always means he's really mad. "Stacey, go up to your room. I'll deal with you later."

"Stacey? Wait a minute, who are these girls?"

"I think you'd better go, Grace. I'll talk to you tomorrow," Grandpa says. He tries to push the woman out of the doorway, but she's strong, a lot stronger than someone who looks like a skeleton should be.

"I'm not leaving until you tell me what the hell is going on!"

"Grace, please—"

"What's the meaning of this?" Grandma asks from behind Grandpa. "Grace? What are you doing here?"

"I want to see Madison. Where is she?" Grace points to Stacey. "This little girl says Madison is here."

"Yes, she is."

"Tess—"

Grandma takes Grandpa's arm. He stops trying to close the door. "Jacob, please. Grace has a right to know"

"Grandma? Grandpa? What's going on?" Maddy asks. She stands beside Stacey. "Who's that lady?"

Grace squats down and her eyes narrow. "Madison?"

Maddy whimpers and then presses against Stacey for protection. "Grandma, who is this? What's going on?"

Grace rushes forward to put her hands on Maddy's shoulders. Maddy cries out at this. Stacey tries to push the lady away, but again she is surprisingly strong.

"Madison, it's me. It's Grace. Do you remember me? I love you."

Maddy starts to sob now and screams at the top of her lungs like they taught in school. "Go away! Stranger! Stranger!"

This deflates Grace. She pulls her hands back. Maddy sprints away and buries her head against Grandma's body while she continues to sob. Grace turns to Stacey and stares at her. Stacey flinches as Grace runs a hand through her hair. "Stacey, do you remember me? It's Grace. We used to work together. At the clothes store. Remember?"

"No," Stacey manages to get out. She wants to run away, but she's frozen in place.

"I know it's you, Stacey. I can see it in your eyes. Even with the glasses."

Grandpa takes Grace by the shoulders, to pull her back. "I think you should go."

"No! I don't know what's happened to them, but I know it's them. Why didn't you tell me? They're my friends!"

Grandpa sighs. He looks really tired all of the sudden. "Let's go talk in my study."

"OK," Grace says. Before she goes, she pats Stacey's cheek. "I'm sorry I scared you. You look very pretty."

"Thanks," Stacey mumbles.

After Grace has gone back to the study with Grandpa, Grandma picks Maddy up. Maddy clings to her, still crying. Grandma touches Stacey's shoulder. "Let's go to your room," she says.

Stacey takes a look towards the study and then nods; she follows Grandma upstairs.

***

Maddy falls asleep after a couple of minutes. Stacey crawls into the top bunk and collects her stuffed monkey Pinky. To her surprise, Grandma crawls into bed with her. It's a tight squeeze because Grandma is so big, but she's able to lie down and face Stacey.

Grandma strokes Stacey's hair as she asks, "Are you all right?"

"Yes." Stacey thinks for a moment and then asks, "Grandma, who is that crazy lady? Why did she say those things?"

"She's just confused, dear. That's all."

"She said she knew me. She said we worked together in a clothes shop."

"As I said, she's confused. She thinks you're someone else."

"But she said she could see it in my eyes. Even with my glasses."

"You don't have to worry, dear. She's not going to bother you anymore. Grandpa will make sure of that."

"OK." Stacey grips the monkey tighter. It's not long before she starts to doze. She's barely aware when the bed creaks. Grandma slides off to leave her to nap. After all, she has a busy night.

There's a crack of light that for a moment gets into her eyes. She hears the crazy lady's voice again. "I'm so sorry, Mrs. Madigan. I didn't mean to create so much trouble."

"It's fine, dear. Did Jacob explain things to you?"

"Yes." There's a pause and then Grace asks, "They really don't remember anything?"

"I'm afraid not."

"Oh." There's another pause before Grace asks, "Are they happy like this?"

"Yes, I think so. They've both made new friends. Madison is the most popular girl in her class."

Grace laughs at this. "Everyone likes Maddy, once they get used to her. What about Stacey? Has she come out of her shell a little?"

Stacey eagerly awaits this answer. Grandma embarrasses her when she answers, "A little. She has a couple of very close friends. One of them is a boy."

"She has a boyfriend?"

"After a fashion. It's just puppy love, really."

They both giggle at this. Stacey wants to protest that her love for Darren isn't something to laugh at, but she can't without giving herself away. Grace says, "I guess it's just as well she doesn't remember her upbringing. Now she can have a normal childhood."

"I'm so sorry, Grace. I know how much you care for them. Jacob and I wanted to tell you—"

"I understand. It's not an easy situation." Grace makes a sound in her throat like she's about to cry. "At least now I know they're all right. Are you going to tell Maddy's mom? She's all but given up hope of seeing Madison again."

"I don't think we can, not right now. You see how difficult it is."

"Yeah, I do." There's another pause. "Can I see Maddy? I just want to say goodbye."

"She's sleeping right now."

"I won't wake her. I'll be quick."

"All right."

Stacey squeezes her eyes shut and pretends to sleep. Grandma must turn the light in the hallway off, because the crack of light goes away. Stacey listens closely as Grace pads across the room. Stacey opens one eye to make sure the coast is clear and then slides as close to the rail as she can.

She watches as Grace squats down beside Maddy's bed. Maddy is still asleep, Mrs. Hoppy tight against her while she sucks her thumb like a baby. Grace leans closer and brushes one of Maddy's pigtails back. Though it's dark, Stacey can see tears run down Grace's cheeks. "Oh, Madison," she whispers. "I'll never forget you."

Stacey's stomach roils as she watches the crazy lady kiss Maddy's cheek. Maddy stirs a little and mumbles something that's unintelligible with her thumb in her mouth. Then Grace stands up. Stacey closes her eyes tightly, but she's too late.

"Hi, Stace," Grace says. A few of her friends on Facebook call her "Stace" but she thinks it's a stupid nickname.

"Hi," Stacey says. "Are you going to kiss me too?"

"Do you want me to?"

"No."

"Then I won't."

"Grandma says you're confused."

"I guess I am." She nods to Stacey's pink monkey. "That's a cute monkey."

"Thanks."

"I like the glasses too. They're very pretty."

"Uh-huh."

"How old are you?"

"Ten."

"Maybe I'll look you up in eight years when you're a grown-up."

"OK."

"Bye." She doesn't kiss Stacey or even try to touch her hair; she just gives a little wave and then turns away.

Grace is almost to the door when Maddy rolls over. She pulls the thumb from her mouth to ask, "Grace?"

Grace doesn't say anything. She opens the door. Maddy rolls out of bed and drops her rabbit on the floor. Grace is halfway through the door when Maddy catches up to her. She clamps herself around Grace's left leg. "Don't go!"

"Sorry, Maddy, but I have to."

"No. I wuv you, Gwace," Maddy says. She uses that lisp she breaks out when she wants people to think she's cute.

Grace bends down to look Maddy in the eye. "Madison? Is it really you?"

"Yes. I remember now."

"You do?"

"We used to be together. In our own place. Above your store."

"That's right, Madison."

"And I was going to college. I want to be a reporter." Maddy looks down at the floor. "I guess that won't be for a while."

"I don't care, Maddy. I'll wait as long as it takes for you to grow up."

"But I'm only five."

"It's just thirteen years. I can wait."

"Oh Grace, I missed you so much."

"I missed you too." Grace smiles and then pokes Maddy's tummy. "At least they're feeding you pretty well."

"I'm not fat!" Maddy shouts.

"I'm sorry. I didn't mean to upset you." Despite this, Maddy starts to cry. "What's the matter, sweetheart? What is it?"

"This is never going to work," Maddy bawls. She runs back to the bed and throws herself on the mattress to turn her back to Grace.

Grace sits down next to her and puts a hand on Maddy's back. "I'm sorry about that. I don't know what to do."

"Just hold me," Maddy says. "Like you used to."

"OK," Grace says. She slips onto the bed and wraps her arms around Maddy's body to press her close. Stacey watches them for a minute and then turns away to stare at the wall until she falls asleep.

***

Grace stays for dinner. She carries Maddy downstairs and then they sit next to each other at the table. Stacey has to sit on the other side by herself. She glowers at her little sister and the crazy lady, not that they seem to notice.

They have lasagna for dinner. Grace studies hers for a minute and then starts to pick at it. She leaves a pile of meat on her napkin. She glances over at Madison, who's devouring her slab of lasagna. "You're eating meat now?" Grace asks.

"So? I ate meat the last time I was five."

"I'm sorry, Grace," Tess says. "If I'd known you were coming—"

"No, it's my fault. It's fine."

Maddy looks over at Grandma. "Gramma, can Grace watch the pageant tonight?"

"Pageant?"

"My class is having a pageant on all the presidents," Maddy says. "I get to be Eleanor Roosevelt."

"Oh, that's great."

Maddy takes the crazy lady's hand. "You got to come. Pwease?"

"They might not have any tickets left," Grandma says.

"It's supposed to be for school families anyway," Stacey says. "Not *strangers.*"

Grandpa gives her a dirty look; the vein on his forehead starts to pulse. "Eat your dinner, young lady."

Stacey looks down at her plate. Has everyone else gone crazy? This stranger sits at their table, complains about Grandma's delicious lasagna, and acts like she's Maddy's mommy. But she's not. She's not anything, just some stranger. Yet if Stacey says anything, she's the one who gets in trouble. It's not fair.

Grandma changes the topic. "Jacob and I visited Dr. Palmer's lab the other day. She had some very exciting things to show us. In a month or so, she might even be able to cure Madison."

"Really?"

"Don't get your hopes up," Grandpa warns. "It's all experimental. They've got to run a lot of tests before they can try it on Madison."

"Oh," Maddy says. She looks down sadly at her plate.

"There's something else the doctor said before that, when we visited her at the hospital. She said, Madison, you're aging much faster than a normal little girl. You're almost six years old right now."

"I am?"

"That's right, dear. That's why your clothes are getting so tight."

"And you eat too many cookies," Stacey grumbles.

"And Stacey is almost eleven." Grandma smiles and then says, "We should have a birthday party for you both. Then Grace could meet all your friends."

"I don't want Grace to meet my friends!" Stacey shouts. "I want her to go away!"

"That's enough, young lady," Grandpa says. He points towards the ceiling. "March up to your room right now. No dessert for you."

"That's not fair!"

"I'll carry you if I have to."

"I hate you! I hate all of you!" Stacey screams and then runs upstairs. She throws herself on her bed to cry. She waits for Grandma to come in to comfort her, but she doesn't. She's too busy with the crazy lady. It's not fair. They want to take Maddy away from her, to steal her sister away. After Mommy and Daddy died, Stacey promised herself she'd never let anyone break them up, but now it seems like there's no way to stop it, especially since Maddy seems to want it; she's fallen under the crazy lady's spell.

She's still sobbing when the light comes on. It's not Grandma or Grandpa or the crazy lady, thank goodness. It's Maddy. She climbs up the ladder, into Stacey's bed the way Grandma did earlier.

"You can't be up here," Stacey says. "You're too little."

Maddy ignores this and squeezes in next to Stacey so that they face each other. "Stacey, why won't you remember?"

"Remember what?"

"Who you are. Your name isn't Stacey Chang. It's Stacey Chance. You're nineteen years old. You're my best friend."

"You're making that up."

"Am not! And we're both friends with Grace. You work in her store."

"Her clothes store," Stacey says. She sticks her tongue out. "Yuck."

"Stacey, please. You got to remember. We're not little kids. We're grown-ups."

"That's stupid," Stacey says. She grabs Maddy's cheek and pinches it until Maddy squeals. "See, you're a little kid."

"That was mean," Maddy says. She crawls off the bed. Stacey thinks she's going to tattle to Grandma and Grandpa the way she usually does. Instead, she goes to her drawers and rummages around in the top of her drawers until she finds something.

When she returns, Maddy has a piece of paper in her hand. She unfolds it so Stacey can see a crude drawing of a woman. She has red hair, blue eyes, and pale skin, just like the woman Stacey saw in the mirror at Dr. Macintosh's office. "See, that's you. I made it so we wouldn't forget, but we did anyway."

"That's not me."

"It is too." Maddy smiles at her drawing. "Your hair isn't always red. It used to be brown, like mine."

She unfolds another sheet of paper. On it is a woman with long brown hair and blue eyes. She holds something yellow in her hand. "See, that's me. I'm holding a pencil because I'm going to be a reporter."

"You can barely read."

"Shut up! I'm the smartest girl in my class."

"Whatever."

Maddy starts to cry again. "Why won't you believe me? I know you remember. Somewhere you have to remember all the good times we had."

"Why are you doing this? Why are you forgetting about Mommy and Daddy?" Stacey points towards the door. "That crazy lady isn't your friend! You're my sister. We came here after Mommy and Daddy died. Why don't you remember that?"

"Because it's not real." Maddy takes the sheets of paper and then folds them up. "I know what it is: your real parents were mean to you. They were so mean you ran away from them. You don't want to remember that, so you won't remember anything else."

"That's stupid."

"Is not!"

"Just leave me alone."

"Fine," Maddy says with a huff. "We gotta get ready for the presentation anyway. If you're still going."

"Yes, but not with *her*."

"I love Grace, even more than I love you. Don't make me choose."

Maddy crawls out of bed. With her nose in the air she stomps out of the room, to leave Stacey alone. Stacey wipes at her eyes. As much as Stacey hates the crazy lady and this new Maddy, she wants to see Darren, to apologize again for what happened the last time they saw each other.

She starts to crawl out of bed.

Chapter 37

The dress Jamie bought for Stacey is even shorter than she remembers. The hem of the skirt is above her knees. It's tight around her stomach too, so that it feels like someone's tightened a rubber band around her middle. I didn't get that fat in a few weeks, did I? she wonders. It's too late for Grandma to let it out at all; she'll just have to make do.

She takes a few minutes to comb her hair until it's perfectly smooth. She fusses with her bangs to make sure they're straight. When Grandma comes in to check on her, Stacey touches her hair. "Can we do something special with it? I want to look really pretty tonight."

Grandma takes a handful of hair and studies it for a moment. Then she opens a drawer on the vanity. She takes out a silver clip shaped like a butterfly, its wings studded with turquoise. "This used to belong to my daughter," she says. "I think it would look very pretty on you."

"OK," Stacey says. She sits down on the stool and tries not to move while Grandma braids a couple tresses in the back. Then she puts the silver clip near the top of Stacey's head to hold down the braid. "That's really pretty. Thank you, Grandma."

"You're welcome, dear. Would you like any makeup?"

"You said I'm not old enough for makeup."

"Tonight's a special occasion." Grandma smiles and holds up one finger. "It's just for tonight, understand?"

"Yes." Grandma is much better at makeup than Jamie. She puts just a touch of rouge and eyeshadow on Stacey's face. Stacey smiles; she feels older now, like a grown-up. She can't wait until Darren sees her like this.

"Are you ready to sing?"

"Yes."

"That's good."

"Do you think Darren will show up?"

"I hope so. You've both worked very hard on this, haven't you?"

"Yes."

"Then I'm sure he will." Grandma takes Stacey's hand to help her off the stool. "Your sister and Grandpa are waiting for us in the car."

***

Stacey is relieved to see the crazy lady isn't there. Though Maddy said she's a grown-up, she still sits on her booster seat; her big butt hangs over the edges. She wears a yellow dress that's even tighter on her belly than Stacey's dress is. Her hair is up in a bun that's supposed to make her look more like an old lady.

"You look nice," Stacey says, to apologize for earlier.

"Tanks. You wook nice too." Stacey knows Maddy said it in that silly lisp so Stacey will forgive her for earlier. The lisp works. "I'm sorry about what I said."

"I'm sowwy too."

"You can stop doing that."

"What?"

"The *wisp*. I know you're faking it."

"Sorry," Maddy says. She emphasizes the R's.

"It's OK." They hug briefly, but barely touch so they won't mess up their dresses or hair.

They don't say a lot as Grandpa drives them into the city. Grandma looks back a few times to check on them. She doesn't say anything either. This gives Stacey time to think about Darren. She hopes he'll be there. If he's not, then she'll know he doesn't really love her. She remembers what Grandma said about them. "Grandma, what's puppy love?" Stacey asks.

"Oh, that? It's just a silly old expression grown-ups use to describe children who are madly in love."

"What's it got to do with puppies?"

"I don't know, dear. I suppose because puppies are children too."

"So when you said Darren and I had puppy love, you meant because we're kids?"

"That's right, dear."

"You and Grandpa aren't puppy love?"

Grandpa snickers at this. "We stopped being puppies a long time ago, kid."

"So what is it when old people love each other?"

Grandpa looks over at Grandma and smiles. "That's true love," he says. He takes his eyes off the wheel to kiss Grandma's lips. "Gross," Stacey mutters.

There are a lot of cars at St. Andrew's. It's impossible to see Dr. Macintosh's SUV among all the other vehicles. She doesn't see Mr. Borstein's car either. Jamie said he would be here tonight, that he promised he would have to die to not be here. Stacey hopes it doesn't come to that.

Grandpa drops them off at the admin building, just like their first day. Also like their first day Dr. Armey is there, but not with her stupid son. She smiles down at Stacey and Maddy. "Hello, Stacey. Hello, Madison. Aren't you both looking cute?"

"Thank you," they say together.

"The parents are all going into the auditorium," Dr. Armey says to Grandma. "Stacey and Madison should report to their homerooms before they go down to the auditorium."

"I'm sure you children know the way," Grandma says. "Stacey, make sure your little sister gets there all right."

"Yes, Grandma." Stacey takes Maddy's hand. "Come on, let's go."

Some of the older kids serve as guides to lead the parents to the auditorium. Stacey looks for Jamie, but doesn't see her until they get to Maddy's homeroom. Jamie waits for her there in the blue dress she bought. She has her hair in a French braid and wears a little more makeup than Stacey.

"There you are. I figured you'd get here eventually." Jamie bends down to pinch Maddy's cheek. "You look real cute."

"Thank you," Maddy says.

Stacey lets go of Maddy. Unconcerned if anyone sees her, she gives Maddy a hug. "Good luck," she says.

"You too." Maddy goes a step farther and kisses Stacey's cheek. Then she rushes inside to show off her dress and hair to all her friends.

"You look cute too," Jamie says. She tries to pinch Stacey's cheek, but Stacey bats her hand away.

"Stop that!"

"I'm just kidding."

They walk down the hall to Stacey's homeroom. "Have you seen Darren?" Stacey asks. "He wasn't at school today."

"I haven't seen him today either. It'd be just like that freak to leave you hanging."

"He's not a freak. He's my boyfriend," Stacey says.

"Fine, you're both freaks." When Stacey frowns, Jamie grins at her. "Gotcha."

"Stop it! I'm serious. I love him."

"I'm sorry. I'm sure he'll be here. Or he might have gone to the auditorium already to tune up the piano or something."

"Maybe." Stacey figures the only way to find out is to go inside. She gives Jamie a hug just like Maddy. "Good luck to you too."

"Hey come on, I'm not hardly doing anything. I just have two sentences about the Berlin Wall falling down."

"Oh."

Jamie leans forward to kiss Stacey's cheek the way Maddy did. "I can't wait to hear your singing. I'm going to record it on my phone so everyone can hear it. Maybe even some record producer will hear it and give you a contract."

"Shut up."

"It could happen."

"Unlikely."

"Well, there's always a first time." They hug again and then Jamie hurries away to get to her homeroom.

Stacey goes into her classroom to find Darren isn't there. She tries not to show any reaction to this. She just goes over to the desk where she usually sits, away from everyone else. She wishes she had her phone, but she left it at home. All she can do is stare at the floor and wait.

"Looks like someone got dumped," Keshia says with a triumphant sneer.

Stacey continues to stare down at the floor. There's nothing she can say. Keshia is right.

***

Darren isn't in the auditorium either. He really is going to ditch her. The fourth grade is huddled in a corner of the backstage area to wait for their turn. Stacey sees Jamie with her class. They exchange waves, but can't leave the group now. Maddy is near the front of the backstage area. She's like a second teacher as she appraises the appearance of her classmates. She actually forces one girl to take out her pigtails so Maddy can retie them to look more even.

From backstage, Stacey hears Dr. Armey's voice say, "Welcome parents, alumni, and future students of St. Andrew's Academy. Tonight we are here to celebrate one hundred fifty years of providing the best elementary and intermediate education in the world."

The headmaster stops to wait for applause. She continues, "Tonight our elementary classes will perform for you as a tribute to the events and people that have shaped the last hundred fifty years. We will begin with the kindergartners performing a skit on the founding of St. Andrew's Academy."

There's more applause while Mrs. Cohen literally pushes the kindergartners onto the stage. Stacey doesn't watch, but she can hear how stupid it is. Most of the babies don't even know their lines. One starts to cry and runs backstage. Stacey hopes Maddy doesn't do that or suck her thumb or any of the other baby things she does.

There's undeserved applause as the babies finish their skit. To make room backstage they go directly to sit in a row reserved for them. Dr. Armey takes the microphone to say, "And now our first graders will present a tribute to the presidents of the United States over the last hundred fifty years."

Stacey breaks away from her class so she can peek through a gap in the curtain to watch Maddy. Since they start with Lincoln, Maddy stands off to the side with the others. Being the bossiest kid in her class, she continues to hiss into the ears of the other kids, probably to remind them of their lines.

After about ten minutes, it's time for Maddy to perform. There's a boy on stage with her to play Mr. Roosevelt. He sits in a wheelchair, which is how he was cast for the part. Maddy delivers her first line on time; she puts her hand to her head and sounds overly dramatic. "Oh, Franklin, I'm so afraid this terrible Depression will never end."

"Relax, Eleanor. We have nothing to fear but fear itself," the boy says. He's robotic, but he gets the lines right. He's probably scared of what Maddy will do if he doesn't.

Another boy holds up a posterboard sign that says in shaky letters, "Twelve years later…"

They couldn't put the wheelchair boy on a bed, so he leans back in his chair as much as he can. Maddy kneels down next to him. She wipes his forehead with a handkerchief. "Oh, Franklin," she says again, "don't leave us. I need you. America needs you to end this awful war."

"I'm sorry, Eleanor, but I can't." The boy is still robotic, even when he touches Maddy's cheek. "But be secure in the know-ledge," he says, tripping over the big word, "that our nation will be in safe hands."

Maddy pushes the boy back to the side of the stage. As she does, she looks back. Stacey gives her a thumbs-up. Maddy smiles and her cheeks redden with pride. Then Stacey retreats to prepare for her part of the show.

***

The second graders do a presentation on inventions of the last hundred fifty years. Stacey doesn't pay any attention to them. She finds a chair to sit on while she worries more and more Darren won't show up. She'll have to go up there alone and stand all by herself on stage with all those eyes staring at her. She won't even have Darren's piano to accompany her.

It's not fair. This is Grandma's fault. If she hadn't been so mean, Darren would be here and they could hold hands somewhere as they wait for their turn. Grandma scared him off, made him afraid to be near Stacey. That or she turned Darren's uncle against them to keep Darren out of the presentation. Does his uncle really want him to fail the project? This is half of their grade for the semester; an F will make it hard for Darren to even pass the fourth grade. Is that what the adults want?

Keshia is happy to add to Stacey's misery. "Your boyfriend hasn't shown up yet, has he?"

"He's not my boyfriend," Stacey says. "I don't even like him."

"That's not what I hear. I hear you two have been kissing all over the place."

"Have not."

Keshia puckers her lips. She kisses at the air. "Oh, Darren, I love you, I love you. I want to have your weird little babies."

"Shut up!" Stacey shouts. She tries not to cry so she won't ruin her makeup.

"You two deserve each other. You're both losers."

"We are not!"

"You're probably going to pee your pants up there and then run away like a stupid little baby."

"Leave me alone!"

Ms. Lowry hisses at her to be quiet. "Stacey, what is the meaning of this?"

"Keshia's being mean to me."

"Both of you be quiet right now or else I'll fail you."

That gets Keshia to shut up. She retreats back to her friends. She does give Stacey a victorious smile. Darren won't be here and Stacey will do terribly and get a D for the entire project.

No longer caring about her makeup, she turns her head to the corner and cries. She probably looks like a baby to the others, but she doesn't care about that either. All she cares about is Darren. Where is he?

***

The thirdies finish their presentation on sports. Dr. Armey announces, "Our fourth graders will now present the arts."

It's time for them to march onto the stage. Stacey is last; she trudges behind the others as if she's on her way to an execution. She might as well not even bother.

Then she feels someone tap her shoulder. Keshia is already on stage so it can't be her. Her heart leaps with joy to see Darren there. "Darren!" she squeals. She throws her arms around his neck. "You made it!"

"Sorry I was late. There was an accident or something holding up traffic."

"Likely story." She motions to her cheeks that are all smudged now from her tears. "Look what you did."

"I'm sorry. It wasn't my fault."

"What about class today? Why weren't you there?"

"I was too nervous." He pats his stomach. "I didn't eat anything all day so I won't throw up later."

"Gross!"

Ms. Lowry appears, her arms crossed and face red. "What are you two doing? Get on stage immediately."

"Yes, ma'am," Stacey says. She takes Darren's hand to lead him onto the stage.

They stand off to the side with the others to wait for their turn. She doesn't pay attention to the others; she whispers into Darren's ear, "I missed you so much. I thought you didn't like me anymore."

"I could never stop liking you."

"Even if I were mean like Keshia?"

"You could never be as mean as her."

She giggles a little and covers her mouth with her hand so they won't get yelled at. "Probably not. Unless you do something like that again."

Keshia's presentation on the 1910s and '20s is right before theirs. Lacy Doubletree is her partner. They're both dressed in period costumes. Keshia sets up a CD player to go with her presentation. It starts to play some kind of marching band music. Keshia just about pushes Lacy forward to begin. "This music was very popular with people a hundred years ago," Lacy says flatly.

Keshia takes over a couple minutes later. Her presentation is on jazz music. "My great-grandpa was a jazz musician in the Roaring Twenties. He played with people like Louis Armstrong and Duke Ellington. This is him playing the trumpet," Keshia says. She stops so everyone can hear the music. "He was one of the greatest musicians of the era. Isn't that right, Great-Grandpappy?"

A spotlight comes on. Stacey sees an old black man stand up at the back of the auditorium. His face is so wrinkled he looks like a raisin. He must be a hundred years old. That doesn't stop him from lifting a trumpet. The notes are a little unsteady, but the audience roars with applause as he plays. Keshia turns to Stacey and grins triumphantly.

"That's not fair," Stacey growls. "He's doing most of the work."

"I can't believe that's her great-grandfather," Darren says.

"It's probably not. It's probably just some old man she paid."

"Don't worry, your singing will make everyone forget about this."

"And your piano playing."

The old man finishes and then takes his bows. The audience still applauds long after he sits down. Keshia applauds too. Everyone but Stacey does. That big rat, Stacey thinks. She hopes Darren is right, though right now she doubts it.

***

It takes three janitors to wheel the piano into place. It's a grand piano like Darren has. In fact, it's exactly like Darren's piano. "Did you bring your piano?"

"Why do you think it took so long?"

She has to resist the urge to kiss him right there in front of everyone. "Here we go," she says. A smatter of applause welcomes them to the stage. As they practiced, Stacey takes the microphone. Darren noodles around on the piano to get his fingers ready to play.

Stacey puts the microphone to her lips. She sees hundreds of faces out there, none of them familiar. She wishes she could see Grandma, Grandpa, and Maddy right now so she wouldn't feel so alone. Out of the corner of her eye she sees Keshia with an evil grin.

"Hi," Stacey whispers into the microphone. She takes a deep breath and tries to focus on the script they wrote. "During the Depression and World War II, America's spirits were very low at times. Music helped them through these troubled times. There was still jazz, but new forms took root as well. Perhaps one of the best-known artists of this era was named Cole Porter. My grandpa says he wrote some of the greatest love songs ever." Stacey pauses to wait for the audience's laughter to die down. Darren wrote that joke; he said it would sound cute when she said it.

Once the laughter has faded, she continues, "We'd like to take a few minutes to introduce you to this wonderful music that lifted so many spirits."

That's Darren's cue. He's right on time. The problem is with her. Her stomach begins to churn so violently she can feel the lasagna from dinner in her throat. She's going to choke—literally if not figuratively.

Darren's such a pro that he doesn't miss a beat; he circles around to pick her up just like they did in practice when she missed something. She's so lucky to have him for a partner. He's so sweet and considerate. Too bad she's such a mess.

She turns to him. He nods slightly to her, not enough anyone should notice. He mouths, "You can do it."

She takes another deep breath. Then she starts to sing. The audience melts away. So do Keshia and the rest of her classmates. It's just her and Darren on the stage. It's just her and Darren in the whole world right then, his piano and her voice in perfect harmony. The beautiful words of Mr. Porter about love become her words to Darren about their love, a love that will last forever.

At the end of the medley she sits on the bench, as if she really is singing to just him. She puts one hand on his head to ruffle his hair. During a pause she kisses him on the cheek and then leaps to her feet. With triumph she sings, "Anything goes!"

A wave of applause washes over her. She blinks her eyes a few times as she remembers there's a whole audience there. The microphone slips from her sweaty fingers; she doesn't bother to pick it up.

Darren comes up next to her and takes her hand. They take a few bows for the audience, which only drives the audience to applaud louder. Stacey can hear a few people shout for an encore. But there won't be an encore; she's much too exhausted for that. She clings to Darren for support as she stumbles backstage.

Jamie is there to help her over to a chair. "Oh. My. God!" Jamie shrieks. "You totally kicked ass."

"Thanks."

"You did too," she says to Darren. "That was fucking amazing!"

Jamie's teacher clears her throat. "Well it was!" she shoots back. She takes her phone out of her pocket. "I got it all right here. Just a few seconds and it'll be on YouTube so everyone can see it."

"Everyone?" Stacey asks. Her voice cracks as she remembers kissing his cheek. Billions of people will be able to see that now.

Jamie puts a hand on her shoulder. "You'll be a superstar by tomorrow morning."

"Great." Stacey runs her hand through her sweaty hair. "I think I need a nap."

***

They stay backstage through the rest of the presentation. Jamie does an OK job with her lines, but she doesn't get any applause for it, except from Stacey. Her reading on the Berlin Wall won't go up on YouTube either. Lucky her.

Before she goes out for her final remarks, Dr. Armey says, "I think everyone would appreciate it if you two went out for an encore."

"Do we have to?" Stacey asks.

"I'll make sure Ms. Lowry gives you extra credit," she says.

Stacey looks to Darren. "What do we do?"

"It's up to you."

Stacey smiles at him. "I know a song we can do."

His face pales. "Not that one."

"Why not? I know the words. You know the music. It's perfect."

Darren stares at her for a moment and then nods. "OK."

Dr. Armey goes out to deliver her final remarks. "We would like to thank all of you for helping to make this possible. St. Andrew's couldn't exist without all of the students, faculty, parents, and alumni throughout the last hundred and fifty years. We hope to continue molding tomorrow's young leaders for another hundred fifty years and beyond."

While the headmaster speaks, Stacey and Darren scamper across the stage to hide behind the piano. She can feel the nervousness in her stomach again. They don't have to do this, but they could both use the extra credit, not to mention Dr. Armey's gratitude.

"And now as a special treat, I'd like to reintroduce a couple of St. Andrew's students with very bright futures. Our little songbird Stacey Chang and accompanying her on the piano, Darren Macintosh."

Darren takes his place at the piano while Stacey goes over to Dr. Armey and accepts the microphone like a baton in a relay race. Stacey clears her throat; she hopes she can go through with this. "Hi again," she whispers into the microphone. "We'd like to share another song with you, a song written by a very good friend of mine."

Darren finishes his warmup. With a flourish he starts into a sunny, up-tempo beat. She doesn't miss a note this time; she wants to make Darren's song perfect. "Stacey, you brighten my days," she begins. She blushes to sing her own name. "Like a summer sun's warm rays—"

The rest of the audience disappears again as she focuses on Darren. He focuses on his keyboard; his cheeks burn red and not from the effort. This is the first time any of his music has been played in public. She just hopes he doesn't trip over any notes.

Of course he doesn't. His fingers are too well-trained for that. She doesn't miss any notes either. Again she sits down on the piano bench, only this time because she's so tired. Though she still sings into the microphone, she feels as if she's whispering the words into Darren's ear. "I hope you'll stay," she sings. She holds out the last word as long as she can. When she can't anymore, she tosses the microphone aside to kiss Darren on the mouth. She doesn't care if everyone can see her, not anymore.

Chapter 38

Darren's uncle is the first of their relatives to congratulate them. He crushes Darren in a hug. "Your mother would be so proud," he says and then tousles his nephew's hair.

"Thanks, Uncle Bob."

Dr. Mac keeps an arm around Darren's shoulder as he turns to Stacey. "And you were amazing. I don't think there's any question about what you'll be when you grow up."

"Thanks." Stacey looks down at her feet. "I couldn't have done it without Darren."

"Of course not. You're a team. Like Simon & Garfunkel or Sonny & Cher."

"Who?"

"Never mind. The important thing is that you two were brilliant."

"Does that mean I can still come over to play with Darren?"

"You'll have to discuss that with your grandmother."

"OK," she says. She gives Darren a hug. "I'll call you later."

"OK," he says, back to the regular, shy Darren. "See you at school on Monday."

"Right."

She finds her family in the lobby. Everyone else has gone now, back to their cars or to wander around the rest of the campus. Maddy runs to her and almost bowls her over. Maddy's arms clamp around Stacey's chest. "You were great!" Maddy shouts. "I knew you could do it."

"Thanks."

Grandma pats her on the back. With far more restraint she says, "You were very good, dear. Just lovely."

"Thanks, Grandma."

Grandpa is next. He gives her a rough hug. "I'm so proud of you, kid."

Then she sees the crazy lady over by a wall. Worse yet, the crazy lady is talking to Jamie. Jamie shows Grace something on her phone, probably her video of Stacey singing. "What's *she* doing here?" Stacey asks.

"Grace came to see me," Maddy says. "And you too. She's our friend."

"She's not my friend." Stacey pulls away from her family to stomp over to Grace and Jamie.

Jamie turns to her and says, "Why didn't you tell me your cousin was so cool? We were just playing Angry Birds and—"

"She's not my cousin."

"She's not? But she said—"

"She's just some freak who thinks she knows us," Stacey says. She takes Jamie's hand to pull her away. To Grace she shouts, "Stay away from my family!"

"Stacey, please—"

"Shut up! I don't ever want to see you again. You're nothing but a mean old liar!"

They leave Grace there to cry. Jamie shakes her hand out of Stacey's. "What the hell? That was way harsh."

"I don't care. She's trying to ruin everything."

"OK. Calm down. Don't freak out on me."

"I'm not freaking out!"

"Yeah, sure," Jamie says in a tone that clearly indicates otherwise.

Stacey turns away from her and heads over to her grandparents. "Can we go home now?"

"Not until you apologize," Grandma says.

"No! I'm not ever going to apologize. I hate her!"

"Stacey Lynn Chang, I have had enough of that. You march over to her and apologize right now or you'll be grounded for a month."

"I don't care! Ground me forever if you want."

Maddy has a far different punishment in mind. She bowls into Stacey again; this time she knocks her over. They wrestle around on the floor; Maddy tries to hit her, but doesn't succeed much. "Get off me!" Stacey shouts.

"No! Not until you apologize to Grace."

"Never!"

They wrestle around for another minute or so, until Grandma and Grandpa separate them. Grandpa takes Stacey and clamps down on her wrist hard enough to make her wince. "That's it young lady. I've had enough of your attitude. You're going to apologize or I'm going to paddle your little ass until it's red."

Stacey tries to shake out of Grandpa's grip, but he's too strong. He drags her over to where Grace is still crying, her face even paler than before. Grandpa shoves Stacey forward. "Go on, young lady. Say it."

Stacey looks down at the floor. "I'm sorry," she whispers.

"Say it like you mean it," Grandpa snarls.

"I'm sorry I've been so mean, Grace," Stacey says. "I don't hate you."

"That's better," Jake says.

"Thank you," Grace says. "That's very grown up of you."

Stacey turns to her grandfather. "Can we go home now?"

"In a few minutes. Why don't you say goodbye to your friend?"

"OK."

She trudges over to Jamie, who isn't crying, but looks almost as pale as Grace. "I'm sorry about that," Stacey says. "You must think I'm a total freak now."

"Kinda."

"I'm sorry."

"Hey, whatever. It's fine." Though Jamie's voice sounds so hollow that Stacey knows it's not fine.

Stacey reaches for her necklace. "You should take this back. I don't deserve it."

"Come on, Stacey, don't be like that. You're still my best friend."

"You mean it?"

"Of course." Jamie sounds more sincere this time. They hug for a few moments. Then Jamie pats her on the back. "I got to go before Caleb drives Daddy crazy with his whining. I'll text you later, OK?"

"OK."

There's one last person to apologize to. Stacey goes over to Maddy, who clings to Grandma. "I'm sorry, Madison. I'm sorry I was so mean."

Maddy sniffles, but says nothing for a minute. She finally peels herself off Grandma's leg. "I forgive you," she says. "But you have to accept that Grace is my friend. My bestest friend in the whole world."

"I understand."

"You're still my big sister, though."

"Thanks." They hug and then everything seems back to normal.

At least until Grandpa comes back, his phone against his ear. "We'll be there in about an hour," he says. He hangs up the phone and then looks down at Stacey and Maddy. "Dr. Palmer wants to see you girls at her lab right away. She says she has some really good news for you."

"Good news about what?" Stacey asks.

"About making you big again," Grandpa says.

"She's going to make us big again?" Maddy says. She starts to jump up and down. "Oh boy!" Then she races across the lobby to Grace. "Grace, did you hear? The doctor's going to make me a big girl again!"

"Now don't get your hopes up," Grandma cautions. "What exactly did she say?"

While her grandparents talk and while Maddy continues to celebrate, Stacey shivers as if a blizzard has suddenly blown in. What if Dr. Palmer really can make her a grown-up? What would happen with her and Darren? She looks over at Maddy and Grace for the answer. Except she would be the grown-up and Darren the kid. They couldn't be together anymore or else people would think it was creepy, like one of those bad people they warned her about at school. She couldn't kiss him or hug him or hold his hand again—

Stacey makes it through the doors before anyone can stop her.

Chapter 39

There are still people out front by the admin building to make small talk like adults do. Stacey sees one of those people is Mr. Borstein. Maybe he wants to get more clients for his business. At the moment she doesn't care because it provides the perfect chance to escape.

She finds Jamie and Caleb in the backseat of Mr. Borstein's car. Jamie screams when Stacey thuds against the side of the car. Out of breath from running so far, Stacey can only stand there and pant while Jamie rolls down the window.

"Stacey, what the hell? You scared the crap out of me."

"Sorry."

"What's going on? Why were you running?"

Stacey isn't good at lying. Her grandparents, teachers, and the reverend all say lying is wrong. In this case, she feels it's necessary. Jamie will never believe her crazy story; not even Stacey really believes it.

"My grandparents are going to get rid of me," she says. "They're going to send me and Maddy to a foster home. Back in California."

"What? No way! Your grandparents wouldn't do that."

"They can't afford us," Stacey says. Now that she's begun, it's easier to lie. "This new family is richer."

"Oh my God," Jamie says. "When?"

"A couple of days." It doesn't take much effort for Stacey to cry. "I'm not going to go."

"Then what are you going to do?"

"I'm going to run away. Me and Darren. We can find somewhere to hide in the city." Stacey leans closer to the window. "They're going to be looking for me here any minute. You got to get me out of here. *Please.*"

"Of course I will. But you can't ride in the car. Daddy will see you." Jamie looks around. Then she leans over the seat, to open the glove box. She punches a button along the side. "Climb in the trunk."

"The trunk? I'll suffocate."

"Only if we leave you in there for a couple of days," Jamie says. "It'll just be until we get home. Then I'll let you out. I promise."

"OK," Stacey says. She doesn't see much of an alternative. She lifts the trunk. It's not very big, but big enough for her to squeeze inside. Jamie gets out to close the lid for her.

She looks down at Stacey for a moment and then says, "I'll ask Daddy to get us out of here right away. Once we're home and everyone's upstairs, I'll sneak down to let you out. Try not to panic or anything until then. Just relax." Jamie hands her phone to Stacey. "Here, you can use this. Just don't post nasty messages on other people's walls with my account."

"I won't. Thanks."

"Anything for my best friend." Then Jamie slams the lid down and Stacey is alone. The only light comes from the screen of Jamie's phone. Stacey takes a deep breath and tries not to think about how small the trunk is or wonder how long she can breathe in here before she suffocates.

She isn't sure how long it is before the car starts to move. At least Mr. Borstein hasn't opened the trunk to turn her over to Grandma and Grandpa. As she listens to the purr of the engine, Stacey tries to piece things together. Why would they want to make her a grown-up? There is a part of her that would like to be grown up, so she can do whatever she wants, but not without Darren. She doesn't want to wait eight years or longer for him to grow up too.

The hum of the engine and the darkness, combined with her exhaustion from the busy night, lull her to sleep. She wakes up with a startled cry as the trunk lid pops open. She braces herself for Mr. Borstein to ask what she's doing in there, but it's not him. It's just Jamie.

"You all right in there?"

"I'm fine." Stacey smiles. "I took a little nap."

Jamie holds up a duffel bag. "I brought you some clothes and shoes and food. There's some money in there too from my piggy bank to help get you started."

"Jamie, no, I can't take your money."

"You have to, Stacey. I don't want you eating out of dumpsters and stuff."

Stacey has to admit Jamie has a point. She and Darren will need some money for food and maybe for somewhere to stay. "I'll pay you back. I promise."

"Forget about it." Jamie sticks out her hand to help Stacey out of the trunk. Once Stacey is out of the car, Jamie hugs her. "You just let me come visit once you find somewhere, OK?"

"OK." Jamie's done so much already that Stacey hates to ask, "How am I going to get to Darren's house?"

"I already called a cab. It'll be here in a few minutes."

"Are you going to get in trouble?"

"Me? Nah." Jamie reaches into the trunk for her phone. "Daddy thinks I came down here to find my phone. He won't miss any of the other stuff."

"That's good." Stacey looks down at her feet and feels suddenly shy around her best friend as it comes time to say goodbye. "I can't thank you enough. You're the bestest friend anyone could have."

They hug again. Jamie sniffles and then says, "Damn it, now you've got me crying. Why do you do that?"

"I'm sorry."

"You let me know you're safe as soon as you can, all right?"

"All right."

They walk up from the garage, out to the front of the building. The taxi pulls up a couple of minutes later. Jamie hands the driver a wad of bills. Then she leans in Stacey's window. "See you later."

"Later," Stacey says. She wishes she could say more, but there's no time.

She turns to look back at Jamie on the curb; her best friend waves to her. She waves back. Then the cab turns a corner and Jamie is gone.

***

The taxi drops her off a couple houses away from Darren's uncle's house. Jamie thought of everything. She's way smarter about this stuff than Stacey. "Thank you," she says to the driver and then climbs out.

Stacey figures by now her grandparents have probably called Dr. Macintosh to ask if she's turned up there. They probably called Jamie's dad too. She hopes Jamie doesn't get in trouble for helping her. No, Jamie is too smart to get caught, not unless Stacey gets caught and confesses.

Dr. Macintosh doesn't have much of a yard. The side yard is more of an alley, where the doctor keeps his trash cans and a grill. She slips past these, into the tiny backyard. She looks up, and tries to remember the layout of the house. Which window is Darren's? If he's even in his bedroom. But if he doesn't have his piano, where else will he be?

She figures it must be the second window. It's dark, but he's probably asleep. Now she just needs a rock. She squats down on the ground and feels around until she finds a stone big enough to make some noise, but small enough not to break the window. She cocks her arm and then throws the rock.

She misses by at least ten feet to the right. She can't see where the rock lands, so she has to find another. She makes sure to get a handful of them in case she misses again.

It takes her four tries before she hits what she hopes is Darren's window. Nothing happens for a minute. She tries again; she just needs two tries to hit the window. After about thirty seconds, the light comes on. The curtains part to reveal she was right about it being Darren's window.

She was right about him being asleep too; he's dressed in his pajamas. She waves to him and motions for him to open the window. He does so and then asks, "Stacey?"

"Darren, you gotta let me in. It's important."

"Can't you just go to the front door?"

"No! I'm running away from home. You can't let your uncle know."

"Stacey—"

"Darren, just let me in. I'll explain everything."

"Well, all right," he says after a minute of deliberation.

"But don't let your uncle know."

"I won't."

She waits for a couple of minutes in the backyard, between some lawn chairs so no one will see her. As she waits, she begins to shiver. It's gotten cold, especially in this dress. She unzips the bag Jamie gave to her. There's a pink hooded sweatshirt inside; Stacey puts it on over her dress, which warms her a little. She really needs to put on some pants. Where is Darren?

The back door opens. Darren sticks his head out. "Stacey?" he calls out much too loud. She hisses at him to be quiet. "Sorry."

"You didn't tell your uncle, did you?"

"No, he's on the phone."

Probably with her grandparents. She scurries over to the door. "Let's go up to your room."

"My room? But—"

"I'll explain up there. OK?"

He thinks about it for a few moments. "OK."

They hold hands as he sneaks her upstairs. They can hear Dr. Macintosh in the living room on the phone. "I'm sure she didn't get too far," he says. "She's just a little girl."

This makes her feel a swell of pride. This little girl got a lot farther than Dr. Mac thinks, right into his house. Too bad she can't walk into the living room to gloat about it. Instead she follows Darren up to his room.

Once the door is closed, Stacey kisses him on the lips. Then they sit down on the bed, but keep their clothes on this time. "Stacey, what's going on? Why are you sneaking around?"

"I told you, I'm running away from home."

"Why?" She gives him the same story she gave Jamie earlier. He believes it just like she did. "That's terrible. How soon are you going?"

"I'm not going to go. That's why I'm running away."

"Where are you going to go?"

"I'm not sure yet." She reaches into the duffel bag. "Jamie gave me some money and stuff. We can find somewhere for a couple of days while we figure things out."

Darren stares at her blankly. "We?"

"You and me. We have to go together."

"I can't run away from home. Uncle Bob will worry about me."

"You can let him know you're safe after we find somewhere."

"But my mom is going to come home in a few weeks."

"Darren, I love you. Don't you love me too?"

"Well sure, but I can't just run away from home."

Stacey hangs her head. She starts to cry. When Darren tries to put an arm around her, she shakes him away. "Stop it! You don't love me. You don't care about me at all."

"That's not true. You know how much I care about you. I wrote a song for you."

"So what? If you really love me then you'll go away with me so we can be together forever."

"But Stacey, we're too little to run away."

"No we aren't. I got this far already, didn't I?"

"I guess—"

She takes Darren's hand again. She looks into his eyes to make one final pitch. "Darren, I love you and you love me. That's all that matters. We can figure out the rest later. Come with me. Please?"

Darren looks away from her, down at the floor. "I'm sorry, Stacey. I can't go, not right now. Maybe in a few months, after school is out—"

She rolls onto the bed and begins to sob. Darren tries to pat her back, to comfort her. She ignores him. "Stacey, don't cry. It won't be so bad. We can write—"

She rolls over to face him again. She slaps him across the face. "Shut up!" she screams. She pushes him backwards, off the bed. "Don't you understand how much I love you? I'm giving up everything for you. My whole life, just for you. And you won't even come with me because you're too scared."

She runs to the door, but doesn't get far. Dr. Macintosh is in the doorway. She tries to dart past him, but he's too quick; he seizes her by the shoulders. He lifts her into the air. She screams and kicks at him, but it doesn't do any good.

"I think it's time we have a talk," Dr. Macintosh says. "Darren, stay here. I'll deal with you after Stacey goes home." Of course that coward Darren doesn't come to her aid. He just stares as Dr. Macintosh carries her away.

***

He carries her down to the living room. "Lemme go! Lemme go!" she screams while she continues to thrash in his grasp. "I wanna go!"

"Not until we've talked about this," he says. He drops her onto an armchair. Before she can spring to her feet, he pushes her back against the cushions. "Stacey, stop it. I can give you something to put you to sleep if I have to, but I hope we can discuss this like grown-ups."

"I don't wanna discuss anything. I wanna go."

He sits on the ottoman for the armchair so he can keep her on the couch. All she can do is curl up into a ball on the chair. "Your grandmother called me. She's very worried about you."

"I don't care."

"I know that's not true. I know you love your grandmother."

"Do not. I hate them. They want me to go away."

"Do they?"

"They want me to grow up so they don't have to take care of me. They don't want me and Maddy around anymore."

"If that were true, she wouldn't have called me, would she? She wouldn't be at home, crying because you ran away."

"It's her fault. They made me do it."

"They only want what's best for you."

"Do not."

"You think remaining a little girl is the best thing for you?"

"I *am* a little girl."

"We both know that's not true."

"It is so true!" Stacey presses her head against the cushions. "Why do people keep saying that I'm not me?"

"Because it's true. Stacey Chang isn't real. You created her when you became little."

"Did not. Mommy and Daddy named me."

"I see. Describe Mommy and Daddy for me."

"What?"

"Tell me what Mommy and Daddy were like."

"Daddy was a soldier. He was big and strong and very brave. Mommy was very nice. She took care of us."

"I see. What were their names?"

"Mommy and Daddy."

"No, I mean what were their real names?"

"Qiang and Steve," Stacey says.

"Those are very nice names. How old were they?"

"I don't know. Old."

"And how did they die?"

Stacey hides her face from Dr. Macintosh and shakes her head. She doesn't want to talk about their deaths. She doesn't want to relive those terrible days. She whimpers when Dr. Macintosh puts a hand on her back. "Stacey, answer the question. How did they die?"

"I won't talk about it."

"You won't talk about it because they aren't real. They weren't really your parents and you aren't really Stacey Chang. It's all an elaborate game of make-believe."

"Is not," she mumbles.

"So answer the question. Prove me wrong."

She looks up at him; tears stream down her cheeks. "Daddy died in Afghanistan. Some mean people killed him."

"What about Mommy?"

"She died in a fire. She got me and Maddy out, but she couldn't get out in time."

"Very good."

"You believe me now?"

"I believe Steve and Qiang did exist, just not as your parents. Qiang was the woman who cared for you and Maddy when Dr. Ling took you captive. Do you remember him?"

"No," Stacey says, but she shudders at the name.

"You're lying. You remember him. He was a very bad man. He did awful things to you and Madison. He injected you with a drug that turned you into little girls."

"Nuh-uh."

"He was going to take you both away to China to continue his research, so Qiang helped you escape. She did die in a fire, a fire she set to cover your escape."

"No she didn't. You're lying."

"Am I? I'm sure your grandfather could get a copy of the police report on an explosion at an old elementary school. A lot of people died there, including Qiang."

"Did not."

"Your 'father' wasn't a soldier. He was a policeman named Steve Fischer. Some bad people did kill him, a gangster named Artie Luther. He put a bullet in Steve's head. He didn't really die, though, did he?"

"I don't know."

"The gangster injected Steve with something, the same thing Dr. Ling used on you. So instead of dying, Steve became a young woman. A young woman named Stacey Chance."

Stacey shakes her head. "You're lying! You're lying!"

"I wish I were. Would you like to see proof that I'm not?"

"No."

"Why not? Are you afraid of the truth?"

"I don't care. I wanna go."

"Where are you going to go, Stacey?"

"I don't care."

"I see. How long do you think you'll last out there? You're just a child."

"I can find a way."

"Wouldn't it be better to go home to your grandparents? They only want to help you."

"Do not."

"Don't you want to be a grown-up?"

"No."

"Why not?"

"I just don't."

"I see." Dr. Macintosh doesn't have a notepad, but he taps his knee as if he has a notepad there. "Why did you come here, Stacey?"

"To say goodbye to Darren."

"Darren is important to you?"

"Yes."

"You care about him a lot?"

"Yes."

"You love him?"

She shakes her head and then looks down at the floor. "No."

"I think you do, Stacey. I saw you onstage tonight. You kissed Darren twice. Why did you do that?"

"I don't know."

"I know Darren cares a lot about you too. After you left my house the last time, he was very distraught about it. He loves you, Stacey. Did you know that?"

"He doesn't. Not really."

"What makes you say that?"

"He won't come with me."

"Where?"

"Wherever. He's chicken."

"I see. You came here to ask Darren to run away with you."

"Yes."

"And he wouldn't go?"

"No. He's scared."

"Why do you think he's scared?"

"Because he's stupid."

"That's not a big girl answer, is it?"

"I don't care. He's a stupid boy and I hate him."

"Now I know that's not true."

"Is too."

"If you hated him, you wouldn't have come here, would you?" When she doesn't say anything, Dr. Macintosh says, "Do you remember our last session? When I had you look in the mirror?"

"Yes."

"You saw another face, a woman's face, didn't you?"

"Yes."

"A woman with red hair and blue eyes?"

"Yes."

"You still don't know who that is?"

"No."

"Her name was Stacey too. She was a patient of mine. A very special patient. She was a very good singer too, just like you."

"I don't care."

"Then one night she was singing and she ran away. She disappeared. No one's seen her since then. Not until you saw her in the mirror."

"So what?"

"That woman is you, Stacey. You can keep trying to fight it, but we know it's true. The question is: why don't you want it to be true?"

"I don't know."

"You can tell me, Stacey. I'm not here to judge you, remember? You're safe here. Why don't you want to go back?"

"I don't know!" Stacey curls up on the armchair to sob again. She wishes Dr. Macintosh would leave her alone. She doesn't want to answer any more stupid questions. She just wants to leave, to find somewhere to rest for a long time, to sort everything out. "Why don't you leave me alone?"

"Because I'm your friend, Stacey. I care about you. I want what's best for you."

"Do not."

"I see. You like being ten years old. You like having Tess and Jake take care of you, cleaning up after you, bathing you, buying your clothes. You like depending on them, don't you?"

"No."

"And you like having Madison as your little sister. You like that she needs you for support, as someone to look up to. You missed that before, didn't you? Madison needing you. She didn't need you when she was just your friend, did she? She could have always made other friends, but she couldn't find another sister so easily, could she?"

"Shut up!"

"Everything is so much easier for you this way. There's no confusion about who you are or what you are. Everything is in black-and-white now. Jake and Tess are your loving grandparents. Madison is your sweet baby sister. Jamie is your best friend. Darren is your boyfriend. You don't have to carry around that guilt anymore about not being a good enough father to Madison or sleeping with Grace or not knowing what to do with your life. It's all so simple for you, isn't it?"

"Shut up," she whimpers. She presses her hands to her ears to block out his words. "Leave me alone."

"I'm sorry, Stacey. This isn't your life. Your life is out there. You can't keep hiding from it."

She can't say anything; her throat is too choked with sobs to speak. As much as she doesn't want him to, Dr. Macintosh continues. "Stacey Chang is a wonderful little girl. I wish she were real. I wish she and Darren could be sweethearts forever. But Stacey Chance is a good person too. She's sweet and strong and bright, in her own way. She's a very good friend to a lot of people. A lot of people will be very sad to lose her. Me included."

"Stop it!" Stacey shouts. She shakes her head violently; she hears not just Dr. Macintosh's voice, but others as well. "Go away! I don't wanna go back!"

With a final scream, she passes out.

Chapter 40

It's like a bomb goes off in my head. A dam breaks open and everything rushes out: over fifty years of memories. It's not like they say when you're about to die; everything doesn't come out in chronological order. It is a flood of random images and sounds, some good and a lot that aren't. One moment I see Maddy at the Kozee Koffee, twenty-two years old with pink hair and a nose ring and the next a doctor passes a newborn Maddy into my arms. All of these things fall into place like pieces of a jigsaw puzzle, until I can see the whole picture: the face of Stacey Chance, the one I saw in the mirror but didn't want to recognize.

When I open my eyes, I'm Stacey Chance again, at least on the inside. On the outside I'm still a little Chinese girl. I see that when I sit up a little to find I still have on a pink sweatshirt over my red dress. Dr. Macintosh's face looms large before me and smiles down at me. "Don't try getting up yet," he says.

I realize then I'm on the floor. "How did I get here?" I ask.

"You ran away from your grandparents. Do you remember?"

"No, I meant how did I get on the floor?"

"I put you on the floor. You were having some pretty bad seizures."

"Oh. Did I make a mess?"

"No, I don't think so."

"That's good."

He holds three fingers up to my face. "How many fingers?"

"Three."

"What's your name?"

I sigh and ask, "Which one? The one I was born with or one of the other ones?"

"So you remember now?"

"Yes."

"That's good news."

"Is not," I say. Dr. Macintosh was right: things were a lot better as Stacey Chang. When I was completely immersed in her life everything was better, simpler. I didn't feel any guilt about Maddy or Grace. I didn't feel confused about who I am or the future. Everything was all planned out, even if it was a silly, childish plan. I had dreams again. I was in love with someone my own age who wasn't involved with anyone else. I was closer to Madison than I had been in thirteen years, if not longer.

"This is for the best, Stacey."

"For who?"

"For you. Remember what I told you when you first came to me as Stacey Chang? We needed to integrate your identities. Not repress them. You have to learn to accept who you are, both the good and bad parts of it."

"Why?" I start to cry again as I think of the last month. "I was happy. I mean, happier than I've been in a long, long time."

"Why is that, Stacey?"

"It's like you said: because it was easy, simple. I didn't have all this baggage anymore."

"But it was a lie."

"So what? It was a good lie."

"Do you think you could have gone on living that lie forever?"

"Why not? If Grace hadn't shown up and if Dr. Palmer hadn't called, I'd still be living it. I'd be home right now, dreaming in my bed. Tomorrow I'd get up and Jamie and I would go shopping and maybe see a movie. And Monday I'd go to school and see Darren." I glare hard at Dr. Macintosh. "That's the reason you wanted me to remember, isn't it? You couldn't stand that your nephew and I were in love. I wasn't good enough for him."

"Why would I think that?"

"Because I'm not rich or beautiful or anything like that."

He shakes his head. His voice is still perfectly calm as he says, "Stacey, you made Darren the happiest he's been in his entire life. He never could have gone out on stage to play the piano tonight if you hadn't been there with him."

"Then why do this? We were all happier with the lie."

"Are you sure about that? Do you think Grace was happy?"

I think of Grace the last time I saw her, how pale and thin she'd gotten. "No, I guess not."

"What about your ex-wife, Madison's mother? She's not happy either. And what about Jake and Tess?"

"They like having us around."

"Are you sure about that? You realize how hard Jake's been working so he can provide for two little girls who showed up on his doorstep?"

"He always works hard. And Tess likes us around. She likes being a mommy."

"Not all the time. Like when two little girls are bickering or when one selfish little girl runs away from home."

"Yeah, so maybe it wasn't a honeymoon in paradise for everyone. But it wasn't a cakewalk for everyone when I was grown up either. Tess and Jake still had to take care of me."

"Not as much, though."

"Yeah, maybe not." The realization starts to sink in. "I was being selfish, wasn't I?"

"Not entirely. As I said, you were very helpful for Darren. And for Jamie too."

"Now I'm going to hurt them."

"Kids are resilient. They'll bounce back."

"Will I?"

"I think you can, if you want to." He takes my hand and helps me sit up. "I'll help you."

***

Tess is ecstatic to hear from me. I can hear the tears in her voice as she says, "Oh, thank God! I was so worried about you!"

"I'm sorry, Grandma Tess. I didn't mean to worry you," I say. I sound every bit like a little girl who's been scolded.

"It's all right, dear. The important thing is you're safe."

"Thanks."

"But when you get home, you're grounded for two months."

"Yes, ma'am."

"Now, your grandfather and Madison should still be at the lab. You can probably meet them there if Dr. Macintosh will take you."

"OK." Before I hang up, I say, "I love you, Grandma."

"I love you too, dear. Come back safe."

I turn to Dr. Macintosh. "Can I say goodbye to Darren? I promise I won't be mean."

"Go ahead. I have to ask Mrs. Finley to look after him for a couple of hours anyway."

I run upstairs and knock on Darren's door. "Darren? It's me. I'm really sorry about what happened. Can we talk about it?"

"Go away!" he shouts.

"Darren, please. I might be going away for a really long time. I just want to say goodbye."

I wait for a minute; each second brings me closer to tears. I may not be a little girl on the inside, but I still love Darren with a ten-year-old's enthusiasm. And maybe some of that love wasn't just a little girl's crush. Darren is so sweet and kind and talented and he's not bad-looking, at least not to me.

The door finally opens. He's still in his pajamas, but I can see he's been crying too. I can't blame him after the awful things I said to him. I try to hug him, but he pushes me back. "What do you want?"

"I want to say goodbye. And I'm sorry. I didn't mean all those things I said. I was just mad." My eyes water. It won't be long until I'm a sobbing mess again. "I was so stupid to think I could run away. I mean, I'm just a little girl. I can't even turn on the stove yet."

Darren smiles for just a moment at this. "It was pretty stupid," he says.

"But it's not stupid that I love you, is it?"

"No."

"Good." I lean forward to kiss him on the lips. It's another dry child's kiss, but to me it feels better than even when I kissed Grace. Maybe because my love for Darren is so much purer.

After we pull apart, he asks, "Do you have to leave tonight?"

"I'm afraid so. I wish I could stay," I say and then remember his song for me. "But it's like you said, we can still write. Maybe chat online and stuff. And maybe you can go to college in California or I can go to college here and then we can be together again."

"Maybe."

"But no matter what, I'm never going to forget you. You're my first real boyfriend."

"You're my first real girlfriend too."

"For the rest of my life, even when I'm an old, old lady I can say, 'Darren Macintosh was the first boy I kissed.'"

"I wish you didn't have to go."

"So do I." We look down shyly at the floor at the same time. "I'll talk to you later, OK?"

"OK."

I give him one final peck on the cheek. Then I go downstairs to wait for Darren's uncle to take me back to Lennox Pharmaceuticals.

**

While I wait, I change out of the red dress into something warmer. Jamie gave me a T-shirt and jeans, both as pink as the sweatshirt. When I see myself swaddled in so much pink, I don't feel as bad as I once did. I look cute.

Not long after I step out of the bathroom, Dr. Macintosh returns with an old woman, his next-door neighbor. "Thank you so much, Mrs. Finley," he says. "It should only be for an hour or so. I'm afraid Stacey here isn't feeling well."

I take that as my cue to cough dramatically. "I want Gwamma and Gwampa," I say. I borrow Maddy's cute toddler lisp.

"Oh, you poor dear," Mrs. Finley says. She pats my head. Then she turns back to Dr. Macintosh. "I'll take good care of Darren for you."

"Thank you so much," he says again.

He carries me out to his Lexus. I lean my head against his shoulder like a sick little girl would. "You're sure she's buying this?" I ask.

"You might have oversold it a little."

"Sorry."

He opens the back door and buckles me in the middle. "Stay right there," he says.

"I know. I'm not going anywhere."

I stay in place as he goes around to the driver's seat and gets behind the wheel. He starts up the engine. A few seconds later we're on the road to the lab, where Dr. Palmer promises to have good news for us.

I know something is wrong when there's no one at the front gate. The gate itself is raised so we can drive through, but there's no one inside the guard shack. At least no one alive. Dr. Macintosh doesn't think anything of it, but he's not as familiar with Lennox Pharmaceuticals as I am.

"Do you have a gun?" I ask.

"No. Do I need one?"

"Right now, maybe."

"What's wrong?"

"There should have been someone manning the gate. They wouldn't just leave it open and untended at night, not after what happened with Artie Luther. They aren't that stupid."

"I see. You think we should turn back?"

"No," I say. I point to Jake's Fairlane parked by the front doors. "We gotta see what happened to Jake and Maddy."

"Maybe you should stay here," Dr. Macintosh suggests.

"You won't know where you're going."

"Stacey—"

"Jake and Maddy went in there. They could be dead or hurt. We gotta find out."

"OK," he says. He gets out of the car. I assume he'll open my door for me, but instead he opens the trunk. He rummages around until I see him hold up a tire iron. "It's something, right?"

"Yeah, something."

I climb out of the car. It feels reassuring to take his much-bigger hand. I lead him up to the front doors, which are unlocked. I remember the first time I came here. Artie Luther's goons murdered the guards on duty then.

Whoever broke into Lennox Pharmaceuticals this time isn't any kinder. I press my face against Dr. Macintosh when I see a guard on the floor behind the front desk. He pats my back as I whimper. "It's all right, Stacey."

"Maybe I should go back to the car," I say. "I'm too little for this."

"You'll be fine," he says. "Just keep your eyes closed until I say so."

"OK."

I do as he says, my eyes squeezed shut as we shuffle away from the desk. When I open them again, I see the elevators. "We should take the stairs," I say. My old cop instincts kick in. "They might have sabotaged the elevators."

"That makes sense."

He opens the door to the stairs. The stairs look so much bigger now, like a mountain. He pats my back. "How about a piggyback ride?"

"Sure," I say, the little girl in me unable to resist. Besides, it'll be faster this way.

He tucks the tire iron into his waistband and then picks me up with a groan. "I'm not that heavy," I say. "I'm not fat like Maddy."

"You could lose a few pounds," he says.

I swat at his head as he puts me up on his shoulders. "That's mean."

"I'm joking. I think your little tummy is cute."

"Thanks." I look up at the steps, which seem a lot smaller now. "It's the fifth floor. Watch out for any guards."

"You'll see them before I can."

"Maybe."

At the fourth floor I start to get nervous. What will we find in the lab? Will it be trashed, Jake and Maddy's bloody bodies on the floor? What about Dr. Palmer? Did they kill her too? Or if someone is after FY-1978 again they might have kept her alive, at least for now.

There's no one on the stairs to the fifth floor. If we're lucky, Jake might have taken care of whoever it was. He might be cleaning up right now. Maddy might be napping somewhere, thumb in her mouth while she sleeps.

As Dr. Macintosh opens the door to the fifth floor, we listen for anyone. There's no sound of anyone alive up here. The lights are out, which leaves just dim red emergency lights. I whimper again and lean down to be closer to Dr. Macintosh.

"It's all right, Stacey," he whispers. "Maybe you should stay here."

"No. It'd be scarier to be here alone."

I ask to be put down and he sets me on the floor. I take his hand again and lead him towards Dr. Palmer's lab. He takes out the tire iron again, just in case. We creep along the dark corridors; my stomach churns more with every second as I wait for something to pop out at us. It's even scarier than when Jamie and I watched *Dream House* by ourselves in the theater. If only I could be back home, in my bunk bed, clutching Pinky while I dream.

No one jumps out at us. We reach the doors to the lab. I back away and flatten myself against the wall so Dr. Macintosh can take the lead. He raises the tire iron as he pushes one door open. I close my eyes and wait for the sound of a gunshot or a scream.

I hear Dr. Macintosh ask, "Mr. Madigan? Can you hear me?"

I hurry into the room. The lab is trashed. Jake is on the floor, surrounded by broken glass. There's a large spot of blood on his right calf and a gash on his head. Someone shot him in the leg and then hit him, probably with something made of glass like a beaker.

I kneel down beside him and put my head to his chest. He's still alive! He seems to be breathing normally. Neither wound is probably fatal, unless he loses too much blood. I look up at Dr. Macintosh. "We need to tie off that wound in his leg and bandage his head. There's probably a first aid kit around here somewhere."

"I'll check," Dr. Macintosh says.

While he does that, I glance around the rest of the room. There's no one else in here. No Dr. Palmer. No Maddy. Did she run away to hide somewhere else? We'll have to search the building. After Jake is out of danger of bleeding to death.

Dr. Macintosh returns with a red plastic box. "I found it," he says. He opens it up. I play Florence Nightingale and clean the gash on Jake's head and then apply a bandage to it. As I finish up, his eyes open.

"Stacey?" he whispers.

"Hi, Grandpa," I say. "What happened? Where's Maddy?"

"Took her."

"Who?"

"Ling," he says and then passes out again.

Chapter 41

Dr. Macintosh ties a tourniquet around Jake's leg while I sit on the floor, knees tucked beneath my chin. It can't be Dr. Ling. He's dead. That prison of his exploded. We saw it. The police investigated it. He couldn't have survived.

The cop in me reminds me we didn't actually see him die. The police hadn't identified all of the remains yet. He could have gotten out in time. He could have been wounded, not killed. Though the question then is why he didn't try to abduct us sooner. He had plenty of chances to pluck us away from Jake and Tess.

"That ought to hold him for now," Dr. Macintosh says. "We should call an ambulance."

"You do that. They won't believe me," I say. It occurs to me then how useless I am right now, too little to be much good to anyone, especially my daughter.

I stay with Jake while Dr. Macintosh uses his cell phone to call 911. I hope Jake will wake up again to provide more details, but he stays unconscious. That leaves it up to me, who until two hours ago thought she was a ten-year-old girl.

As I do on stage, I take a couple of deep breaths to try to relax. I close my eyes and try to think. Maddy needs me right now. Not Stacey Chang, her big sister. She needs Detective Steve Fischer, her daddy. First, what does Ling want Maddy for? The FY-1978. I remember what Qiang said, that Ling planned to take us to China so he could run more experiments before he had us killed and dissected.

He'll take her to China. He probably wanted both of us, but he'll settle for just Madison. He'll want to get there before anyone can catch up to him. He'll be safe in China, free from extradition. So he'll take a plane. Commercial flying is out; it's too risky to keep a toddler—even if he drugs her—with him on a plane full of strangers for thirteen hours.

A private jet. There's less security on the smaller airfields. Plus he won't have to worry some do-gooders on the flight will try to stop him. And God knows he can afford to charter a private jet from here to China.

I leap to my feet. I run down the hall and slam into Dr. Macintosh with childish enthusiasm. "Dr. Mac, Dr. Mac! I know where he's taking her!"

"Where's that, sweetheart?"

"Dixon Field."

"You're sure?"

"Yes."

"We should call the police."

"They won't believe us! And we gotta hurry. He's taking her to China!"

"China?"

"He's going to dissect her!"

"You're sure?"

I take his hand and start to pull him towards the door. "Come on, we gotta go!"

"What about Mr. Madigan?"

"You called an ambulance, right?"

"Yes—"

"Then he'll be fine. Let's go!"

I don't ask for a piggyback ride. It's easier for me to run down the stairs than up them. I actually make it down ahead of Dr. Macintosh. He's going to his car, but I stop and point to Jake's. "This will be faster."

"I don't have the keys."

"I do! I took them before I left."

Dr. Macintosh tousles my hair. "You are one clever little girl."

***

Dr. Macintosh hasn't driven a stick in fifteen years. That explains why we're thrown against our seatbelts every time he has to shift for the first couple of miles. "Maybe I should drive," I say sullenly.

"It's coming back to me. Don't worry."

"Will that be before or after I barf?"

"So why Dixon Field?"

"It's the closest. He's going to want to make a fast getaway. Soon as he's over international waters, no one can touch him."

"I hope you're right."

"So do I."

Dixon Field is about ten miles away. Once Dr. Macintosh gets the hang of driving a stick, it only takes us about five minutes to get there. The airfield is located at one end of the island; it faces the ocean so anyone who misses the runway can end up in the drink. It doesn't have terminals or anything like that, just hangars for the companies who keep a plane there.

The gates are locked as we approach. "You think we should run through them?"

"Yes," I say, though I know how pissed Jake will be about his precious Fairlane getting dinged up. But if it lets us save Madison, then it'll be worth it.

The Fairlane roars into the gates. We're lucky this is a private airport that doesn't have anything stronger than a chain-link fence with barbed wire. The car slams through the left side of the gate; it almost bends in half before it bounces away from us. I let out a scream of joy at this, even as I'm being thrown hard against my seatbelt.

"Let's do it again!" I scream.

"Not on your life."

The question now is which hangar belongs to Ling. The easiest way to find out is to zip around the place to look for which doors are open. That's what Dr. Macintosh does. At two in the morning there aren't many hangars to choose from, only one with its door open, a plane being readied for takeoff. There are two big guys near it who sure as hell aren't flight attendants.

"There it is!" I shout. I point to the hangar. Dr. Macintosh skids to a stop and cuts his lights. They've probably heard us already, but if the plane's engines are on, they might not have.

"What now?" he asks.

I reach down to open the glove compartment. I rummage around until I find the spare gun I know Jake keeps in there. A cop in this city can never have too many weapons close at hand. And since he hardly ever took us girls in the car, he didn't have to worry we might find it—until now.

"Here," I say. I pass the gun to him.

"I don't know how to use a gun," he says.

"It's not that hard. I can show you."

It's probably a surreal experience for him to have a ten-year-old girl show him how to use a pistol. I give him the basics about how to turn the safety off and cock the weapon. "It's totally not hard," I say. "Didn't you ever play video games?"

"Not really. I'm a child psychologist."

"Well, do your best."

"Right." He opens the door. "I'll go get her. You stay here."

"Sure." Before he can get out, I lean over to kiss his cheek. "Good luck."

I watch as he creeps towards the hangar. I wait until he's a good fifty yards from the car before I reach into the backseat for the tire iron. Then I get out and run.

***

I don't run straight to the hangar. A little girl all in pink would be pretty damned easy for anyone with eyes better than mine to see. I go around another hangar to take a circuitous route. I cut across the back of this hangar to head for the one where Ling's plane waits. I hope there's a back door I can use to get inside.

By the time I make it to the hangar I'm covered with sweat and panting worse than a dog that's been locked in a car with the windows up on a summer day. My short legs aren't used to running this much, nor is my potbelly. "I really need to work out," I grumble.

There is a back door to the hangar. Unfortunately it's locked. I stare at the door for a moment before I heft the tire iron. I strike the door handle as hard as I can. That isn't very hard. I barely scratch the metal handle. I hit it again with the same result. "Come on!" I tell myself. I gotta get in. I gotta do it for Madison. She needs me.

I hit the handle again and let out a groan as I put all of my weight into the blow. This time I hit the sweet spot so that the handle drops to the ground with a clang. I hope I haven't made too much noise or else this will be hopeless.

The door must not be used much; it creaks as I push it open. I crouch down so I'm less visible and so I don't get a face full of engine exhaust. I hear a shot. It's far enough away that I know it must be Dr. Macintosh or someone shooting at him. Either way, there's not much time to spare. I have to get on that plane.

Though I'm exhausted, I force myself to run as fast as I can towards the plane. There's no one between the door and the ramp of the plane. Apparently Dr. Macintosh has their full attention. I hope he can keep them busy long enough.

I scamper up the ramp, into the plane. Right away I see Maddy. Except it's not the Maddy I left a couple of hours ago. She's shrunk into a baby, an actual baby probably no more than a year old. Her yellow dress has become so big that all I can see is her pudgy face, crowned by a sparse cap of black hair. Her fat cheeks are red; tears stream down them. There's tape over her mouth that muffles her cries. Ling has her buckled into a seat, but her tiny hands are too weak to unfasten the seatbelt.

I hurry over to her. It's not hard to free her from the seat. "This is going to hurt a little," I say. I grasp one edge of the tape. "Try not to make any noise, OK?"

She nods to me, which tells me her mind isn't that of a baby. I pull the tape off in one swipe. More tears bubble up in Maddy's eyes, but she doesn't scream. "It's all right," I whisper to her. "We're going to get out of here now."

"Stacey," she chirps as I pick her up. Even though she's a baby she's still heavy, probably because my muscles are so weak. It's tough to cradle her in my arms, but there's no way she can run under her own power.

I turn around and start for the door I came in through. I skid to a stop when I see someone in the doorway. It must be Dr. Ling, though I can't be sure. He looks like the Invisible Man, his face wrapped in gauze and sunglasses on despite that it's dark. He also wears a suit with gloves that cover his hands so that all I can see are his lips.

"This is a pleasant surprise," he says. His voice sounds rougher than before. "I thought I would have to arrange for your disappearance separately."

When she hears Dr. Ling's voice, Maddy starts to wail like a fussy baby. I pat her back, to try in vain to comfort her. "What did you do to her?"

"I gave her a booster," he says. He reaches one gloved hand into his pocket. It comes back with a needle filled with dark red liquid. "Now it's time for you to take your medicine."

I try to run, but being little and with a baby in my arms, I'm not very fast. Dr. Ling isn't very fast either; he lurches after me like the Frankenstein monster. His longer strides catch me as I reach the galley. One hand seizes the hood of my sweatshirt and yanks me back hard.

Somehow I manage to keep hold of Maddy as I hit the floor. I even roll to land on my side so she's not hurt. She still screams; her face goes from red to purple. "Stacey!" she wails as Dr. Ling tears her out of my hands.

I claw at him, but it doesn't do any good. I'm too weak. He bats my hands aside and holds me down with one arm. All I can do then is whip my head from side-to-side to try to avoid the needle. It's only a matter of time, before my luck runs out. I feel the needle plunge into my neck.

The pain is just as intense as back in Ling's dungeon. It feels like my entire body is being squeezed in a vise. Something different happens this time: my teeth fall out. Ling lets me go, which allows me to roll over so I can spit out a mouthful of teeth. Through a red haze, I see glossy white teeth dotted with blood on the carpet.

As if that's not bad enough, my gums burn with pain. I know what this is: my baby teeth are coming back in. I'm becoming a baby again, like Madison. Through the red haze, I see my hands shrink until they retract into my sweatshirt. It won't be long now until I'm just as tiny and helpless as Maddy, not that I was much good to her anyway.

When my arms become too weak to support me, I collapse onto the floor; fallen permanent teeth press against my cheek. I twitch on the floor while Maddy continues to scream. There's nothing I can do for either of us now.

And then it's over. The pain turns off and leaves only numbness. I try to move, but the only muscle that responds is my tongue. I probe my mouth and find most of my baby teeth, all except my front ones. I'm not a baby, just a little girl maybe seven years old.

Dr. Ling grabs me by the hood of my sweatshirt. When I stare up at him, my eyes tingle. My glasses have become too strong for my younger eyes. I can see well enough to see Ling study me, though I can't read his expression behind the bandages and sunglasses. "Perfect," he says. "Now, young lady, it's time to go for a ride."

He drags me by the sweatshirt while he carries Maddy with his other hand. She continues to scream until he finds the piece of tape to stick over her mouth again while I'm left on the floor, still too numb to move. I feel tears run down my cheeks as I know in thirteen hours or so Maddy and I will be in China, little more than lab rats until we're finally executed and dissected.

Dr. Ling straps Maddy back in. Then he grabs me by the front of the sweatshirt. He tosses me onto another seat as if I'm a rag doll. I feel like a rag doll, like my limbs are filled with stuffing right now. There's nothing I can do while he arranges me in the seat and buckles me in. He stares at me again and then tousles my hair. "Be a good girl until I get back."

I don't have much choice about it. Ling limps over to the door. As he pulls it up, I hear gunshots. Dr. Macintosh is still out there. He can save us. That seems unlikely; he's a child psychologist, not a Navy SEAL. He's never going to make it in time.

Ling seals the door and then heads into the cockpit. He screams something in Chinese at the pilot. The pilot says something back in a softer voice. The discussion continues for a minute until Ling finally shouts, "Take off, now!"

The plane lurches forward. There's a metallic crash that must be the steps hitting the ground. Apparently Ling won the argument and we're going to take off right now. He's going to leave his minions behind to make sure he gets us back to China.

I desperately want to get out of here while I still can, but my body won't respond. The numbness has become a gentle tingle, like when your foot starts to fall asleep. Feeling is coming back to my limbs now that my nerves and veins have compacted. It won't be too long until I can move, but by then we'll be airborne.

Even over the plane's engines I hear a familiar rumble. I'd know the engine of Jake's Fairlane anywhere. Dr. Macintosh must plan to run the plane off the tarmac.

It turns out he has something more desperate in mind. There's a roar, followed by a crash. The plane lurches. The entire fuselage drops sharply; my glasses are catapulted from my face. I see them land by the cockpit door. For the first time in five months, I can see clearly without the glasses. At the moment all I can see is Maddy screaming against the tape on her mouth as the plane skids.

The plane begins to go around and around in a flat spin. It's only a matter of time before we flip over or wind up in the ocean or crash into another hangar. No matter what, there won't be much Maddy and I can do about it, not like this. It'll be a contest to see whether we burn or drown.

As far as I can tell, none of that happens. The spin begins to slow until finally the plane stops completely. Then there's silence except for Maddy's whimpers. We're still alive, at least for the moment.

I get to savor that for two seconds before I smell smoke. I'm not sure where it's coming from; probably the engines if they're still attached. With a full tank of gas, it won't be long until the plane goes up in a fireball that will turn Maddy and I into cinders. Like Qiang, the police will probably never be able to identify our remains, what little will be left of us.

The tingle in my limbs gets stronger. I close my eyes and will my body to move. There's a little twitch in my right arm. I concentrate harder to convince my arm to swing into my lap. I have to coax my fingers out of hiding in the sleeves that are too big for me. Slowly, an inch at a time, my fingers emerge. I feel the cool metal of the buckle. I have to focus really hard in order to work a simple mechanism that would take me two seconds to operate any other time.

But then I'm free. I open my eyes and see smoke begin to drift into the cabin. I have to get Madison out of here. She needs me, her big sister. I concentrate to move my legs. It's not easy to stand since my sneakers have become like clown shoes now. I wobble for a moment as if I'm a baby like Maddy.

When I see her swamped in that dress, her purple face stained with tears, it provides all the motivation I need to take those few steps over to her seat. "It's all right," I say, my words slurred a little. "I'm going to get you out of here."

I promised that before and didn't deliver, but this time I'm determined to do it. The tingling is almost gone now; I can move more or less normally. I still fumble a little with the buckle; I need a full minute to get Madison free.

There's no way I can carry her this time. I'm too little and my muscles much too weak from the transformation. "You gotta walk," I tell Maddy. "Can you do that?"

She nods. I take her hands and help her slide off the seat, onto the floor. She rests there for a moment. Then, while I still hold her hands, she levers up to her feet. She's even unsteadier than I was, but she manages to stand.

We toddle over to the door. I let Maddy lean against the wall while I try to open it. Of course it won't give. I'm too weak. I try not to panic, so Maddy won't start to scream again. "It's all right. We'll find another way out."

The smell of smoke is stronger. It's good we're both so short now, so it'll take longer for the smoke to scald our tiny lungs. I tow Maddy back towards the galley. We're almost there when the cabin door bangs open. I hope it's just the pilot, but of course we aren't that lucky.

The bandages on Ling's face are torn, so that I can see bits of red flesh. Blood stains the gauze in other places. Yet he's still alive. Not only that, he has a pistol in his hand. "Get back here!" he says.

"No!" I shout, although it's a feeble comeback. And there's nowhere to go. Even if we can find another exit, Ling will catch up to us.

I start to drag Maddy. Ling moves slower too; blood drips from tears in his pants after the crash. Ahead of us I see another door outlined in red, the emergency exit. That's our ticket out of here, not that it will matter.

I give the handle a tug. It's no good. I'm too weak for this door too. I turn and see Ling's reached the galley. He could probably shoot us, but he doesn't want to damage his prizes. I give the door another tug with all my might. Nothing happens.

There's only one thing left to do. I pull Maddy into the very back of the plane, into the lavatory. I leave her on the floor, while I sag against the door and turn the lock. Since I probably only weigh sixty pounds, I doubt I'll be able to keep Ling out for long. Even if he doesn't break in, the plane will probably explode in a couple of minutes.

"I'm sorry, Maddy," I say. "I didn't want it to end like this."

"Stacey," she chirps again. She crawls forward, to hug my leg. "Wuv you."

"I love you too," I say. I tousle her short hair.

Ling bangs against the door. "Come out, little ones," he says. "Come out before I have to break down the door."

"You go ahead and try," I shout back.

"I'll give you to the count of three. One."

Maddy snuggles up closer against me, like when we shared a bed. "It'll be all right," I tell her. "Everything will be fine."

"Two."

"We'll go to a better place. To Heaven," I say.

"Three." I close my eyes. There's the sound of a gunshot. I hear a thump outside the door as something hits the floor.

I still have my eyes shut when I hear a knock on the door. It's not the angry pounding of someone who wants to break the door down, but a gentle tap. "Stacey? Madison?" Dr. Macintosh says. "Are you all right?"

"We're fine," I say.

I scoot away from the door and push Maddy along with me. The door opens and I see Dr. Macintosh in the doorway. His hair is mussed and face stained with blood from a cut on his forehead, yet he still has that air of calm from his office. His eyes widen when he sees us.

He doesn't let this bother him too much. He reaches down to scoop Madison up; he cradles her to his chest. She coos softly at this and wraps one pudgy arm around his neck. He holds out his hand to me. I take it and he helps me to stand. "Can you walk?" he asks.

"Yes."

"Good. We have to get out of here very quickly."

"OK."

On the way out, we pass the body of Dr. Ling. There's no coming back for him this time, not with a bullet through the chest. Dr. Macintosh is a pretty good shot for someone who never used a gun before.

In the movies we would make it off the plane seconds before it explodes, our bodies thrown through the air by the blast before we land unharmed. In reality we make it off the plane with a few minutes to spare. The crash has tilted the door down enough that we don't need the steps. Dr. Macintosh leaves Maddy and me in the doorway before he jumps down. Then he takes Maddy and sets her on the tarmac. I'm the last one off; Dr. Macintosh grabs me around the waist. I collapse against him and feel safe for a moment.

Then he lets me down to pick Maddy back up. We run across the tarmac, over to where the Fairlane—what's left of it—rests. The front of the car looks like someone smashed it with a really big hammer. That hammer would be the front landing gear of the plane.

The car's doors still work fine. Dr. Macintosh climbs in the front seat, Madison cradled against him. I get in on the passenger's side. Dr. Macintosh puts an arm around my shoulders. I'm more than happy to scoot over until I'm snuggled up against his warm body, where I feel safe again.

The same time the plane explodes, every nerve in my body does too. The pain sends me rolling off Dr. Macintosh, onto the floor. Maddy starts to scream again; from the way she thrashes around, she feels the same pain. Dr. Macintosh sets Maddy on the seat. "Madison? Stacey? What's wrong?"

I'd like to answer what's wrong is my body feels like someone lit it on fire, but I can't because every muscle cramps all at once. I manage to get out one scream before everything goes dark.

Chapter 42

The first thing I notice when I wake up is that my throat is sore. It feels like someone's filled my mouth with cotton. I try to work up some spit. It doesn't do a lot of good. My tongue is thick and heavy, but as I flick it around, I feel all of my teeth. How old am I now?

I start to sit up, but I don't get very far. Something holds me down on the bed or table or whatever I'm on. I manage to turn my head to the side and see a beige blur that I assume is a wall. At least there's no chalkboard or factory equipment so I'm not back in one of Ling's prisons.

"Hello?" I call out, though it's more like a whisper. But even from the sound of it, I know I'm still a girl. "Is anyone there?"

I hear a door open, followed by the squeak of rubber soles on tile. A face appears over me. It's a turquoise-and-brown blob at first. As it gets closer, I can make out Dr. Palmer's face. She wears a surgical mask and a shower cap, but I can recognize her eyes. Her gloved hands touch my cheek. "Welcome back," she says. To my relief she inserts a straw into my mouth. Water courses down my throat, to expel the dryness. "Is that better?"

"Yes," I say. My voice sounds even higher than before, like the voice of a cartoon rodent. "Where am I?"

"At Lennox Pharmaceuticals. You're in quarantine."

"Quarantine? Am I sick?"

"No. It's more like we're protecting you from the rest of the world."

"What happened?"

"I'll explain that in a little bit. What do you remember?"

"Dr. Macintosh and I went to rescue Maddy. I got on the plane and Maddy was there but she was a baby. I tried to save her, but Dr. Ling showed up. He gave me a shot and I became littler. Then Dr. Macintosh saved us. He crashed Grandpa's car into the plane. Maddy and I hid in the potty. Dr. Ling tried to get in, but Dr. Macintosh shot him. Then he helped us off the plane and we watched it explode. I fell asleep after that."

"You weren't really sleeping, Stacey. You've been in a coma."

"A coma? Why?"

"I'll explain later. You've been in the coma for two weeks."

"Two weeks?" It seemed like just a few seconds. I open my eyes again to study Dr. Palmer's face. "What about Maddy? What happened to her?"

"She's still sleeping."

"Is she in a coma too?"

"Yes."

"And Dr. Macintosh?"

"He's fine. His stitches came out yesterday."

"That's good. And Grandpa? Did they get to him in time?"

"He's fine too. He's still on crutches, but he'll pull through."

"Good." I take a deep breath and then ask, "Dr. Ling?"

"He's dead. We're sure of it this time."

"So why am I tied down?"

"You were having some bad seizures. We didn't want you to fall and hurt yourself."

"Oh." I try to see myself again, but I can't. "What's been happening to me?"

"I'm not sure we should get into that yet. You just woke up."

"You gotta tell me! How little am I?"

Dr. Palmer touches my hair and even through the mask I can see her smile. She holds up her other hand and in it I see the monitor she used to check our ages. She turns the screen and holds it close enough so I can see it. The digital numbers read: 17.2.

"I'm seventeen?"

"That's right. You're a grown-up now—more or less."

"Can I see?" I ask.

"I'll take the straps off, but be careful. You're going to be weak."

"OK."

Dr. Palmer's right that I'm weak; I can't even sit up on my own. She adjusts the bed so the back reclines to put me in an upright position. Then she turns the bed around to face a mirror. I can't see anything at first, just a blur. I feel something touch my face and everything comes into focus. I gasp at what I see.

I'm still mostly Stacey Chang. I've still got her black hair, almond-colored skin, tiny nose, and football-shaped eyes. The big difference is that those eyes are blue now like they were before Dr. Ling got to me.

"Are you all right?" Dr. Palmer asks.

"I'm fine," I say.

She runs her hand through my black hair, which is back down to my waist; I'll need to get it cut again. "I think you look very pretty."

"Thanks."

"And seventeen's not so bad. You might even get a year or so older over the next few days."

"I guess."

She puts the bed flat again. "You should get some more rest."

"I want to see Maddy."

"Not right now. When you're stronger."

"But—"

"No buts, young lady. You can either go back to sleep or I'll have an orderly bring a syringe in here. Got it?"

"Yes."

"Good. You're still in a state of flux right now. We have to be careful."

"OK." I could try to argue, but I'm pretty much at Dr. Palmer's mercy at the moment.

"I'll have them bring in a TV and some other creature comforts for when you wake up."

"Can't you put me in a different room?"

"Not yet. We don't want any germs getting in here while your immune system is so weak."

"Oh." That's all I can say before I fall asleep again.

***

I'm not sure how long I'm out this time. Not two weeks. I'm a little stronger when I wake up, able to sit up on my own. As I do, I notice a couple of other things. One is that my breasts look smaller than before. I'm not flat like when I was ten, but they don't look like C-cups either. The other thing is that I'm short. My tiny feet are a good foot away from the end of the bed, maybe more than that. That will be clearer if I'm ever able to stand.

There's a TV now in one corner of the room. Someone brought in a stand to sit next to the bed too. I find a remote control and a plastic water cup. I drink most of the water and then turn on the TV. I flip through the channels until I get to Nickelodeon. There's an episode of *iCarly* on, an older one I watched with Jamie. I sigh as I wonder what I'll do now.

Dr. Palmer shows up after the episode is over. She still wears her mask and shower cap so she doesn't infect me with her germs. "Feeling better?" she asks.

"A little."

"It's going to take time. You've had a big shock to your system."

"Tell me about it."

"The important thing is to relax and rest so you can get your strength up."

"I guess."

Dr. Palmer comes over to the side of my bed. "I've got a surprise for you," she says.

"What is it?"

"You'll see."

She wheels my bed across the room, to the opposite wall from the mirror. A curtain pulls back and I can see another room. It's pretty much like mine after I woke up the first time with just a bed and some monitoring equipment.

On the bed is a very fat woman. There's a big mound of flesh around her midsection that rises and falls as she breathes. Her flabby biceps are each as big around as my head. I can't see her neck because of the double chin surrounding it. Her cheeks are flushed even though she's asleep. About the only thing even somewhat recognizable is the long brown hair. "Is that...Maddy?"

"Yes," Dr. Palmer says.

"But she's so...*big*."

"I know." Dr. Palmer puts a hand on my shoulder as I start to cry to see my baby like that. "The important thing is she's healthy, right?"

"How old is she?"

"She's up to nineteen so far. The reaction seems to be slowing, so we're expecting her to wake up in a few days."

"Can I be there when she wakes up?"

"I'm not sure that's a good idea. It's going to be enough of a shock to see herself without seeing you too."

"I'm not that different."

"You are from two weeks ago."

"Good point."

"I'll leave you here for a while so you can watch her. If you want."

"Yes," I say. After Dr. Palmer's gone, I watch my sleeping beauty. No matter what, she'll always be my little girl.

***

Two days later I hear the scream as I watch TV. I'm strong enough now that I can hop off the bed. I can't really run, but I can hobble over to the window. I'm just in time to see Maddy take hold of her gut with both hands. "No!" she wails. "It's not fair. I don't wanna be Fatty Maddy anymore!"

I can't hear what Dr. Palmer says, but Maddy doesn't like it. "Healthy? Look at me, I'm a whale! You call this healthy?"

Tears stream down her pudgy cheeks as she says this. Dr. Palmer says something to her, probably to reassure her that everything will be fine. "Shut up! You're not the one who has to live with it." Dr. Palmer tries to calm her down again, but it doesn't work. "Normal life? What kind of normal life am I going to have? What do you think Grace is going to say when she sees *this*?" Maddy says. She shakes her stomach again. "She won't even be able to find my vagina."

I'm sure Dr. Palmer tells her the same thing I would, that Grace will love her no matter how big she is. "Yeah, right," Maddy says. I can hear her sigh even through the glass. "What did you butchers do to Stacey?"

I wait for Dr. Palmer to push Maddy over by the window or at least turn her so she can see me, but she doesn't. Whatever she says calms Maddy down a little. "Can I see her?" Dr. Palmer shakes her head. "What, you're worried I'll scare her?" Dr. Palmer says something else. Maddy sighs again. "Just leave me alone for a little while."

Through the window I watch Dr. Palmer leave. Once the door closes, Maddy starts to cry. She's still crying as she leans back on the bed and goes still.

Dr. Palmer comes into my room then. "That was pretty bad," I say.

"It could have been worse."

"Do you think she'll try to *do* something?"

"I don't think so. Madison is resilient. I think she got that from her dad's side of the family."

Resilience and stubbornness were about the only things I gave her. "Can't you suck some of that fat out of her?"

"I could, but liposuction is dangerous. Especially in her volatile condition. It'll be better to wait and let her lose it the old-fashioned way."

"Yeah, I guess," I say. I promise right then I'll do everything I can to help Maddy lose as much weight as she wants, until she's happy again.

***

Another two days go by before they move Maddy into my room. To keep out any germs, they have a plastic bubble over her gurney. An orderly takes off the bubble once Maddy is securely in my room. It takes two hefty orderlies to steer the gurney into place beside my bed, the nightstand between us.

"Hi!" I say, my voice squeakier than usual.

"Hi," she says, her voice gloomier than usual. She pats her gut. "So I guess I'm the big sister now, huh?"

"I guess so." I clear my throat and then say, "I'm only seventeen anyway, so you're older than me again."

"I'll try not to push you around too much."

I reach across the nightstand to find her hand. I give her pudgy fingers a squeeze. "I know it's weird right now, but we'll get through this. And no matter what, we'll still have each other."

"You mean after Grace dumps me?"

"Grace loves you. More than anything in this world. She's not going to care even if you're a thousand pounds."

"I might take you up on that."

"Maddy, come on. She's been worried sick about you for almost six months now. You think she's going to dump you just because you're a little heavier?"

"A little heavier? I'm two hundred fifty pounds! That's like twice what I used to weigh."

"I'm sorry."

I let go of Maddy's hand. I pick up the remote to flip through the channels until I find some cartoons Maddy used to watch. Despite the change, I can still see something of the toddler I knew for six months in the way her face lights up. "You think they could sterilize Mrs. Hoppy and bring her in here?" she asks me.

"Probably."

After a few minutes, Maddy shifts a little to look at me. Past the flabby red cheeks, her eyes are still the same as the baby her mom and I brought home from the hospital. "I know I've been a little preoccupied feeling sorry for myself. I didn't even thank you for coming after me."

"I would never leave you behind." I smile at her. "I didn't do much anyway. Dr. Mac did all the hard work."

"Yeah. I never thought of him as the action hero type."

"Me either." I sigh as I remember the lavatory door opening and him in the doorway, blood on his face and gun in hand, our valiant rescuer. "That was pretty awesome."

"It was." Maddy reaches out to take my hand. "You look cute. Not like little, I want to pinch your cheeks cute. I mean like if you weren't my big sister and I didn't look like Shamu I'd ask you to come back to my place."

My face warms at this. It's surreal to have my daughter talk about picking me up like that. "Thanks," I squeak.

We both turn back to the TV screen. We continue to hold hands, even after Maddy falls asleep.

***

A couple of days later we're strong enough to go back to school. Not St. Andrew's Academy, but a very special class in our hospital room. Dr. Palmer has an assistant bring in a laptop and a projector so we can watch her presentation from our beds.

"I know it sounds weird," she begins, "but in a way you're lucky Dr. Ling gave you that shot."

"Yeah, real lucky," Maddy grumbles. She jiggles her stomach for Dr. Palmer.

"What I'm saying is he sped up the process for you." She turns down the lights and then starts with her presentation. A lot of it is science stuff Maddy and I don't understand.

Dr. Palmer breaks it down more simply. "They might have told you that both of you were aging at an accelerated rate. What we didn't realize yet is the effect was working at an exponential pace. What that means is you were going to get older, faster. In a couple months, Madison, you probably would have been older than Stacey. From the notes Ling had on him, he knew what was happening. That's why he made that booster shot and set that trap, using my voice to get your grandpa to bring you here.

"But either he was in too much of a hurry or didn't have the right equipment because he miscalculated. Instead of keeping you younger for months or even forever, the booster shot interacted with what was already in your system and actually sped up the destabilization."

"That's stupid," Maddy says.

"Think of it kind of like a pool game," Dr. Palmer says. She's come prepared with a diagram of a pool table on the laptop. "Say this 2-ball here is the first shot he gave you and this 8-ball behind it is the second shot." She clicks a button so we can watch as a computer figure takes a shot. The cue ball hits the 8-ball, which speeds into the 2-ball and knocks it into the corner pocket. Then the 8-ball, too much momentum behind it, drops into the pocket too. "The second shot essentially erased the first shot in your systems. But its matrix became unstable and so you started to grow up again even faster."

"But if it left our systems, why didn't we go back to how we were?" I ask. In my case, why didn't I go back to being a man?

"We're still looking into that, but our best guess is that this wasn't a clean process. For you, Stacey, that Chinese DNA remained. And for Madison, there was probably a stimulation of certain glands and hormones that changed her metabolism and caused her to gain so much weight."

"Can't you fix us?" Maddy asks. "Give us another shot to make us normal again?"

"I wouldn't right now even if I could. You're both far too weak to endure another dose of that stuff. In the meantime we're still working on the serum, but it'll take a while to have something ready for human trials." Dr. Palmer sighs. "I know you don't want to hear it, Madison, but it'll be a lot better to lose the weight naturally than play Russian roulette with another shot."

"Easy for you to say. You're not the one who has to go back out into the world like this."

"Don't get mad at her. She's just trying to help."

"Yeah, she's been a lot of help so far."

"That's not fair. It's not her fault. She didn't do this to us."

"Oh sure, take her side. Everything's just hunky-dory for you. You're not a blimp."

My eyes water. "It's not easy for me. You can always lose the weight. I can't get new eyes. I can't stretch myself out to fit in my clothes again or be able to look you in the eye without standing on my toes. So don't act like you're the only one who's got problems."

Now Maddy starts to cry. "I'm so sorry," she says through her sobs. "I'm being such a total bitch to everyone. I just wish things could be the way they used to be, you know?"

"I know." I think of what's happened in the last eighteen months and say, "But sometimes change is a good thing. Sometimes you find something that makes it all worthwhile, like a little sister."

She wipes at her pudgy cheeks and then smiles at me. "Thanks, big sis."

Epilogue

Dr. Palmer keeps us under observation for two more weeks. Every day she checks our ages with the monitor. Since the results are the same and since we're strong enough to move around, she tells us we can finally go home. "But I'm going to want to see you both at least once a week to start with and then if things remain steady we can make it once a month."

"OK," we say in unison.

"I had someone do a little shopping for you two," she says. She hefts a couple of shopping bags. "These might not be the most stylish, but it's better than a hospital gown."

Maddy's face reddens as she holds up a turquoise dress that looks big enough to cover a Buick. "Is this supposed to be for an elephant or what?" The panties that come with it are almost as big. She says to me, "Jesus, we could probably fit three of you in there."

I'm not much happier about my new clothes. Whoever bought them for me must still think I'm ten years old. There's a pink T-shirt with a cartoon monkey on it and a set of pink overalls. There's a tiny pair of pink Keds too. The underwear have Disney princesses on them; whoever did the shopping didn't think I need a bra.

Maddy can't stifle a giggle when I come out of the bathroom. "Oh my God, you're so cute!" she says. She laughs even harder. "You look like you're in kindergarten."

"Shut up!" I squeak.

Maddy runs a hand over her loose-fitting dress. "At least you don't look like the Blob." She turns in the mirror and puts a hand on her gut.

It's about an hour later when Dr. Palmer escorts us out of the subbasement that's been our home for the last month. We take an elevator up to the lobby. I try not to think about the last time I was in this lobby with Dr. Macintosh.

There aren't any dead security guards, just Jake, Tess, and Grace. Their eyes all go wide for a moment when they see us. I'm not sure what Dr. Palmer told them to expect, but this isn't it. Grace is the first to recover; she races forward to throw herself at Maddy. She showers Maddy's chubby face with kisses before she plants a final emphatic one on Maddy's lips.

Feeling even more awkward now, I shuffle over to my former grandparents. Tess just kisses me once on the cheek and then hugs me. "Welcome home, dear," she says. "You look so pretty."

"I'm still little," I say.

"That doesn't matter, dear. Just as long as you're healthy."

"I guess."

Maddy and Grace have finally come up for air. Maddy puts a hand on her stomach. "I guess there's a lot more of me than you expected, isn't there?"

"I don't care about that," Grace says. "All I want is you, however you look."

"We'll see about that tonight, won't we?"

I squirm out of Tess's grasp to face them. "You're going with Grace?"

"Well, yeah. We got a lot of catching up to do."

"Oh," I say. My voice catches in my throat. I look down sadly at my Keds. "I thought you'd come home with us."

Tess gives my shoulder a squeeze. "Madison and Grace need some time alone, dear."

"I guess."

Maddy squats down so she can look me in the eye. "Hey, come on, we can still come over to dinner and stuff. And you can come see us. You're big enough to ride the train by yourself."

"I know." I should have seen this coming. Maddy and Grace are practically married. They haven't seen each other in six months, at least not as grown-ups, so of course they want to be alone. Maddy's a grown-up now. So am I. I do what grown-ups are supposed to do and force myself to smile even though I want to cry at losing Madison again. "I guess it'll be more room for me then."

Maddy crushes me in a hug; she squeezes me so tight I expect my skeleton to pop out like in a cartoon. "I love you, big sis."

"I love you too, little sis."

Then we go our separate ways, me to Jake and Tess's station wagon and Maddy to a cab with Grace. I turn in my seat to wave at Maddy. She doesn't see me; she's already cuddling against Grace.

***

I feel a little more like a big girl a week later. I wear a pink T-shirt, but no cartoon character on it. I've got a bra on underneath it too, not that I really need it. Instead of overalls I wear blue jeans. The Keds have grown on me so I decide to keep those for now. I got my hair trimmed to just past my shoulders, but I kept the bangs. I still have my red-framed glasses, only with new lenses in them.

The overall effect is that as I sit in Dr. Macintosh's waiting room I feel at least fourteen now instead of ten. It helps me to feel more grown up not to have Tess with me. She wanted to come upstairs, but I told her I could do it by myself, so she waits for me in a coffee shop.

It doesn't take long for me to regret that decision. As soon as I see the patient register sheet, I feel a nervous flutter in my stomach. After some discussion with Jake and I, Tess made the appointment under my old name of Stacey Chance. It feels weird to write that name in the space on the sheet. I keep my face tilted down and hope the receptionist doesn't remember me from before.

The receptionist isn't the one I have to really worry about, though. I sit in a corner of the room to play with my phone a few minutes later when the door opens. Caleb trudges into the office, eyes fixed on his cell phone screen. To my horror, Jamie is behind him. I'm on my phone, so I can't even hold up a magazine to my face. I just stare at the screen like Caleb is and hope for the best.

While on the outside I pretend to play Angry Birds, on the inside I berate myself for being stupid. Why didn't we think to check if Jamie had an appointment today? Why didn't we get another psychologist? The answer for the latter is there's not another shrink I can go see, not unless I want to spill all my secrets again. The former we just didn't think about with so many other things going on.

My heart starts to race when I see Jamie coming over here out of the corner of my eye. It's probably the stupid glasses. I should have got different frames, but I still feel I owe it to Qiang to keep her daughter's spirit alive in some small way.

"Stacey?" Jamie asks.

I look up at her so she can see I'm not the same girl who slept over at her house and talked about kissing boys with her. "Yes?"

She stares at me for a moment; her cheeks flush. She smiles a little. "Sorry. I thought you were someone else."

"That's all right," I say. The butterflies in my stomach have turned to ice now. I hate to trick Jamie like this; I desperately wish we could still be best friends. I even still have her necklace on, though it's hidden beneath my shirt. "It happens."

"But it's weird because your name is Stacey too and you've got red glasses just like she has. What are the odds of that?"

"Well—" I brace myself to run if Jamie figures it out. I've continued to post status updates on my Facebook page as Stacey Chang, to say what a great time Maddy and I are having at our new house in San Jose. I even found some pictures online of a mansion by the ocean to post on my wall. This might not be enough to fool her.

"Hey, you're playing Angry Birds?"

"Yeah."

"That's my favorite game." Never all that shy, Jamie sits down next to me. She takes her phone out. "You want to play against me?"

"Sure," I say. "But my appointment's in a few minutes."

"That's OK. I can probably beat you before then."

"I don't know, I'm pretty good at this."

"We'll see."

I have gotten a lot better at it since that first time in the waiting room. I'm still not as good as Jamie. To put it mildly, she kicks my ass.

Just like when we talk on Facebook, I feel ten years old again when I play Angry Birds against her. It's only afterwards when she says, "You're a lot better at this than the other Stacey," that I remember I'm not ten. I'm some stranger Jamie just met who bears a resemblance to her former best friend.

The receptionist calls my name and I stand up. "It was nice to meet you—"

"Jamie," she says. We shake hands, like strangers. "Maybe we can play again next time."

"Sure. I'll make sure to practice before then."

"You'll need it," Jamie says. Then she goes over to sit by her brother. I make sure to turn off my phone because I know she'll send Stacey Chang a message on Facebook to tell her about the freakiness of seeing another girl named Stacey at Dr. Macintosh's office with the same geeky glasses.

I tuck the phone into my pocket and go in to meet with Dr. Macintosh.

***

I hope after all we've been through together he'll run up to me and give me a hug or at least shake my hand. He doesn't. He sits in his usual chair, notebook on his knee like I'm another patient. He points to the other chair, "Have a seat, Stacey."

I sit down opposite him, on the very edge of the cushion. I'm glad my feet can touch the floor now, if just barely. It takes an act of will for me to look at him. He doesn't have a scar or anything, no reminder at all of the night he saved me and Maddy. "You're looking good," I say and then feel my face turn warm. "No worse for wear, huh?"

"I could say the same about you."

I toss my hair and smile. "You like the new look?"

"The important thing is whether you like it."

"It's growing on me. I mean, it's better than being a little kid, right?"

"Is that right?"

I can't meet his eyes anymore; I look down at my pink Keds. "Well, yeah. I mean, I get to stay up late now. I have my own room. I don't have to get up early to go to school."

"Those sound like pretty superficial reasons."

"Maybe I'm just shallow then," I snap.

"There's no need to get upset. I only want you to think more deeply about the question. Are you happy to be an adult again?"

"Sometimes," I mumble.

"Not all the time?"

"No. Like just a couple minutes ago I was playing Angry Birds with Jamie in the lobby and that felt really good. We were having fun like we used to."

"I see. You miss your friend."

"Yeah. Is there anything wrong with that?"

"Of course not. Jamie was very important to you, wasn't she?"

"Yes. She was my best friend in the whole world." I take out the necklace so he can see it. "I thought about getting rid of this, but I couldn't. She's still my friend, you know?"

"I see. But you still have other friends, don't you? Friends closer to your own age?"

"Sure, there's still Grace."

"What about Madison? Isn't she your friend?"

My face turns warm again. I nod. "I kind of forget that she's my friend now, not my little sister." I laugh stupidly. "Pretty dumb, huh?"

"Not at all. You were sisters for almost six months. I'm sure you forged a bond during that time."

"I thought we did."

"But you didn't?"

"As soon as we got out of the hospital, she went to stay with Grace. I mean, that same day. She hardly even said goodbye to me, she was in such a hurry to get back to that smelly old apartment." I put a hand up before Dr. Macintosh can say anything. "I know it's wrong to think that. I know she loves Grace."

"And she doesn't love you?"

"Not in that way."

"So you're feeling something akin to empty nest syndrome? Your little bird has flown the nest and you're all alone?"

"I don't know. Maybe. It's just that for those few months we were so close, probably closer than when I was her dad." I cross my arms over my little B-cup breasts. "Now I'm back to being the third wheel."

"I'm sure Madison still values your friendship."

"Yeah, right. She's only sent me one text since we left the hospital. You know what it said: 'Fat sex is great!' Oh, that's kind of a spoiler, I guess. You haven't seen her yet, have you?"

"No, but Dr. Palmer told me she's put on a bit of weight."

"Yeah, a bit."

"How does it make you feel that she's put on that weight?"

"It sucks."

"Very succinct."

"What else can I say? It sucks she's fat. I would have given anything to make her just the way she was before all of this. Before I—"

I start to cry. Dr. Macintosh brings me a box of tissues. "You still feel it's your fault all of this happened?" he asks me. I can only nod in response. "Speaking from personal experience, Dr. Ling was a very sick individual. He would have gotten to you eventually."

"But not Maddy. He didn't want her. Just me."

"Maybe. Maybe he did want her. Or maybe if he didn't get her he would have taken your friend Grace or Mrs. Madigan or Mr. Madigan."

"So you're telling me it could have been worse, right? Everything more or less worked out for the best, except Maddy is shopping at plus size stores and I'm—"

"You're what?" he asks.

"I don't know." I wave at myself. "I don't even know who I'm supposed to be anymore."

"Who do you want to be?"

"I don't know," I say again.

He reaches beside him for the mirror. I'm reluctant to take the thing, worried about what I'll see. "Go on, tell me what you see."

I force myself to look into the glass. In it I see the pieces of myself: the glasses and Asian features of Stacey Chang; the shy smile of Stacey Chance; the steel in my eyes of Detective Steve Fischer. "I see a girl who's sweet and a little shy, but who's tough when she has to be. I see a girl who cares about her friends, especially Madison."

"Is that all?"

"No. I see a girl who loves to sing. Maybe she won't ever be a famous singer like Lady Gaga, but she wants to go on stage and make people happy, like she did at that presentation."

"That's very good, Stacey."

"I passed the test?"

"You're getting there."

I clear my throat. "I was looking online the other day at the schedule for my old school—community college, not St. Andrew's. Did you know they have a lot of classes about music? Not just listening to it or playing an instrument either. I saw this songwriting class I thought might be interesting."

"You want to be a songwriter?"

"I don't know. I think at least I'd like to know how to do it. I mean when Darren wrote that song for me—the one we did for the encore—I looked at it and it was like Greek, you know? All those squiggly symbols and stuff. If I'm going to sing, it might be nice to know what all those mean."

"I think that's a good idea."

"If I can still sing. I'm not sure I can even do it anymore. It'll probably sound like one of those Chipmunk songs."

"Let's find out. Go ahead and sing something."

"Now?"

"Why not?"

"Well, OK, but don't be too hard on me." I clear my throat a couple of times. I take a deep breath. Then, like the last time I sang in his office, I do "Twinkle, Twinkle Little Star." It sounds a little screechy to my ears.

Dr. Macintosh is far more forgiving. "That's very nice. With some training you could be a soprano."

"You mean like a gangster?"

"No, I mean like an opera singer. Soprano is the highest range."

"Opera? Yuck."

"You can sing popular music too. Or maybe you could be an actress on Broadway."

I shiver at that and remember how hard it was to be on stage the last time. If Darren hadn't been there I'd have probably run away again. "I don't know, maybe." I laugh stupidly. "You see what I mean, though? You say soprano and I think you're talking about TV."

"Do you think you might want to get a degree in music?"

"I don't know about that. It's a little soon to decide."

"True. You're young. You have time."

"I guess." I clear my throat again. "I never really got the chance to thank you for saving me and Maddy. If you hadn't shown up then, he probably would have shipped us both to China. Or just killed us."

"It was my pleasure."

"Jake's still pissed you totaled his car to do it."

We share a smile at that. "I'll have to reimburse him for the repairs."

"Or you could help him fix it. You two could go work in the garage, a couple of manly men getting all greasy." As I say this, I start to see the scene in my head and my face turns warm out of embarrassment. I squeak, "Or not. Whatever."

"I can't promise I'd be a lot of help. I don't know much about cars."

"Yeah, you can't even drive a stick." There's something else I haven't told Dr. Macintosh: ever since that night he saved us, I've dreamed about him. It's more like I've *fantasized* about him. After I woke up, I kept seeing him in my mind, in the doorway of the lavatory, the blood on his face and gun in his hand, like James Bond. I remember how warm and safe I felt to be with him.

That explains why I shoot out of my chair to kiss him. It's kind of like when I kissed Darren, at least until he opens his mouth. Darren and I were too little to ever use tongues. We never made a kiss last this long either, to the point where I'm about to pass out.

Only then do I pull away, to sag onto my chair. "I'm sorry," I whisper once I've caught my breath.

He straightens his tie, smoothes down his hair, and then says, "I think that's it for today."

***

Despite how my last gig ended, the karaoke bar is eager to take me back. The price is down to just one hundred dollars. That's OK; I don't care about the money so much as to see if I can really do it. For the next week I practice the songs Darren and I used to do, except I don't have him to accompany me. Tess is the closest I have to a music coach, though she'd applaud if I burped the alphabet.

On the way to the karaoke bar I think about Dr. Macintosh. I sent him an e-vite, but I doubt he'll show up. He's probably too embarrassed about it. I'm a little embarrassed too. That was really the first time I acted like I was seventeen, doing something stupid and impulsive. Maybe me being so young is part of the problem. Technically it's illegal for us to kiss, at least until I'm eighteen. But my ID says I'm nineteen and inside I'm over fifty, which I'm sure he knows too.

My fan club is already at the bar; Grace and Maddy are in the front row like last time. They've got seats saved for Tess and Jake. "You look great," Grace says.

Then it's Maddy's turn. She still isn't used to being so big; when she hugs me it's so tight I expect to hear bones snap. "Go get 'em, big sis."

"Thanks, little sis," I say and we both smile.

From there I'm on my own. Before my knees would be jelly and my stomach doing flips. Not this time. I feel pretty good about it. When I worry about it, I remember that applause during my presentation with Darren. I remind myself I can do this; I can be a singer. It's my gift. Not the best gift I've got from all this. That gift sits in the front row: my daughter, my best friend, and my surrogate grandparents. Eighteen months ago I had no one but Jake and a bottle and now I have a whole little family. What's not to like about that?

I go off to a corner backstage so I can run through my scales. This new voice takes a little getting used to. As I continue to practice, I hear the emcee say, "Ladies and gentlemen, tonight we have a special treat. Back for a return engagement, Miss Stacey Chance."

There's a smattering of applause, most of it probably from my family. I take a couple of deep breaths and then go out there. There are a lot of people in the bar, a lot of eyes on me. A month ago I would have been terrified, but now I just smile. I can do this, I tell myself. After all the weird shit I've been through in the last eighteen months, this should be easy.

I count off to three and then signal the emcee to hit it. The karaoke machine isn't much of an accompaniment. It's just a dumb machine, not at all like Darren, with his passion for the music I could feed off of. I do the best I can; I close my eyes and focus on singing "Anything Goes."

The song ends and the applause goes way up from when I was introduced. Now they see I'm not the usual drunk girl here to make an ass of herself. "Thanks," I say. "I'm glad you enjoyed it. Now here's one of my personal favorites."

About halfway through my performance, I notice someone in the back of the bar. Not some drunk college kid who wants me to take off my clothes. It's much better than that. Dr. Macintosh leans against the back wall. He smiles at me and nods his head in time to the music. I stop looking at the rest of the audience and just focus on him, to watch his reactions. He must love it, as he applauds and even whistles at me.

I remember the last time I was up here, how I thought of Dr. Macintosh kissing me backstage. That thought had scared the hell out of me, which had prompted me to run away and get into this whole mess. This time I'd like nothing better than for that fantasy to come true.

By the time I finish, my face is covered in sweat and I feel like I've run two marathons back-to-back. Not that the audience cares. They of course want an encore. I'm off to the side of the stage, chugging a bottle of water, when the emcee asks if I'll do an encore. I nod to him. When I can talk, I say, "But it's not in your machine, so I'll do it unaccompanied."

"Sure, why not?" he says.

Before he can go back out, I whisper in his ear, "And I think I deserve a big fucking raise." I let him digest that and then walk back to the center of the stage. It takes a minute for the applause to die down. I hate how young my voice sounds when I say, "Hi everyone!"

I take a deep breath and then focus on Dr. Macintosh. He stares back at me with anticipation. I'm not about to disappoint him. "This next song was written by a good friend of mine. He's a really bright young songwriter with a great future ahead of him."

It's too dark in the bar and the stage lights too bright for me to see Dr. Macintosh's reaction. I close my eyes then and bob my head as I hear the intro in my mind. "Stacey, you brighten my days—"

Also By P.T. Dilloway:

Chance of a Lifetime (Chances Are #1): When Detective Steve Fischer investigates a robbery, he's murdered by a gangster and injected with an experimental drug known as FY-1978. Thanks to the drug, Steve comes back—as a woman. Now Stacey Chance has to find those responsible and make them pay.

Last Chance (Chances Are #3): Five years after she first became a young woman thanks to an experimental drug, Stacey Chance has come to enjoy her new life. That life gets even better when the man she loves pops the question. But when that experimental drug starts to wear off and an old enemy from Detective Steve Fischer's past resurfaces, Stacey's wonderful new life is thrown into chaos.

A Hero's Journey (Tales of the Scarlet Knight, Volume 1): Dr. Emma Earl never wanted to be a hero. But when she finds a magic suit of armor that can deflect bullets and turn her invisible, she becomes part of an ancient war between good and evil. It's up to Emma as the latest incarnation of the heroic Scarlet Knight to save Rampart City from the fiendish Black Dragoon and his plan to rule first the city and then the whole world.

Acknowledgements:

I'd like to thank Jean Seiler-Bonifacio for beta reading this and the first book in the series. You rock!

About the Author

P.T. Dilloway has been a writer for most of his life. He completed his first story in third grade and received an 'A' for the assignment. Around that time, he was also placed in a local writing contest for a television station, receiving an action figure in lieu of a trophy, thus securing his love with the written word. Since then, he's continued to spend most of his free time writing and editing. In the last twenty years, he's completed nearly forty novels of various genres.

In 2012, Solistice Publishing published P.T.'s superhero novel *A Hero's Journey, Tales of the Scarlet Knight #1*. That same year, December House Publishing included P.T.'s flash fiction stories as part of the collection *We Are Now*. Also in 2012, P.T. created the imprint Planet 99 Publishing to publish the remainder of the Tales of the Scarlet Knight series as well as a variety of other novels, all of which can be found at http://www.planet99publishing.com.

When not writing, P.T. enjoys reading and photographing Michigan's many lighthouses. In order to pay the bills, he earned an accounting degree from Saginaw Valley State University in 2000 and for the past ten years has worked as a payroll accountant in Detroit. Visit his website: http://www.ptdilloway.com

Made in the USA
Charleston, SC
24 August 2013